"... (Trouble in Mind) skillfully blends alien abduction conspiracies, political intrigue, space battles, and epic romance into a psychic police procedural that also packs an emotional punch." – *Publishers Weekly*

"If you are a fan of Star Trek, Firefly, The X-Files then you will love the world that Ms Frelick has created, and of course want more of it too!" – *Nerd Girl Official*

"...a gripping story packed with plenty of action, suspense and science-fiction-style creativity." – *RT Book Reviews*

Books by Donna S. Frelick

The Interstellar Rescue Series:
Unchained Memory
Trouble in Mind

By

Donna S. Frelick

First INK'd Press edition February 2016.

ISBN-13: 978-0692460955
ISBN-10: 0692460950

To the far-seeing children of both past and future.

Fear not, for your courage can vanquish all monsters.

CHAPTER ONE

Nashville, Tennessee, Earth, Sector Three

A phone buzzed, intruding in the intimacy of the darkened living room. Alana struggled to escape the languid embrace of her companion. "That's mine."

"Don't answer it." Mark's voice was a breathy murmur in her ear.

"You know I have to." She wriggled in his grasp. "I'm on call this weekend."

"Oh, hell." He exhaled, letting her go. "Probably just some 7-11 robbery that skipped over the state line."

She reached for the cell, confirmed the display read "FBI Nashville." "Matheson."

"Hey, Lana, this is Cheryl in Dispatch. I've got Sheriff Thomas Radford of Cheatham County on the line. Says he has a kidnapping."

Lana felt a swift kick of adrenaline as she went into professional mode. "Put him through." She made signs for a pencil and paper. Mark grabbed them off the kitchen counter. "Sheriff?"

"Well, look who drew the short straw tonight."

Radford's drawl was deep and familiar. "At least I won't have to break in somebody new."

"After all we've been through together, Tom?" A meth bust. A nasty porn ring. "You ought to be tired of me. Dispatch said something about a kidnapping?"

"Yep, looks like it. Details are a little hinky, though. I'll fill you in when you get to the scene."

"Works for me. Tell me where you are." She wrote down the directions, then ended the call.

Mark almost looked sober. "I'll go with you."

Jamisky was an experienced agent, but Lana declined. "Two martinis and wine with dinner, Mark. Besides, you know Ballard is going to stick me with the kid as soon as this is logged in."

"Shit, the boss still has you babysitting that rookie?"

"Somebody has to do it." Lana moved to her bedroom to change out of her date-night clothes into something more appropriate to a rural crime scene. Mark was at her back as soon as the dress hit the floor, his hands warm on the bare skin of her shoulders. She leaned into him, tolerating his kiss on her neck, but she couldn't suppress a tiny flare of annoyance. Her mind was already on the job ahead.

"I could wait around. Save something for you." He pressed against her, making it clear what would be there for her when she got back.

She turned into him and forced a smile. "It'll probably be a long night, babe." She gave him a quick kiss and pulled back.

He watched her as she finished getting dressed and tamed her unruly blond curls into a disciplined French twist. "Ever thought about giving all this up, Lana? Taking on a normal lifestyle?"

She didn't even spare him a glance as she sat to lace up her hiking boots. "Do I look like the desperate-housewife type?"

"No, you look like the desperate-agent type. You let these cases get to you—the murders, the kidnappings. You take them personally. If I was the Supervisory Special Agent around here, you'd only be allowed to use that famous intuition on white-collar crime."

She shrugged into her shoulder holster and kept her mouth shut. She refused to apologize for loving her job.

She pulled her Glock 23 down from its spot on the shelf, loaded it and slipped it into the holster. Then she scooped up some extra ammo, threw it into her bag with her credentials and her cell phone and turned to go.

Mark frowned at her from his post against the doorjamb. "Now you're mad."

She closed the distance between them and brushed her lips over his. "No. Just grumpy at having to go out. Call you later?"

He smiled a little. "If I don't answer, it's because I've found somebody else to occupy my time."

She grabbed his crotch and gave him a squeeze. "Y'all have fun."

Purple night was gathering in the hollows as Lana and her partner rounded the bend in Highway 70 and saw the little store that was the staging area for the investigation. Cars filled the cramped gravel parking lot in front of Dalton's Market and lined the curve on that side of the road. She pulled off the opposite roadside and parked her FBI-issue Chevy sedan behind a State Police car.

Her nerves hummed with anticipation. Catching a major case on complaint duty had made her night. She felt a brief flutter of regret over Mark, but it didn't last. Anyway, if she had any sense, she'd be looking outside the Bureau for dating material. Way outside. Like maybe Mars.

Her partner sat up in the passenger seat and yawned. "Looks like the locals are having a party. I bet the scene's a freakin' mess."

Rick Mason was still on probation, fresh out of Quantico. He had a lot to learn, and Lana was tired of teaching him.

"You forget I'm a local, too, rookie." She'd grown up around Nashville, spent hours on the back roads of Middle Tennessee. She was the reason a man like Tom Stafford could call the Feds for help without choking.

The kid rubbed a hand across his buzz cut. "I didn't mean—"

"Just follow me and pay attention." Lana grabbed

her creds and cell phone and led Mason across the road to the store. Inside, in a cluttered space that smelled of country ham and coffee, she found the controlled chaos of a police command center: State Police, sheriff's deputies, fire and rescue squad volunteers, a couple of suits with Tennessee Bureau of Investigation badges, store personnel and one guy who looked like he'd been worked over pretty good—the victim who'd been left behind to tell the tale. No media yet, though, thank God.

A tall, beefy redhead in a brown uniform separated himself from the group. He grinned and stuck out a hand.

"Good to see you again, Lana."

She answered the grin and took his hand. "Hey, Tom. This is my partner, Rick Mason." She waited for the nods and handshakes to be done before she asked, "So where are we?"

Radford handed her a clipboard with the preliminary report. "Victim, Dr. Ethan Roberts, found wandering along the road just outside the store here, injured and mentally altered. No phone, no ID. Folks called 911. EMTs called our office when the guy finally remembered what happened, at around 4:47 p.m."

Lana glanced from the report to the battered man on the stretcher in the corner of the room. "Altered how?"

"Couldn't remember any details about what had happened to him until the EMTs got here. He'd been hit in the head bad enough to have been unconscious for at least an hour. Should be in the hospital, but he wouldn't let us take him."

Ah, hell. Her heart contracted as she read further. "His wife and child were taken?"

Radford nodded. "TBI Crime Lab is already at the river where he says they were attacked, but there were at least four or five vehicles down there today. Not unusual in the summer. Lots of folks use that area as access to the river. We're canvassing for witnesses. Nothing yet. My guys found what looks to be his car about two miles from there. Torched."

"He's got a lot of blood on him." She kept her voice steady. "All of it his?"

"Haven't gotten that far."

"We'll need his clothes, samples. Think he'll agree without a warrant?"

Lana saw sympathy on the sheriff's ruddy face. "Whatever happened down there, I don't think he's part of it. I think he'll agree to just about anything if it'll help."

"Okay. Amber Alert?"

"Yep. He's given us pictures of his wife and son."

Lana turned to her partner. "Rick, you stay with the locals putting in the Alert. Call it in to HQ and provide whatever help they need. I'm going to talk to our man."

Disappointment crossed Mason's youthful features before he nodded and followed the sheriff. Lana turned to look at the man she would be interviewing.

The two black eyes, the busted lip and the bruises on his face made it difficult to imagine what he actually looked like, but the strong jaw and the cleft in his chin were still visible. Maybe he'd started the day out a handsome man, maybe late thirties, early forties. Despite his injuries, he had fought back—his knuckles were scraped and bruised. They'd finally had to hit him from behind to take him down.

The real question was why they hadn't just killed him outright. She knew the usual answer, though she hated it. Whoever had done this wanted him alive to come up with the goods. The wife and son were just the collateral. The thought of the boy, only six years old, defenseless and terrified, brought old panic screaming up from where she kept it hidden. She shoved it back down and went to work.

The man lay propped up on the stretcher, the IV still counteracting his dehydration. "Dr. Roberts?"

He opened his swollen lids, revealing bloodshot blue eyes.

"I'm Special Agent Alana Matheson of the FBI, here to help with the investigation." She showed him her credentials. "I have a few questions for you, if you're up to it."

He nodded. "Have they found anything?"

"We're doing everything we can. Can you remember anything about the men who attacked you? What they looked like? The vehicle they left in?"

Roberts exhaled slowly and closed his eyes again. "I've tried. I don't remember anything beyond being at the river with Asia and Jack this morning. I asked for a blood test. I think they may have drugged me."

"Before or after hitting you in the back of the head?"

"After. I think I was out a long time—longer than the head injury accounts for."

"Interesting theory. What kind of doctor are you again?"

He looked at her, his gaze sharp despite his puffy lids. "A psychiatrist."

She smiled. "So you would know, huh, Doc?"

"Yeah. I would."

"How long do you estimate you were out?"

A muscle jumped in his jaw. "At least two hours, maybe longer."

She stared at him. "Damn. That's quite a head start. Did you tell the sheriff this?"

"I tried. Not sure he believed me."

She turned to look for her partner. "Hey, Rick!"

"Yo!"

She moved her head to bring Mason over. "Dr. Roberts says he thinks he was out at least two hours, maybe more, down by the river. By the time he hiked all the way up here, the perps were probably gone with Asia and Jack for three-four hours. They may even be out of state by now. We need to expand the search net."

Mason nodded. "I'm on it."

"Doctor, if you want to help your wife and your son, you have to be honest with me. Can you think of any reason why someone would want to hurt you by taking Asia and Jack?"

Roberts looked at her for a long moment, and in his

face she saw anger flicker and be extinguished. "No."

"Do you owe anyone money? Are you involved with drugs or gambling?" She asked the questions, but somehow she couldn't believe this man would answer yes. He was too self-possessed, his emotions too tightly controlled. If he was into anything like that, he was in deep and at the top. Psychiatry wasn't the usual cover career.

"Why ask me these questions again, Agent Matheson, when you know if I was involved I'd lie? You'll be looking into my background anyway."

"And what will I find when I look into your background, Doctor?"

"Nothing that will help you find my wife and son." He was growling now, everything about him showing anger and bone-deep fatigue. "This is not about drugs, or loan sharks or my first wife, who is dead, by the way, or my wife's ex-husband, who she hasn't seen in maybe five years."

"All right." The more questions the man answered, the more issues he seemed to raise. "What about your patients? Any of them crazy enough to want to hurt you?"

He appeared to consider it, but at last the question seemed to defeat him. "I don't think any of my patients are capable of this. They're harmless neurotics, not dangerous psychopaths."

Lana let the silence hang between them for a moment. "Everything all right between you and your wife, Dr. Roberts?"

His reaction was immediate—but it wasn't the outrage she expected. He closed his eyes and drew in a quick breath, his face frozen in a mask of pain. Unable to hide his misery, Ethan Roberts simply lay on that stretcher and tried to breathe. Lana found it damn hard to watch.

At last he opened his eyes to look at her, and she saw nothing but truth. "I love my wife, Agent Matheson. I would have died to protect her and my son, if I could have. She loves me; she wouldn't have left me. She and my son were *taken*. Tell me you can bring them back."

Lana looked at Roberts' battered face and thought maybe Mark had been right about her. Because this hunt had just become more than a case. For no reason she could explain, it had become personal.

Xorinxe Spaceport, Savagne Planetary Governance, Sector 13

Gabriel Cruz stood in the understated luxury of the XEX Corporation lobby, the sweat trickling down his spine the only outward sign that he did not belong there. His visitor's badge had already survived examination at the security desk, helped along by a discreet pass over the guard's mind. Gabriel knew he couldn't blend in here. Whatever impression he made while he waited for his client had to be the right one. He'd made sure his clothing showed plenty of credits and class; his face wouldn't show up on any criminal databases, so he was just vain enough to consider his dark good looks a valuable asset.

Outside, past ten centimeters of clear, protective trans-steel, Savagne's incessant wind howled. The phosphorescent sand lifted off the dunes and rode the swirling gusts, painting the night sky in riotous color. Those winds, the scouring sands—that was the reality of this planet, not the pampered life XEX had made possible beneath the environmental domes and the planet surface. Something in Gabriel that wouldn't be tamed watched the raging desert and howled along with it.

The elevator chimed its arrival from the lower levels, and Gabriel turned to meet his client at last. Martin Blake was a smallish human, nearing middle-age, hardly impressive. Yet Gabriel knew if this unassuming genius escaped the planet tonight as planned, the biggest corporate giant in the quadrant would wake in the morning to find its golden-egg-laying goose missing.

He met Blake halfway across the lobby with a big grin and a firm handshake. "Martin! Good to see you again. When was the last time—that nanovirals conference on Prena, wasn't it?" He sent a subtler message directly to the communication centers of Blake's brain. *Easy now. Remember the plan. We're colleagues, remember? This is a social call. Go through your usual checkout. I'll handle the guard.*

The guard monitored them closely, suspicious that

the employee under his watch might attempt to pass sensitive material on to this "friend." Gabriel backed off to a proper distance and urged Blake forward.

"Yes, uh, excuse me just a minute, John." Blake indicated the guard. "I've got to check out."

"Oh, sure, sure. Do whatever you need to." Gabriel sauntered up behind him while the checkout proceeded, appearing only to be ready to follow his friend through the exit gate.

At the last minute he laid a casual hand on the guard's arm. "You don't need me for anything do you?" He sent a light suggestion through the man's mind, erasing the details of his face and name. In minutes, the guard would not be able to recall his presence at all.

The guard shook his head as his eyes glazed over.

Gabriel guided his man through the gilded doors leading out into the dome. "Let's go."

Stealing Blake from right under the nose of the CEO of XEX had been the easy part. Keeping him safe from Chairman Xe, who'd come out of Savagne's desert and had all the instincts of his sandcrawler ancestors, would be a different matter.

Like XEX Corporate, the workplaces and playgrounds of the elite sat on a broad thoroughfare around the outer rim of the dome, each claiming a wedge of stark desert view above and multiple levels below ground. But Gabriel sought fewer lights on a street less traveled. He ducked into a dusty alleyway and led his lamb across the less-fortunate center of the dome. No place inside the domes was truly wretched, but behind the restaurants and prosperous businesses, the garbage still stank and the shadows were thick enough to hide in.

Blake finally found the courage to speak. "Couldn't we have just taken the sub line from XEX?"

"Yes, if we'd wanted Corporate Security on our tails. That's your usual way home, isn't it?" Gabriel approached the end of an alley and scanned the street beyond. Clear. He emerged, Blake close behind him.

"You mean I'm being watched, despite all my precautions?"

He glanced down at the little man. "You're Xe's most valuable engineer. What do you think?"

"Are you sure Security's not waiting for you?" Blake was scowling now as he struggled to keep up with Gabriel's long strides. "You're the one with a 20,000-credit bounty on his head."

"True enough." His own father had put it there, and though the bloody bastard was long dead, his two half-brothers and plenty of others were still trying to collect. "But I'm still alive, and people have offered me good credit to make sure you do the same. I always earn my pay."

"Well, I'm supposed to be paying for the best." Blake hunched his shoulders. "And I *need* to get on that ship."

The street had become narrow and winding, crowded with people stumbling in and out of the bars on either side. Loud music and the sour smell of cheap synthohol spilled from the doorways. This was the heart of the dome, as dangerous as it got inside, but Gabriel wasn't watching for prostitutes or pickpockets.

Four more pylons to mark before they reached the sub line that would take them to the port. Five minutes' walk. And then Gabriel saw what he'd been looking for—a hulking bounty hunter lurking in the shadows cast by the lights over a bar. Two party girls hung on his arms, their attention on the passing crowd. Gabriel grabbed Blake and melted into the dark on the opposite side of the street.

Blake protested. "What the fuck?"

--Shut up! Someone's on to us. Who have you been talking to?

--No one! I swear, no one knows! I've been careful.

--Not careful enough. He nodded in the direction of the bounty hunter.

Blake shook his head, his eyes wide.

--We have to make it to the sub line without being seen. Follow me, and do not *get lost.*

Gabriel slipped into a fetid alley leading off the street they'd been walking. Once he was well away from the noisy bar strip he began to run. Blake was hard put to keep up with him, but he didn't wait for the little man. His client's life depended on speed. If Blake thought he'd be left behind he'd run faster.

The four pylons went by like a shot at running speed, and Gabriel dashed down the steps into the sub line with a sense of relief. No one was behind them. He scanned the crowd on the sub platform and didn't see the bounty hunter. Their luck was holding.

The sub train pulled up. People got off. He pushed Blake forward and got on after him. The train took off with a jerk and rapidly gained speed. Then it surfaced like a sand dragon breaching, and skimmed along the surface, headed for one of three stops outside the domes. All around them the battering winds wailed and moaned. The neon sand streaked overhead and scratched at the windows, finding its way in through the seals. The sub wheezed to a stop in the shadow of a sand-blasted butte, and a handful of workers got off at the shantytown station, headed home from jobs too menial to support housing in the domes.

Even so, they were luckier than some. The train began to roll again and slid past a low-slung complex of lighted buildings surrounded by razor wire. Inside the wire, plasform barracks huddled around a mine tipple and a heap of slag. Gabriel cursed.

Blake followed his gaze, but he didn't see. "What is it?"

"Fucking Minertsan slave mine. Like to blow it to hell."

"Don't think my boss would appreciate that much." Blake offered a sardonic smile. "He has a cozy relationship with the Grays. Slave labor is cheap, if you don't count what he pays the Minertsan fleet for protection from the Interstellar Council for Abolition and Rescue."

"The Grays steal people off Earth and wipe their minds and work them to death in mines like that one." Like his own Cuban grandparents. Until Rescue got them out. "Let's hope what Xe pays isn't enough."

They rode on in silence in the full sub car, the passengers with them a cosmopolitan mix of humans, reptilian Savagnoirs, tall Ninoctins and a few others. The second and third desert stops came and went. As the train neared the port complex, Gabriel began to think they might make it without trouble. The first port stop, in the dome housing the freight docks, was coming up in less than a minute.

Then the door between cars opened with a whoosh. "Ah, hell."

The bounty hunter stalked down the aisle toward them, a grin cracking his grizzled face. His hands were empty, though, and that was his mistake.

"Up. Move!" Gabriel pushed at Blake. "Now!"

They scrambled out of their seats and down the aisle. Behind them, the hunter took up the chase. Gabriel grabbed the first thing he could lay hands on— someone's duffle—and threw it at the hunter's feet, tripping him up. He heard a curse and a thud just as they reached the door at the end of the car, then they were through to the other side. They kept moving, through that car and into the next one. But as they neared yet another door, their luck ran out. With the bounty hunter closing in from behind, sub line security had entered the car in front of them. His client couldn't afford to be taken into custody; Chairman Xe owned the law enforcement on Savagne.

Gabriel yanked open the door and surveyed the exit between the cars. "We'll be exiting a little sooner than expected."

Blake stared at him in horror. "You can't be serious!"

The station announcement came just as the train entered the dome and began to reduce speed. Gabriel checked the security men in front, the hunter nearly upon them behind. People preparing to exit had filled the aisles, slowing them down, giving Gabriel and Blake a few more precious seconds before they had to jump.

Gabriel could hear the security guards yelling for people to make way, but no one was moving. Outside the train, the station came into view. The train slowed, slowed. Gabriel kicked open the exit door, grabbed Blake and jumped, dropping into a roll as his feet, then his shoulders, hit the hard platform with bone-crushing force. The breath left him, and he heard Blake shout something. Then he was on his feet, dragging the little man behind him, searching for the stairs that led out of the station.

There—up ahead! But—*damn it!*—the bounty hunter had already caught up with them. They pelted up the stairs to the main level, their pursuer's boots heavy on the treads behind them. Gabriel steered his man to the left at the top and turned to plant his foot in the hunter's chest. The hunter parried and sliced his calf with a 20-centimenter blade. Cursing, Gabriel snatched his leg back and punched hard at the man's nose. The hunter kept coming. And he still had the knife.

Gabriel scrambled back as the blade swept in

towards his gut. The swing just missed him, and he rushed the man, pinning the hunter's knife arm to his chest and twisting his wrist. The knife slipped out of his grip. Gabriel let go of the pinned arm long enough to smash his elbow into the man's face, but *Jesus!* he just wouldn't go down. And now the sliced muscle of Gabriel's calf was giving way, refusing to hold him. He went with it and dropped to the ground with the man's jumpsuit in his fists, flipping him over his head. By the time he'd rolled out of the throw, the fucker had nearly gotten to his feet.

To hell with this. Gabriel pulled the stunner from inside his jacket and squeezed the trigger. The hunter went down in a rigid convulsion of agony.

Gabriel grabbed his client by the arm and hustled him into a side corridor as alarms began to blare at the discharge of an unauthorized weapon. He got them out of sight, and wrapped a strip of his shirt around his wound so he wouldn't leave a blood trail. Then they navigated a maze of stacked containers into the quietest part of the automated freight docks. All the while, Blake trotted at his side, wordless and pale.

In range now, he made his connection. "Cruz to *Shadowhawk.*"

"*Shadowhawk* here. Stand by for Captain Murphy."

Sam Murphy growled his displeasure. "Where the hell are you? And is all that comm noise I'm hearing because of you?"

"Just get me onboard and get us to the jump ASAP. I've got the whole damn planet after my ass."

"Can you get to a D-mat pad? We'll register you as cargo transfer."

He saw one of the larger units meant for cargo up ahead, deserted at this hour. "Yeah, we're good." He and Blake stepped up on the pad. "Ready on your mark."

The freight dock disappeared and the *Shadowhawk*'s D-mat pad resolved in a shimmer of consciousness. Gabriel limped off the pad, but got no further before the ship's captain flung open the hatch and strode in to meet him.

"Cutting it a little close, aren't we?" Murphy looked him over with a critical eye before he slipped a well-muscled arm under his shoulder and helped him to the corridor. He ignored Blake.

"We? Where were you when that hunter tried to slice me in half?"

"Bounty hunter?" Murphy shot a glare at Blake. "Yours or his?"

"His, we think. But no matter. Where's the better half?"

"Rayna's on the bridge, trying to talk us out of orbit. Space Authority wants to shut down all departures for some reason." They turned into a hatchway labeled "Crew Lounge", and Murphy lowered Gabriel into the nearest seat. "Figured you wouldn't let me take you to Sickbay."

Gabriel grunted. "You figured right. Could use some skinseal, though." His leg still hurt like a sonofabitch.

Murphy came back to the table with a medkit, a

tumbler for Gabriel and two mugs full of grog for himself and Blake. "Spit in Xe's eye!"

They all raised their glasses to that.

Gabriel grimaced. "Synthohol? I know you keep the good stuff."

"In my cabin. I'll share later. First we need to talk."

"Look, I wouldn't have pulled the stunner if that hunter hadn't come at me with a knife." He bent to clean and seal the rip in his leg.

Murphy waved a hand. "Necessary. No, I have another job for you."

He sat back. "Don't need another job." What he needed was a bed. And a woman. And the time to enjoy them both. Sam had it right—partner up with your mate.

But Murphy wasn't taking no for an answer. "This one is special. A woman and a six-year-old child were taken. Returned slaves—and personal friends."

"How long ago?" Time was key.

"About ten hours planetary by now, I guess."

"Where?"

"Earth."

Gabriel's eyes opened wide in shock. "Say again?"

"You heard me."

When he wasn't providing transport for Gabriel's clients, Sam Murphy served an organization with a very narrow view of where you could go and what you could do. "I thought Earth was off-limits for Rescue."

"It is. This isn't a job for an official Rescue team." Murphy caught his gaze. "It's strictly a one-person operation, very low-profile. The local authorities are already involved."

Before Gabriel could respond, Blake broke into the conversation. "I've heard rumors that the Minertsans have been stealing returned slaves back from Terrene. Maybe the Grays are taking them from Earth, too."

Gabriel had been raised in Terrene's colony of former slaves, a polyglot of cultures forever cut off from their home planets. He'd heard the rumors, too.

He looked at Murphy. "Well?"

The captain frowned. "Could be, but Asia . . . well, let's just say she has special talents of interest to certain Earth-based groups. They tried to take her once before. We think this is a repeat."

Dios, *she's resistant to the mindwipe. No wonder they want her.* Even the Grays would find that interesting.

Gabriel shook his head. "Sam, you know I hate working on Earth." Black ops agents who knew too much. Overfed dirtside cops with small minds and provincial attitudes.

"Yeah." The captain ran a hand through his black hair, turning it into spikes. "But she's a good friend, Gabriel. And the boy's only six."

Damn it, Sam really knew how to push his buttons. Even Blake was looking at him like a lost mooncat.

"And there's something else." Murphy shifted in his seat. "Our intel says the *Bloodstalker*'s headed for the Sol system. Kinnian and Trevyn Dar are in command."

Blake went pale. "Jesus, those killers? The Thrane

hunters?"

Gabriel's teeth clenched hard in his jaw. Rescuing this mother and son from Earthers with a hard-on for UFO's would be all in a day's work. Saving them from his alien brothers would be a matter of personal honor.

He tossed back what remained in his glass. "I'm in. Set course for Earth."

CHAPTER TWO

Trin, Center for Administrative Control, Consortium of Minertsa, Sector 10

The Minister of Labor considered his options. In the wake of the attack on the processing center at Del Origa, they were limited. Demand was up all over the Consortium. Supply was correspondingly short. And the traditional sources for slaves, thanks to the mud-sucking pirates who called themselves abolitionists, were drying up.

His fellow ministers in charge of mining, industrial production and agriculture continued to raise production quotas. The new numbers for this interval taunted him from the upper left quadrant of his visual field, the holo-display accompanied by an encouraging message from the Consortium Oligarchy. For a swift second he lost control of his emotions and the air around his body churned with black and hideous purple.

Director Prime Sennik composed himself, adjusting the colors of his aura to reflect only calm neutrality. There was no use mourning the loss of Del Origa now. And, in fact, most of the facility's functions—the mindwipe procedures, the medical screenings, the labor allocation—could be taken up at other sites. He had already begun rerouting newly acquired slaves to compensate.

But Del Origa had been important for another reason, one only he knew. He meant to keep that secret to himself.

He opened his mind in summons and waited until he saw his second-in-command appear in the doorway of his office.

--You needed me, Director Prime?

Sennik let the female be aware that he approved of her prompt appearance. In fact, he approved of Ardis's appearance in all aspects—her smooth, light skin, her long-fingered hands, her large, liquid, black eyes. Her aura, as usual a delicate lavender shot through with deeper tones of violet and midnight blue, communicated just the right combination of respect and ambition, of eagerness and ruthlessness. Then there was that intriguing hint of sexual interest that sometimes seemed to curl around the edge of his perception.

He monitored his own vibratory emissions and was pleased to note none of his observations had colored his aura. He remained an even-toned silver-gray.

--What is the status of our search for the slaves stolen in the raid on Del Origa?

--We have identified all those taken, sir, and we have begun reacquisition of all the test subjects who remain in accessible territories.

--Excellent. When do you anticipate completion of this task?

Director Second Ardis's aura blushed with an uncomfortable salmon. *There are many who have been resettled on Terrene. Taking them all at once would raise questions. The teams have been forced to be discreet.*

--Blast Terrene! Nothing but a poison pool where fang-eels slither to hide! Take the slaves or kill them outright if taking them is impossible. Sennik noted the boiling black in his aura and struggled to calm himself. He amended his order. *Except, of course, the immature ones. Those we must have. We have too much invested in them to lose them. What news of the coordinator?*

Ardis's aura flashed green with fear. *The Thranes report he may have been among those who have been sent back.*

--Sent back?

--You are aware the abolitionist organization Rescue often tries to send the slaves back to their home planet?

Sennik waved a hand. *It's not as if that ridiculous speck of dust they all come from—what is the name of that stupid place? Erp?*

--Earth, sir.

--Yes, well. It's not as if the place is at the far end of Zfar's Galaxy. The ball of dirt practically sits on top of one of our busiest jump nodes. It should be a simple matter to get my property back. I sent Thrane hunters after the boy for a reason. Contact the Bloodstalker

and tell Kinnian Dar I am waiting for him to earn the credits I'm paying him.

Nashville, Tennessee, Earth, Sector Three

Ethan Roberts sat on the couch of the big, open room that served as his office, his injured leg stretched out on the worn leather in front of him. A grating pain in his knee kept him in place and in torment. The throbbing pain of his cracked ribs made it impossible to sit comfortably. But the fearful pain in his chest where his heart should have been was nearly unbearable.

His wife and his son were all he could think about. Where they were. What was happening to them. Not knowing what had happened at the river was a special kind of torture. Had they been hurt? He would give anything to have Asia and Jack safe in his arms at this minute—*anything*. He ached for it with a longing so strong it seemed to rip his soul into pieces.

Ethan had little confidence in the police and FBI agents who were establishing operations in his secretary's office on the other side of the entryway of his home. Except for the two cats, J.J. and Merlin, who prowled mournfully around the living room looking for their lost humans, he was alone with his agonized thoughts despite the dozens of officers all around him. He'd given some thought to calling his friends, or Asia's, but there'd been time for only one contact, a desperate one. He wouldn't rest until he'd seen some results from that nearly-hopeless plea.

"Ethan? Where are you, man?"

Thank God, Sam Murphy at last. Ethan inhaled a shaky breath and clamped down hard on his emotions as he struggled to his feet. Sam was frowning down at one of the police officers, who was making a futile attempt to stop and question him in the hall. The tiny woman at his side was already ignoring the brewing dispute and hurrying in Ethan's direction.

Sam's wife and Rescue partner wrapped her arms around him. "Ethan, I'm so sorry. How are you?"

"Rayna. I'm glad you're here." He ignored the pain as she squeezed his battered ribs, taking the warmth she offered him.

Sam evaded the police officer at last and replaced Rayna's with a hug of his own. "We bent the jump frame a little to save some time." The big man gripped him hard. "We got here as soon as we could."

Ethan dragged in a breath against the fresh pain and stood back, his muscles rigid with the need to control his emotions. He nodded to show he understood and was grateful, not trusting his voice to say what he felt.

Someone had come in with Sam and Rayna. A tall man, lean and dark, he stood off to one side and watched with somber patience, waiting for them to have time for him. Ethan straightened and caught the man's gaze.

Sam followed his stare. He slipped a hand around Ethan's upper arm, a gesture both comforting and gently controlling.

"Want you to meet a friend. He's here to help us." He lifted his chin and the man came closer. Ethan himself was over six feet tall, and Sam was easily 6'3", but the man seemed somehow larger than either of them. Ethan realized at once that it wasn't his height, which was only slightly above his, or the fact that his frame was packed with muscle, or that he moved like a fighter.

This man had something else—a darkness that was deeper than the pantherish black of his hair or the mahogany glitter of his eyes. There was something in him, a dense inner core, not of cruelty, but of ruthlessness, as if he were a weapon that, once released, could never be called back.

"This is Gabriel Cruz," Sam was saying. "Gabriel, Ethan Roberts."

Ethan shook the man's hand, found it strong and warm. Ethan knew immediately why the man had come. And he realized maybe he needed a weapon like Gabriel Cruz.

"Do you also work for Rescue, Mr. Cruz?"

"Occasionally."

"And you think you can find my wife and son."

The corners of Gabriel's mouth quirked upwards. "A man who comes right to the point."

"Gabriel is the best extractor in the galaxy." Rayna laid a hand on Ethan's arm. "He can find anybody, anyplace, anytime, and bring them home. I've seen him do it."

Ethan considered him. The police weren't going to like the fact that he'd brought in someone from the outside. He himself was already a suspect. What was this going to look like? And once they'd unleashed this bloodhound, would he answer to anyone's command?

"You don't trust me, Dr. Roberts." Gabriel's gaze held his.

Ethan didn't look away. "I don't know you, Mr. Cruz."

The man shrugged. "There are people who have been of my acquaintance for years who still don't know me, Doctor. It's not necessary for the work I do. Sam and Ray, on the other hand, are my friends."

Ethan nodded. "They're good friends to have. And because I trust them, I have to believe you can help me. *Can* you help me?"

"Yes." No hesitation. No fear.

Ethan watched the man for a moment longer, found Gabriel returning his consideration evenly, then dropped his eyes. In contrast to the extractor's confidence, Ethan felt so tired, so *defeated*. He hurt in so many places, only some of them physical. He fell into the familiar comfort of the armchair beside his desk and ran his hands through his hair.

Sam and Gabriel found places on the couch and tried not to make it obvious they were watching him.

Rayna perched on the desk beside Ethan. "When was the last time you ate anything?"

He shook his head. His stomach lurched just thinking about it.

Sam's eyes lit up. "Oh, damn! Gabriel, did you know they bring the food right to you? Pizza! God, I *love* pizza! Ethan, what place is good, man?"

"Check the menu by the phone." Ethan had to smile. He noticed even Gabriel was grinning at Sam's enthusiasm. The flash of white teeth in the tan skin of his face transformed him, softened him, subsuming the killer below the man that held that killer in control. A killer that Ethan now realized was engaged in service to his family.

"It's a very good thing we do not live on this planet of wonders." Rayna sighed. "Sam would weigh 150 kilos."

"Dr. Roberts, you told Sam and Ray you think you know who took your wife and son." Ethan felt the intensity of Gabriel's gaze. "Tell me about these people."

"Gabriel, let's skip the titles, okay? Call me Ethan." He tried to focus his mind. "How much do you know about Asia and Jack's history with the Grays?"

"I know Asia was in a labor camp on Gallodon IV for several months before Ray got her out." Gabriel settled back on the couch as he spoke. "I know Jack was rescued as part of the operation to take out the Del Origa processing facility. I know they both have a resistance to the deep psychological programming the Grays use on their slaves to keep them docile."

"The same kind of programming Rescue uses to help returned slaves reintegrate into their home societies." Ethan couldn't keep the bitterness out of his voice.

"A necessary evil." Gabriel's expression was carefully neutral.

"So I keep telling myself." Ethan wanted to choke on the words. How much of this was his fault? He and Asia were still involved with Rescue, still helped settle returnees back on Earth by making sure they had no memory of their alien abductions. If the two of them had just refused that job and disappeared when they had the chance, would this even be happening now?

Rayna's hand was gentle on his arm. "Ethan, you know how much good you do for people, how much they—and we—need your help. Hiding wouldn't have helped Asia and Jack. They would have found you eventually."

Gabriel brought him back on track. "Who would have found you?"

Ethan allowed a tiny smile to lift his lips. "Asia calls them the Men in Black. Black ops government agents with an interest in extraterrestrial intelligence. About 18 months ago a group of them took Asia, but Sam and Ray and I rescued her and dismantled the organization. We thought that was the end of it."

"We should have known it went further than the two research facilities we found," Sam explained. "There are many more of these people out there, working with unlimited resources. They want what Asia has—first-hand knowledge of life on other planets and an ability to resist alien technology. They must be the ones who have taken her." A look passed between Sam and Gabriel that Ethan could not interpret.

Gabriel looked back at Ethan. "You've told the authorities nothing of this, I take it."

"As if they would believe any of it." Ethan gave him a grim smile. "But even they aren't dumb enough to think there's *no* reason for a kidnapping like this. They suspect I'm involved with drugs or gambling or worse."

"And your son?"

He was suddenly unable to speak around the emotion gripping his throat. "Rayna brought him to us five months ago, after the raid on Del Origa. I don't think the ones who want Asia know about his ability. I mean, how could they? They identified Asia from her psychological records. We were careful to protect Jack."

Gabriel considered. "Probably just collateral damage."

Anger flared white-hot, and Ethan gripped the arms of his chair. "What did you say?"

Rayna put both hands on Ethan's shoulders. "Ethan, he didn't mean—"

"I'm sorry. Poor choice of words." The extractor held out his hands in apology. "I just meant they probably grabbed him by mistake." He immediately switched gears. "What kind of vehicle did they use?"

"Shit!" Ethan got to his feet and began an awkward pacing, though the agony in his knee nearly took him to the floor. "I don't remember anything. They hit me in the back of the head. Then they drugged me. I insisted on a drug test—the results aren't back yet, but I'm sure I was drugged. I was out for two or three hours."

He came to a stop and turned to see Gabriel staring at him.

"You fought them." The man inclined his head at Ethan's knee and his hands.

"It didn't do any good."

"They didn't have any weapons?"

Ethan's brows came together in puzzlement, his heart still pounding. "I don't—that doesn't make sense, does it?"

"I can help you remember."

Ethan stared at him. "Hypnosis?"

The other man shook his head. "It's much more . . . pro-active . . . than that. Some people would say invasive."

"What are you talking about?"

Rayna looked up at him. "Gabriel is a touch telepath, Ethan. A very good one."

He heard the words. At some level they even made sense. But Ethan remained unable to understand what she was telling him.

"A touch telepath?"

"I read minds." Gabriel's tone was matter-of-fact. "But only if we're skin-to-skin. And only if we both agree." His lips curved. "All the intimacy of sex—without the payoff."

CHAPTER THREE

The Nashville bungalow where Ethan and Asia Roberts lived was easy to find, even at an hour of the early morning when nothing but the streetlights were on to show the way. Two Metro Police Department squad cars, a deputy sheriff's vehicle from Cheatham County, a black sedan with a TBI sticker and a gray one with a Bureau shield crowded the street and the driveway. If that weren't enough, the house itself was still blazing with lights. Lana couldn't help a small sigh of sympathy for the poor man who'd been beaten senseless as his wife and child were taken and was pinned down now in the middle of all that glare.

She pulled up to the curb and killed the engine, trying not to let her own energy die with the sound of the motor. She reached for the 7-11 cup and downed the last bitter gulp of cold coffee to brace her for the next round. The boys inside would have a fresh pot brewing, and she could fill up if she had to stay. She'd check in to make sure the phones were set up, see how Roberts was reacting, then head home for a few hours of sleep.

Rick met her at the door, looking like a toddler

who'd been allowed to stay up late for a grownup party. "Tellmer's here. He's got the phone lines all set, but nothing's come in yet."

Lana nodded. "You look like shit. We keeping you up past your bedtime?"

The youngster rubbed at his jaw. "Oh, uh, I didn't get much sleep last night either, I guess."

"Welcome to my world." She pushed past him into the entry. "Where's Roberts?"

"Vic's in the big office there. He's got some friends in with him."

Lana turned on him. "Hey. Once we get a name for someone, we use it. This guy's name is Ethan Roberts. Dr. Roberts to you. He's had the day from hell, and so far we are not making things any better for him. We can at least show him some respect."

"Come on." Rick's mouth twisted with disgust. "You gotta like the guy for this thing. He probably owes somebody money and they're holding the wife and kid until he pays up. Maybe he gambles or something—"

Lana jacked the kid up by an elbow and backed him down the hall until he slammed against a closed door at the end. She kept her voice low, but there was no question of her emotional level.

"One: we have no evidence that he's involved. Two: if we did have any evidence, we wouldn't go blabbing it around that we know. Three: there is such a thing as innocent until proven guilty. Four: I'm tired of your shit-for-brains attitude. So keep your mouth shut and your ears open and you might make it through probation. Are you hearing me?"

Anger flashed in the kid's eyes, but he had little choice. "Yes, ma'am."

She let the cloth of his windbreaker slip from her fingers and stepped back. She noticed she was shaking. *Must be the caffeine*, she thought. *Didn't really mean to shrink-wrap his tiny little balls.* "I'm going to see Dr. Roberts."

Roberts was waiting by the bay windows in the former living room that served as his office, staring out at the night. A woman and another man Lana didn't know were sitting on the couch that dominated the room, bookended by two cats. She noted those things, but only as peripheral details, bits and pieces she would collect and store in case they became useful later. Because in the center of her consciousness, at the focus of all her attention, was the man who rose from behind the doctor's desk. On one level, her training was still operational—the man was about 6'2", black hair, brown eyes, athletic build, possibly Hispanic, black tee shirt, dark jeans.

But, my God, that said nothing of the *impact* of the man. From the slow thud of her heart in her chest, she would have to start all over with a totally different kind of description to come close to explaining how he affected her. The muscles of his chest and shoulders moved under the silky fabric of his shirt like a jaguar's under its fur. His eyes regarded her with an intensity that lit her from the inside and sent the warmth to her face in a rush. The smooth honey of his skin made her want to touch—everywhere. And she didn't dare think about what might be inside those jeans.

Lana swallowed against the sudden dryness of her throat. *Get a grip, girl*, she admonished herself. *You're supposed to be a professional*. She forced herself to ignore him, though he stood no more than an arm's length away, and spoke to the battered man by the window instead.

"Dr. Roberts?" She was pleased to note that there was no sign of a tremor in her voice. *Thank you, God*.

"Agent Matheson." Roberts turned from the window and limped in her direction. "Any news?"

She shook her head. "Nothing substantive. I do have a few things to tell you." She glanced at the others in the room. "Do you mind if we speak in private?"

"These are my close friends." He nodded at each of them in turn. "Sam and Rayna Murphy, Gabriel Cruz. Whatever you would say to me, you can say in front of them."

Lana frowned. "I understand your need for support at a time like this, Doctor, believe me I do. But for the good of your wife and son, the fewer people who know the details of our investigation, the better."

Roberts opened his mouth to protest, but Cruz stepped in and placed a hand on his shoulder. "Don't worry about it, Ethan." His voice was quiet and deep, with an accent she couldn't place. "It's time we all got some sleep anyway. I'll be back in the morning, when the drugs have worn off. We can talk again then, okay?"

It seemed to Lana that Roberts wasn't particularly

looking forward to that conversation, but after a moment he agreed. She flicked her eyes in Cruz's direction, meaning only to acknowledge his cooperation. She found him watching her intently, some inner amusement lifting the corners of his mouth. Without the involvement of her brain, her own traitorous lips smiled at him in response.

"Thank you." She shocked herself when the words came out in a murmur more appropriate to a bedroom than a . . . well, than anyplace else.

The man's smile widened. "Certainly, Agent Matheson. Good night."

Lana didn't trust herself to say anything further. This time she kept herself to a nod.

The Murphys both hugged their friend and promised to see him again in the morning, then the three of them found their way out through the maze of officers in the hall. Roberts looked like they had taken the last of his strength with them when they left. He dropped into the armchair near the desk and scrubbed at his face with a shaking hand.

"I just wanted to tell you that the electronic surveillance is all set on your phones." Lana watched his reaction, which was minimal. "When the kidnappers call, we'll be in position to trace the call back to its source."

Roberts lifted his eyes to look at her. "You're assuming they will be asking for a ransom."

"That's what we expect."

"And if they don't?"

"Dr. Roberts." She paused, searching for the right words. "Right now we don't have a lead on the vehicle they're driving. We don't know the direction they may be headed. We don't even have a description of the men who took your family." Lana paced a few steps, ran a hand over her forehead. "We have to hope they do call us. Otherwise, we're going to have one hell of a time finding them."

Interstate 40, West of Memphis, Tennessee, Earth, Sector Three

Asia Roberts opened her eyes and saw a single square of light above her: a tinted skylight showing a patch of clear, moonlit sky and little else. The silver light from above was enough to show her the empty interior of the van—metal walls, a thinly carpeted floor, a solid sliding window into the cab, now shut tight. The van was moving, the engine a loud growl through the frame, the tires a rhythmic whirr and tick beneath the floor.

She tried to move, an effort that brought on a wave of dizzy pain and nausea. She recognized the dry mouth and metallic aftertaste of the sedative that had been used to drug her. The dose had been a big one, judging from the headache and the night sky. It had been early afternoon when they'd been taken.

Slowly she sat up. "Jack?"

No answer. Her heart exploded in her chest. "Jack!"

Her head swiveled to look for him, though the sudden movement was like shaking a skull full of broken glass. *There! In the corner!* She scrambled across the floor to him.

"Jack, answer me, baby. Are you okay?" Boy-sized arms shot out to circle her neck as she pulled Jack into her lap and rocked him close.

"There you are! Were you hiding?" She kept her tone as light as she could, refusing to let him sense her fear. Jack had known enough of terror in his short life. He had just gotten a taste of what love and normalcy could be like before this second trauma had struck. Damn it, how could this have happened? They were supposed to have been done with all of this!

Asia stroked his hair. "You were very brave at the river, Jack. A fighter, like Daddy. There were a lot of bad guys, and we lost the first round, but Daddy will find us and get us back home, don't you worry."

She fought to hold her tears back. She couldn't let Jack know how worried she really was. Ethan would have fought until they beat him unconscious. *Please, God, tell me it ended there. Tell me he's still alive.*

Jack clung to her without a word. He had been just as silent when he'd first come to them. He hadn't talked for weeks, hadn't slept a night through without waking to scream in rigid horror, hadn't smiled or played with toys or done any of those things that a six-year-old boy could be expected to do. Ethan and Asia weren't surprised by his behavior. They knew what he'd been through—stolen from his home in the middle of the night by creatures from some grown-up nightmare; torn from his parents in the midst of bloody chaos; subjected to procedures that would make any lab animal cringe in the corner of its cage.

Asia knew from her own abduction what it was to be forced to carry those memories, though they ate at your heart with corrosive power. It was one reason Rayna had brought Jack to them.

Ethan, of course, was the other reason. Ethan, who had helped her find her own way back to sanity. He had used all his professional knowledge as a psychiatrist and all his warmth as a man to bring the boy out of his shell. Now she was afraid the little guy would never speak another word after this new violation.

"Mom?"

"Jack!" Asia sat up and held him at arm's length to examine his expression in the wan light of the moon. "Hey! You okay?"

"I'm thirsty and my head hurts. Are we gonna stop soon?"

"I don't know, baby. I hope so."

He climbed off her lap and sat next to her. "We can talk if you want to."

She looked at him. "Okay. What do you want to talk about?"

He shrugged. "Nothing. But you don't have to worry. I'm not going to stop talking now."

Ice slid down her spine. "What are you . . . what do you mean?"

He sighed in exasperation. "You know. Like before.

When I first came to live with you and Dad?"

"Oh. Yeah. I remember."

"I didn't talk then because I thought you could hear me without my voice. But you couldn't. So I had to use my voice again."

Asia shook her head. "I don't think I understand, buddy. How could we hear you without your voice?"

Jack sat for a moment, his brows drawn together. Then his face lit up.

"You know how Dad says you have to listen to that little voice inside you that tells you what's right and what's wrong?"

Asia nodded, not even remotely certain where the boy was headed with this.

"Well, I thought I could just use that voice to talk to you and Dad, but you couldn't hear it, so I had to use my regular voice. The loud one."

"You mean your *thoughts*, Jack? You thought we could hear what was going on in your mind?"

"Well, yeah. I guess so."

Asia looked at her son, her eyes wide. She was almost afraid to ask the next question.

Before she had even opened her mouth to ask it, he had answered: "Yes."

"You know what I'm thinking?"

"Not all the time. Just like when you're getting ready to say something." He grinned. "Or when you're really mad, or happy, or like that."

"Oh, my God!"

"Did I do something wrong?"

She dragged him into her embrace. "No, honey. No, you didn't do anything wrong." She kept the surface of her mind carefully neutral, while the depths of her consciousness were in turmoil. What the hell did this mean? And how had she not noticed it before?

She tried to keep her tone casual, as if she was asking him about his favorite TV cartoon. "Have you always been able to listen to people's thoughts, baby?"

Jack stared at the floor of the van and didn't answer.

Asia tried to meet his downcast eyes, but he looked away. "Jack?" There was a stubborn set to his features that she had begun to recognize after their time together. She didn't press. "Okay. It's not important. Any other superpowers you want to tell me about?" She grinned and poked at his ribs.

The teasing earned her a shy smile and half a shrug.

Oh, God. If the men who wanted her because of what she knew found out about Jack . . . Until now he'd just been an inconvenience to them. If they found out what he could do, Jack could become the focus of their "scientific investigation." The Men in Black had just hit the Bonus Round. *Shit!*

She did her best to scan the interior of the van— corners, ceiling, seams in the metal sides. She checked the seal of the sliding metal window connecting the rear of the van with the cab in front. Still shut tight. There was a vent for the circulation of air, but her inspection revealed no obvious monitoring devices.

She kept her voice just loud enough for the two of

them to hear. "Jack." She put both hands on his shoulders and squared him up to look in his face. "Promise me you will never tell anyone else about this. Except for Dad, when we see him again. You can tell him, but no one else, okay? Especially these men. If they find out about it, they might hurt you. So it has to be our secret. Do you understand?"

The youngster matched her grave expression and nodded.

Asia thought a moment. "Have you heard anything from the men in the front?"

Jack shook his head. "I can't hear people I don't know very well. I have to try really hard."

"Do you think you could listen to them if you were a little closer?" Asia twisted to take a look. "Or if the wall wasn't in the way?"

"Maybe. Then we could find out who they are."

Asia grinned at him. "Smart boy. Or where they plan to take us."

"I could do that!"

"Okay. But you have to be really careful." Her throat went dry as she understood the fine line she walked between encouraging him and exposing him. "Remember what I said. They can't find out what you can do, right?"

"Right. Maybe I should pretend I can't talk again."

She nodded at him. "And we'll wait for a chance to listen to them, okay?"

Not long afterward, the van veered off the highway and slowed down. It came to a stop at last, and a face appeared in the window. Despite the dark, the man wore sunglasses, and his buzz cut made it impossible to determine his hair color. Otherwise, he'd made no effort to hide his features—a bad sign, Asia realized.

"In a minute we'll come around to open the back. We'll walk you to the restroom when there is no one inside. You won't have a chance to speak to anyone or leave a note or do anything heroic, you understand? We're in control here. Anything jumps off and Junior dies first, get it?"

Asia nodded. She had no doubt that the man meant what he said. He'd been the one driving, and he was in charge, in all the ways that counted.

They waited in the van for an endless time, the sounds of other cars, of people talking, all around them. Asia gritted her teeth, shaking, her hands clenched into fists in an effort to keep from pounding on the side of the van and screaming for help. She knew it would do no good; that kind of move would only get them killed. But the evidence of life flowing in an undisturbed stream around the island of their misery nearly sent her over the edge. She took a deep breath and convinced her rebellious mind to stick with the plan—get a precious break, get close enough to their captors for Jack to "hear" something.

Finally Asia heard the two lesser partners return and report that all was ready. Another minute and the doors in the back of the van swung open and let the night in—the damp smell of diesel exhaust and freshly mown grass, the glare of the lights in the parking lot, the oddly comforting glow of the Interstate Visitor Center. Despite the noise she'd heard in the van, they were parked at the far end of the parking area, and there were few people in the vicinity.

Asia crawled out of the van and found her feet, stretching as much as she could before she was pushed toward the restroom. Her legs wobbled, not wanting to cooperate until they got a decent supply of blood. When she made it to the Women's, she saw the team had found the custodial closet and posted a "Closed for Cleaning" sign to keep people out. One of them knocked loudly on the door to confirm the restroom was empty, and when he got no reply, he walked Asia and Jack inside. His companion stayed outside to guard the entrance.

The chance to use the facilities was such a relief that Asia gave little thought to anything else. Even if she had given it a thought, the man watching her gave her no opportunity. He stood right outside the stall and checked it afterward, making sure she'd left no plea for help on a scrap of toilet paper or scratched into the wall. He did the same for Jack. As soon as they washed up, he ushered them out and back toward the van again.

Asia had nearly given up on the idea of leaving any sign behind when she caught sight of an older woman walking a dog not far from the van. The woman and her poodle were dappled in shadow on a grassy strip near a stand of trees; Asia's guards were watching their charges. There was a chance she could attract the woman's attention without their knowledge. Without further thought she sneezed—loudly, twice.

The guard just in front of her turned as he felt something wet hit the back of his neck. "What the fuck!"

"Sorry! Did I spray?"

"Get in the fucking truck! Now!"

She kept her head down, but she managed to glance toward the woman at the edge of the trees. Sure enough, she had seen them. Maybe it had been enough to matter.

As they climbed back into the vehicle, the driver handed them several bottles of water and some wrapped sandwiches and snacks from the vending machines.

"Make those last. We won't be stopping again for a while." To emphasize the point he shoved a large bucket filled with a noxious, pine-scented disinfectant cleaner lifted from the custodial closet into the back with them. "For emergencies." He gave them a last emotionless glance and disappeared around the front of the van. Then the doors swung shut with a heartless clang, and she and Jack were left alone.

Alana was relieved to find her apartment empty when she got home past two a.m. She was looking forward to sinking into bed—alone. She didn't feel like dealing with Mark right now, with his questions and his teasing and his insistence. The man knew his way around the bedroom, but, damn it, she was tired, and he seldom took no for an answer.

Besides, there was one little job left to do before she slept, an itch she meant to scratch or she knew it would keep her up the rest of the night. Lana shrugged out of her jacket and holster and threw them on the bed, then went back out into the living room and booted up the computer in one corner of the room.

It wasn't long before she found him, courtesy of the Department of Motor Vehicles of the State of Florida: Gabriel de Santos Cruz, born March 21, 1979, Miami, Florida. His record was clean in Florida and everywhere else. He had a gun permit and a Private Investigator's license. She Googled the name of the PI firm on the license (Guardian Angel Investigations) and found a nicely designed website with an understated brief of his scope of work (broad), his qualifications (impressive) and several of his clients. One of his specialties was locating missing persons.

She searched her desk for a pen. Maybe she should talk to one or two of those clients. Before she could find something to write with, her cell bleated at her, making her jump. Cursing, she reached across the desk for the damned thing and thumbed it open.

"Matheson."

"Hey, baby." She could tell by the husky whisper that Mark was calling from bed.

"Mark, do you know what time it is?"

"I can tell you're not asleep yet. You don't have that

little sleepytime purr in your voice."

"I'm about to have that little fuck-off growl in my voice." She sighed, but she allowed the corners of her mouth to lift.

"All right, I know it's late." He sounded appropriately contrite. "I just wanted to see if you were okay. Rough night?"

"I've had better. There's a kid involved." That sense of panic rose again. She crushed it.

"Yeah. Ballard will be using everybody on this one."

Lana sat up. "You got a call?"

"Nah, I just checked in with dispatch to see where you were. Asked a few questions."

"And they told you what was going on?" Holy shit. If security was this lax, the media would have the whole story by tomorrow morning.

"Like I said, Ballard's planning on calling everyone in on it. Got a staff meeting set for 8:00. Hey, you're the lead on this. I figured you knew."

She ran a hand down her face. "Of course I know about the meeting, Mark. I just didn't think the old man would have everybody and his brother there."

"Well, shit, girl, thanks a lot."

"No, I didn't mean it like that. Look, I'm just tired. And that meeting's coming up really early . . ."

"Yeah, I know. I'll let you go. Hey, and don't worry about tomorrow. This one's open and shut. You know the husband's got to be good for this somehow."

Anger flared at hearing this bullshit for the second time tonight. "Actually, Mark, I don't know that at all."

"Oh, you've got to be kidding me, Lana." There was both disbelief and condescension in Mark's voice. "Don't tell me you've got another one of your famous hunches."

"My hunches usually play out pretty well, you know." She tried swallowing the hurt his disdain caused her. It didn't go down so well.

"Yeah, except when they don't."

"But in this case, the evidence so far is on my side. The husband looks clean."

"Looks can be deceiving, darlin'. We haven't even begun to look into him. Don't you dare go into that meeting tomorrow defending his ass. Right now he's your best hope of finding that mother and her son."

Shit. "I know." She blew out a breath. "I gotta get to bed."

"You're right, sweetheart. Wish I was there with you. Good night."

She ignored the honey in his voice and answered with a single, curt, "'Night."

She keyed off the phone and stared bleary-eyed at Gabriel Cruz's handsome image on the screen in front of her. He was grim and unsmiling in his DMV photo. She couldn't help remembering how his slow, incendiary smile had transformed that predator's face earlier, how it had ignited something deep in her chest. And yet there was no question. The man was a hunter.

Damn it. Ethan Roberts had brought in a ringer. To help find his wife and son? Or to run a very elaborate and professional interference?

CHAPTER FOUR

Gabriel Cruz had spent time dirtside on most of the planets clustered around the galaxy's busier jump nodes. He'd pulled a few tours on some of the worlds of the distant Outer Reaches, too. His job required plenty of travel and a familiarity with many of the galaxy's exotic locales and bustling centers of commerce, the slums and the luxury resorts, the slave markets and the sex trade. Gabriel hadn't seen it all, but he'd seen a lot of it. And he could still find much to admire in a summer morning in a temperate climate zone on the planet its inhabitants called Earth.

The yellow sun was shining out of a flawless blue sky as he got out of the car and followed Rayna up the sidewalk toward Ethan's house. It would be hot soon, but Gabriel didn't mind the heat. He hated the cold of ships and space stations and dank colonial outposts, always balancing the scarcity of resources against the needs of many. Here he could smell the rich earth, the vegetation growing in it, the asphalt and the car exhaust. He could hear the birds singing, the neighbors mowing lawns and taking out the garbage. For one minute, he could pretend his life was like anyone else's. Gabriel took that minute. Then he took a deep breath and went up the steps into Ethan's house.

A young man in the white uniform shirt of a Metro Nashville PD officer stopped them at the front door with the usual bluff and bluster. Gabriel could see Ethan start toward them from the office inside on the right, but FBI Special Agent Alana Matheson was quicker.

She waved them in from a desk in the smaller office to the left, dismissing the uniform. "It's all right, Officer. They're friends of the family." She nodded as she came to join them. "Morning, folks."

"Agent Matheson." Gabriel was intrigued by the way her grass-green eyes locked on to his. They studied him as if they'd never quite encountered anything like him before. He didn't know whether to be flattered or insulted by the thought, but he recognized he had that much in common with the FBI agent. He'd never seen local law enforcement like her before either.

Slightly unnerved, he said the first thing that came to mind. "Have you been here all night?"

She smiled, her fatigue showing. "No, I did get a little sleep. Don't think your friend got any at all, though. He's looking pretty slammed." She indicated the office where the doctor was talking with Rayna.

Gabriel noted the signs of weariness in Ethan's body that went beyond the obvious need for sleep and healing, his bone-cracking tension and heart-rending pain, his desperation. He felt his own chest tighten in sympathy. He turned back to Alana to see her watching him.

"How long have you known Ethan Roberts, Mr. Cruz?"

He held her gaze to see what her reaction would be and was delighted to see the color rise in her face in the seconds before he answered her question. "Not long. Sam and Rayna are mutual friends. They asked me to see if I could be of help."

"In what way?"

"You might say I specialize in recovering what is lost."

"As in missing persons." She gave him that thorough once-over again. "I'm aware you're a private investigator. Has Roberts hired you to find his wife and son?"

Gabriel smiled. It hadn't taken her long to find his data plant.

"As I said, Sam and Rayna asked me to help. I'm not being paid."

"Mr. Cruz, I hope I don't have to tell you that interfering with a Federal investigation is against the law."

Somehow, he found her warning intensely sexy. "I have no intention of interfering. I'm simply here helping a friend recover something he's lost. In this case, starting with his memory of what happened yesterday at the river."

Alana's gaze narrowed. "Are you also a psychiatrist

of some sort, sir?"

"No."

"A hypnotherapist?"

"Not really."

"Then how do you expect to be able to help?"

He shrugged. "I have my ways. Some people would consider them somewhat . . . unconventional."

Her lips curved. His breath stopped.

"Really. Okay. Maybe I should sit in on your meeting today, see for myself."

He almost laughed. He hadn't planned on this, but he could see no real harm in it. He would leave her behind long before he got to the point where the chase got dangerous.

"Why not?"

Her smile widened, revealing white, even teeth, and she waved a hand toward the office. "After you, Mr. Cruz."

"Thank you, Agent Matheson. And, please, call me Gabriel."

"Might as well call me Lana," she murmured as he passed her. "We're going to be very close friends from now on."

The words, the breathy whisper of their delivery, her scent, caught in the air as he passed—all sent the blood rushing to Gabriel's groin so fast his head spun. He had to force himself to keep walking against an irrepressible urge to take her in his arms, to bend his head to those lush, full lips and drink until they were both dizzy and falling down drunk. He looked at Lana in alarm, unsure of himself, unsure of her. This was not something he experienced. Ever. Interest, yes. Lust, even. But this? This was . . . God, what the hell *was* this?

She was watching him again. "What?"

He shook his head. "Nothing."

Gabriel admonished himself to forget about the woman for a moment and get down to business. Ethan was so clearly in need of help, and it was past time he got started. He approached the man and laid a hand on his shoulder.

"Morning, Ethan. Did you sleep?"

Ethan shook his head. "I've got some pain meds. I'll take some later."

Rayna, watching them from a post by the window, didn't bother to hide her concern. "That's the best idea I've heard all morning. I'll be here in case anything happens. You need to get some rest."

"I'll be all right." Ethan glanced at Gabriel and managed a brief smile. "Maybe you shouldn't have compared this to sex. I'm feeling like a virgin, and, no offense, but I'm not sure I even like you."

Gabriel laughed, impressed by Ethan's attempt at humor. "Don't worry. I'll be gentle." He found a seat on the couch and gestured for Ethan to sit next to him. Then he saw the shocked look on Lana's face and wanted to laugh again. "Are you sure you want to be a part of this?"

She hooked a hip up on the desk, folded her arms over her chest and gave him a sultry smile. "Oh, I wouldn't miss this for the world."

"I do love an open mind." His own smile began to fade as he settled into himself in preparation for what he was about to do. Rayna closed the doors to the room and took a seat in the armchair next to the desk. The room was quiet, expectant, the sounds of the morning filtering in from outside like the sunshine through the windows.

When he was ready, Gabriel laid a hand on Ethan's forearm and closed his eyes. "What's the first thing you remember about yesterday, Ethan?"

There was chaos in Ethan's mind for a moment, a riot of images, most of them passing too quickly for Gabriel to catch them. Anything that stood out was from more recently—this morning, last night, yesterday afternoon as he'd talked with the police.

Gabriel spoke to him again, his quiet voice leading him. "Try to calm down and just think of one thing. The first thing. Waking up yesterday morning."

The images slowed, focused. *A face—her face, so sexy and warm, just coming out of sleep. He bent to kiss her and the touch of her lips was all it took to ignite the fire in him. She breathed his name and moved to straddle him, taking him in as his body went up in flames . . .*

"Son of a bitch!" Ethan pulled his arm back like he'd been bitten and curled his fingers into a fist. Their connection broken, he sat glaring at Gabriel, his chest heaving.

Gabriel met the man's gaze without heat, though

his own throat strangled his breath. His heart hammered, he was hard and aching, as if *he* had been making love to Asia Roberts that morning. He felt Ethan's love for her; he knew the depth of their intimacy. As always, he felt like the worst kind of voyeur.

Rayna simply waited, watching. She'd been through this with him before.

Lana looked from Ethan to Gabriel to Rayna, seeking an explanation. "What the hell happened?"

It was some time before Gabriel looked up to answer her. "We're, uh, we're making progress."

"Like hell we are." Ethan moved to stand up. "We're finished here."

Rayna put a hand on his shoulder. "Ethan, honey, you have to let him work."

"I'm sorry, Ethan." Gabriel held his gaze. "We can't censor what you show me. I'm either in your head or I'm not. If we want to find out what happened at the river, I'll have to be with you."

The doctor made a visible effort to control his anger, forcing the tension out of his shoulders. But Gabriel could see the lingering sense of violation sparking in the man's eyes. He would never forgive Gabriel for it, no matter what the outcome of this session.

Gabriel held out his hand. He saw Ethan take a breath, then take the hand. The connection was immediate, and Gabriel felt Ethan's resentment—and his determination—burning through.

"Let's try to go directly to the river, Ethan. Where did you go? Show me."

Again, there was a jumble of images, then the slow resolve to a single impression: *a grove of smooth-barked trees beside a broad, shallow river, sandy soil leading down to a pebbly shoal under a bridge on the left hand, bushy undergrowth and a muddy approach on the right. A picnic table with food laid out. A blanket spread out under a big oak set back from the river. Asia laughing and splashing with Jack in the water.*

Gabriel's heart twisted in his chest as he felt with Ethan what he'd lost that day—the joy, the love, the simple closeness. The longing he felt for it now was like a black void in his soul, a hole that devoured all light, worse than any Gabriel had seen in space. It was one thing to be lonely when you had nothing and no one. It was an entirely different thing to have everything and lose it in one moment of horror.

Gabriel swallowed his own fear and pulled Ethan back on track. "What happened next?"

This time as he entered Ethan's mind he sensed a new level of intimacy, of trust. The man had decided to let him in, no matter what.

"Mom, can I go back in the water?"

His son's hopeful face hung over them, blocking out the sun winking at them through the trees. His wife looked up at the boy with a drowsy smile.

"We just ate, Jack. Give your food some time to digest. Come back in fifteen minutes."

"How long is that?"

With an effort he moved to help. "Here, son. Take my watch. Be careful with it. Right now it's exactly one o'clock—see? So when this big hand is on the three, come back and ask again."

"Okay!" He could hear the excitement in Jack's voice.

"Jack! Don't go too far."

"I won't."

"Ten to one the watch lands in the drink." Asia's murmur was sleepy and sweet.

Ethan shifted so his body lay touching hers along one side, his arm curled across her ribs. "It's waterproof. And shockproof. And, uh, mudproof."

She turned her head to smile at him. "Then you're a genius."

"Finally, the recognition I deserve." He bent his head to brush his lips across hers.

"Just wait 'til I get you home." She wove her fingers through his hair to pull him closer. "I'll show you what you deserve."

She offered her mouth for another kiss, and he took it, deeper this time, his tongue stroking hers with velvet heat. He settled his weight over her, pressing the hot ridge of his erection against her thigh. She arched under him, encouraging him with a sigh.

Eventually Jack appeared over him with an expression of glee. "The big hand is on the three!"

Ethan groaned and sat up, reluctantly releasing his hold on Asia.

"So it is," Asia confirmed. *They stood up, just as a white van turned from the main road onto the river access, tires squealing.* Gabriel felt Ethan's apprehension; he knew what was coming. Something was wrong about the van from the beginning. Gabriel watched the van as it came into the clearing, hoping for an identification plate, but the kidnappers had been careful. There were no plates, front or back.

The van slid to a stop in front of their car and three men in ski masks jumped out. He grabbed the closest thing he could find—a branch he knew would do little good—and pushed Asia and Jack behind him. They backed up to the big oak and made a stand.

Gabriel took a minute to note the three attackers' height and approximate weight, the way they moved, their skin color where it showed between mask and shirt. He could see they'd had combat training and had worked as a team before. Professionals.

The closest man pulled a gun from his waistband. "Don't make this any harder than it has to be, Roberts. The woman comes with us. You and the boy take a nap. Nice and easy."

Gabriel looked closely at the weapon, made certain of its shape and size and caliber so he could have Lana run it through ballistics later. Then he felt hesitation and doubt as a shadow of disbelief flitted through Ethan's mind. He pressed on, hoping for clarity, praying for rescue.

"He pointed the gun at you. What happened then, Ethan?"

The gun that had been pointed in their direction twisted out of the attacker's hand and flew into the thin stand of trees near the river. The two men, connected in mind and spirit, gasped in surprise almost as one. Gabriel imposed his will on the scene in Ethan's mind once more, slowing the action, and replayed it, watching again as the gun was wrenched by an invisible force from the man's hand and landed somewhere in the undergrowth near the water's edge. He could see nothing that could have caused what Ethan remembered, but there it was. He shook his head and moved on.

Their attackers closed in as one and made a rush for them. He swung the branch hard and took out the closest one at the knees. A second man hit him before he had a chance to pull back for another swing, slamming him so hard in the gut he thought the fist might punch through to his spine. He doubled over, losing his grip on his only weapon.

Asia screamed his name, frightened for him, though she was the one in danger. He struggled to keep his feet, blocking the worst of his attacker's blows, and ran in her direction. She had Jack in her arms—the little boy refused to let her go—and was running for the car. Dragging one man with him, he tackled the man pursuing her and went down with both of them in a tangle of elbows and knees. Then he became Ground Zero of a shitstorm of pain, attacks coming at him from every angle, until the back of his head exploded in agony and everything went black.

Gabriel let go of Ethan's hand and sat back, breathing hard. Ethan slumped against the pillows of the couch, his eyes closed, his face haggard with loss and re-emergent pain.

"Okay, that's it." Rayna took immediate charge of the situation. "You're going upstairs to bed—now!" As she slung Ethan's arm over her shoulder and urged him to his feet, she cast a glance at Alana. "Can you handle Gabriel?"

Lana's brows were drawn together in confusion, but she nodded. "No problem. What about Ethan?"

"I'll get some of those pain pills into him and make sure he sleeps most of the day." Rayna steered Ethan toward the stairs. "He should be a little better by this evening."

Gabriel let the conversation drift by him for a while, closing his eyes as the room emptied. He didn't know how Ethan was still standing. He had taken a brutal beating, but that was the least of it. What his body was suffering was nothing to what his heart was enduring. If it was the last thing he did, Gabriel would find this man's wife and child. He would never be able to live with himself if he failed Ethan in this and left the man alone with his guilt.

"Hey." He opened his eyes to see Lana's face above his, her honey-colored hair backlit by the morning sun coming in the windows. "I brought you some coffee."

He sat up to take the mug from her hands.

"Okay, that didn't look like a whole lot of fun." Her tone was light, but concern put two lines between her brows. "Not that I could tell what was going on. What were you doing exactly?"

There was no use trying to gloss over what he was. He came out with it.

"I'm a touch telepath. If I'm in physical contact with someone I can sense what's in his mind. In cases like Ethan's where memories might be lost, I can provide a little push to help them remember. I can read details others might miss."

Lana regarded him, disbelief lifting one corner of her mouth. "A telepath. Really. So you weren't kidding when you said you had to be in his head?"

"No. I wasn't kidding."

"I take it he didn't like it much, especially at first."

He gave her a tight smile. "You might say that."

"What was it that pissed him off?" It was obvious she didn't believe what he'd told her; she was testing him.

The image came to his mind again of Asia, caught in the power of that moment with Ethan—the passion, the hunger, the depth of love in her eyes for him. Gabriel suddenly wanted to see that look on Lana's face—for him. His body flushed with heat and a desire so intense he could barely speak.

"That's between him and me."

Her eyes widened in understanding. "Oh, so things can get personal, I guess." She made a little speculative hum deep in her throat. "All right. Let's say I believe this is something you can do. What can you tell me about the kidnapping?"

"Let me tell you something else first." Gabriel took a big gulp of his coffee and met her eyes. "If you have any thought that this guy is involved in his wife's disappearance, forget it. He loves her and his son. He would do anything to get them back—including something stupid. If we have anything to watch out for with him, that would be it."

"If you say so." She searched his face, her expression giving away nothing. "What else?"

"We're looking for a late model white van, the kind used by businesses, no windows in the back. No markings on the side. It didn't have any plates. A . . . Ford Econo . . . something."

"Econoline."

"That's it."

"You could *see* that?"

He shrugged. "People retain every detail of what they see. They just can't recall everything. When I go in, I can take my time, slow things down and look."

"Wow. Now that's a talent we could really use in the Bureau." She crossed her arms and frowned at him. "Assuming you're not completely full of shit."

Gabriel raised an eyebrow. "You don't believe me?"

"How the hell am I supposed to believe you just pulled this out of a man's brain like . . . like Spock on some dumb *Star Trek* episode?"

"Huh?"

"Forget it. The point is I can't put out an APB based on your reaching inside Ethan's head and pulling out a plum."

Dios, the woman made him want to laugh, though the look on her face told him that just might get him killed. "So I guess you wouldn't be interested in a description of the kidnappers, then, either."

"You saw the kidnappers?" Skepticism overrode any hope in her tone.

He shook his head. "They were wearing ski masks." The term rolled off his tongue like he knew what it meant, but the knowledge had been freshly plucked from Ethan's mind along with the image. "There were three of them, two white males and one black male, all six-foot or better. The black guy had to be"—he hesitated, making a quick conversion to local equivalents—"over 240 pounds, the others were medium build."

Lana gaped at him, then reached in her pocket for a notebook and a pen. She wrote it all down.

"I swear, Cruz, if you're blowing this out your ass, I'll have you in lockup so fast it'll make your pretty head swim."

Gabriel couldn't hold back his grin. "I'm not sure I know how to respond to that comment, Agent Matheson."

"Just tell me how I'm supposed to explain where I got this information."

"Tell the truth. Your victim remembered. He's much clearer today than he was yesterday And it's not just because of the knock on the back of his head. He really was drugged. You'll get confirmation of that when the drug tests come back.

She searched his face, her pen poised over the page in her book. "You could see that, too?"

"No. But I could feel it in him." He paused, wondering how much to tell her about the gun. "Can you take me to the crime scene?"

She shut down at once, her face shuttered with suspicion. "I can't do that, Gabriel. We're still combing the area for evidence."

"Evidence is what we're after, Lana." He sat forward and would have reached for her until he caught himself and pulled back. "I saw something I think is important."

"Tell me and I'll have the evidence team look for it."

"No," he insisted. "It'll be faster for me to look myself. I'll recognize the location when I see it, but I won't be able to describe it."

"You better damn well describe it or you'll be withholding it." Her green eyes flashed fire. "I can't let you on the scene, so do you know something useful or don't you?"

Goddamn, pig-headed, narrow-minded, dirt-sucking locals! This was why he hated working with them. "I can't be certain of what I saw, Agent Matheson." He deliberately kept his voice low and even to try and balance the impatience that drove him. "Telling you would make no sense."

The agent got up and headed toward the door. "Well, you got that right, Mr. Cruz. None of this makes any sense. I'm heading out to the crime scene now. If I see anything unusual—white rabbits or anything—I'll let you know. Maybe it'll match whatever it is you caught a glimpse of while you were having your magic vision."

Gabriel's hands clenched into fists as he watched her go. Damn it, he'd thought there was a chance he could work with this one . . .

She stopped and turned back to him from the hallway. Looking a little embarrassed, she waved her notebook at him. "Thanks for the description of the van and the perps, by the way. I don't know how you got it, but *that* we can use. We'll put it out right away."

Heat flashed through his body, but he was no longer certain it was anger fueling the fire. He only knew Alana Matheson was going to be a problem, one he'd have to get rid of as soon as possible.

CHAPTER FIVE

Trin, Minertsa, Home Planet of the Consortium, Sector 10

Ardis found her way to her usual seat in the fourth row, first balcony of the Lorenda Excelsis Presentation Venue, as she did every tenth solar cycle. She was a regular patron of the entertainments staged at the Venue—the historical reenactments, the auditory performances and, like tonight's scheduled event, the color spectrum orchestrations. Those had been her favorites, in a time when her attendance at the Venue was simply for pleasure.

The Director Second of the Ministry of Labor watched as the great hall filled with beings of all descriptions. The entertainments were popular not only with her own people, but with the many outsiders who now crowded the central governing planet of the Consortium. The audience even included a number of humans. There had been a time when a human could not have moved freely anywhere in the worlds of the Consortium. But now, though the slave trade still flourished, the descendants of Earth's people and their humanoid allies throughout the galaxy had broken many barriers. They were everywhere, even here in the heart of Minertsa.

The color spectrum shows were appealing to the humans, for whom entertainment of any kind seemed to be addictive. Ardis found this somewhat puzzling, as the humans could only perceive the visual aspects of the presentations. From what she understood, they "saw" the colors with their eyes, pronouncing them "spectacular," and claimed to "hear" certain of the auditory frequencies in the vibratory spectra. These they described as "eerie" or "compelling." Yet they completely missed the tactile nature of the vibratory spectra and were not capable of interpreting the emotional or sensual content of the colors. Frankly, she did not see the point of attending a performance handicapped in such a way. She imagined it would be like trying to experience the humans' beloved statue of David wearing a blindfold. Possible, but inadequate.

The time for the show to begin approached, but still the seats on either side of Ardis remained empty. This was as planned. She waited, keeping her aura within careful bounds. She could allow a tiny amount of deeper violet to tinge her usual lavender; the excitement surrounding the entertainment would naturally heighten her color. But no more, or her mission would be in jeopardy. She cast a discreet glance at the others in her section. No one was looking in her direction. Satisfied, she kept her eyes on the stage until the lights in the hall began to dim for the start of the performance.

As the Venue went black, someone slipped into the seat to her right. She knew immediately it was not her usual contact. The human was larger. Male, not female. She kept her aura a neutral lavender-gray and challenged him.

"You have the wrong seat. Please check your ticket."

"This ticket was given me by a friend." The man kept his voice low. "You may check it yourself."

Once her eyes had adjusted to the darkened theater, Ardis peered down at the hand he held out to her. In his palm was a tiny data crystal. She met his even gaze and accepted what he offered, slipped the crystal into the port in her wrist and confirmed his identity. Then she removed the crystal and swallowed it.

"Where is my regular contact?"

"We fear she has been taken."

Bright green fear streaked through Ardis's aura before she could control it. "Then we may have been compromised!"

"No. She would never betray us."

The performance began, colors washing through the air around them, auditory vibrations a low thrum through the seats. Ardis ignored the emotional beginning to the piece, her mind in turmoil. She didn't want to trust this man with her report, but she had no choice.

She handed him the precious data crystal. "You must tell your people time is running out. Sennik is impatient, and he is under pressure. I won't be able to deflect him much longer."

"We understand." The man downloaded the data from the crystal into the port at his wrist, then disposed of it, as she had done with his.

"He has sent Thrane teams everywhere, even to Earth. They have been very successful at recapturing the adults." Ardis glanced up, pausing as two latecomers were shown to their seats not far away. Then she continued in a rush. "We must protect the rest. The searchers are closing in. Once the Director Prime has the young ones it will be impossible for any of us to stop him."

"We'll do the best we can."

Ardis caught the hand of her human companion, as an emotion she could not control turned her aura the flaming colors of the setting sun. "Make certain your best is good enough. Or the galaxy will soon be at war."

U.S. Interstate 40, Arkansas, Earth, Sector Three

Asia lay motionless in the back of the van, sweat dripping from her skin to pool beneath her where her body met the floor of the vehicle. The temperature in the metal coffin of the van was rising with the morning sun outside. If the engine had been running, there would have been some movement of air in the back of the vehicle; at least, there had been yesterday—air coming through the vent high up on one wall of the steel box that held them. Today, the endless motion of the van had stopped, the engine had been silent for hours now, and the heat was suffocating.

Jack raised his head beside her. "You okay, Mom?"

"Yeah, baby. I'm just hot. You?"

"Yeah. Can I have some water?"

The stench of the slop bucket in the corner hit her nostrils as she got up to give him a swallow of water from one of the last of their precious bottles. She tried to ignore it.

"You hear anything from up front?"

"No. The man is sleeping. The other two are outside, still trying to fix the van." Jack smiled. "I don't think they can, though."

"I don't think they can, either." Asia sighed, her head falling back against the van wall. "They would have done it by now if they could."

"That's because nothing is really broken."

She looked at the little boy. "What do you mean?"

He shrugged. "It's not broken. It just won't work right now."

Asia's heart kicked in her chest. The look on Jack's face was more than a little frightening.

"Jack. Did you do something to the van?"

"Yes." He giggled.

She stared at him, not sure how to react. "Tell me, Jack. Tell me what you did."

He stared back at her, his eyes big and round. "I—I don't know. I thought it was a good idea."

Asia scooped him up and held him tight. "Jack, it's okay. You're not in trouble. I'm just a little . . . confused. Explain it to me. How did you stop the van?"

He pulled back to look at her, still trying to determine whether what he'd done was against the rules or not. "I was wishing we were home. And I thought, I wish this old van would just STOP. And I thought about it really hard, like Teacher told me to. And then the van stopped."

Asia swallowed, fear clogging her throat. "Teacher?"

Jack refused to meet her eyes.

Holy Christ. The ability to resist mental programming. Telepathy. And now telekinesis. Her son was truly exceptional. Had the Grays tried to exploit his talents in the short time they'd had him in their custody? Rayna hadn't been certain how long he'd been at the processing center before his rescue. The Minertsan centers processed large numbers of newly acquired slaves before distributing them throughout the planets of the Consortium; they usually didn't hold them for more than a few days.

"Mom? I'm getting kinda tired. Should I make the van go again?"

"Does it make you tired to do these things, buddy?"

He nodded. "It was real hard at first 'cuz they were trying to start it a lot. They haven't tried in a while, but they might again soon, and then I could let them."

Asia agreed. "It's getting really hot in here, baby. I think we should probably get going again."

Suddenly there was movement in the front of the van—the man in the front seat coming awake with a curse. He thrust his face in the window between the sections of the vehicle and hissed at them. "Keep your mouths shut!" The window slid closed again with a snick.

Asia hunkered down, holding Jack close to her chest. Outside the van, she heard a car pass close to the van and come to a stop in the gravel of the roadside ahead of them. A minute passed in tense silence.

Then the voice of the driver, just outside the driver's side door: "Everybody keep quiet and let me handle this. Morning, officer!"

"You fellas having some trouble?"

"Well, we stopped to switch drivers a minute ago, and now we're having a little trouble starting her up again." The driver's voice oozed oily calm. "I'm sure she'll kick over here in a minute."

"You need a jump? I've got cables in the cruiser."

"Mom!" Jack was shaking in her arms. She put a finger in front of her lips, trying to quiet him, but he insisted. "They're thinking of killing the policeman! We have to stop them!"

Shit! "Start the van, Jack. As soon as they try, start the van." It was the only thing that would save that patrolman's life.

"That shouldn't be necessary, officer." The driver was closer now. "Let me just try it one more time before you go to all that trouble."

Asia felt the van rock slightly as the man stepped up

inside. He muttered a curse as he fumbled with the key in the ignition. Jack closed his eyes in concentration. Then the engine roared to life, and all three of the men in the front seat laughed with relief.

"See there! Third time's the charm, eh, officer?" The driver's voice was edgy and harsh, despite his attempt to appear relaxed.

"Guess so. Next time you want to switch drivers, though, you need to stop in a rest area. Road shoulder's for emergency only."

"Yes, sir. Been overseas for a while with the military. Guess I didn't think."

"Oh, yeah? Whereabouts?"

"With the Marine Corps in Afghanistan."

"Well, I sure appreciate all you're doing for us over there, soldier. You gentlemen have a nice day."

"Thank you. You, too."

Asia held her breath while the men in the van waited silently for the patrolman to walk back to his cruiser. She heard the scratch and pop of gravel as he pulled out.

Then she heard one of the men in the front: "Fucking bastard's lucky I didn't drill him where he stood."

"Yeah, and how would we have explained a dead Arkansas State Trooper to HQ, you idiot? Now let's get back on the road. We're way behind schedule. Hilliard, you drive for a while."

There was more shifting of weight and doors slamming in the van as the men changed positions.

After a moment, the van started moving again and cooler air began to filter into the back of the vehicle.

The window between the sections slid open and the leader's face appeared. "It was a good thing you stayed quiet. If you had tried to contact that trooper, you'd have forced me to kill him."

Asia looked at him. "That wouldn't have been my fault. But I stayed quiet to protect my son."

"A good move anyway. You probably noticed he wasn't looking for this vehicle, either. There's been no report issued with our description. Wonder why that is, Asia?"

She felt rage heat her blood until she shook with it. "Did you kill my husband, you bastard?"

The man laughed, and slid the window closed.

The sun was already climbing toward noon by the time Lana parked her car behind the police barricade at Harpeth Narrows and walked down toward the river. Under the dense grove of trees near the water, though, it was still cool, the air smelling of mud and green life. A half-dozen TBI forensics officers dotted the open area from the gravel turn-out to the water. As Lana approached, one of them turned and waved at her—Janet Goodman, from the state crime lab.

Lana slowed as she got within speaking distance, looking for evidence flags. There were none.

"Hey, Janet. You all find anything interesting?"

Janet shook her head. "We sent the clothes you gave us yesterday off for analysis, along with some little blood splatters we picked up down here. Normally wouldn't have that back for weeks, but given that it's a kidnapping I've put a rush on it, sent it to the top of the pile. Took some casts of tire tracks, but there was a lot of traffic. Don't think that's gonna help much."

Lana knew the Narrows; she wasn't surprised. "Think we caught a break there. The husband gave us a description on the vehicle this morning."

"Oh, yeah? Great. 'Cause, otherwise we got shit. No footprints. Sure as hell no fingerprints. They didn't drop a damn thing. Looking for hair and fiber's like looking for a needle in a friggin' haystack, but that's what we're doing now."

"Husband said they wore ski masks and gloves."

"Report didn't say that." Janet looked back at her notes. "Are you sure?"

Lana felt for Janet; her job had just gone from difficult to impossible. "Roberts was drugged at the scene. He's only now getting this back."

"Shit. Might as well pack this up then."

Lana looked around at the shady expanse of ground, peaceful except for the team of specialists trying desperately to find a clue to what had happened there, and felt a familiar weight settle over her shoulders. From past experience, she knew she'd be carrying that load until the case was over.

On the road above the barricade, a black Ford Explorer slowed and turned in. Two men got out and headed her way.

"Oh, that's just fucking perfect." She put her hands on her hips and watched the pair approach.

"Friends of yours?"

"My idiot rookie partner and the private dick the family's brought in on the case."

"You're kidding."

"I wish." She moved to meet them before they contaminated the scene. "What the hell are you doing here, Rick?"

"I couldn't get through on your cell." The rookie swallowed and held out a sheaf of papers. "And the guys said you needed this."

She took the stuff from him and looked it over. Routine phone and communication logs indicating Ethan Roberts had received and made no phone calls in the hours since the kidnapping. Very funny.

"They were yanking your chain, Rick." She glared at Gabriel. "And you. I told you specifically I couldn't allow you to be here."

"Did you?" The man actually smiled. The effect was dazzling. "I'd understood you couldn't bring me to the crime scene. I found another way."

She ignored the way his grin made her feel and pointed up the access road. "You need to get your ass on the other side of that barricade before I have you arrested for interfering in a Federal investigation. Rick, turn your butt around, take him back to Nashville and get back on the job at Roberts's house."

"Yes, ma'am." The kid started to grab Gabriel's

elbow to do as she said, but Gabriel shrugged him off.

"Alana, please. Since I'm here, let me do some good." When she hesitated, he pressed on. "Your search pattern, for example. Maybe I could help focus it a bit."

Lana glanced back over her shoulder at Janet, who was watching with brows lowered, but wasn't close enough to hear the details. "We're doing just fine, thank you very much."

Gabriel got the message and leaned in so only she could hear him. "You're scattered everywhere. And they haven't found anything, have they? I *saw* what happened. Let me help you."

Her wide-eyed partner stood looking from Gabriel to Lana now, wondering what had been said in private, waiting to see how this would fall out. Lana blew out a breath.

"All right. Hell. Rick, go on back. I'll bring Cruz when I come. And, for future reference, civilians don't belong at a crime scene. Don't bring them along with you. Got it?"

"But he said—"

"I don't give a shit what he said. I'd already told him no."

The kid nodded at last. "Got it." He turned and trudged up the rise to his Explorer.

"I'd thank him for the ride, but I suppose that would only pour salt on the wound."

Lana felt an unexpected bubble of laughter rise up in her in response. She smothered it.

"You'd damn well better make yourself useful,

Cruz. I wasn't kidding when I said you don't belong here."

He was already scanning the grove with the intensity of a bird of prey. He went from charming rogue to professional tracker in a heartbeat, the change in him instantaneous and thorough. And as she watched him work, she caught his logic.

"The search pattern, you said." She looked up at him. "The men who took Asia and Jack were professionals. They didn't leave much behind, but Roberts gave those guys a run for their money. He fought them. Could be he shook something loose?"

Gabriel considered her, a smile tugging at the corners of his mouth. "The fight took place just in front of that big oak—from there to approximately here." He paced off the area.

She called the forensics chief over. "Janet, this is Gabriel Cruz. He's, uh, he's consulting on the case for the family." Janet frowned in Gabriel's direction, but softened when he gave her a smile. "He got some more info from the victim this morning. Try concentrating your hair and fiber search in this area. Maybe something will turn up. At least you'll be finished in time to enjoy your Sunday dinner."

"Works for me." Janet stalked off to redirect her crew.

"There's something else." Gabriel started walking. "This way. Near the river."

Lana followed him away from the location of most of the action. "What the hell are we going to find way down here?" *Except maybe a copperhead or two*, she thought, as they began to encounter mucky, reedy swampland near the river. The fetid stench of decaying vegetation and a cloud of flies rose to meet them as they waded into the undergrowth. "Shit. If there's anything in here, it's in a foot of water. We'll never find it."

"You're right." He stood for a moment, eyes closed, then splashed back out of the muck. He pointed a few steps downriver, to a drier piece of ground covered with low bushes.

"Gabriel." She refused to follow him this time. "If you would tell me what we're looking for, I could help. Better yet, let's get some people over here."

Lana was getting the sinking feeling that she'd taken this huge risk for nothing. She wasn't on the best of terms with Ballard as it was, and if he caught wind of this . . .

"Gabriel! *What* are you looking for?"

"This!" He stooped to retrieve something with a length of dry pine branch. He turned and held it out to her in triumph. There, dangling on the end of the stick by the trigger guard, was what appeared to be a shiny new Sig Sauer semi-automatic.

She stood staring at it, unable to come up with any explanation for its presence. "You want to tell me how this got here?"

"I need an evidence bag." Gabriel stood looking at her, still holding the weapon at the end of the stick.

Lana swore and ran a few steps back toward the

others. "Janet! You got a bag?"

The TBI agent joined them, her eyebrows disappearing into her auburn bangs. She snapped open a plastic evidence bag and held it under the weapon, nodding to Lana. "Here, hold this." She grasped the gun in one gloved hand, released the magazine neatly into the bag, ejected the last cartridge from the chamber and placed the gun inside the bag with its ammunition. Then she sealed the bag and pulled out a Sharpie to mark it.

When she'd done her job, she finally thought to ask, "Where the fuck did you get that?"

Lana indicated the patch of ground where Gabriel had found it.

Janet's eyebrows came together. "How the hell did the gun get way over here if they were fighting over there?"

"Ethan wasn't clear on that point." Gabriel offered no further explanation.

Lana's voice rose a full octave. "Are you kidding me?"

He shrugged. "It happened during the course of the fighting. That's all I know."

"So, what, Ethan took the gun off the guy?" Lana knew her expression must have reflected her belief that Gabriel had lost his mind. "Then I guess he just threw it away? Sure, that makes perfect sense."

"That's not what I said."

Lana took a deep breath and turned to the TBI agent. "Janet, could we have a minute?"

Janet gave them both a look and retreated.

Lana turned on Gabriel with a flash of temper even she wasn't expecting. "What the fuck are you trying to pull?"

"Take it easy." His hands went to her shoulders. "We got the gun, didn't we?"

Lana looked down at his hands, at the place where he was touching her, and she was suddenly flooded with a puzzling wave of emotion. Anger made up the most of it, and exasperation, and plain old confusion. The whirlpool sucked her down, and she forced herself back up, coming out of it sputtering and mad. She got herself under control by glaring at his hands until he let go.

She found her voice. "How did the gun get there, Cruz? What did you see?"

"You wouldn't believe me."

Her voice was steel. "I already don't believe you. Try another one."

Gabriel shook his head in defeat. "I don't understand it myself."

The man looked like he was ready to offer an explanation, but he never got a chance to deliver it. Lana glanced over his shoulder and groaned. Another FBI vehicle had just parked beyond the barricade, and a familiar figure was unfolding from behind the driver's side. Mark Jamisky waved at her and started in her direction.

Lana held up a hand to Gabriel. "This isn't over. It's a long drive back to Nashville."

"Lana!" Mark huffed as he got closer. "You weren't answering your cell. What's up?"

He came close, aiming maybe for a hug or a peck on the cheek, but she sidestepped him. She muttered, "Working here, Mark," and her expression held a warning. "This is Gabriel Cruz, he's consulting on the case. Special Agent Mark Jamisky."

Gabriel and Mark shook hands, circling each other like two wary wolves. Lana caught the scent of testosterone on the air and tried not to roll her eyes.

"I've been trying to get hold of you," Mark repeated. "Dispatch told me you were down here."

"I've been a little busy." She realized she'd been avoiding him since the staff meeting. She'd let his phone calls roll over to voice mail—had it really just been because she'd been working?

"So, Janet's team come up with anything?"

"Mark, you know I can't give you any details on this, unless you're telling me you've been assigned to the case?"

"Not yet, but that can always be arranged." He grinned.

Lana felt a sting of irritation. "I'll let you know when I need your help."

Mark's grin slid off his face. He turned to the taller man standing at Lana's side. "So, Gabriel. What kind of consulting work do you do, exactly?"

Lana shot him a glare, but Mark was making a point of ignoring her.

"Oh, a little of this, a little of that." Gabriel stood

with his feet planted, his body relaxed, like a fighter's. The curve of his lips showed he was enjoying this. Maybe too much.

"Uh-huh. Like what? Detective work? Security? Babysitting?"

"Mark." Lana could tell what he was up to, and it was likely to go too far. Mark didn't like to be cut out of the play, especially if some new number was called instead of his.

"I do whatever my client pays me to do, as long as I agree it's worth doing." Tone still even, but the eyes were sharp. You could cut glass with the intelligence in those eyes.

"What about this case, Gabe? Care to tell me why you've got your nose in a Federal kidnapping case?"

What the hell? Lana stared at the man who she could usually depend on to have her back. This time he'd as good as put a knife in it.

"I prefer Cruz. But it seems to me that would be the business of the agent in charge, wouldn't you say, Mark?"

Yes. Thank you. "Mark. With me. Now." She took the agent's arm and hauled him to one side, far enough to be polite, but not quite far enough to be completely out of earshot. "What the hell do you think you're doing?"

"Me? I'm doing my job, Lana. What the hell are *you* doing? You bring this guy here to a crime scene; you let him interfere with an investigation. God knows what kind of information you've let slip. And who the fuck is he anyway?"

"Hold on just a goddamn minute." Her anger was at full boil now. "You think you can walk up in here, throwing your weight around, barking like a big dog. But you know what? I'm in charge of this case. I'm the one who decides who gets to look at the crime scene and who doesn't. Gabriel led us to a key piece of evidence today. What are *you* doing here, besides giving me an ulcer?"

"I'm here saving your ass, that's what," Mark shot back. "How are you going to explain all this shit to Ballard?"

"That's my business." She looked brave, but the thought had been on her mind, too. She could only hope her boss would be happy enough with the results that he wouldn't worry about the methods she used to get them. "And I'd thank you to stay the hell out of it, especially around the hired help."

"Well, don't come crying to me when he wants to know what you've been up to with pretty boy over there." Mark spiked a glare at Gabriel, then turned on his heel and stomped off to his car without another word. The car door slammed, and he kicked up a cloud of dust as he peeled out onto the paved road from the river access.

Lana watched him go with a mixture of regret and relief. Somehow she'd known this was coming, and it had little to do with Gabriel. Mark's only saving graces were his humor and the fact that he was good in bed. That had been enough for a while, but suddenly it just wasn't. Lana sighed.

"Are you all right?" Gabriel was at her side, close enough to touch her, but keeping a careful distance.

She looked up into his face and saw a stream of emotions too quick to interpret run through his eyes. "I'm fine." She surveyed the grove, saw that the TBI team was still working their systematic magic, quartering the area of the fight between Ethan and kidnappers. "Are we done here?"

He nodded, starting back toward the car. "Lunch?"

Her eyes came up to meet his, trying to read his intent. He looked . . . hungry. "On one condition."

He smiled, shaking his head. "I can't explain how that gun got there, Lana."

She blew out a breath. "Well, there's at least one explanation for its being there," she muttered. "But I damn sure don't like it."

Gabriel stopped walking and stared at her. "No."

"Yes. Ethan could have planted that gun. Though why the dumbass threw it way over there is beyond me."

"Alana, you know Ethan had nothing to do with this."

The FBI agent lifted her arms in frustration. "Actually, Gabriel, no, I don't know that. I don't know that at all. It's pretty rare when *strangers* kidnap someone in this country, and this case has all the signs of the more usual circumstance. Somebody owes somebody else money or drugs or blood. Just because I haven't figured out yet what Ethan owes and who he owes it to doesn't mean he doesn't fit the profile."

"You're wrong about him." His whole body was taut with conviction. "There is a reason these men want Asia, but it has nothing to do with money or drugs."

She stared at him, eyes narrowing. "What, then?"

He appeared to think, then shook his head. "I don't know. I only know what I saw in Ethan's mind this morning. He's not involved with this. You can believe me."

"And what about the gun? Tell me what you saw."

"I could show you."

She stopped, gaping at him. "What?"

"I could show you what Ethan showed me."

She started walking again, double-time. "And be privy to everything in his head—and yours—like you were this morning? No, thank you!"

He grabbed her arm, and there was a swift jolt of electricity through the point of contact. She gasped and pulled away from him, her skin tingling with warmth where his hand had been. She stared, and found him staring back in a shock as obvious as hers.

"Sorry . . . I, uh, didn't mean for that to happen."

"What? You didn't mean to grab me? Or you didn't mean to electrocute me?"

"Both. Either." He exhaled. "I mean that's never happened before. I'm usually able to control . . . contact."

She shook her head once to clear it of the confusion that threatened to swamp her. "And you expect me to let you do the mindmeld thing? Forget it."

"A mindmeld sounds both dramatic and permanent." He looked at her as they reached the car. "This is neither. I can control this. And it won't be like this morning. Ethan couldn't filter what I saw because I was in his mind. I'll be letting you into my mind, and I'll just let you see this one thing. I won't be in your mind at all. I promise."

She snorted. "Like I'm supposed to trust you?"

He took her by the shoulders and looked down into her eyes. She felt rooted to the spot.

"You can trust me in this, Alana."

She noted the careful choice of words—"you can trust me *in this*"—as if there were some rules he saw fit to break, some conventions he felt free to flaunt. As if he had a foundation of ethics all his own, a structure of right and wrong upon which his entire life was built and from which he did not depart. Evidently anything having to do with his mind reading fell within that structure.

Too bad the rules aren't posted somewhere on the outside of the building for everyone to read, she thought.

Lana knew she should say no. For chrissakes, she had known this man fewer than twenty-four hours, she knew nothing about him, and now he was asking to swap brains with her. But her curiosity got the better of her. How many times had she wanted to get inside someone's head—a perp in the interrogation room, a witness at the scene, a victim so much in shock she couldn't get past the blood to remember anything about the man who'd killed her loved one? Gabriel was offering her that chance, if she could believe he was for real.

"Okay," she heard herself say. "But not here. On the way back."

Gabriel smiled, the corners of his mouth lifting just enough to show he was pleased. How was it that when he smiled like that he looked so sad—and made her want to kiss him until she couldn't draw breath?

CHAPTER SIX

His room was dark, quiet, a sanctuary of lonely peace in the crowded battle zone his home had become. But when Ethan emerged from a cocoon of drug-induced sleep and his eyes opened onto that comforting space, he was not comforted. God! it hurt to be in this place—in their room—without her. He breathed deep and smelled her sweet scent of desert spice and honey. His eyes roved from the bed to the dresser, from the closet to the bathroom, and everywhere he saw her ghost, smiling at him, watching him with love in her eyes, inviting him with a lift of her eyebrow or the parting of her lips.

He couldn't bear to think about where she was, what could be happening to her—or to Jack—while he lay helpless here. Every muscle ached to defend the wife and son he was supposed to protect. Instead, he was bound with heavy chains of guilt and left in this prison where there was only the endless waiting. The horrible speculation. The feeling of futility, knowing there was not a fucking thing he could do to help.

An old and familiar demon raised its filthy head in Ethan's belly. His knee and ribs were on fire, aching with fierce reality in this second hour past the time when he could have taken another dose of Vicodin, even according to the conservative instructions on the bottle. His friend and fellow therapist Dan Parker had known about that demon, the threat of dependency born of a horrible accident in what had once seemed like a previous life. Dan had taken it into consideration when writing the prescription, but even so, Ethan hadn't wanted to feed his old craving that often. So the pain had grown instead, until it was like a living thing that clawed at him almost badly enough to make him think of something other than Jack and Asia. Ethan considered taking another dose of the pills, trying for another few hours of sleep.

He clambered to his feet, favoring his swollen knee. He staggered to the bathroom and shook out two of the white caplets into his hand. And as he stared at his battered image in the mirror, he heard Jack's voice.

--Dad. Please don't be dead.

Ethan gasped and his hands began to shake; he lost the pills he was holding down the sink. Tears started in his eyes, threatening to spill over onto his cheeks. His son's voice was so clear, so present in his mind, that it was almost as if the boy was in the room with him. He closed his eyes and drew a ragged breath against the pain.

--Please, Dad. You can't be dead. It's not fair.

"Oh, God, Jack." His knees buckled, and he grabbed

at the counter to keep from slipping to the floor in a boneless heap. Jesus, this was bad. He'd expected depression, extreme anger, antisocial behavior, withdrawal, even a return to his addictive tendencies. But a full psychotic break? And if auditory hallucinations were the first sign, what was next? God knows the reality of Asia's kidnapping sounded enough like a paranoid fantasy to have him committed in any normal universe.

--Dad? I can hear you! Where are you?

There was a pause, as if Jack was waiting, listening. Ethan's wild gaze scanned the bathroom, searching for an anchor for his sanity. His mind careened from one thought to another, unable to focus.

--Dad? Are you still there? Can you hear me?

He didn't know what else to do. He answered the voice in his head. *Jack?*

--Dad! You can hear me! Mom's sleeping. I got lonely.

--Where are you, son?

--In a van. We've been riding in it since those men took us. Forever ago.

Ethan didn't know whether to laugh or cry. The sound that came out of him was something of both. *Yeah, it does seem like forever ago, doesn't it?* Logic warred with hope in his heart. This couldn't be real. He had to be creating this as a way of dealing with his grief. And yet, Jack's voice seemed so close, so warm, so alive. He ignored the growing pressure in his head and continued.

--Are you and Mom okay? They haven't hurt you, have they?

--No, we're okay. They stopped and let us go to the bathroom. They gave us some sandwiches. But the man said we wouldn't be stopping again for a long time. And I listened in their minds, and now I'm scared.

Ethan's heart stopped beating. *What do you mean, son? You listened?*

-- Like we're doing now.

--Oh. And you could hear them . . . thinking? Ethan recognized he was at a crucial point in his fantasy. Either he'd created a wonderfully artful way to explain how this could be happening, or his son had powers of the mind none of them had ever suspected.

--Uh-huh. Dad. I'm tired of riding in the van. When are you coming to get us?

Ethan's gut clenched. He struggled to direct his thoughts so he communicated none of his fear. *Soon, buddy. Just as soon as we can. The FBI is looking for that van right now and you know they always get the bad guys, right?*

--I guess so.

--Do you know where you are?

--No. We can't see out.

--Can you ask Mom?

A pause. *Mom says a gas station.* Jack's voice was fading, as if he was growing tired.

Ethan's head was splitting with pain now as he fought to hold their connection. *I'm not going to let*

them hurt you. I love you and your mom so much. Tell
her. Tell your mom I'll find you.

--*Hurry, Dad.* The voice was faint, almost gone. *I*
heard them say they don't need me.

"Mom!"

Asia was being shaken out of a restless half-sleep,
Jack's enthusiastic grin hovering in the dark above her.
"What is it, Jack?" She whispered the words, conscious
of the fact that the van had stopped again.

"I'm talking to Dad! He's alive!" The boy's voice was
an excited squeal. "Where are we?"

She shushed him and sat up, trying to gain a hold
on reality. She could smell gasoline, hear the sound of
cars passing close by.

"A gas station." She glanced up to see the window to
the front of the van open a crack, a face scowling at her.
She nodded to show she understood and placed a
quelling hand on Jack's arm. He settled down.

The van rocked as the driver jumped into the seat
and slammed the door. "Goddamn it!" The van started
up with a roar and the vehicle lurched forward.

"What the hell?! That coffee was hot!"

"Fuck the coffee, you moron! They're on to us. We
need to make it to the safe house, and we need to call
for a pickup before the Feds track this piece of shit
we're driving."

"What happened?"

"They had the news on in there. The FBI has an Amber Alert out, and they somehow got a description of this vehicle and the three of us."

"Shit!"

"Shit is right, Sherlock! Get me the directions to the closest safe house."

Hope injected adrenaline into Asia's veins, kicking her heart into overdrive. They had a description. That could only mean that Ethan had survived. Tears pooled in her eyes as she offered a silent prayer of gratitude. He was alive, and there was a chance now that this nightmare might end. She was shaking with relief.

"Fuck! Close that window, you stupid idiots!"

The window between the sections of the van slid shut, and Asia lost her insight into whatever strategy the men might be devising to deal with their sudden exposure. She couldn't make herself care.

Jack stirred beside her. He looked tired and drawn.

She gave him a squeeze. "Good news, buddy. The FBI is looking for us. They know what kind of van we're in and what the men look like, and they're asking people to watch for us. That'll make it hard for them to hide us."

"I know." Jack nodded. "Dad told me."

"What do you mean, Dad told you?" Asia was beginning to feel like every conversation with her son led her further into uncharted territory. Her tolerance was being tested with every observation, and more each passing hour.

"I tried to tell you before. I was talking to him in my

head. He told me the FBI was looking for us."

This was too much, even for Asia's newly expanded frame of reference for the boy. "Jack. Your father is miles away now. You couldn't have talked with him. I think maybe this time you were just dreaming."

The hurt and betrayal in Jack's face pierced her to the heart. "It *wasn't* a dream. You were sleeping, but I was awake. I was lonely, and I was thinking really hard that I hoped Dad wasn't dead. Then I heard him say my name. And I started talking to him, but only for a little while because I got tired. It was hard to do."

Asia couldn't speak. She could only stare at her son, her breath caught in her throat. *Ethan*. In a flash of longing so intense it made her want to curl into a trembling ball, she felt the fragile connection that had somehow come into being between Ethan and Jack. She understood on a primal level how it must have hit Ethan in the depths of his despair to hear his son's voice in his mind, how he would have first denied it, then reached for it in irresistible need. She understood, because she would give anything at this moment to hear Ethan's voice in her mind, to be able to tell him the things that were in her heart.

She gave in. "What did he say to you, sweetheart?"

"He said he wouldn't let them hurt us." Jack's small hand rested on his mother's shoulder as if it was his responsibility to keep her calm. "He said to tell you he would find us."

Asia nodded. She gathered her son to her and hugged him hard, her need to protect him like a searing flame in the center of her chest. "Yeah," she whispered. "That sure sounds like your dad."

The Narrows was a classic horseshoe bend in the Harpeth River, a canoeist's dream. It was possible to put in on one side of the horseshoe, float for a couple of hours in the green, rippling Harpeth and take out on the other side. Then you could hike over the high bluff in the center of the horseshoe, get your car where you'd parked it at the put-in site, and bring it around to pick up your canoe, all in a lazy afternoon. Lana had done it with more than one boyfriend over the years growing up, with plenty of stories, at least one broken heart, and a scar or two to show for it. She loved the place.

So Lana didn't go far when she and Gabriel left the grove on one side of the horseshoe that had become a crime scene. She simply drove around to the other side and parked the car at the river access there, grateful that the police activity around the Narrows had spooked the usual crowd of teenagers and river enthusiasts for the day.

Gabriel got out of the car and took the path through the high grass down to the river bank before she had a chance to say anything to him. He began to wander the shoreline, picking up stones to skim across the sun-splashed water. Lana followed him, found a flat rock to squat on and sat watching the river flow for a while. As always, the sound of water over stone, the smell of wet mud and growing things soothed her.

After a while she roused herself enough to speak. "So were you born with this ability you're about to demonstrate on me, Gabriel?"

He looked back at her from a spot on the bank a few feet away. "Yes. I had to learn to control it."

"Must have freaked Mom and Dad out a little."

One rock skipped across the river, then another. "Let's just say Mom was expecting it. Dad was a no-show."

Lana gave a short, humorless laugh. "Yours too, huh?"

His head snapped around to look at her. Then a slow grin spread across his face.

"And here I thought you were some pampered suburban princess."

She barked out a laugh. "Oh, yeah, that's me. Remind me someday, I'll give you the whole, sad story." *But not today. Not while the sun is shining, and I have a chance at feeling good for half a second.*

Gabriel's eyes lingered on her face for a long moment before he sauntered over, jumped to the rock and lowered himself beside her. "Someday I'd like to hear it."

That's all. He said nothing else, did nothing else. But warmth spread through her like melting butter, and she had to look away before she did something she would regret.

The world was still, waiting. The Harpeth sluiced over the shoals, gurgling and lapping in endless rhythm. The sparrows and finches, the redwing blackbirds and cardinals and jays challenged and called in the rising midday heat. Lana didn't want to get down to the business they had come to this lovely spot for, but she knew better than to put it off. Despite her reluctance, despite his deep brown gaze on her face and the way he made her feel when he looked at her like that, she said the very thing she did not want to say.

"So. What happened with that gun, Gabriel?"

His lips curved upward for the briefest second. Then it was as if he had never smiled in his adult life. The lines of his face were taut, hard, almost cruel. *But his eyes!* Lana thought. It was as if his eyes held all the grief of the world. What had this man seen in his life to give him eyes like that? Yet even as she lost herself in their mahogany depths, they changed, and whatever she had seen was gone.

Gabriel held out his hand to her. She felt herself tremble, and clamped down hard to control it before she reached out to take what he offered. She stilled, breathing, not sure what to expect. At first she perceived only his hand—warm, strong, closing over hers as if he would protect her from harm. Then she felt a jolt, like the one she'd felt earlier when he touched her, only stronger. And the world dissolved . . .

Three men in ski masks stood in a loose ring around his beleaguered family. Asia and Jack were behind him, backed up against the big oak. Jack was whimpering with fear. The sound tore at him, ripping a bleeding hole in his heart. He gripped the branch, determined to do what he could, refusing to think beyond the next second.

Lana squirmed inside Gabriel's mind. She didn't want to see this. She didn't want to feel this. Her heart twisted in her chest—for Ethan, for Asia and Jack. Anger rose to meet the fear. She wanted to kill those men. She *would* kill them. Her hand clenched around Gabriel's.

The closest man pulled a gun from his waistband. "Don't make this any harder than it has to be, Roberts. The woman comes with us. You and the boy take a nap. Nice and easy."

Like Gabriel had done, Lana focused on the weapon. It was the same one they'd found by the river, the same shape and size and caliber, there was no doubt. She felt Gabriel's presence as he made certain she saw clearly what happened next.

The gun that had been pointed in their direction twisted out of the man's hand and flew into the thin stand of trees near the river.

Lana shook her head, not believing what she'd seen. The action in the scene stopped at that point, Gabriel taking control of the "playback" so they could both be certain. Then he showed her again. And there was no question. For no reason at all, the gun wrenched itself out of the man's hand and hurtled into the underbrush where they later found it.

Lana broke her connection with Gabriel and sat gawking at him. "What the hell was that?"

He shook his head. "I don't know."

Her cheeks flushed with heat. "You don't know? What do you mean you don't know? How the hell am I supposed to explain that to my superiors? 'Oh, yeah, well, then the gun just up and took itself out of the guy's hand and tossed *itself* into the fucking bushes.'"

She got up, too angry to stay in one place, and found a level space to pace along the bank. She pushed both hands through her hair, a gesture she was aware turned her blond waves into feral curls in an instant, and exhaled with enough frustration to end up in a snarl.

"How am I going to explain any of this?" She glared at Gabriel. "And don't say Ethan took the gun off the guy and threw it. No one's going to buy that either."

He shrugged, his lips curling with poorly-concealed amusement. "Um, the guy had a seizure?"

Lana stared at him for a second, then caught the gleam in his eye. She had to admit the image of a masked assailant going into spasms and losing his weapon was funny. She relaxed, laughter bubbling up through her chest.

"Very funny. Thank you, Jimmy Fallon."

Gabriel stood and leapt from the rock to the bank in one easy movement. Lana drew in a breath watching him. The way he moved—Jesus, he was beautiful. Like a big cat, all grace and power, with nothing wasted. He was standing next to her in a heartbeat, so close she had to keep herself from stepping back—or closer.

"Just tell them Ethan's not sure what happened. He hit the man with the branch and the gun went flying.

It's Ethan's story, not yours. And he was hit on the head and drugged, remember?"

She considered that option. "It might work." One hand went through her hair again, taking her styling beyond all redemption. "At any rate, it's all we've got. I'm sure as shit not giving them a word of what I saw."

"That would be my advice, also." He reached out and stopped just short of touching her hair. His voice went soft. "I didn't realize it was so curly."

Lana did back up, then, her cheeks growing warm. "Yeah, well, a legacy from my Granny Jen. And no thanks to her for that." She turned toward the car, desperate to hide the emotion he'd brought to the surface. "I'm starving. How about you?"

He said nothing until he was in the car with her and she'd started up the vehicle to head out. "I like it." His voice was even softer than before and his gaze stroked her unruly mane from the crown of her head to the curly tips. "You can definitely tell Granny Jen thanks from me."

She was going to tell him that was grossly inappropriate. She was going to tell him to keep his preferences to himself. She really was. But before she could find the breath to do it, he'd withdrawn his attention. He turned his face to stare out the window, as if his mind was a million miles away.

In the empty silence that fell between them, Lana could only wonder why she suddenly felt so alone.

CHAPTER SEVEN

Gabriel let his soul take in the healing energy of the lush Tennessee countryside and mulled over how this job had so quickly gotten out of control. Dirtside tracking was difficult enough without the complication of local authorities sniffing around. They got in the way; they compromised evidence; they wanted bribes to do their jobs or they threatened to jail him or kill him for one reason or another. But this was even worse. In this case the local authorities were actually competent—and Alana Matheson was not going to be as easy to lose as he'd once thought.

He thought of the touch of her mind in his, her discipline and intelligence, her humor and courage, so tangible despite the shields he'd held in place to limit their contact. She had been so open, almost as if she had psi talent of her own. It would have required the slightest caress of thought to know her—her frivolous likes and dislikes, her deepest desires, her secret fears. He'd found himself wanting to let her into the vault of his own psyche in the same way, a temptation he had never felt before.

Gabriel breathed, seeking to clear his mind with the fresh smell of the red clay and deep green vegetation outside the car, but Lana's warm ginger-cream scent overrode all else and heated his blood. It made him want to bury his face in the hollow of her neck, to lick and nip at the throb of her pulse there while he drew that delicious scent into his lungs. He shifted to reposition himself in jeans that were suddenly too tight and tried to get his mind back on the business at hand.

So far, he had to admit, his alliance with Lana had been useful. His usual practice was to avoid any police presence, and he almost never had access to anything they knew. He rarely needed the help. Yet until Sam came back from delivering Martin Blake to safety on Terrene, Gabriel had limited technology at his disposal. Tracking the kidnappers' vehicle would be impossible without the sensors aboard the *Shadowhawk*. He could only hope Lana and her colleagues would do that for him.

"Hey." Lana's light touch on his shoulder interrupted his strategizing. "I'm too hungry to wait until we get all the way back to town. This place has some decent home cooking. Wanna stop?"

"Sounds good to me." He smiled at the unassuming little place she'd picked. The parking lot was almost full of older sedans and pickup trucks. "Looks like a popular place with the locals."

"Should be. Been here since I was a kid." She slipped the Chevy between two battered Jeeps and switched off the engine. She glanced once at him in invitation and was gone. He followed her across the parking lot and into the restaurant, anticipation tugging at him for no reason at all.

The girl who served them looked to be no older than 18 and was as thin as a refugee, but she was friendly enough. "Hey! Can I get y'all something to drink?"

"Iced tea, unsweetened," Lana said, her eyes on the menu.

Gabriel had no time to decode that phrase, but he nodded to indicate he'd have the same. The girl disappeared in the direction of the kitchen.

His gaze roved over the menu offerings, most of which were at least recognizable as food. This wasn't his first job on the planet many of the peoples of Terrene had once called home, and he'd explored the origins of their transplanted culture before.

His real attention was on Lana—her hair a temptation of soft curls, not uniformly one color of blond, but streaked and interwoven with light and dark, honey and pale gold. Her skin glowed with the kiss of the sun, as if she lived her life outdoors, instead of behind a desk. And her eyes—he was waiting for her to lift those wide green eyes from the page she was studying just so he could see them again.

He realized he was acting like a fool, and looked down again at his menu just as Lana looked up. "What's good here?"

"The barbecue's great. The chicken's pretty good. And the cornbread's to die for. Save room for pie."

"Spoken with authority." He thought it might be safe to find those eyes now. "Come here a lot?"

"I was on a case down here last year." She made herself comfortable in the booth. "This is one of Tom Radford's hangouts."

Gabriel felt a pang. "Oh? A friend of yours?"

Her lips curved upward. "County sheriff."

The waitress returned and took their order. When she left, Gabriel got to the point.

"What do you do for fun, Lana? Are you married? Got a boyfriend?"

She grinned, as if she knew what he was up to. "Not that it's any of your business, Gabriel. But no, I'm not married. And after this morning, I can't say I have a boyfriend, either."

"Mark?"

She shrugged, but offered no further details. "Tit for tat, Mr. Cruz. You married? Got a girl back home?"

"No wife, no girl back home." It had never bothered him until now.

She considered him, the smile lingering around her lips. "Let me guess. You're the kind with a girl in every town. Or do you just love 'em and leave 'em?"

He laughed. "Neither. The nature of my work makes it hard to form relationships."

"Ah." She nodded. "A hard case. I believe I know the type."

His eyes locked onto hers, the connection made at once. Warmth blossomed in his chest, even as his lungs struggled to take in air. His heart stuttered, then began to gallop, pumping blood to the growing ache in his groin.

He was grateful for more than one reason when the waitress brought their food.

Lana attacked her meal for a while before she got back to her questions. "So how long have you been doing this kind of work, Gabriel?"

"Most of my adult life." This was one question he could answer honestly. "I worked for someone else for a while. Started my own business about ten years ago."

"That's awfully young. You must be pretty good at it."

He shrugged. He had talents he couldn't tell her about and clients who paid him well to use them.

"In my experience the best PI's are the ones who aren't afraid to take the crazy cases, the cases likely to get them killed." She looked at him for a long moment, assessing him. "Would that be you, Gabriel?"

The question was a little too close for comfort. He deflected it.

"Are we talking about this case?"

Her eyebrows shot up. "Are we?"

"Not as long as you let me tag along with you." He gave her what he hoped was a disarming grin.

"I wouldn't count on that."

"You have to admit I've been helpful."

"So far," she admitted. "But once my boss hears about this, I'm up shit creek."

There was a pause, the two of them eating in silence, Lana's forehead creased in thought. After a while she appeared to dismiss her concerns with a tiny sigh. She looked up at him again.

Whatever she might have said was lost as her cell phone trilled at her waist. She got up to take her call outside, ruining Gabriel's chances of catching any of the conversation.

He signaled the waitress for the check and pulled his own phone out of a holster at his hip. No one questioned why he focused on it for minutes at a time; they assumed he was using its many capabilities to access data. But the device was largely unprogrammed, capable only of limited-range communications. For anything else he used his own brain's wetwire cyber-enhancements and his exceptional psi skills. He'd found the phone useful when assigned to planets at Earth's stage of development before. Staring into space while he accessed data had almost gotten him killed one too many times.

He checked his bank balance—the diamonds he'd arranged to sell through intermediaries in New York had brought enough to cover his expenses for as long as he needed to stay.

Gabriel smiled when he saw the "readouts" from the crime scene. His sensor implants had detected faint echoes of the electromagnetic signatures he'd been looking for. The traces had been broken, scattered, much too scant for his own senses to have detected them, even though he'd been scanning every second he'd been in the riverside grove. Still, the biosensors had picked them up; they were so obviously different from the others. He'd be able to identify Asia and Jack—and their unique psi signatures—whenever he got close enough now.

He checked his messages. There was one waiting from Sam.

"Package safely delivered. All involved say thanks. *Bloodstalker* confirmed within Sol system hunting our prize. Watch your back. See you in eight hours. Sam."

Gabriel closed his eyes and forced himself to breathe. The *Bloodstalker*. Once his father's ship, now his brothers', Kinnian and Trevyn. Two of the deadliest, most inescapable trackers of a race of undercover warriors, men whose brutality and single-minded devotion to violence were legendary, even among those following a violent profession. Full-blooded Thranes with psi talents likely twice the strength of his, with a team and plenty of technology to back them up.

This simple kidnapping was now a game with multiple players. And as Gabriel well knew, his half-brothers played rough—and they played to win. The only question was, what was it about Asia that made her worth the game?

"Ray, have you ever experienced what Gabriel does?"

Ethan had taken more pain pills against the agony in his ribs and his leg and splitting skull. He had slept and showered and shaved. He had even forced himself to eat, and now sat over the remains of a simple meal with Rayna in his dining room, struggling to make sense of what had happened to him hours earlier.

She shook her head. "Never had the need. Why?"

"Have you ever heard . . ." He groped for the words he needed. "Is it possible that in opening myself up to him, I might have opened myself up to something else?"

"What do you mean?"

"I've never been sensitive to extra-sensory stimulation before, but today . . ." He stopped, recognizing how unstable he sounded.

Ray reached out to take his hand. "What is it, Ethan? You look better, but something's on your mind, I can tell." She looked him in the eye. "Are you worried about the drugs?"

He shook his head, a smile tugging at his mouth. "I may be crazy, but the drugs aren't the cause. They aren't known to cause hallucinations."

"Hallucinations? What are you talking about?"

"What would you say if I told you I'd just had a conversation with Jack upstairs?" He said it, then sat looking at her, waiting for her reaction.

Her expression showed first alarm, then pity and at last a quickly-conjured neutrality. Ethan would have found it amusing, had the subject been anyone else but himself.

"Ethan, sweets—"

"I know what it sounds like, Rayna, believe me. I'm not sure I don't agree with your first reaction."

"Reaction?" She tried for an innocent expression. "What reaction?"

"You think the stress has driven me over the edge. That's what I thought, too." He stood up and moved in an awkward limp to the living room, his damaged knee making him slow. "It wasn't like I heard him in the room. He was in my mind, I was clear on that. But his voice was so real, Ray, so *present*. He didn't sound like my *idea* of Jack. He sounded like *Jack*. Do you know what I mean?"

Rayna shook her head. "Not really. What did he say?"

"Nothing much. He complained about riding in the van. He said Asia was sleeping, and he—" He took a deep breath, clamping down hard on the emotion that threatened to choke him. "He wanted to know when I was coming to get him."

Rayna got up and put her hand on his arm. "Ethan, you want so much to know he's okay. And I'm sure he is."

Ethan accepted the comfort of her touch, but he wouldn't accept her view of what had happened. "His voice faded after a moment, like he was tired. And my head was killing me trying to keep up the contact. If this had been just a figment of my imagination, I could have been a lot easier on myself."

Rayna pulled back to consider him, her expression somber. "So . . . what? It's your theory that you developed special powers after your session with Gabriel this morning?"

His shoulders lifted. "I don't know. Maybe. We do know that Jack is resistant to programming, like Asia is. Maybe *he's* the one with special powers."

"Resistance is one thing. Psi talents are something else entirely. What Gabriel does is just not that common among humans."

"What do you mean?" Suspicion put an edge to his voice.

Ray ignored it. "I mean he's got a rare skill set. One you wouldn't expect to pop up unannounced—either in Jack or in you."

"And yet, if those skills were latent in either one of us," Ethan insisted, "the kind of session I had with Gabriel this morning might have been enough to open new pathways for telepathic communication, especially between people in close relationships."

"Then why wasn't it Asia who contacted you?"

Ethan's heart stopped. He had no answer for that question.

Rayna shook her head, sympathy in her eyes. "I'd like to believe you, honey, I really would. But you're the psychiatrist. If any of your patients came to you with a story like this, would you believe them?"

Ethan turned away from her and stared out the window at the lowering sun. He knew what his answer would have to be if logic were applied to the question. Yet logic had let him down before. When Asia had first come to him, a rational woman with what seemed to be a delusional pattern of memories, he had been forced to abandon logic for the dictates of his heart. He'd been rewarded for that decision over and over again, every time he'd looked at her, or touched her, or heard her whisper his name as he made love to her.

Logic told him Jack could not possibly have reached across miles of empty space to speak to him, but his heart told him it was so. And illogical or not, he believed what his heart told him.

Lana put away her cell phone and turned to see Gabriel coming through the door of the restaurant onto the covered porch. He caught sight of her and smiled, but the smile didn't reach his coffee-colored eyes; he seemed preoccupied, his mind bent on solving a puzzle for which only he had all the pieces.

She stifled a sigh. Damn, the man was easy to look at; the darker his thoughts, the more attractive she seemed to find him. She shook her head and took the few steps required to close the distance between them.

"Got a phone call from Rick." She was all business now. It just seemed easier. "Tip from the Amber Alert puts our vehicle at a rest stop in Arkansas at about 10:00 last night. The woman who saw them has details and lives just this side of Memphis."

Gabriel brightened. "Close enough to speak to her in person."

Lana strode across the parking lot to her car, knowing he would be right on her heels. She opened the car door and waited a second for the overheated interior to cool. She looked at him over the roof.

"I'm going to drop you off at the river. Someone

there can give you a ride back to Nashville."

"Like hell. You're going to take me with you." The grin he offered up with this prediction was devastating.

She dropped into the driver's seat and started up the engine, setting the A/C on full blast. "You know I can't do that. Interviewing a witness is Bureau business. It would be way over the line for you to be there."

"Lana, you want all the details from this witness, don't you? Not just, 'Oh, I think it might have been a white van and three men,' but the license plate, the scratch on the left front bumper, the way Asia and Jack are holding up. If this witness actually saw something, I'll know it just by shaking her hand."

"Christ, Gabriel, I can't be a part of that." Something close to horror seized her heart. "If we ask for her permission, the Bureau would have my badge by tomorrow morning. If we don't ask . . ." *He wouldn't do that, would he?* The thought of what he could do was frightening enough without wondering how those powers might be used in the absence of ethics or conscience.

Gabriel considered her. "Fair enough. You interview her your way. Then you leave the room. I'll ask for her permission. If she gives it, I'll go in and get what we need. That way you're legally off the hook."

"Are you kidding me?" Lana shook her head. *Why am I even listening to him?* "You're not supposed to be with me, don't you get it?"

There was anger in his voice now—and frustration.

"Do you want to find Asia and Jack or not, Lana? We can work together on this, or we can waste time while the wolves pick up their scent."

"What the hell are you talking about?"

He huffed out a breath, but refused to explain. His face could have been carved in granite.

"Gabriel?"

His eyes, when he looked up to meet hers, had gone nearly black. "Just take me with you, Alana. You won't regret it."

They were approaching the turnoff for Harpeth Narrows. Lana knew she should make that turn. She should take this man with his troublesome talents and his disturbing good looks and drop him into someone else's lap down at the river. She had no logical explanation for why she thought she could trust Gabriel Cruz. It was just her damnable intuition at work again—the same spooky sixth sense that gave her the best solve rate in the Nashville office, but lost her every partner she'd ever had. No one else wanted to trust her gut like she did.

Maybe that's why despite everything she'd been taught, despite every rule in the book, in defiance of all good sense and responsible judgment, Lana passed right by the turnoff for Harpeth Narrows and kept driving west toward Memphis with a near-stranger in her government-issue vehicle. *Some days you just have to listen to that little voice inside you, even when all you hear is crazy talk.*

CHAPTER EIGHT

Beyond the Oort Cloud, Sol System

The ship materialized on the outer lip of jump node A10, one instant *not-there*, the next instant *there*, in the usual way of internodal space travel. A miracle to behold. And an even greater miracle to accomplish, for without it the sentient species of the galaxy might well be confined to tooling around their own little solar systems, pining for the glory of the stars.

The discovery and mapping of the nodes, which formed short connecting "jumps" between otherwise widely-separated areas of space, had been the singular lasting contribution of the long-departed Tularian Empire. A more aggressive species used against them the information the Tularians had so painstakingly acquired, jumping into the heart of their empire in force to destroy them.

Trevyn Dar, staring at the viewscreen at the evidence of their genius, had always thought the story of the Tularians a sad and telling episode in the history of the galaxy. They had given sentient-kind so much, and had received such poor thanks in return. Of course, his brother would have said it was no more than they deserved for paying so little attention to their own security.

"Confirm arrival at jump terminus, Commander. Stealth shielding engaged, per your orders." The lieutenant at the helm was newly assigned, a Ninoctin, not a Thrane, and her mental protections were almost non-existent. He could read her nervousness clearly, almost as clearly as her attraction to him and her struggle to control it. Trevyn stifled a sigh. He had spoken to Kinnian about hiring crew members without the psi talents of their people, but his brother had laughed him off. Kinnian *liked* being able to read others easily, especially women, and for the same reasons Trevyn found it uncomfortable.

"Very good, Lieutenant. Set course for the third planet. Three-quarters ID."

"Aye, sir. Setting course. Three-quarters ion drive." A heartbeat later she looked up from her instruments. "Commander. We failed to navigate the jump according to MEA calculations, sir. We're well outside parameters."

Trevyn turned to see the numbers himself. The nodes had funnel-like openings; they allowed for some variation in the approach a ship took in hitting them. But too much deviation from the Most Efficient Approach and a ship could be thrown off course at the outlet or torn to pieces in transit. *Shalssit!* They were so far off they were lucky they'd arrived at all.

His helm had kept her voice low, but every soul on the bridge had heard her. And every pair of eyes was now on the navigator who had made the near-fatal error. That navigator was glaring at the lieutenant with undisguised rage. Trevyn heard him curse the helm officer under his breath as his commander approached the nav station.

"You have something to say, Navigator?" He stood over the man and used his height to intimidate. "Perhaps you'd like to explain how we nearly missed such an easy jump?"

"I gave that bitch the proper calculations." The man was sweating under his heavy beard. "Can I help it if she didn't enter them correctly?"

Trevyn turned his head, but his gaze never left the navigator's face. "Is that true, helm?"

"No, sir! The log shows what he gave me and what I entered. They are the same."

He looked at her now. "But they are incorrect. Am I to understand that you only detected this error when you began to calculate your course for Earth?"

"Aye, sir." To her credit, the Ninoctin's voice did not tremble. She met his gaze without flinching. "I should have double-checked the navigator's calculations before we entered jump."

"Yes, you should have." Still, Trevyn found it easy to be lenient with her. "Except for meals, you will confine yourself to quarters during your off-duty shifts for the remainder of this assignment."

The woman accepted her punishment with nothing

but a movement of her pretty throat to show she had swallowed hard. "Yes, Commander."

The navigator, on the other hand, deserved much harsher punishment, more so since he was watching now with a self-satisfied smirk. "You find this amusing?"

The man's expression turned sullen. "No, sir."

"No, and you won't like this, either. You're relieved and sentenced to fourteen ship cycles in the brig." He glanced toward the brute clad in body armor stationed near the bridge exit. "Security, get him off my bridge."

The navigator leapt to his feet. "The fuck you say! You give that cunt a slap on the wrist yet you send me to the box for a half-moon for a cursed math error? Your brother would never allow—"

Trevyn ended it by backhanding the man across the mouth. The navigator staggered back into his console, his knees buckling, blood spurting from his split lips. He stared at his commander with eyes wide, saying nothing. Trevyn gestured for Security and the huge officer scraped the navigator off the control panel to put him in restraints.

"My brother would never allow insubordination on the bridge of his ship. And neither will I. Thirty cycles now, and the only reason you're not dead is that I don't have another navigator."

He waved a hand at his security officer. "Get him out of here." Then he turned to his helm. "Estimated time of arrival at the third planet, by local equivalent?"

"Approximately four hours, thirty-six minutes,

Commander."

Steady. Trevyn admired her poise. "I'll report to the Captain, then I'll be in my cabin. You have the conn."

"Yes, sir." He noted her emotions: a flush of surprise. Relief that she would no longer have to deal with his presence. Fear when he mentioned Kinnian.

Trevyn took the short flight of stairs and the passageway down to the captain's quarters. He knocked on the metal of his brother's cabin hatch and opened it when he heard Kinnian's gruff voice answer.

"Four-and-a-half hours to target, my lord." He closed the hatch behind him.

Kinnian Dar glanced up with a scowl from the holomap laid out before him. "On schedule, then. Good enough."

Trevyn indicated the map. "Have you found the place?"

Kinnian sat back and scratched at the thick black beard covering his jaw. "You couldn't find Felzac's ass on these maps. I can't tell whether it's that there are no roads or towns or landmarks, or that the map doesn't include them. This . . . North Da-ko-ta . . . looks like an uncharted planet in the Outer Reaches."

Trevyn helped himself to ale from the pitcher that sat on the counter next to the desk. He sat and stretched out his long legs.

"The information that Sennik provided is no help?"

"Sennik!" Kinnian nearly spat. "That overevolved slimehog has done nothing but make my life a living hell. If the credits were not so good on this job, I would throw it back in his moony face."

Trevyn ignored his brother's outburst and stuck to the point. "I assume the target had an identification chip."

"The target's chip was removed when he was repatriated by Rescue, of course, but even so it was specially encrypted." Kinnian frowned at the map. "I have his original identifying information from Sennik—it was kept separately from that of the other slaves in the Del Origa facility."

"Why?"

"How the fuck should I know? Sennik plays his little games with the slaves; that's his business. All I know is that the information he gave me isn't helping me find the fucking piece of dirt the brat was whelped on."

"You're thinking Rescue would have sent him back to relatives near where he was born?"

"Of course. Where else?"

Trevyn swallowed a mouthful of ale. For some reason it left a bitter taste on his tongue.

"Give me the boy's name. The humans have an antiquated communications delivery system. In such a sparsely populated area, it should be easy to find others with his name. I'll have a location for you in less time than it takes to fuck a whore."

Kinnian smiled, an expression Trevyn knew meant no good for those they hunted. "My brother! You continue to be of such tremendous use to me."

Gabriel had been brooding for the two hours it had taken them to close in on the address Rick had given her over the phone. Lana thought once or twice to ask if he was all right, if he'd gotten bad news from home or some tragedy had befallen the world while she was out on the porch talking with Rick, but his silence was a wall she couldn't begin to scale. There was something on his mind, something dark that was usually buried deep and kept away from prying eyes. She left him alone until they got within a few miles of the little town where the witness lived.

"Hey, do me a favor." She turned on the GPS navigator on her dash and waved at the controls. "Are you familiar with one of these?"

Gabriel peered at it, his brows drawn together. "I'm familiar with its function."

Lana glanced at him. "I'll take that as a yes." She flipped her notebook open with one hand and pointed to a scrawl halfway down the page. "That's the address. Enter it in the navigator for me."

When he hesitated, she gave him the sequence of instructions. It took him a minute, but he finally accomplished the task and looked back at her with a grin.

"If I'd known you wanted directions, I could have gotten them for you in half the time."

"Your phone has a nav app?"

"What?"

"Nav app. GPS. On your phone."

"Oh. Right. Yes."

Lana turned her eyes back to the road, but her attention remained on the puzzling man in her passenger seat. There had been times in this strange day when she'd felt so connected with Gabriel it was as if they'd known each other all their lives. Then there were the moments, like this one, when it seemed as if he'd come from another planet. He didn't seem to understand the most basic things, and yet he knew things it should have been impossible for him to know. He was so unlike any other man she'd ever met. And she was drawn to him in a way she'd never experienced before. She had no idea if the irregular leaping heartbeat she kept feeling was a result of legitimate fear or unthinking exhilaration. Or both.

At least the distraction of the navigator had lifted his mood for the time being. He even smiled as the feminine voice of the device instructed them to turn off the main highway onto a secondary road.

"It talks." He seemed captivated.

"Saves the driver squinting at the dashboard and causing a ten-car pileup." Lana shook her head. "Yes, it talks. You don't get out much, do you?"

His smile grew wider. "Technology is not my field of specialty."

Why did she get the feeling there was something left unsaid in that comment? "I'd have to agree with you there, though just what we could call your specialty, I wouldn't know."

Gabriel grunted and turned back to the window. They were within a few turns of their destination now and a strategy had to be decided upon.

"Let me take the lead on this," Lana said. "We'll see how much this . . . Mrs. Clark . . . remembers on her own first."

Her companion looked at her. "If you say so."

"Gabriel, I don't feel comfortable having you probe this woman—"

"Is that what you think I do?"

"Isn't it?"

When he didn't answer, Lana glanced in his direction. His face was unreadable, but his eyes, when they turned to meet hers, flashed with what looked like anger.

"I would ask her to show me what she saw. That's all. Unlike Ethan's case, where the memories had to be retrieved from deeper in the mind, this woman is more than willing to tell us what she remembers. It's right there on the surface for the taking. I could do it without her being aware of it, but I wouldn't. Do you know why, Alana?"

She pulled up in the woman's driveway and stopped, waiting to hear the rest of it.

"Because I think it's wrong." He held her gaze for a heartbeat, plenty of time to make her burn with shame. "Are we clear on this?"

"Yeah, we're clear." It was an apology. "When I'm done, I'll leave and let you speak with her alone."

He nodded. "Thank you."

The two of them left the car and approached the tidy ranch house together, but Lana led the way up on the covered front porch to ring the doorbell. A small, determined bark sounded inside, followed within seconds by a female voice, telling the dog to "shush!" The door swung open to reveal a short, plump woman of about 70 in a Graceland tee-shirt and polyester pants. A tiny, white poodle circled her feet, pausing occasionally in its dance to bark at the visitors.

Mrs. Clark gave them a ten-megawatt smile and opened the storm door to invite them in. "Y'all must be the FBI folks! The young man on the phone said y'all would be coming. I'm Kathy Clark. Come on in and sit down." She ushered them into a living room that was J.C. Penney's idea of French provincial, mixed with a few pieces of Americana from Grandma's attic. "Would you-all like something to drink? It's awful hot out. I can get you some lemonade or a cold drink."

"No, ma'am, no, thank you." Lana pulled out her credentials and notebook and took a seat on the damask sofa. "I'm Special Agent Alana Matheson. This is Gabriel Cruz."

Gabriel gave the woman a smile that would have melted the heart of any heterosexual female between the ages of three and 103 and murmured a hello before he sank into the chair next to the sofa. Mrs. Clark's cheeks blushed a girlish pink. Lana could tell she was completely won over as soon as Gabriel reached down to pet the dog.

"You called some information in to the Amber Alert hotline this afternoon, Mrs. Clark, is that right?" Lana eased her into it, as if they had all the time in the world. "Can you tell us what you saw?"

The woman was distracted; her poodle had settled at Gabriel's feet. "Why, I've never seen Pookie do that with anyone before!"

Gabriel shrugged. "I have a way with pets."

"Well, you surely do, Mr. Cruz." Their witness seemed to recall why the FBI was in her living room and turned to Lana. "Oh, yes. Well, I was walking Pookie at the rest stop."

"This was the rest stop at mile marker 114 on I-40, west of Memphis?"

"Yes, that's right. Last night about ten o'clock. My husband, Harold, and I were coming back from seeing my sister in Little Rock."

Lana looked up from her notebook. "Mrs. Clark, I hate to stop you, but that rest area is on the interstate headed west."

The woman's hand went to her throat and fluttered there. "Yes, that's right," she started, then followed with a rush of explanation. "But, you see, we'd passed the last rest area on our side a long time back, and there wasn't another one for a while, and Pookie *really* needed to go and so did I, so I made Harold turn around in the median and go back, and I know that's illegal except in emergencies, but this *was* an emergency, really it was."

Lana ignored the grin threatening to break through

Gabriel's control. "Well, ma'am, next time you, uh, you might want to plan ahead."

Mrs. Clark found her smile again and patted Lana on the knee. "Oh, thank you, honey, I'll do that. So, anyway, Harold was in the restroom, and I was walking Pookie over in the grassy area, under these trees, away from everything, you know? I suppose that wasn't very smart, being away from everything and everybody, but I wasn't thinking about that. I was just thinking that Pookie needed to go. So I was out there, and all of a sudden I hear this loud sneeze—ah choo!—like that! And I look up and there's a young woman about your age, dear, and a little boy about five or six, and a couple of big men with them. Then she sneezes again really loud, and it was like one of the men got kind of mad at her, I thought, and he almost pushed her in the back of this white van. And that's why I noticed it, you know, because he seemed so mad, and the woman and the little boy were in the back of the van, but the men got in the front. That just seemed so *odd*."

"Did you notice anything else about the men? Can you tell us what they looked like?"

"Well, no, I can't say as I can, Agent Matheson." She frowned. "They were awfully tall and, you know, they looked like those fellas on the wrestling. Big, you know. One of them was black, I think. But I was too far away to recognize them or anything."

"What about the woman and the child. Did they appear to be injured in any way?"

"No, they looked all right to me. They weren't tied

up or anything. The little boy looked right brave."

"And the van, Mrs. Clark—can you tell me anything about the vehicle? License plates? Identifying marks?"

"Oh, dear, I'm sorry, I didn't see a thing on that van." Mrs. Clark's face reflected her distress. "It was just plain white, no writing or anything. And I'm no good with makes—I couldn't tell you if it was a Ford or a Chevy. You know, I don't even think they had plates on the front at all. Maybe just the back, but I didn't see the number." The woman actually wrung her hands. "I'm afraid I don't make a very good witness, do I?"

Lana smiled reassurance at her. "You've done very well, Mrs. Clark. Just one more question. Did you see the van leave the rest stop?"

"Why, yes, they left before we did. They went out the other way, headed west. We turned around and went back east, of course."

"Thank you, Mrs. Clark. This has been very helpful." She glanced at Gabriel, who gave her a barely-perceptible nod. "Ma'am, would you mind if I used your bathroom?"

"Oh, certainly." She rose to lead the way. "It's right in here."

Lana lingered in the floral-scented and pink-and-green wallpapered powder room for as long as she dared, trying to give Gabriel enough time with Mrs. Clark. When she came back to the living room, she found the two of them chatting like old friends.

"Mr. Cruz helped me remember a few things about last night while you were gone." The woman's sunny smile was full of pride. "He said you wouldn't mind."

"Oh, no, that's fine." Lana shot Gabriel a look. "Do I need to write anything down?"

"No, I think I have it." Gabriel stood up.

Lana held out a hand. "Thank you, Mrs. Clark, you've been a terrific help."

"Well, thank you for coming so quickly." Mrs. Clark shook her hand, then Gabriel's. "I sure hope you find those folks."

"We will." Gabriel's dark eyes captured hers.

Shameless, Lana thought. *Absolutely shameless.* The older woman was blushing again as she showed them to the door, her poodle weaving in and out between her ankles. They said their goodbyes and got back in the car. Lana waited until they were out on the road before she asked Gabriel to account for himself.

"Well?"

He shook his head. "Not much more than she told us, I'm afraid. These men are being very careful. The vehicle has no distinguishing marks—it's probably new. Mrs. Clark wasn't wearing her glasses, so she couldn't read the license plate or provide any details for the description of the men. They didn't have their masks, but they still had dark glasses on, even though it was after sunset. One of the two had light hair, clipped very short. The other was black. The third was in the van, couldn't get a look at him."

"Shit. This was a wasted trip, then."

"No. We've confirmed this is Asia and Jack. We know which way they're headed. I might be able to learn more if I could see this place."

"What, the rest stop?" Lana turned her head to stare at him. "You're kidding, right?"

"Yes, of course, the rest stop."

"First of all, once again, it's a Federal crime scene, which, need I remind you, you're not supposed to have access to. Secondly, it's at least three hours' drive from here, on the other side of Memphis."

Gabriel shrugged. "If you need to go home, you could drop me at the nearest car rental."

"As I believe you said recently, *like hell*." Lana noticed she was making the turns that would take her in the direction of I-40 West, against her better judgment. What was it about the man that made her want to do things like this? "What do you need to see this place for anyway? It's a freaking rest stop." A flash of insight pulled her up. "Wait. You're not looking for another gun, are you?"

He almost laughed. "No. I doubt we'll find any tangible evidence this time."

"Then, what?" She glanced from the road to his profile seeking some clue. "Damn it, Gabriel, you are the most puzzling partner I have ever had the misfortune of working with."

One black eyebrow arched toward his hairline. "We're partners now?"

"Hell, no, we're not partners—not until you start telling me what the fuck is going on in that mind of yours."

She could have sworn he looked startled for half a

second, as if her comment surprised him. Then he sighed. "Alana. You won't understand."

Anger stirred in her chest. "You think I'm stupid?"

He gaped at her. "No! Far from it."

"Then tell me. Because I'm getting pretty pissed off here."

He ran a hand through his thick, black hair, an action that accented the waves framing his face and just touching his collar. Lana swallowed. Angry or not, she could hardly ignore *that*. She saw him take a breath.

"I have other . . . talents, Lana. I can sense things—electromagnetic markers, for example—even if the living being that left them has been gone awhile. It's part of what makes me the tracker I am."

Lana felt her world tilt off its axis. "Electromagnetic markers."

"Yes."

"You want to start by explaining that?"

He stared up at the roof of the car for a second, obviously unhappy, with himself or with her, she couldn't tell. Then he looked back at her.

"Every living thing is distinguished by an electromagnetic signature or marker unique to that individual. They are as different as, say, fingerprints. Traces remain behind in a space an individual has occupied and can be detected with certain devices or by people with the appropriate psi talents."

"Psi—psychic? That would be you?"

"Yes."

"So, your psi talents make you a good tracker?"

"Among other things."

She pinned him with an unrelenting stare. "Don't stop now, you're on a roll. What other things?"

He exhaled, a breath of sound in the intimate confines of the car. "I don't just use my talents to find people. In the business, I'm known as an extractor. I find people, then I help them escape whatever difficult circumstances they find themselves in."

Lana almost slammed her foot on the brakes. She wanted to bring the car—and this whole misbegotten day—to a screeching halt. Instead, she slapped her palm on the steering wheel and cursed.

"Holy fucking shit! And that's what you plan to do when and if we find Asia and Jack, I suppose! Just waltz in there and rescue them, all on your own, a civilian, right from under the noses of the FBI, the State Police of what looks like at least two states now and whatever local police might be involved, huh? Are you freaking insane?"

She looked for a place to turn off, saw one up ahead and slowed down, pulling off onto the side of the road, gravel flying as she slid to a stop.

"Lana—"

"Don't even start. I'm turning this car around and taking you back to Nashville right now. We're done, Gabriel."

He put a hand on her arm. "Wait a minute, Lana, please."

She refused to look at him. Somehow she knew if she did, she wouldn't be able to maintain the level of anger she needed.

"Damn it, Gabriel, you used me. You have to know I can't possibly allow you to do what you're thinking of doing." She did look at him, then, hoping to convince him of the foolishness of what he was planning. "It's not just that my job is on the line here—and for damn sure, my job is in jeopardy. If you're thinking you can 'extract' two kidnap victims without bloodshed, you're just plain crazy. The real world doesn't work like that. Think of that woman. Think of her little boy. If these men are as professional as you say they are, do you think for one minute they'd hesitate to kill their captives if they suspect a rescue attempt?"

Gabriel took her hands in his. His hands were warm, his fingers and palm rough against her skin. She didn't want to notice, but she did.

"You have to trust me, Lana. I know what I'm doing. I wouldn't put Asia and Jack in danger. I wouldn't put you in danger. I wouldn't risk your job. No one but you will ever know the extent to which I was involved here. I'm only here to help you, not to get in your way. You're in charge, not me."

"That is such bullshit." But, God, she wanted to believe him.

"You'll be watching me every minute." His thumb stroked the back of her hand. "How the hell will I be able to mount my own rescue?"

He did have a point there. If she cut him loose, there was no telling what he might be up to without her knowledge.

"Have you benefitted from my help so far, or not?"

"You know I have. That's not the point."

"But it is the point. The point is we have to find Asia and Jack, and I can help you do that. Take me back to Nashville and you'll be wasting precious time. They're heading west, not east."

"God *damn* it!" She pulled her hands out of his and put them to her head. "Swear to me you will not take one step without my knowledge or consent, Gabriel. Swear!"

Eyes as dark as midnight met hers. "I swear you won't regret this, Lana."

Her heart thumping a warning in her chest, she shifted back behind the wheel and turned out onto the highway, headed west.

CHAPTER NINE

Near Orrin, North Dakota

Kinnian Dar's temper was growing shorter by the hour. Trevyn could feel the rage building in his older sibling, the hellish heat of it boiling just under the surface of his thoughts, ready to explode outward like the release of superheated gasses from the death of a star. He knew the three others in the team with them could feel it, too. Their uneasiness clung to the back of his mind, though he could do little to soothe it. Kinnian would find what he was looking for, or they would all suffer for it.

"I tire of an endless trekking across a desolate waste in this antiquated hulk, Trevyn." The farmstead receded in the rearview mirror of their rented SUV, quiet now. "Too much more of it and I won't care who notices we are here—I'll use all the resources at my disposal to find the brat. How many more of these households are there?"

Trevyn hesitated. There was danger in the truth. They had already visited eight isolated houses, some of which appeared to be attached to agricultural enterprises. None of them had harbored a six-year-old boy named Ashton Bailey. People seemed to remember a boy and his family had disappeared in the area some time back, but they weren't related to that side of the Baileys. There were only two addresses left, both within a few miles of each other on the other side of the town they'd just passed through. If Kinnian knew his options were running out, his interrogation methods would become intolerable.

"Well?" His brother turned in the seat to shout at him.

"Two. A short drive from here."

"One of these had better be the right one." Kinnian's right hand—his weapon hand—clenched and unclenched against his thigh. Trevyn knew that sign of agitation well. It would be all he could do to protect these humans they were going to "interview."

The troop in the car was silent, heavy with foreboding, as they pulled up in the yard of a large, prosperous farmstead. Two healthy canines came from the area of a mechanical shed, barking a warning at them, but stopping well before they were in arm's reach. Kinnian growled at them, then laughed as they shrank back under a glancing blow from his mind.

A middle-aged man came out onto the porch from the house, a frown on his weathered face. "Can I help you folks?"

"My name is Kinnian Dar. Are you . . . ?" He turned to Trevyn.

"Arnold Bailey."

Kinnian turned back to the man.

The man's frown deepened. "Yeah, that's me. What can I do for you?"

"I'm in need of information concerning a six-year-old boy named Ashton Bailey. Do you know him?"

Bailey paled and his knees wobbled. "Ashton? What do you know about Ashton? Are you the police?"

Kinnian drew closer to the man on the porch, taking one step at a time up onto the wooden planks until he stood toe-to-toe with his victim. Trevyn shuddered as he watched him, praying for restraint, knowing there would be none.

"No, Arnold Bailey, I'm not the police. And I don't know anything about Ashton. That's what you're going to tell me."

The man backed up, but he made the mistake of showing his anger. "Ashton's been gone for almost two years, him and his mom and dad. They disappeared on an overnight trip up to Bismarck. His dad was my brother, so if you know anything about that, mister, you better be saying something quick or get the hell off my property."

Kinnian put out a hand and caught Bailey's wrist in a grip strong enough to break bones. The man gasped and went to his knees.

"Do not take that tone with me, human. What you would tell me easily, I already know. What I want to know, I will take from you, easily or not."

And then it began. Trevyn strengthened the shields

in his own mind to block his connection with Kinnian, but it did little good. The ice storm of the man's pain beat at Trevyn's protections while Kinnian tore at his defenseless mind. Trevyn felt the human's horror, his helplessness and rage as Kinnian ripped through him, shredding his consciousness, his memories, his emotions. Sickened, Trevyn stood by as his brother took everything from the man that made him a sentient being, until there was nothing about him that Kinnian did not know.

Bailey's scream brought his wife to the door. Trevyn knew his duty. He directed the others to secure her for Kinnian. Then he went to see if there were children in the house. That was his only salvation when his sibling was in one of his killing rages. Kinnian sometimes ignored the children and left them to Trevyn.

Upstairs in one of the bedrooms, Trevyn found two girls huddled in a closet. They were shaking and crying, hysterical with fear, but they were old enough to understand him and follow his directions. From the porch below, they could all hear the brief silence that followed the end of their father's torture pierced by the beginning of their mother's. He took one of their hands in each of his and compelled the girls' attention.

"You must listen to me now." He spoke softly, reinforcing what he said through a shallow mindlink. "There is a bad man downstairs who will hurt you if he finds you. You must hide and be very quiet. You will go to sleep now and when you wake up, he'll be gone. Then you can call the police. Do you understand me?"

The two girls sniffed and nodded. "Did he hurt Mommy and Daddy?" the younger one said.

Trevyn looked at her. "They are sleeping, too. Hush, now."

He watched as the two drifted off under his compulsion, then he made certain the closet was shut against prying eyes. As he came down the stairs he ordered his troops out of the house.

"The house is empty. Lon and Tyr, call for transport and take the two bodies back to the ship for disposal."

Gabriel dropped to his knees, felled by a scream of agony that ripped through his mind like a jagged blade. His brother's face filled his vision, lined with cruelty and unrelenting will, his lips curled with disgust. Kinnian wanted; he demanded; he would take what he needed. Nothing would stand in his way, neither strength of body nor power of mind. Gabriel felt the laser of Kinnian's will spearing through the layers of his mind, searching, sorting, discarding, burning everything in its path. It was horrifying, excruciating, as if he had no blocks, no protections at all. He groveled on the ground, grasping for the core of his being, desperate to shield himself.

"Gabriel!" He heard the voice from light-years away. "Jesus Christ! Tell me what's wrong. Look at me! Gabriel!"

Kinnian's face faded from view, but for some

seconds nothing replaced it. There was nothing in his world but the pain.

"Gabriel! Look at me! Come on!"

With an effort that took everything he had, Gabriel lifted his head. He opened his eyes and blinked until they focused—a woman's face, eyes the color of emeralds, skin kissed by the sun, lips . . . lips too close to his.

"Lana."

"Thank God! What the hell happened?" She crouched in front of him on the ground, concern drawing down her features. There was grass under his hands and knees, the smell of diesel fumes in his nostrils, the sound of traffic, lots of it, nearby.

He rocked back to sit, his hands cradling his aching head. "You tell me."

"You were walking around the rest area—scanning, you said." She sat next to him. "Then you yelped, grabbed your head and fell on your knees."

Gabriel looked around, remembered the rest area, tried to bring back what he'd been feeling in the moments before the attack.

"Was it something you picked up? The EM markers?"

His heart jumped. If Kinnian already had Asia and Jack . . . "No. This was something else. The only markers I felt here were Asia's and Jack's."

Lana's brows came together. "Were you expecting to pick up someone else's?"

"What?" He realized his mistake and backpedaled.

"No. Though I recognize the three men who have them now, too. I caught the same signs back at the river." His head was splitting in two, and he needed time to sort through what he'd felt. He tested his shields. They were intact. But he had a connection with his brother, one that ran deeper than blood or bone and easily crossed the light barriers he had in place in his mind. Though it had seemed as if his own mind had been invaded, he had been feeling the impact of Kinnian's violation of another. Not Asia or Jack, he was certain. The mind he'd felt disintegrating under Kinnian's ruthless probe had been defenseless. From what he knew of them, the two they all sought so desperately would have offered more resistance. Not that it would have done them any good.

"Gabriel?" Lana was searching his face as if she might find an answer there to the questions in her eyes. "You don't look so good."

He rubbed a hand across his forehead. "Just a headache. I'll be all right."

She stood and held out a hand to help him up. He swayed as he pulled himself to his feet, and she slipped an arm under his shoulder to support him.

"Come on. Back to the car."

He didn't really need her help, but it felt good to feel her arm circling around his back, the warmth of her body along his side. He allowed his arm to drape across her shoulders, and drew her in as close as he dared. Her spicy-sweet scent caught at his senses, distracting him.

But something still tugged at his consciousness, and all at once he perceived a new link to his brother that remained open despite the reinforcement of his shields. The alternate pathway wormed its way through his protections, intricate, secretive and deep—Kinnian's work. He couldn't leave it in place, but he couldn't shut it down without Kinnian knowing it instantly. Perhaps he could use it to his advantage, but adapting it would take time and concentration.

They reached the car, and Gabriel allowed some of the weakness and nausea he was feeling to show. He slumped into the passenger seat as Lana went around to the driver's side.

She considered him. "You really don't look good."

"I just need some sleep."

"Migraine?"

He looked at her, a slight smile lifting his lips. "Something like that."

"Look, it's late and it's a long way back to Nashville. How about we find a motel?"

"Sounds good to me."

She nodded and backed out of the parking spot. Then she nosed onto the entry ramp to get back on the interstate headed west.

Gabriel used the time while she drove to the closest exit with a decent motel to examine the telepathic conduits Kinnian had established between his mind and his brother's. They were built along long-unused neural pathways that had existed between his two half-brothers and himself since before they were born.

Those networks had been programmed into their brains by their DNA, part of the patterns that allowed for the development of their psi talents.

Had his father still lived he would have been part of that genetic web. With the talents it was said he wielded, he could have directed communication between the siblings, focused and fused it into a powerful weapon for good or ill. Together, they might have ruled Thrane. From what Gabriel knew of his father, it was well he had died years ago, before his younger sons had come into their full power. Kinnian's brutality was but a shadow of his father's.

What is your father's name, boy? the teacher had asked him. Gabriel had been ten. He'd never met his father, but his mother had told him what to say. The training was necessary, and to get the training, his lineage as a Thrane had to be undisputed.

"Kylan Dar, Captain of the Bloodstalker, *Psilord of Thrane." He was small, but his voice did not waver.*

There was a collective gasp among the others seated at the table before him, though the teacher betrayed no emotion. "That is not possible," one man said. "Captain Dar's mate is Thrane, not human. His sons are not yet of trainable age."

Gabriel lifted his chin. "My mother said I should give you this." He pulled a medical sampler from his pocket and stuck it in his thumb. It didn't hurt, really. The device drew a droplet of his blood and held it in a sterile capsule for analysis. "She said you would have a reader available."

The teacher's eyes narrowed, but Gabriel thought he saw his lips curve upward as he reached down to take the sample. The man turned to give the sample to someone at the table, who placed it under a scanner for the computer to read. When the computer indicated the results, there was another murmur of reaction around the table.

A woman at the table looked to the others. "The law is clear. The boy is obviously Dar's, half-human or not. Whether or not he claims him, we are obligated to train him."

"A law foisted on us by the weaker minds in the galaxy." An older man stared at Gabriel with distaste.

"A law nonetheless," another said with a sigh. "What do you say, Rodyn?"

The teacher turned to him, a glint in his gray eyes. "I say we owe the galaxy a civilized Thrane to make up for the butcher that is his father. What is your name, boy?"

"Gabriel Cruz, sir. And I am human, not Thrane."

Rodyn had beaten him for that impudence, the first of many beatings Gabriel was to suffer at the old Thrane's hand. He had explained why later, and even at ten Gabriel understood his reasons. In fact, they had understood each other quite well, all in all. Gabriel had been a quick study, and Rodyn had been waiting a lifetime for a student like him. They had loved each other almost from the first.

Rodyn had taught him some of the tricks he was using now to untangle the threads Kinnian had left in his mind. By the time Lana turned off the interstate, Gabriel had teased the knot apart. He rewove the net of Kinnian's invasion so that it brushed a harmless corner of his mind rather than stretching across the main line of his thoughts. The false signals his brother received would be enough to keep him connected, but not enough to allow him fully into Gabriel's mind.

As he finished his task and worked to make his way back to the surface of his mind, Gabriel caught the presence of another consciousness. He'd seen the pattern before, always overridden by Kinnian's. It was distinct, even if it was rarely separate from his brother's. Trevyn Dar's signature was there *beneath* Kinnian's, and apart from the trap that Kinnian had woven later to maintain the link between them.

"Gabriel?" Alana's voice was soft. Her hand on his face was warm. "We're here. I'm just going to go in and register, okay?"

He sat up and rubbed a hand down his face. "Okay. Um, I've got cash if you can put your card down for both rooms."

She just nodded and pushed the car door closed.

He watched her go, then using all his skill to avoid activating the link, Gabriel explored Trevyn's shadow in his mind. There was tremendous emotion behind it—horror, revulsion, guilt, anger, self-loathing. It was as if Trevyn had tried so hard to shut himself off from Kinnian and what he was doing that he had punched through to Gabriel without even being aware of it. But as soon as the link was open, Kinnian had felt it and used it—which meant he was watching Trevyn now, monitoring his thoughts, following the link between them.

Gabriel's forehead wrinkled in a frown. His two half-brothers had always worked together, since the day Trevyn had reached maturity, just two years after Kinnian. Trevyn's reputation was nearly as bloody as his older sibling's. What could have caused this change of heart? And how could he find a way to contact Trevyn without putting his younger brother in greater danger?

He saw Lana come out of the motel office and realized he'd have to leave this problem for another time. He was tired; he needed food and sleep before he dared try to work around Kinnian to reach Trevyn. And there was Lana, who would need some kind of explanation for his . . . headache.

Lana drove around the building to their rooms and handed him a key card. "That's it—yours is 122. I'm going to head out for some food while you finish your nap. When I get back we need to talk. What do you like on your pizza?"

He managed a smile. "Anything but anchovies." He said it because he'd heard someone say it in the hallway at Ethan's house the night before. He had no idea what anchovies were, but Earthers apparently either loved them or hated them.

"I'm so glad you said that," she concurred with a grin and took off as soon as he shut the door.

Trevyn found his brother on the porch of the Bailey farmhouse in a sober, though no longer a murderous, mood. Kinnian pivoted on his heel and regarded him with an air of speculation.

"Ah, there you are, brother! Is all secure?"

"Yes, my lord. There were only the two of them in the dwelling. Did you get the information you needed?"

"No, damn the gods. The boy is not here. By which I mean, he has not been returned here."

Trevyn met Kinnian's dark gaze, wondering in the depths of his mind why his brother's rage was not burning hot enough to scald them all. "So, now what?"

"We may have an opportunity to snatch victory from the jaws of defeat, brother." Kinnian's voice was like oil over wet ground. "As these humans screamed out their deaths, I caught the echo of a long-lost voice in the back of my mind. It was as if this ghost saw my handiwork from afar and despaired. I felt it distinctly. I'm sure I could not be mistaken."

Trevyn fought to control his body's reaction, knowing Kinnian was watching for it. "What ghost would haunt you, my lord? And how?"

Kinnian grinned and came closer to put a hand on Trevyn's shoulder. His fingers closed in a grip as tight as an *orphyl's* claws.

"Why, none other than our lost brother, Gabriel. In my mind, watching. All caught up in our little drama without the least invitation. It appears he is here on this planet, hunting this boy, as we are. The bastard, as always, seeking to take from this family what is rightfully mine. As to how . . ." His grip tightened. "It is no secret to me that you disdain my methods, brother. You think to hide your weakness from me, but I see it. I feel it. And so, it seems, does Gabriel. Perhaps he used you to get to me."

Trevyn pulled away from Kinnian's hold. "You think me disloyal?"

"If I thought you disloyal, you would be dead."

"I serve you and no other." Trevyn kept his voice steady, his gaze unswerving, hiding his turmoil. Were his shields so weak he'd reached out to Gabriel without knowing it? If so, it was the first time it had happened. "But my mind is my own. If you ask me to tell you what I think, then I'll share my thoughts. Until then, I'll keep them to myself."

Kinnian's face came so close, his beard brushed Trevyn's clean-shaven chin. "See that you do. You understand that we must control our link with Gabriel? Perhaps it is our new proximity to our long-lost brother that has drawn him into our circle. Still, I can't have him tracking us through you." He bared his teeth in a smile that could not be misinterpreted. "Your efforts to leash me would be ill-served from the confines of the ship's brig, would they not, Commander?"

"My lord." Trevyn acknowledged his brother's meaning—and his power—with a slow nod.

"For now, it is fortunate that we have established a

link with Gabriel, no matter how it happened." Kinnian turned and led the way back to the rented SUV. "His unguarded mind has given me a name. It may be enough to lead us to the boy."

Trevyn made sure to reinforce the shields in his mind before he followed his sibling to the back seat of the vehicle. With a thought, he activated the computer network connections wetwired into his brain.

"What is the name?"

"Asia Roberts. And the boy is called Jack, now." Kinnian seemed pleased that Trevyn was already settled in to work. "There was some anxiety around this knowledge, but I was not connected long enough to detect exactly what it was. When I have time to explore, I intend to find out more."

"Of course." Trevyn began a search for the name in all the local databases he could access.

Doors slammed as the other members of the landing team returned. Trevyn heard his brother give the order to move, felt the SUV roll over the gravel drive as they left the farm behind.

It was not long before his search produced results. "There is a reason for the anxiety you detected." He glanced up at Kinnian. "Asia Roberts and her son Jack have been reported kidnapped. The governing police authority for this sector of the planet has posted a special alert regarding their disappearance."

Kinnian's face reddened. "Someone else has the boy? Who?"

Trevyn shook his head. "If the answer even exists in

the information matrices of this world, it will take more than a few minutes to find it, my lord."

"Portol's balls!" Kinnian slammed a hand on the back of the seat. "Ditch this fucking kidney crusher and get us back to the ship. I want them found *now*, Trevyn. We've spent too much time in this ass-end of space."

Gabriel woke to the sound of heavy pounding. At first he was sure it was inside his head, where the pain was still a dull weight swinging around the inside margins of his skull. When he heard his name being repeated with some urgency he realized it was the door, and he staggered out of bed to answer it.

"Hey." Lana pushed past him with a huge, flat cardboard box and a pack of six chilled aluminum cans in her hands. "I thought I was going to have to call 911." She put her burdens on the table in the corner of the room and turned to look at him. Her eyes widened and her mouth fell open. "Oops."

That was when it occurred to him that he was dressed only in his boxers. He mumbled something apologetic and reached for his pants.

"I took a shower and thought I'd lie down for a minute. Guess that was about an hour ago."

"Don't blush on my account, GQ." She stifled a grin and turned to pull a beer from the pack. She handed it over once he'd zipped up. "Just think of me as one of the guys."

It was the last way he wanted to think of her. "A gentleman always dresses for dinner." He set the beer aside to pull on the same soft white shirt he'd been wearing all day. Lana had exchanged her collared shirt with the FBI logo and practical pants for something much softer and more feminine. He thought instantly of touching her. "Did you go shopping?"

She laughed. "On my salary? No, just the value of foresight. I always keep some things in the car—for emergencies."

"Smart." He tipped his beer in her direction.

A smile lifted the corners of her mouth. "You must be feeling better. Headache all gone?"

"Mostly." He felt like he'd been on a three-day bender, but he was damned if he'd admit it.

She examined him a minute longer, judging the depth of the lie, then turned to open the pizza box. "Eat. Something on your stomach will help."

He was ravenous and wolfed down two pieces of the strange flat bread covered with meat and cheese before he thought to speak again. He paused to take a breath and looked up to see Lana watching him in amusement.

"This is good!" No wonder Sam raved about it.

"It's Pizza Hut, all I could find. You must be starving." She squinted at him as if he had sprouted antennae. "Are you sure you're all right?"

"I'm fine. I think you're right. I just needed food." He took another piece of pizza, but he ate this one slowly, savoring it, appreciating the way the flavors blended in a riot of sensation. Tangy. Salty. Satisfying.

There was nothing subtle about it.

He glanced back at Lana just as the pink tip of her tongue came out from between her lips to collect a tiny dribble of red sauce before she dabbed at her mouth with a napkin. Gabriel's breath exploded from his chest as his groin tightened in painful response, and he was forced to bite down on a groan. For no reason he could explain he had become acutely aware of her, of the way an errant curl escaped from her pinned-up control and teased her neck, the way her creamy skin was flushed with the color of ripe *aluria* fruit. His senses were wide open, picking up every thread and nuance in the room. It could have been an aftereffect of the psychic overload he'd experienced earlier, but—

"You know you scared the crap out of me with your little performance this afternoon, right?"

The way she was looking at him set off any number of alarms. The spark of concern he saw in her eyes just didn't match the bite of anger in her voice.

He opted for honesty. "You weren't half as scared as I was."

Oh, hell. Now the concern had morphed into something deeper, and her gaze was sharp, full of hooks to catch the unwary.

"Okay. So what's your explanation?"

"I'm not sure." He shook his head. "All of a sudden it was like my head was caught in a vise and someone was turning the crank."

"Uh-huh. And this has never happened to you before?"

"No." That, at least, was the truth. He and Kinnian had never come so close before, and his brother's power had grown since their last, brief encounter.

"This, uh, attack. It wasn't accompanied by any, say, visions or anything, was it?"

He met her eyes and found both knowledge and certainty there. "Why would you think that?"

"Gabriel. You have talents. You admit it. And you forget I was on the outside, observing this attack of yours." She leaned closer. "You *saw* something. You were *watching* it happen. And it was horrible."

She got up, leaving Gabriel shaken and staring after her. She paced for a moment, then turned back to him.

"I don't believe you saw Asia and Jack. You wouldn't keep that to yourself. But whatever you saw, it has you tied in knots. You pretended to be asleep, but I could tell you sat in that car all the way here trying to solve some kind of problem. Now, I risked my job to bring you here, knowing what I know about you. I could be risking lives to keep you here. You need to trust me. Tell me what you saw."

Everything in him wanted to respond to what she asked of him, to give her what she needed. The words were at the tip of his tongue, ready to spill out of his mouth into the air between them, changing what she knew of the universe forever. But he couldn't trust her yet. And worse, he knew better than to trust himself. It was far too early for the truth, if the truth could ever be spoken between them.

He gave up a part of the story. "What I felt was an

interrogation," he admitted, "but not of Asia or Jack and not by the people that hold them. There's another group out there looking for them."

Lana regained her seat across from him and raised her eyes to his. "I hardly know where to start asking questions, Gabriel. I haven't figured out yet why *one* group of kidnappers would want to snatch this woman and her son. Now you're telling me there's a second bunch out there that wants them? And this second bunch is 'interrogating' people in such a way that you can feel it psychically somehow? You do know that Mulder and Scully don't really work for the FBI, don't you?"

Gabriel considered half a second, then dismissed the last question as rhetorical. He was getting used to Lana's sense of humor. Behind her sarcasm, he sensed her frustration. She didn't want to believe that Ethan was involved in the kidnapping of a wife and son he so obviously loved, but she lacked alternative explanations. Knowing he shouldn't, he decided to give her one and see how open her mind might be.

"On the other hand, your colleagues believe Ethan is the reason Asia and Jack have been abducted."

Lana's eyebrows lifted. "What do you mean?"

"That's the usual motive, isn't it? The husband's involved in something illicit. The loved ones are held for collateral until the kidnappers get what they want from him. But there's a problem—you haven't been able to dig up anything suspicious in Ethan's background."

"Doesn't mean it's not there." She couldn't meet his

gaze. "Give us more than 24 hours to look and God knows what we might turn up."

"You don't believe that."

She blew out a breath. "If you have another theory, I'm listening. Right now, I've got squat-all else."

"What if Asia was of interest because she is unique in some way?"

Lana stared at him. "You're thinking psi talents? Telepathy, maybe?"

Gabriel shrugged. "It's a possibility, at least."

"Ethan *has* been hiding something." Lana got up to pace again. "Maybe that's it. Asia had been his patient . . . could have been one reason she came to him. And the boy . . . just scooped up with her, you think?"

"Probably." But the scene he had witnessed told him Kinnian had been sent for Jack, not Asia. His brothers had somehow found Jack's relatives— something Rescue had been unable to do—most likely with information provided by the Grays. And thank God for that, because it meant they knew nothing of Ethan.

The FBI agent in the room was still working out her own investigative problem. "Who would be so interested in psi talents that they'd grab a woman and a child and nearly kill a man? In broad daylight."

"Trust me, Lana, the list is endless if the talent is great enough."

She rubbed a hand over her face. "That's not much help. This little theory of yours needs some evidence if I'm going to convince my people. Maybe I should run it by a guy I know in military intelligence."

"No." He stood up, as if he could physically stop her. "Some of these groups could be operating deep inside your government."

She threw a sharp glance in his direction, and he cursed himself for the slip. But she missed the "your" and focused on "government".

"You mean black ops? If we suspect that, then I definitely should brief my boss."

He touched her arm. "Lana, it's too early to share this. You don't want to tip your hand before we're sure."

Her lips thinned in anger. "Asia and Jack wouldn't say it's too early. In fact, they'd say we need to get up off our asses." She turned again to take up her agitated pacing. "We need a break, Gabriel. I feel the time slipping away from us."

He caught her by the shoulders. "We'll find them. We're only a step behind; I can feel it."

She pulled back to look up at him, her eyes locked on his. She trembled under his hands, vibrating with what he thought at first was the frustration of the case, but quickly realized was something much more dangerous.

"Aw, hell." She shook her head and stepped back.

He couldn't help himself; he followed her, closing the distance. "What's wrong?" His voice came out lower, softer than he intended. He touched her face. She frowned at him. But those eyes . . . *Dios*.

She held her ground. "I'm trying to focus here.

You're distracting me."

"Maybe we both need a little distraction." He stroked her cheek. *So soft.*

She allowed it. And, at last, she moved closer, bringing their bodies together.

"Distraction can be dangerous."

"It can also be an unexpected pleasure." He bent his head to her, his lips nearly touching hers. "Why not indulge yourself?"

She brought her mouth to his, as he had known she would, and opened her lips to receive him, welcoming him with a taste that was sweet and hot and all her own. His tongue swept her mouth and withdrew, slipped again past her lips for a longer exploration, teased her, tempted her. Her mouth, her body melted under his assault, growing hotter, softer, her arms rising up to ring his neck and draw him closer, enclosing him in her spicy, ginger-cream scent.

He couldn't control his response. His body was on fire for her, his heart thrashing in his chest, his fevered blood filling him until he was heavy and aching. His hands wandered down her back and over the swell of her hips to pull her into him, and he shifted so that their hips were aligned, hard to soft, heat to heat. A gasp escaped her, and he groaned as he took her mouth again. Her taste—God, he loved the way she tasted.

A subtle vibration shook him, something shared between them that sizzled like the flow of current along a circuit. Something was connected, completed in the press of their bodies, in the velvety tangle of his tongue with hers. His shields were under assault, but from her mind or his own needs, he could not tell. He could feel her need for him, her longing to surrender, beating against him like the waves of a sea storm against a sandy shore. And he was crumbling, sliding into her surging waters, wanting to open his mind and let her in. So he could feel everything about her. So she could know everything about him.

But, suddenly, almost as quickly as it had begun, it was over. Lana pulled back, reluctance and something close to fear shadowing her green eyes. She licked her lips. Took a breath. Touched his face.

"I think that's probably enough self-indulgence for tonight, don't you?"

"If you say so." He kept the words light, but his heart battered his ribcage, wanting more.

She shook her head, stepping back. "I'll see you in the morning."

And then she was gone.

Jesus, what the hell was I thinking?

Lana slammed the door to her room behind her and collapsed on the bed. She stared up at the dingy motel ceiling, her heart bumping so hard it rocked her entire body. She had broken so many rules today she'd stopped counting, but this one—God, *this* one took the prize. Not only had she let a civilian so far into this investigation she might as well have issued him credentials. Now she was ready to drop her pants for him, too? *Holy shit!*

But, my God, was she ever ready! If she hadn't run, she'd have been out of her clothes and in his bed in less time than it took for one of those slow smiles to spread across his beautiful face. She laughed out loud in the silence of the room at the ridiculous situation she found herself in. She was 32 years old, for chrissake, and she was mooning over this guy like a kid in braces. And all it had taken was one kiss!

She jumped as the cell phone at her waist began trilling. She yanked it free and groaned when she saw who had broken the giddy spell Gabriel had woven over her.

She hit the talk pad and spoke into it. "Hey."

"Hey, baby. Where are you? Thought you'd be home by now." Mark sounded put out. "I felt bad about earlier. I was gonna stop by and apologize."

Lana knew all about Mark's apologies. Once upon a time they'd been fun. Good thing she was a long way from home. She didn't seem to be in the mood for one tonight.

"Yeah, well, looks like you'll just have to grovel over the phone tonight, babe, 'cuz I'm spending the night in Memphis."

"In Memphis? What the hell for?" He was pissed now, she could hear it.

"I had to interview a witness on this case, and I was too damn tired to drive all the way back to Nashville, that's what for." Did she sound pissed, too? She thought so.

"A witness? All the way to hell and gone in Memphis?"

"She saw the van at a rest stop down here. They're headed west on I-40."

"Well, good. They're Little Rock's problem by now, then."

"It's still my case, Mark."

"That's my little agent, always on the job." He chuckled, but there was a nasty edge to his teasing that made her teeth clench.

"It's been a long day." She yawned. "I'm going to bed."

"All right, honey. Just make sure you get there by yourself."

Her temper flared hot enough to fry him over the 200 miles that separated them. "What the hell is that supposed to mean?"

"Means you damn well better not have that fucking Mexican with you there in Memphis—for more than one reason."

Blind with rage, she fought to control the tremor in her voice. "First, he's Cuban-American, not Mexican. Second, whether he's with me or not is *my* business, not yours. Third, don't threaten me. Ever. I don't belong to you, Mark. I never did. And now we're done."

Lana thumbed the phone off and just kept herself from hurling it across the room. She jumped up from the bed and began to pace the length of the motel room, curses falling from her mouth in an unending stream. She could only wish she'd used some of them on Mark directly. It was too late now. She didn't plan to speak to him except in a professional capacity ever again. The asshole.

And, of course, if he ratted her out to Ballard about Gabriel, there was a good chance that professional capacity would be threatened, too.

CHAPTER TEN

Trin, Center for Adminstrative Control,
Consortium of Minertsa, Sector 10

The Minister of Labor's right hand sat at her desk
and stared at the data crystal, a thing that held the fate
of worlds in a latticework of mineral no bigger than the
tip of her finger. The significant facts for each of the
adult subjects of the Del Origa project—slaves retaken
from planets all over the galaxy and now in place
according to the original master plan—were there in
the heart of the crystal. The data was what Sennik had
been waiting for. Director Second Ardis could delay
giving it to him no longer.

Ardis had tried by all the many means at her
disposal to root out the purpose behind the project. She
had sought some reference to it in all the databanks to
which her inventive and intelligent mind could secure
access, and that was almost all of the Consortium's vast
storehouse of knowledge. If there was any record of the
project in computer storage, it was secured beyond
retrieval by her considerable skills. Ardis suspected

there *was* no official record. Del Origa had been Sennik's personal project, protected under his own special protocols.

Ardis had ended as she had begun, with no coherent picture of what Sennik had in mind for his specially-programmed slaves, now that he had stationed them on the many planets of the Minertsan Consortium. From what she knew of him, only two things seemed certain: Sennik himself was the only one who knew the final plan. And disruption on an epic scale would be its inevitable outcome.

Ardis stood, the crystal in her hand. She adjusted her emotional composition, jettisoning all fear, all doubt, all hesitation. She had worked long and hard to be in place when the time came. Still, nothing could have prepared her for this moment now that it was here. The humans spoke of selling one's soul to the devil. And though her people believed in neither soul nor devil, Ardis thought she understood the despair the phrase evoked. She felt lost, perhaps for all eternity.

She enhanced the colors of her aura with confidence and sexuality and pressed her hand on the sensor requesting entrance to the Director Prime's office. His answer came at once, and she entered, closing the door with care behind her.

--You have news for me, Second? His aura was darker than usual, the silver shot through with ominous black.

She allowed her lavender to lighten with pleasure. *The data you have been waiting for, Director Prime.*

All of the adult subjects of Del Origa have been reprogrammed and reassigned. All are in place, awaiting your orders. These are the preliminary reports from each of the placements.

Sennik stood and came around his desk to her. His aura lit up from within until it shone with golden highlights.

--At last! We were able to recover all of them?

--Yes, Director Prime. All fifty-six.

The golden streaks in his silver aura swirled and danced. *Excellent. You have done your job well, Ardis. What of the young ones?*

Ardis held on to her emotions, refusing to allow any reaction. *The* mrill-*cursed pirates have protected them well, sir. We have recovered thirteen of them. Four remain at large in various sectors of the galaxy. Three are dead.*

--What of the coordinator? Has he been found?

--The boy is as yet unrecovered, but Captain Dar reports he has found the beginnings of a trail.

Sennik brightened. *Indeed. If Dar says so, we should have him shortly, then. All is well.*

Ardis lifted her color and subtly altered her hue.

The male noticed at once. He stepped closer, the silver of his aura tinged with a bright blue. *Ardis, perhaps you would join me in a celebratory drink? I think we both deserve it, don't you?*

She ducked her head submissively and sent a flush of purple through her aura. *I would be honored, Director Prime.*

Sennik waved her toward the heated rest platform at the opposite end of his well-appointed office. She curled up on one end of it while he poured the *mrikis* from an antique decanter into two delicate flutes. She watched him, suppressing a tiny tremor of revulsion. He could not be allowed to detect the slightest hesitation in her mind.

By the time he handed her one of the glasses and sat down very close to her on the platform, his aura was stained dark blue with arousal.

Just this once, my dear, I believe it would be acceptable for you to call me by my egg name. Ren.

She took a drink from the flute—it was very good *mrikis*—and because she knew it was inevitable and necessary, she let herself feel the beginnings of arousal. Her head grew lighter, her breath became short, her heart rate rose. She began to hunger. Her aura deepened like twilight.

--Ren. I have practiced that name on my tongue.

--Have you, my dear? His fingertips stroked her temple. *Tell me your egg name.*

--Ilia.

--It seems as though I have noticed your interest in me before, Ilia. Have you thought of me and let yourself become aroused?

Yes. She felt him in her mind, watching her reactions as his hand slid lower to her neck, her throat. Flames followed the touch of his fingers.

His aura burned blue as he removed her clothing and his, exposing their skin, their bodies to each other.

His mind reached deeper, heightening her pleasure at the sight of his nakedness. His hands stroked lower, touching, inflaming. His mind circled her pleasure center, teasing.

Have you held me in your mind, Ilia, as you pleasured yourself? Like this, perhaps?

Yes, she answered, *yes, yes*, pressing his hand against her pulsing core as she shuddered with need. Her aura flowed with the dark purple and midnight blue of intense stimulation. He was deep in her mind now, spearing into her pleasure center with brutal intimacy.

Yes, I feel it. Sennik moaned, his other hand stroking his own engorged sex, out of its sheath now and demanding attention. *Give me more, my love. Give me everything.*

And because he asked it, because she could refuse him nothing, she showed him her naked need, coming for him in a raging storm of blind desire, his name on her lips.

She felt Sennik's triumph as he found his own release, his seed spilling through his fingers onto her belly. But in his mind, open for a few brief, unguarded seconds, she also found the clues she needed. And in the deepest, most heavily shadowed recess of her mind, behind every shield and barricade, behind even the self-loathing she would save to endure later, Ardis smiled.

Outside Memphis, Tennessee, Earth, Sector Three

Gabriel greeted the dawn naked on his knees on the floor of his motel room. If he'd had more time he would have sought out a more appropriate place for this task—a high point overlooking a valley, a quiet spot near water. Even a cave would have been better than this cramped, unnatural monument to humanity's lack of energetic sensitivity. But he didn't have time. He needed to know now what he was up against.

In the posture required by the Disciplines for the deepest levels of mind work, he settled into the breathing pattern. Long years of training, reinforced by painful punishment, had shown him the path. Maturity, habit and the reinforcement of need had carved the path into a broad roadway, easy to follow even in the dark of physical stress or the storms of emotional upheaval. He tracked it down through his conscious mind, past his subconscious, into his unconscious, seeking out the traps and barriers he'd erected against his sibling's incursions the day before.

There, in a remote corner of his mind, he saw a golden net stretched like a spider's web between two marble columns. The black threads of his brother's attack writhed within the sparkling strands of Gabriel's trap, struggling to be free in his mind. Entangled there, they saw and heard only what Gabriel wanted them to see and hear. Satisfied that his snare held, he went on to seek out the separate trail that led back to Trevyn.

There! He saw Trevyn's energy like a gateway leading out onto a long narrow bridge. He followed it, oblivious to the long fall into nothingness on either side, his attention on the stone at his feet, drawn by the warmth and light of an unseen sun in the air around him.

And then he saw him. Tall. Fair, where he and Kinnian were dark. His face holding a smile, tentative and sad, as though he expected nothing.

"Trevyn."

His brother inclined his head. "Gabriel. I didn't know if you'd come."

"Where is Kinnian?"

"Close, as always." He looked over his shoulder. Behind him was a garden, overgrown with dense vegetation. A high wall stood in the thick of it. In the distance, Gabriel could hear a thunderous roaring.

"We don't have much time," Trevyn said.

"Why did you lead me here?"

"To warn you. To help you as much as I can."

Gabriel laughed. "You've never helped me before. You didn't help me the night our father butchered my sister's husband."

"I was a boy, Gabriel. You can thank your God that butcher never claimed you as his son."

"Claim me? From the moment he knew I existed, Kylan Dar wanted only to kill me. Do you know how many children he killed at the Academy looking for me?" Rodyn had given his life that night to save Gabriel's—and set him on the road he travelled now.

"Because he feared you. As Kinnian does."

Bitterness rose in Gabriel's throat. "I was a reminder to Kylan of a youthful mistake, a moment of vulnerability, nothing more."

Trevyn shook his head. "You don't see it even now. What you could become."

"I rejected my Thrane inheritance a long time ago."

"You're still a threat to Kinnian. You have no idea how strong he is, how powerful." He straightened and lifted his head to meet Gabriel's gaze. "That's why I called you. He knows you're here. If he breaks through your defenses—"

"I'm aware of his attacks."

Gabriel started to turn back toward the bridge, but Trevyn grabbed his arm. "No, my brother. You don't understand. Come with me."

He pulled out of Trevyn's grasp and looked around, suspecting a trap. "The longer I stay here, the more dangerous it is, *brother*."

"If Kinnian had known you were here, you would be his by now." He turned away. "Come."

Trevyn led the way into the tangled undergrowth, a narrow path opening before him. Wary and reluctant, Gabriel followed him, his mind alert to traps in the clinging vines and grasping bushes all around him. They pulled up when they reached the towering stone wall.

The noise on the other side of the wall was now a

steady roll of howling and shrieking, of growling and baying and ear-splitting roars. And underneath it all, there was a sound like drums pounding and the earth beneath their feet shook.

"What the hell is that?" Gabriel had to shout to be heard.

Trevyn pointed to a tiny chink in the stone. Gabriel bent to put his eye to the hole and looked.

On the other side was a creature two stories high and as broad as a starship, with toothy jaws as wide as an asteroid miner and a tail that could flatten a building with a single sweep. It paced on four legs, but seemed capable of standing on two of them. All four appendages ended in deadly-looking claws.

Gabriel backed away from the wall, his heart in his throat, but before he could say anything, he found himself back on the other side of the garden with Trevyn.

"My God!"

"Do you remember the creature from your training?"

He swallowed. "The VRadkrystion. Symbol of the power of the Blood Legion."

"It has paced and grown behind that wall since the time of our father's death."

"Do you mean to say that Kylan's murder was the price of Kinnian's induction in the Legion?"

Trevyn lifted a shoulder. "If that's so, the galaxy was done a service. It's not usually the Legion's way, though they may have had their own reasons for wanting Kylan dead. Kinnian, for all his power, is not nearly as intelligent as the old man was."

"Or as unpredictable." Gabriel's lips curled in a wry smile. "And yet here you sit, under that creature's very nose. Watching. And waiting. For what, Trevyn? Are you too weak to put an end to it—or too afraid?"

Fury flashed in Trevyn's eyes and every muscle went taut as if he would launch himself at Gabriel's throat. But he held himself still, and in time the steel melted from him.

"I have endured the hell that is my life in order to save who and what I could from the savagery of our blood. I've been forced to watch because I've been waiting for *you*. Since the age of 12, when I saw my friends die that night at the Academy, I've been waiting for you. Yes. I'll admit I'm too weak to stop this on my own. I need your help."

Behind him the roar of the VRadkrystion pealed like distant thunder. Gabriel studied his brother's face, saw the pain in it. But in the end, he shook his head.

"It may be too late for that now. With the Blood Legion behind him, Kinnian may be too much for both of us."

Trevyn nodded, as if he'd expected Gabriel's answer. "Then at least you can end this for me, Gabriel. I'm so damn tired."

The trill of her cell phone woke Lana out of a

restless sleep. She slapped at the table beside the bed in the dark motel room until she found the beeping device and hit "talk".

"Matheson."

"Sorry to wake you, ma'am. It's Rick Mason."

She sat up, clearing the cobwebs from her head. The overlarge dial on the motel clock told her it was crazy early by most standards: 4:30 a.m.

"S'okay, Rick. I was just getting up." God knows why she told *that* lie. "What's the news?"

"Two reports came in overnight. I waited as long as I could before I called."

Lana bit back the urge to cuss the rookie thoroughly for waiting any time at all. *Let's see if the reports are worth anything first.*

"Tell me."

"Arkansas State Trooper encountered a van matching our description yesterday around eleven a.m., 120 miles west of the Tennessee state line on I-40."

"Shit! How long did it take Arkansas to wake up and figure out they'd seen our guys?"

"Twelve hours."

"Jesus. Okay, what else?"

"Citizen called in from a gas station off I-40 past Russellville, Arkansas, at about three p.m. with a similar description. Said they'd been there an hour before."

"And when did we get that one?"

"About midnight."

"Holy fucking shit! Why the hell do we even bother

with these alerts if the state assholes dick around for hours before they pass them on! And why the *fuck* didn't you call me?"

"Agent Jamisky was on duty. He said he'd take care of it, ma'am."

"Oh, he did, did he?" Lana shook with righteous anger. "Fine. Connect me with SSA Ballard."

"Now?"

"Yes, now, Agent Mason." She held on to the phone as if she was afraid it might fly out of her hands and shatter against the nearest wall.

"But, Agent Matheson, there was something else—"

"*What?*"

"The TBI lab called with preliminary results of the blood work from Roberts' clothing. Identified a former SEAL who was listed as medically discharged in 2006, Tyler Mahone."

The information threw cold water on her building tantrum. The evidence she needed was starting to drift in and was settling out in the pattern Gabriel had predicted.

"That was fast—and just what I needed. Thanks, Rick. Okay. So, now you can wake Ballard up. I promise not to chew his ear off."

"Yes, ma'am."

Lana used the few minutes it took to transfer the call to switch on the light and clear the last of the fog from her brain. She would need all her wits to get what she wanted from Supervisory Special Agent Frank Ballard.

Her boss's voice was thick with sleep and gritty with unhappiness. "Matheson? What the hell?"

"Sorry, boss, I know it's early. This couldn't wait."

"This about the Roberts case?"

"Yeah. We've had a few breaks overnight."

"So good of you to join us, Agent. Jamisky brought me up to date hours ago. Where the hell have you been? Wasn't this supposed to be your case?"

"I've been—"

"—Yeah, I know, interviewing a witness in person down in Memphis. What the hell for? You need to get your ass back in Nashville and get something on Roberts or we won't have a chance in hell of catching these guys."

"With all due respect, sir, I don't think Roberts is involved." It was too soon to lay that out, all her instincts said so, but she had to say something to justify her line of investigation. "We got the blood work back on one of the perps—a former SEAL named Mahone. I need to run him down."

"Good. You can do that from here."

"Yes, sir, but all the information we got overnight indicates these guys are headed west as fast as they can go. They're on I-40 and they're not stopping for anything. We need to mobilize to identify and track that van. I can do that better from out here—maybe Little Rock."

"Shit, Matheson, those sightings are more than twelve hours old." Ballard's impatience came through the phone in a growl. "That van could be any-fucking-where by now. What do you want to do—set up a roadblock *behind* the damn thing? Trust me, you'll do more good chasing your own tail than trying to chase these guys down the road with what we've got right now. The answers are here with the husband."

Lana gripped the phone, desperate to hold on to her temper. "How about we attack the problem from both sides, sir? Let Agent Jamisky follow any leads he can find on Dr. Roberts there in Nashville. I'll move on to the Little Rock Bureau office and coordinate our efforts to find the van from there, at least until we're sure that it's out of the state. In the meantime Agent Mason can continue to monitor the Amber Alert response and see if we can dig up anything on Mahone."

Ballard was quiet for so long, Lana was sure he was going to say no, but he conceded at last. "All right. I'll approve expenses for a few days—but that's it. Wrap this fucker up, Matheson, you hear me?"

"Loud and clear, boss. Thanks."

Lana exhaled her relief and swung her bare legs over the side of the bed. Now that she had what she wanted, she couldn't have said just why she was so reluctant to go back to Nashville. The only thing she knew was that her intuition screamed for her to pursue her quarry west; if she went back east she'd lose them. She'd relied on her gut for every one of her ten years as an agent. She wasn't about to give up on it now.

She went to the sink, flipped on a light, splashed cold water on her face. She studied her face over the edge of the towel as she dabbed at her wet cheeks. Was that a hint of shadow under her eyes, a line or two of stress around her mouth? She blew out a breath and reached for the toothbrush.

Lana knew what this was about. Not the case. At least, not *just* the case. She hadn't slept well, but it hadn't been because she was worried about finding kidnappers. She'd tossed and turned half the night thinking about a certain PI in the next room over, the one whose broad expanse of bare chest narrowed to a hard, smooth belly, whose silky boxers rode so low on his hips they just covered the delectable package beneath, whose kiss, as brief as it had been, had signaled the beginning of something unstoppable.

Lana had forced herself to pull away from him out of simple self-protection. Another minute in his arms and she would have been lost. Even now, just the thought of that kiss was enough to make her burn. It was as if Gabriel had reached inside her mind and opened a Whitman's Sampler box of sexual fantasies. Only these were no cheap candies. They were rich with the exotic bittersweet of raw cocoa, the dark swirl of molasses, the velvet smoke of Cuban rum. She could still taste his heat on her tongue. And she wanted him. God, how she wanted him. If it weren't for this case . . . her mind exploded with the things she would like to do to, for and with the man in the next room.

She exhaled again and shook her head at her reflection in the mirror. It was no use following that line of thinking any further. There was the *case* to think about, and what she should be doing was finding a way to get Gabriel back to Nashville as quickly as possible. There would be a car rental agency in Little Rock, maybe closer. She ignored the weight of . . . regret? loss? . . . accumulating in her belly and made up her mind to drop him off as soon as she could.

No more than ten minutes later, Lana stood outside Gabriel's door, shivering in the early morning chill. *God, please let him have some pants on this time*, she thought, not at all certain of her resolve at this ungodly hour. She didn't realize she was holding her breath until he opened the door and she saw that he was fully dressed. She scraped up an awkward smile.

"Hey. Sorry to roust you out so early."

He didn't seem nearly as uncomfortable as she was. "I figured you'd be anxious to get started." He nodded at the coffeemaker. "How do you take your coffee?"

"Fully loaded." She stepped inside the room. "And you are my hero."

Gabriel smiled as he turned to doctor the coffee with cream and sugar. "An easy quest this morning." He handed the cup to her. "My lady."

"Thank you, kind sir." She took a sip, letting the hot liquid warm her chest. "We got confirmation that the van is moving west through Arkansas with two sightings yesterday. And some info on one of the kidnappers that goes along with the profile you came up with. I'm headed into the Little Rock office to monitor operations from there." She stopped, reluctant to get to the part where she planned to dump him.

Gabriel studied her over his coffee. "What aren't

you telling me, Lana?"

"We should be able to find a car rental agency on the way somewhere. Or in Little Rock." She couldn't meet his eyes. "I hate to do that to you, but I don't have any other way to get you back to Nashville. I'm sorry."

He didn't look worried. "I'm not going back to Nashville."

Anger sparked, but Lana tamped it down. "Of course, I can't make you go anywhere. But this . . ." She gestured, unable for a moment to describe just what it was they had between them.

"Collaboration?"

"Okay," she accepted, "collaboration. This collaboration can't go on. It was one thing to have you tag along on my own turf. I'll be in someone else's yard in Little Rock, asking them for help in this investigation. I can't explain your presence in the middle of a Federal investigation to people I don't even know."

"Understood."

That surprised her. She narrowed her eyes at him.

"So you agree?"

"I'm not expecting you to introduce me to the boys in the Little Rock office. It serves my purposes that no one else knows I'm involved. If you want I'll even rent another car."

"But you still plan on following me to Little Rock."

He shrugged, the movement a smooth ripple of muscle beneath his shirt. "If you mean do I plan to stay close to you, no matter where this investigation leads, then, yes, Alana, that is my intention."

Lana blew out a breath and ran a hand across the top of her tightly-wound French knot. She didn't know where to start. The man was impossible.

Gabriel moved closer to capture her upper arms. "We've been over this, Lana." His voice was smooth, seductive. "We need each other. Now is not the time to break up a working partnership. Not when we're so close to finding Asia and Jack."

He was standing so near she could feel the warmth coming off him. She could smell the clean tang of hotel soap mingling with the enticing scent that was his alone. She looked up into eyes so dark she could have lost herself for hours, and she wanted him so much she ached with sudden need. Shaking, she forced herself to take a step backward.

Gabriel's hands dropped from her arms, and he stood regarding her, his expression unreadable. She turned away, struggling for the objectivity she needed to bring some order to the chaos in her mind. Only one argument seemed to make sense. Short of locking him up for interfering in a Federal investigation, she had no control over his actions. And if his actions were going to include shadowing her anyway, she had to keep him close enough to know what he was up to.

"All right, let's go." She held up a finger in warning. "But you stay in the hotel room once we get to Little Rock. You can catch up on Ellen."

Ethan drifted between sleeping and waking, unable to find true rest, unwilling to leave the world of his dreams for the waking nightmare his life had become. While he floated he could still hold onto an illusion of a place where pain seemed far away, where a soft touch could soothe his aching heart and a murmured word could bring him solace. If he opened his eyes, he knew, he would be alone, waiting, with only his anger and his guilt for comfort.

--Dad? Are you there? It's me, Jack!

Ethan sat up in the twisted sheets, one hand to his head. *Jack?*

--Dad? You feel sad. Are you okay?

--Sure, buddy, I'm fine. I'm just . . . I miss you and Mom. Are you both okay?

--Mom's right here. She says to say she's fine. They haven't hurt us. She misses you, too.

Ethan's heart turned over in his chest. Asia's face filled his mind, her golden-brown eyes shining with laughter, her fine, high cheekbones blushing with joy, her soft lips smiling at him.

--Tell her I can't wait to see her. And you, too, Jack.

--I know. I wish we could just come home.

The boy's weariness bordered on despair. Ethan felt the emotion being communicated straight to his heart, bypassing the words he heard echoing in his mind. He struggled to conquer his own answering pain and sent back a wave of reassurance and love.

--*Soon, Jack. It won't be long, I promise.*

--*Mom says to tell you we're not in the van anymore. We're in a house somewhere, but we don't know where.*

--*A house?* Hope sparked in him. If they'd stopped moving, Gabriel might have a chance to catch up with them. *Is there anything you can tell me about the house? Can you see anything outside?*

--*No. They covered our eyes so we couldn't see. But I can hear trains. They're really close, and there are a lot of them. All the time.*

--*Trains! That's good, Jack. That's really helpful.*

--*Yeah. Mom said to tell you 'cuz it might help you find us.*

--*Mom's smart, buddy. We're lucky to have her, aren't we?*

--*Yeah. I gotta go. I'm starting to feel pretty tired.*

--*Okay, Jack. Thanks for talking to me. I feel a lot better now.*

--*Okay, Dad. 'Bye.*

"I love you, son." Ethan said it out loud, knowing Jack had faded from his mind, needing to say it anyway. His chest expanded with the feeling, and he allowed himself a shaky breath. They were still alive. They hadn't been hurt. And now they had given him a way to reach them.

When Ethan went downstairs, dressed and with new hope in him, Sam was with Rayna in the living room. He flashed a grin at his friend.

"When did you get back?"

Sam glanced at Rayna before looking back at Ethan. "Early this morning. What's going on?"

"We need to get in touch with Gabriel." Ethan headed to the kitchen for tea. "Jack told me something that may help us."

Sam and Rayna had been trailing him, but now Sam stopped dead and gaped at him. "*Jack* told you?"

"Ethan . . ."

Ethan put a hand on Rayna's shoulder. "Ray, I know how you feel about this, but right now I don't have time to convince you I'm sane. I need to speak to Gabriel."

Sam's head swiveled from Ethan to Rayna and back. "Will someone please tell me what the hell is going on?"

Rayna turned to him, unhappiness written into her dark features. "Ethan says he's been . . . communicating . . . with Jack. Ever since he let Gabriel scan him. That's not a common side effect as far as I know. What do you think?"

Sam shook his head. "Ethan, man, you've been under a lot of stress. And those pain pills—"

"Don't cause hallucinations. Ray and I have discussed this already. Now, it's true I've been under a lot of stress. For that reason I can't remember where I put Gabriel's cell phone number. Can you two please stop worrying so much and help me?"

Sam and Rayna exchanged another look, then Sam

took a slim black case out of his breast pocket and punched in a single digit. He handed the unit to Ethan.

Ethan spent a few seconds admiring the device before putting it to his ear. "New comm unit? Never seen one like this before. Nice." He waited a second. "Gabriel?"

"Ethan? I was going to wait until a bit later to report on our progress. I didn't realize you were an early riser."

"Actually, I have something to report myself. I didn't feel it could wait." He could sense the other man's interest sharpen, almost as if their minds were still connected.

"Tell me."

"First I need to ask you a question. Is it possible that by opening my mind to yours I might have tapped into some latent telepathic talent? Could you have somehow made me more receptive to alternative forms of communication?"

There was a moment of silence on the other end of the line. Then Gabriel spoke very slowly.

"You'll have to be clearer than that, Ethan. Maybe it would just be easier if you explained what happened to make you ask me such a question."

Ethan shot a look at Sam and Rayna, who were keeping a wary watch on him from across the room. "Gabriel, I've been speaking with my son, and he's told me something that may help us find him."

Gabriel went very still. There was every possibility, of course, that Ethan's hold on reality had slipped. The man had suffered severe emotional and physical trauma. Gabriel had borne witness to it in his mind, knew intimately how close Ethan was to collapsing under the weight of guilt and worry. But he also knew the strength that was Ethan's to draw on, the love that sustained him, the determination that fueled his endurance. And he knew an opening of the mind such as Ethan described was possible, in theory.

Rodyn had explained it to him in the earliest days of his training. A similar process of expanding the latent communications pathways that existed in his own mind had been the first step in acquiring those powers that were the legacy of his Thrane genetic code. But this was the first time he'd heard of a full-blooded human responding with an expansion of telepathic ability. The likely explanation for what had happened was Jack's abilities. That one so young and with no training at all could make contact from such a great distance would indicate phenomenal power.

Gabriel drew a breath and glanced at Lana. Her eyes were on the road, but the tension in her body showed she was aware something significant had transpired in the phone call. She turned to meet his gaze, searching. How could he explain? They had both thought Asia to be the prime target of this kidnapping. Perhaps she had been. But if the men who took her found out about Jack, they would quickly be much more interested in him. And there was no doubt Jack was the one Kinnian was after.

"Gabriel? Are you still there?"

"I'm here. Tell me what has happened."

Ethan talked and the extractor listened with more than one sense, probing for signs of strain and instability behind the calm, self-assured voice. Gabriel used the single, silken link that still connected his mind to the doctor's to determine how much to believe of what the man was telling him. He found Ethan excited, anxious for his family despite his hope, desperate to be believed—but he did not find him crazy.

"And what did the boy tell you that makes you think we can find him?"

"They've stopped moving." Ethan couldn't hide his emotion. "They're in a house now, and Jack says he can hear trains close by."

Gabriel frowned. What he knew about the transportation systems of Earth would fit on half the screen of a very small datapad. *Trains*—plural—more than likely meant some sort of depot or hub. He needed a map. Better yet, he needed Sam.

"Is Sam back yet?"

"Yes, he's here."

"Let me speak to him. And Ethan." Gabriel looked again at Lana, who was glaring at him now. "Trust in yourself. Trust Jack. What is happening between you two is extraordinary, but it is not impossible. There are precedents for it. You should know that Jack is very special."

"I already knew that, Gabriel. You need to bring him back to me."

"I'll do everything I can." He waited, staring at the road ahead, while the comm changed hands.

Sam's voice was low and incredulous. "Are you saying you believe all this?"

"Yes. Why do you think we've had certain complications?"

Sam's response was brief, an attempt at discretion. "You mean Kinnian?"

"Yes. He wants the boy."

"Do you think anyone else knows about Jack?"

"Not yet, but it's only a matter of time. I need some technical help. I'll send the specifics through."

"We're standing by. Good hunting, *amigo*."

"*Gracias, mi capitán*. I'll talk to you soon."

Gabriel disconnected the call and appeared to use his phone's data functions while he contacted the *Shadowhawk* through his wetware for a detailed sensor scan of the area around Little Rock. He gave Sam's crew the search parameters for a large rail depot, and he gave them the description of the vehicle they were tracking, in the hope the van was moving or was parked somewhere in the area.

"So are you going to tell me what the hell that was all about?" Lana's voice was deceptively soft.

"It may be nothing."

"Not judging by the look on your face. You know more than you're telling me about these others who are stalking Asia and Jack. Who are they?" Her green eyes had gone dark and there was steel beneath the velvet in her voice.

He shook his head. "I can't be certain."

"You're lying." Her eyes sparked with anger. "I've been a cop for a long time, Gabriel. I can read the signs. Who wants the boy? What's so special about him all of a sudden? We've been assuming he was just picked up along with Asia. If you've learned something that changes that assumption, I need to hear it."

He put a hand on her shoulder to calm her. "The conversation I just had with Ethan changes nothing about what we need to do next, Lana. It only confirms that we're on the right track heading into Little Rock. Sam has access to some fancy satellite equipment. I've asked him to do a little scanning of the area for us. Ethan and I . . . well, we just have a feeling the kidnappers may have gone to ground, that they're no longer on the road."

Alana stared at him. "You mentioned trains."

Gabriel sighed. "Is there a depot of some kind in the area?"

"Why?"

"Just trust me, Lana. It may be important."

"Are they holed up near a train yard, Gabriel? Is that what you're trying to say?"

"I don't know. Maybe."

"How do you know? Where did you get that

information?"

"That's just the problem, my little terrier. You wouldn't believe me if I told you how I came by that particular piece of information. I'm not even sure I believe it until I prove it. So let's just take it one step at a time, shall we?"

Lana smacked a hand against the steering wheel. "God, you are the most exasperating man I have ever run into! You can't give me a straight answer about a goddamn thing! And I'll show you little terrier—I'll take a piece out of your ass, you big ugly hound!"

Gabriel laughed, the unaccustomed sound riding on a bloom of feeling welling up out of his chest. It had been so long since he'd allowed himself the luxury of letting down his guard, he was surprised at the emotion that spilled out. He couldn't remember the last time he'd laughed without irony.

"I take it back. You're not a terrier. You're more like a *targa*, a wildcat with poisonous fangs from a . . . place . . . I once visited. Small, but very dangerous."

"You're making that up." But she was smiling at him, disarmed by his reaction. She licked her lips, as if her mouth had gone dry, sending a shaft of hot desire spinning through him. He saw her throat working as she swallowed. "By the way, laughter becomes you, Mr. Cruz. You ought to try it more often."

CHAPTER ELEVEN

Aboard the Bloodstalker, in Orbit, Earth, Sector Three

Trevyn Dar sailed an endless sea of data, sifting the currents for the information he needed. He was naked as he navigated that vast ocean, stripped of the insignia of his rank, the responsibilities of his station. He was no longer commander of the *Bloodstalker,* brother of Kinnian Dar, second son of a great house of Thrane. He was free. He could almost imagine himself to be happy. It was with disappointment, even a sense of desolation, that he recognized his search was over almost before it had begun.

For someone of his talents, the information systems of this planet were elementary, almost crude. Encryptions were easily broken, firewalls quickly collapsed. Trevyn could follow the name he had been given like a hungry seathrasher follows chum, even though the files he had cracked were encumbered by layers of security encoding. He had found the orders given to take Asia, the men assigned to the job, the passwords and code names and accounts associated with the task. Now it only remained to find the men Earthers called "black ops." The job the Thranes were on Earth to do would be finished within hours; the boy would be in Kinnian's hands onboard the *Bloodstalker* before another day had broken on the planet below.

Trevyn took care to reinforce the shields at several levels of his conscious mind. Kinnian's snares were everywhere, the threads of his intrusive control forming a sticky web ready to catch any unwary thought, any unlucky emotion that strayed outside the proscribed pattern. For Kinnian's benefit, Trevyn went over his search for information on the whereabouts of Asia Roberts in the upper levels of his mind, step by painstaking step. And while the search replayed on an endless loop for Kinnian's diversion, Trevyn hid deeper in his mind to consider what could be done to lessen the stain of this job on his immortal soul.

The boy could not be saved, that was a given. They had been paid a generous retainer upfront and promised a small fortune on delivery of the package to Sennik on Minertsa. But Sennik had not mentioned the woman. Kinnian would consider her expendable. If she was attractive, he would use her himself for a while, then sell her for a profit. Unless he thought Gabriel had some interest in her. In that case, he would torture her, then kill her, just to spite their half-brother. Trevyn would spare her that fate, if he could.

He could not risk another direct contact with Gabriel. He still maintained a fragile link with his sibling, camouflaged within a tangle of meaningless threads leading nowhere, but to use it too often invited Kinnian's attention. Instead Trevyn went deeper into his mind, to a level below verbalization, below visualization, to a place free of conscious thought, free of emotion, a place of pure energy and light. From that place he sent out a call, a beam of formless energy directed at that like place in Gabriel's mind, bypassing all of Kinnian's traps, both in Trevyn's mind and in Gabriel's. When he had made the connection, he rose to the subconscious level of his half-brother's mind and left a message, one calculated to lead him in the right direction without placing him in too much danger.

Then, as swiftly as he had come, Trevyn withdrew, and prayed that Gabriel would understand what he had been asked to do.

Gabriel stared at the sensor data as it scrolled across his compscreen, wishing he had a larger holographic unit with him. Another disadvantage of working with a local—he had to pretend to use their outdated technology. Details were hard to resolve on the screen, and the details were what he needed. The rail depot was dotted with and surrounded by warehouses and industrial buildings and within earshot of any number of residential neighborhoods. Looking for a white van in all that territory was like trying to find the proverbial lump of coal in an asteroid belt.

Sam's first officer on the *Shadowhawk,* a huge, dark-skinned Partaran with a mind like a criminal chess master, had sorted through the images first and sent Gabriel only the most promising scans. Commander Maatik had even devised an image recognition program to further reduce the number of scans anyone would have to look at. Still, the images rolled on, with no white van to be seen. At least no white van in any pattern that made sense—nothing parked in front of a house or a warehouse, nothing leaving and coming back regularly from one location, nothing helpful for the last twenty-four hours.

Gabriel pushed to his feet and began a short-leashed pacing in the limited confines of the motel room. His muscles twitched with restless, unfocused energy; his skin chafed under the weight of his clothes. Something he could not grasp teased at the back of his mind—a name he couldn't remember, features that wouldn't resolve into a recognizable face, a date, a time, a bit of data out of place. Exactly what he had forgotten was lost to him. He only knew there was something he needed to—

Damn it! I don't have time for this!

If he hoped to clear his mind by stepping away from his work, he was quickly disabused of the notion. Any calm he managed was shattered with a single riveting thought—Alana Matheson. She had left him alone at the motel while she got established at the Little Rock FBI office, but she refused to leave his mind. Gabriel wasn't used to working with a partner, especially one who looked like an angel and smelled like heaven. He had to ask himself if the limited information he'd managed to glean from her was worth the risk of having her so close he could taste her.

Christ! Just thinking of her made him so fucking hard he couldn't stand up.

Gabriel's pacing brought him back up against the desk and in sight of his compscreen. Again, he felt the squeeze of desperation around his heart. Now that Kinnian was involved, time was running out. If his brother found Asia and Jack first . . . *blood, red and liquid as wine, pooling at his feet, his sister screaming, his mother moaning over and over again,* Dios! Dios!

The Blood Legion could not be named even as his sister's husband lay dying at their hands on the cold stone of his mother's entry floor. Everyone knew who was responsible, but no one would part their lips to speak the name of the society that ruled Thrane in secret. It was said that Kylan Dar was not just a member of the Legion, but its Master, until his death. But even a Master would have his enemies, and his son might have his uses.

And now the one who had taken his father's place— and his power—hunted Gabriel's own quarry.

"No!" he muttered, sitting down at the desk again. "You won't have these two, *ri shalssiti pultalfa.* These two are mine!"

There was a rapid pounding on the door behind him, startling him nearly out of his skin. When he yanked open the door, Gabriel was surprised to see the afternoon had advanced to sunset in the world outside.

Alana stood framed in the last of the sun's buttery light, her eyes narrowed to read his body language. His pulse and respiration shot up to accommodate her.

"Hey." Her slow drawl turned him inside out. "Kinda hot out here. Can I come in?"

Gabriel forced himself to relax into a grin. "Sorry. Of course." He stepped aside; her body brushed his as she passed, and he gritted his teeth.

She stopped short in the middle of the room, her glance darting from the compscreen on the desk to the satchel containing his clothes on the bed. She turned an astonished face up to his.

"Where did all this stuff come from?"

"I had Sam and Rayna send it out from Nashville." His only elaboration was an innocent shrug. He didn't care to explain the delivery service had made use of technology onboard Sam's *Shadowhawk,* a technology unknown to Earth science.

"Same day delivery?" Lana tilted her head at him. "Damn, that must've cost you. I'm clearly in the wrong business."

Gabriel shook his head. "Not the wrong business necessarily. Just the wrong employer."

She grinned at him, lighting up the room. "So true." She turned back to the compscreen. "Whatcha looking at?"

His foul mood returned with a vengeance. "Sens— uh, satellite photos of the area around the railroad yards."

"Oh, that again, huh? I see you're not having any luck."

"I suppose you can say you've had a breakthrough?"

She straightened from the desk and blew out a breath. "No. Can't say as I have. Little Rock bureau has been cooperative enough. We've set up a pretty good surveillance net on the main roads in and out of town with state and locals, but we have no idea if they're even using the same vehicle. We haven't had any sightings all day. Even bogus ones."

He ignored an illogical urge to break something. "They've gone to ground."

"I believe you, Gabriel, but what am I supposed to do?"

He had no answer for her. He could only stand glaring at the compscreen, willing it to speak to him. They were there somewhere, his gut told him so. But where?

She put her hand on his bicep. "Come on, *mi Cubano*. Let's go for a ride. This motel room is way too small for you and all that dark energy, too."

"*Gracias a Dios, querida*." He felt his heart grow lighter in his chest. "I am more than happy to be out of this dungeon. Maybe we could get something to eat, too. I'm starving."

With a press of a finger, he shut down the compscreen, leaving his fruitless search behind. Then he followed Lana out the door.

"Feel better?"

Gabriel looked up at the twilight streaking purple through the orange and pink of the lost sun. "Much. At least I have no fear that I will starve to death anytime in the next solar orbit."

"Solar orbit," Lana repeated. "If by that you mean year, I agree with you. You ate like you might not get another chance." She slid into the driver's seat and smiled at him as he settled in next to her.

He shrugged. "You never know what could happen. I walked out of a restaurant one night and woke up in a prison on another . . . uh . . . continent the next morning. I didn't eat again for five days."

She stared at him. "You're a dangerous man to go out with, you know that?"

He looked back at her, a smile tugging at his mouth. "Are we going out?"

"No, but I'm not sure your enemies would make the distinction."

"You're right. Still, I think you're safe for the moment. Where to now?"

"Thought we might cruise the neighborhoods around the rail yard, what do you say?"

His grin revealed a wolf's eagerness. "I thought you'd never ask."

"Sometimes it helps to get a feel for the territory. Just being there can give your intuition a kick, you know? Like there's some kind of vibe to pick up." She glanced at him. "Something like you were doing at the rest stop, I guess."

"Yes." She had her own abilities, he realized. Untrained, likely discounted and ignored by others, but real, nonetheless. He wondered how much she relied on them without even being aware of it.

"I play this little game with myself." She threw a shy glance his way. "Wanna play?"

Querida, *there are so many games I would like to play with you.* "Why not?"

"Okay." She settled in behind the steering wheel. "There are two freight depots in town. The larger Union Pacific yard in North Little Rock and a closer, smaller yard near the airport. Which one strikes you first?"

Not what I had in mind. Gabriel's brows came together in a puzzled frown. "Closest, I guess."

She nodded at the exit signs above the highway ahead of them. "There are three exits that can take us in that direction—Ninth Street, Roosevelt Road and Frazier Pike. Which one comes to mind first?"

"Roosevelt." His smile returned as he caught the spirit of the game.

"Roosevelt it is." She passed the Ninth Street and the airport exits. The exit for Roosevelt came up right away, and she gave him another choice. "East or west?"

He didn't hesitate. "East."

"No waffling. I like that." The exit ramp dumped them out onto a busy commercial street clogged with evening traffic, businesses vying for attention on both sides. "My gut says we'll need to get off this street into a residential neighborhood. North or south?"

"North."

"How many blocks up? Give me the first number that pops in your head."

"Three."

"Shit! You're going to make me turn left across all this traffic without a light?"

"Sorry. Just take the next light. We can circle back."

She did as he suggested and almost immediately the traffic dropped off. Convenience stores and gas stations were replaced with duplexes and bungalows on a broad, two-lane street lined with parked cars. Lana slowed the car and lowered the window, scanning from one side of the street to the other.

"This is still too visible for a safe house." Gabriel's arm hung out the window as he took in the night air. "They'd be further off the main road."

Lana nodded. "Turn now? Or give me a number."

"Turn left in four blocks."

They went on like that for a while, zig-zagging across the residential blocks, letting their instincts lead them. At last they sat at the end of a street, lingering at a stop sign with another choice before them. Across the street, a fence and a field of patchy grass and broken bottles separated the neighborhood from the rail yard. Gabriel could hear the trains braking and scraping along the rails.

"Left or right?"

The feeling he had forgotten something returned to

haunt him, stronger now than ever. He'd had a few hours of relative peace, but now Gabriel felt as if his skin was on fire. A sense of intense déjà vu hit him, as if he'd been here before and left something behind, though he'd never seen the place before.

"Gabriel?"

He shook his head. "Left."

She turned, and within a block he heard a whisper, deep in his mind. *Save the woman, if you can.*

"Meadowlark."

Lana's head snapped around. "What?"

"We're looking for Meadowlark—street, drive, road."

"How . . .?"

"Don't ask." A sense of dread gathered in his chest.

She turned back to the road. "There." She pointed. A street sign indicated Meadowlark Drive to the left.

"Take it." His heartbeat accelerated. "Number fifty-seven."

Lana craned her neck to read the numbers on her side of the street. "Eighty-two. . .three blocks down, then. On the right."

Night was descending in a rush now, the late summer sky a deep purple overhead. Shadows were thick along the street, among the parked cars and on the slumping porches of the tiny, ill-kept houses. The neighborhood looked worn out, ready to give up, besieged by the noise and the fumes of its industrial neighbors.

And there was something else here. Gabriel felt it

grow closer, sharper, as the car slowly rolled toward Number 57. His eyes strained to make out any movement along the street, any shadow cast against the light. Nothing moved.

He strengthened the protections in his mind and sent out a gentle, tentative feeler. *There*. A hum, as of high tension wires. A crackle and a buzz warning of danger. *Kinnian*. There was no way to tell how many were with him without a visual count. Gabriel had to remain shielded; he didn't dare use his mind and risk exposure.

"Drive past the house without stopping, and try to find a place to park the car around the block."

Lana looked at him. "Why are we whispering?"

His lips quirked upwards. "Sorry. There are others watching the house." He held up a hand.

"I get it. Don't ask you how you know." Her voice was as quiet as his now. "Watch me driving past the house."

As they drifted past Number 57, Gabriel took note: no lights on in the house; an innocuous, grey rental sedan in the drive; a large, black SUV on the curb opposite; a closed garage; blinds shut tight on all visible windows; no name on the mailbox; no flowers, no toys, no random items of any kind in the yard or on the porch. Also no shrubbery and nothing close to the house to provide a hiding place. The house itself was set a bit apart from its neighbors in the middle of the lot, with a chain link fence surrounding the back yard.

But in the farthest corner of the neighboring yard a

shed huddled against the fence. It was enough to provide some cover if they could reach it from the alleyway behind the houses without being seen.

"Take the next right. Park the car."

Lana looked past him, saw what he saw and nodded. She slid to a stop around the corner, just in front of the entrance to the alley.

They sat, motionless, watching the street for a long moment. The cars parked along the street were empty. The alley was dark and still. Two houses up, a driveway was full, people congregated on the porch and inside the brightly-lit house—a party in progress. Further down, children played on a scraggly front lawn. No one turned a face in their direction.

"You know they have someone watching the back of the house."

Gabriel nodded. *Unless Kinnian is already inside. Unless it's already over.*

"And you have a plan for getting close enough to confirm Asia and Jack are in this house without being seen?"

"Yes. Be very careful."

Lana shot him a glare. She started stripping off her shirt. When she was down to her tank top, she got out of the car and wrapped the shirt around her waist, concealing the Glock she had stuck in the waistband of her jeans.

"I have a better plan."

He scrambled out of the car after her. "What the hell are you doing?"

"It's a public alley. People must use it. I'm just another neighborhood girl." She grinned at him. "When the man on the back door shows himself, you take him out. I'll circle back around the block and meet you behind that shed."

Before he could tell her about Kinnian, she was ten paces up the alley. *Christl!* Telling her now would only lead to an argument—an argument that could get them killed. He ran after her, keeping to the shadows of the ramshackle garages and sheds that lined the alleyway. As Lana approached the back of 57 Meadowlark, a man stepped off the rear porch and ambled toward the fence line. There was a gate near the corner where the shed stood, a rear outlet to the alley from the driveway. As she passed, Lana flipped the catch and swung it open.

"Hey, mister," she called, pointing. "Your gate's open."

From his position in the alley behind the shed, Gabriel heard the man curse, heard his footsteps approach, saw him step out into the alley to retrieve the swinging gate. Gabriel shot out, grabbed the man's gun hand and wrenched it up behind his back, then covered the man's mouth and eyes and took him to the ground. A strike to the throat and he was done. Gabriel dragged the body behind a line of garbage cans, swung the gate closed and retreated behind the shed where he could see the back porch of 57 Meadowlark without being seen. He lifted the flap along one thigh that concealed his stun gun and freed the weapon from its holster. Then he prayed he wouldn't have to use it—or explain it.

A minute later a warm breath kissed his ear. "I take it my plan worked?"

"Like a charm." And thank God, no complications. But they were still a long way from knowing what was inside the house.

"Are you picking up any . . . what did you call them? . . . EM signatures?"

He shook his head, frustrated. "I can't just scan. The others . . ." He stopped, unwilling to give away too much. "They have ways of detecting it. I have to hide what I'm doing."

She looked at him, her eyes shining with what could be read as admiration even in the dark. "Jesus."

He bent his head in concentration and reached inward for the traps he'd set for Kinnian. They were vibrating wildly in response to his brother's presence, receiving and sending constant pulses of false information in answer to the insistent requests for data. He'd let his brother believe he was one step behind him at all times, no further along now than Memphis. The traps were holding; there had been no breaches in his defenses.

Now he went down another level in his mind and opened himself to the outside world. Information flooded his mind in a hot rush—emotion, sensation, thought and data streaming from uncounted sources threatening to overwhelm him. Then he began the filtering process, eliminating all artificial sources, all nonhuman sources, all sources from more than one hundred meters, and finally, all sources except the ones identified specifically as those of Asia and Jack. When the filtering process was done, there was nothing but silence in his mind.

Carefully, with a touch no heavier than a butterfly's wing, he sent out a scan, hoping for an answering echo in an EM range that matched Jack or Asia. Nothing.

Gabriel came back to himself and turned to look at Lana. He shook his head.

Then, from inside the house, gunfire erupted.

With a curse Lana pulled her gun and started for the house, but he grabbed her arm. "No!"

"What the hell?! Jack and Asia—"

"They aren't there." He struggled to keep his grip on her.

"Then what the fuck is going on?"

Blue-white light flashed in the dark house—laser rifles. Kinnian had made his move. Gunfire answered as the fight went from room to room, but Gabriel knew the humans had no chance.

"We have to get out of here."

"The hell you say." Lana pulled out her cell phone. "I'm calling for back up."

"Damn it, Lana!" He caught her arm and swung her to his side, picked her up off her feet and started running. They made it as far as the alley before she twisted out of his grip and dropped to her feet.

"Son of a bitch!" She held out a hand toward him. "Stay the hell away from me or I'll shoot your ass!"

His lips curled upward. "That's the cell phone, not

your Glock."

"Lucky for you, asshole." She looked down, started to key in the number she needed again, but a sound behind her made her drop the phone and turn. A man was clambering over the fence, his face white with terror. She pointed the gun at him. "FBI. Stop where you are!"

The man looked over his shoulder at her, but hit the ground and started to run.

She swore under her breath and took off after him.

A sound, no more than a creak of hinges, and Gabriel felt the moment shatter like so much glass. The foundation of reality slipped, gravity failed and the world went spinning off its axis to collide with the sun. Two Thranes in the combat jumpsuits of a ship's landing party stepped out onto the back porch of the house. One pointed a laser rifle at the fleeing man, at Lana, who almost had a hand on the man's back. The other turned in Gabriel's direction, his weapon rising.

Gabriel fired as he ran. The man who had been aiming at him dropped.

"Lana! Down!" He threw himself at Lana's feet, caught her ankle and tripped her just as the blue-white arc of light flashed above them. She screamed, and he smelled the acrid tang of burning flesh.

He scrambled up and over her back, his skin crawling, anticipating the spearing burn of laser fire. It didn't come, and he rolled the two of them into the shadow of a board fence in the yard next to Number 57. He couldn't see around the fence, but he could hear the pounding of boots on the ground. The trooper was pursuing. He waited. One breath. Two. Movement showed at the edge of the fence line. Gabriel fired, and the trooper's convulsing body pitched forward into the alley.

Lana stared at him, eyes glassy, in shock. A scorched furrow ran across her right shoulder blade. He pulled her to her feet, wrapped an arm around her ribcage and steered her back down the alley.

"What the hell, Gabriel?" Her voice was nothing more than a rasp.

He had no intention of explaining anything before they got their asses out of there. What came after that was another problem.

They came to the end of the alley. He paused, pressed against the rusting steel of a garage door, to scan the street beyond. Then a blast of fiery rage punched into his brain and obliterated all thought. He dropped to his knees, taking Lana with him. His mind exploded with pain, and Gabriel crashed into a black pit of unconsciousness.

CHAPTER TWELVE

"That's a pretty bad burn, there, ma'am. You really need to let us transport you to the hospital."

Lana gritted her teeth as the EMT finished dressing the blistered skin across her right shoulder. "Much as I'd like to cut and run, I think the man headed in our direction is going to want to talk to me."

The kid turned to glance at the Little Rock FBI Bureau chief striding across the lawn towards them, a scowl darkening his features. "I could put you on a stretcher, take you out right now." He slipped her a sympathetic grin. "That'd get you a few hours, anyway."

Lana shook her head. "Might as well face the music. Maybe the war wound will get me some sympathy, huh?"

"I'd play it up big, if I were you. And I'd still recommend you check into the ER as soon as things die down. I don't think a couple of Tylenol is going to keep you comfortable tonight."

"Sure thing. Thanks."

"You bet."

Lana stood as the EMT moved off and instantly regretted it. The burned patch on her shoulder flamed with miserable fury. But she needed to be on her feet when Supervisory Special Agent Wallace Trent lit into her. Her pride demanded no less.

Trent started in as soon as he got close enough. "Agent Matheson, are you responsible for this monumental cluster fuck?"

"No, sir."

The answer seemed to infuriate him even further. "No? Then how do you explain the fact that four people are dead in that house, the house itself is burned almost to the ground, along with whatever evidence it *might* have contained, and the kidnap victims we're trying to rescue are nowhere to be found?"

"The only explanation I can offer, sir, is that a rival gang attacked the house before we were able to confirm the presence of the victims and effect a rescue."

"A rival gang! What the fuck? You haven't figured out who took these people in the first place and now you have a rival gang?" Trent's jowly face hung like a blotchy red moon over his damp collar. "In my district? I don't think so!"

Lana stood at parade rest and let him pace in front of her. He didn't think so? Then let him come up with an explanation, the dumb fuck.

"You know what I think, Matheson?" He loomed over her as if he could threaten her with sheer bulk. "I think this is a surveillance gone horribly wrong. Instead of asking for help and setting this up right, you decided to go it alone and get all the glory. But you blew it. You got too close and spooked whoever was in that house. They started fighting amongst themselves, some of them took off with the vics and somebody else lit a torch. How you like that explanation, you stupid—"

He caught himself just short of the one word that would have bought him a reprimand. He glared at her for a long minute, then gave her a twisted smile.

"That's what's going in my report, along with anything that was in that van we found in the garage. You were found here where you shouldn't have been when fire and rescue and local police arrived. You're wounded, so you obviously engaged in a firefight with the perps. That's all the evidence I need that you started this whole meltdown. You can forget about any more cooperation from my office, missy. Take your sorry ass on back to Nashville." With that, he turned and stomped off toward the alley.

Lana closed her eyes and endured the flush of anger and shame that washed through her battered body. As much as she knew Trent was ignorant, unfair and just plain wrong, a part of her agreed with him that this was her fault. Jack and Asia were gone, she'd missed them by a hair, and now she had no way to pick up the trail. *Damn it!* She turned the night over and over in her mind, but she just couldn't see how it could have come out any differently. Like throwing a pair of loaded dice, things just kept coming up craps.

She knew one thing though. She knew who had handed her those loaded dice. She stalked back to the car to find Gabriel, determined to get some answers. He was standing with one hip against the hood and his arms crossed over his chest, wearing a frown so deep it might have been carved into his face.

She launched her attack before she even reached the car. "What the fuck happened back there?"

"Do you mean the part where we just missed Asia and Jack and got caught in the middle of a firefight, or the part where you wouldn't listen, and I almost got killed trying to save your *mulaak* ass?"

Even though she knew it was a pose, his casual sprawl infuriated her. "How about the part where you curse at me in some strange Cuban dialect, you asshole! And I think we're even on the life-saving thing. I just had to wake you up out of another coma."

"Let's just call that sensory overload. Someone in the house was unhappy that Asia and Jack weren't here."

"Someone in the house. The safe house, the exact address of which you somehow pulled out of thin air. How does that work, Gabriel? More of your special skills, I suppose?"

"You've benefitted from my special skills all along, Lana. Would you rather we hadn't found the place?"

"A lot of damn good it did us. The house is blown to hell—and us almost with it."

Gabriel's dark eyes sparked with dangerous fire. "I tried to warn you."

Lana remembered the urgency with which he'd tried to get her to leave. He'd *known* what they were dealing with.

And there was something else. "That EMT who patched me up thinks I got burned in the fire, but I was a long way from the house. I hit the ground, and when I looked up the guy I'd been chasing was nothing but smoke. I didn't get caught in the tail end of an explosion, did I?"

Gabriel looked for a moment as if he wouldn't answer. Finally he glanced her way.

"No."

"What, then?"

"You were tagged by a laser rifle. The guy you were chasing got hit center mass."

"Laser rifle." The term bounced around in her skull, but found no definition slot to land in. "And what kind of space cowboy uses one of those?"

"The kind that is after Jack and Asia."

"Are you saying—"

"Let's just say these guys have access to stuff that makes the latest media mix look tame, okay?"

"Media mix?"

"Movie."

God, he made her head hurt sometimes. "So we're talking black ops? Super secret shit? Regular weapons aren't good enough for them?"

Gabriel sighed. "Something like that."

"And what about that *pistola* you were using, *amigo*? Same deal?"

"A glorified TASER. Wireless tech. A friend makes them special for me."

"Sure." She couldn't get past the feeling that he was hiding something from her. It was there in the set of his shoulders, the hard line of his jaw. "You've got a fucking answer for everything, but I know there's more to all of this."

He shook his head. "None of that is important. We need to find Jack and Asia."

Lana's simmering anger abruptly boiled over. "You think I don't know that? We have nothing, Gabriel, *nothing*! Not even a vehicle description now. And I'll be lucky if I have a job in the morning."

At last he turned to look at her. "Alana. None of this was your fault. Asia and Jack were gone before we got here, and thank God for that. If they had been here when those men arrived there would have been no way to save them. We might both be dead, and Asia and Jack lost forever. This way we still have a chance. We just have to find them before the others do."

"How? We don't have the beginning of a clue."

"I have some resources. We might have something by morning."

Fatigue suddenly washed over her, and she swayed. He caught her. "Come on. I have something for that shoulder back at the motel."

"Please say it has a label that reads 80 proof."

He almost smiled. "That can also be arranged."

She started for the driver's side of the car, but he steered her to the other side and dropped her into the passenger's seat. "My turn to drive," he said.

For once, she didn't give him an argument.

Lana's mind still buzzed with unanswered questions an hour later. She'd managed to clean up and wrap herself in a towel, despite the dressing on her shoulder, and she knew she should be thinking only of trying to get some sleep. But the things she had seen, the pieces of the puzzle that just wouldn't fit, put her on edge. It would be a long time before she slept.

Still, she didn't welcome the knock on the door to the adjoining room. It was late; she wasn't dressed. Whatever Gabriel had to tell her could wait until morning. She opened the door a hand's breadth, and one look at him on the other side—his mouth curved upward in the barest smile, his body a temptation of coiled muscle under a soft tee-shirt and workout pants—and her resolve faltered.

He held up a small jar in one hand and a bottle of rum in another. "Medicinal aids."

She wanted to make him work for it. "It's late, Gabriel."

He nudged the door. "You need this. Trust me."

She exhaled and swung the door wide. He slipped past her without a word, crossing the room to find the glasses. He poured them each a healthy slug of the rum and handed her one.

"Drink."

She tipped the glass in his direction. "Cheers."

"*Salud.*" He sipped, his eyes locked on hers.

She let the liquor and the warmth in his dark gaze sink deep into her chest. "That's good," she breathed.

He nodded. "It's from Barbados. Very nice." He set his rum down and took her hand to lead her toward the sink. "Now let me take a look."

"Is this really necessary?" She frowned at him in the mirror. "You could leave the stuff; I could take care of it."

"Yes, it's necessary. No, I can't leave the stuff, and no, you can't." He turned her toward the mirror with a sure touch. "Stop being stubborn, and let me help you."

He gently lifted her still-damp curls from her back and swept them to the left, baring the skin of her neck and right shoulder. She shivered. Despite her protests, she wanted to feel his hands, the stroke of his fingers. He stood just at her back, so close they were almost touching. She longed to lean against him, to feel the press of his hips against her buttocks, to feel his heat through the fabric of his pants and the single layer of the towel.

He was focused on the dressing at her shoulder, carefully removing the tape and gauze pad. Lana watched him in the mirror as he worked, noting the small frown of concentration between his brows.

The pain flared as air hit the damaged skin once he removed the dressing, and she sucked in a breath. She took another drink, welcoming the numbing alcoholic haze rising in her brain.

His gaze rose to meet hers in the mirror. "It hurts."

"Shit, yes, it hurts."

"Crybaby."

"Asshole." A tiny smile lifted her lips.

He dropped a kiss on her other shoulder, surprising her. She moved just slightly from the temptation of his lips on her skin and swallowed the emotion that rose in her throat.

"Guess you saved my ass with that tackle."

A smile came and went on his face. "It was the only thing I could think to do. The *targa* was on the hunt and there was no stopping you."

He dipped two fingers in the ointment he'd brought and began to dab ever so tenderly at the burn. The skin under the ointment immediately stopped hurting. Cool relief spread as Gabriel worked, the sizzling burn subsiding to a dull heat, then to a slight itch.

Lana stared at his reflection in amazement. "What the hell is that?"

He shrugged. "Something from home. It's good for burns and bruises. As you might imagine, I have a lot of use for it in my line of work."

"You should patent the stuff. You'd make a fortune."

He finished and set the jar aside, but he didn't leave her. Instead he shifted so his body was closer, warm and intimate against her back. Her gaze met his again in the mirror, and she read his intent in the mahogany depths of his stare. His hands traveled down her bare arms and back up across her collarbone, and she sighed, loving the feel of his fingers on her skin. He bent his head to trail his lips from the top of her shoulder to the side of her neck, to her ear. And then his hand was turning her face to his, his mouth slanting across hers to take her deeply and oh, God, so sweetly, tasting of rum and male and long-held need. She closed her eyes and kissed him back, relaxing into him, letting his strength support her, wanting this, so wanting this.

With a languid, almost unconscious movement of her hand, she released the towel and let it fall. He sighed, a sound she felt against her lips as he pulled away from their kiss, in his body as the breath left him.

"Beautiful." His lips moved against her ear, his hungry gaze swept down the length of her naked body in the mirror.

This wasn't like her, to stand trembling, wordless and aching, while his hands fell over her ribcage to her hips, down the outside and over the tops of her thighs, joining to press low across her belly. It wasn't like her to wait, feeling his hard length pushing up behind her, longing to turn and cradle it against the pounding pulse between her legs. But his slow worship of her body held her powerless, poised at the brink of some dizzying precipice, arms open, embracing the fall.

She gasped with sudden, spearing desire when his fingers grasped her nipple and squeezed just hard enough to thrill. She moaned as his other hand cupped her mound and pulled her closer.

One finger slipped into her cleft, then two, stroking in and out of her silken heat while his thumb circled the glistening pink nub of her clitoris. She couldn't stop watching what he was doing to her—his arm snaking down her body, his hand between her legs. He squeezed her breast. She writhed, wanting more.

"Gabriel." She breathed the word, his name, unable to manage more. Her heart thudded inside her chest. She could have him here and now, with no more foreplay than this. Her mind readily supplied the visions—Gabriel stripping out of his clothes, springing free, huge and eager. Gabriel taking her from behind, hard and fast, her hands gripping the sink as she braced herself against his thrusts. She saw herself coming for him, her head thrown back against his chest, screaming in ecstasy.

She moaned again, so close her womb clenched and pulsed in need. She put her hand over Gabriel's and felt him shudder as he held her. Then she turned and led him to the bed, curling up to wait while he stepped back to shrug out of his clothes.

Her breath caught as she saw him outlined between the harsh light of the motel vanity and the shadows of the bedroom. He had the body of a warrior—broad shoulders tapering to narrow hips, the muscles of his chest and biceps and stomach as defined as if they'd been sculpted in stone. The column of flesh that rose between his strong thighs was long and thick, crowned with a broad tip that even at a distance seemed to pulse and strain with his need.

As he drew near to the bed, she sat up to meet him, running her hands across his chest and down his sides. Jagged scars marred the smooth skin under his ribs; as she touched them she felt him draw in a breath, even as glaring images streaked through her mind. *Fields of blue ice under a black sky. The diamond-bright flash of knives. Blood on the snow, on his hands. Deep, unyielding pain. And someone, some*thing*, dead beneath him.*

Gabriel grabbed her hand, stared into her eyes. The images flickered out.

She shook her head, disoriented. "What happened?"

"It's nothing, *querida.*" He managed a smile. "We've all had our bad days, huh?"

She searched his face for a long moment, but in his eyes there was nothing but a desire so primitive there were no words to express it. Lana bent her head to kiss the ugly welts on his side, then let her lips trail lower, across his belly, toward the rigid shaft arching upward. She grasped him hard and licked at the swollen tip. The taste of him set fire to her blood, bringing heat to her breasts and deep into her belly. She took him fully in her mouth, letting her tongue explore in a velvet swirl of sensation. She groaned, savoring the feel of him in her mouth, letting it fuel the pulsing ache between her thighs.

"Ah, God, Lana! Much more and I'm going to lose it."

She grinned, pulling back. "Maybe I'd like to see you lose control."

He was breathing hard, his chest laboring to pull in air, but his answering smile was wicked, seductive. "You first, *mi amor.*"

He pulled her down to the edge of the bed and knelt between her knees, settling her calves on his shoulders. Her heart pounded in anticipation as his hands toyed with her thighs, stroking and spreading her outer lips, opening her for the press and play of his thumbs. Her sex thrummed and swelled in response to his teasing, eager for more. At last he dipped his head, and his tongue lapped at her, curling around the swollen center of her desire over and over. The need deep inside her sharpened and roiled until her breath came in keening gasps, until her very blood was running like molten lava from her pulsing core out to her fingertips.

His tongue swirled over the engorged pearl of her clit, and her hands twisted in the sheets, wanting, *so close*. Then he slipped two fingers inside her and *God!* It was just right; it was perfect. She bucked toward his mouth, letting it happen, letting him take her, and she heard herself from far away, moaning his name as the intensity built. She heard him, too, somehow, almost as if he was in her mind, encouraging her, urging her to give in to him, to come for him. And she wanted to, God, yes, she wanted to. He kept taking her higher, kept giving her more until finally she couldn't stand it; her body shattered into a thousand quivering pieces as she came at last, arching up off the bed, writhing around his fingers, struggling to find enough breath to cry out his name yet again. Even then it wasn't over. She still wanted him.

Her body was splayed out below him, open, ready for him, and it was all he could do to hold on to his control for the few seconds it would take him to get inside her. The round, smooth globes of her breasts called to his hands, the taut, rosy peaks of her nipples tempted his mouth, the plump, wet lips of her sex drew him like a magnet. And yet he couldn't stop looking at her.

Everything inside him roared savagely that she was *his,* his in a way no female had ever been before, or would ever be again. The part of him that spoke only the language of instinct told him he had to claim her, to mark her, to find his way to her soul and merge with her there. The way she called his name—*his* name—the way she met his eyes with a need that went beyond the flames that burned between them—God, she made him want to lose himself inside her forever.

He lowered himself between her sweet thighs, felt the liquid fire of her core envelop his tip as he positioned it at her entrance. Then with a low growl of possession he plunged deep inside her, burying himself to the hilt in her welcoming heat. She was hot and fit him like expensive leather, and for an exquisite moment all he could do was revel in that silky, snug heat. Then he began to move, slowly at first, pulling all the way out so he could push all the way back in and feel every inch of her slick sheath.

Her hips rose up to meet his every stroke, her breaths came in erotic little whimpers. The heat built between them, and her juices drenched his shaft. *Dios*, she was coming again so soon! A fierce grin lit his face as he increased his pace and watched her catch fire, her eyes closed in ecstasy.

Her body arched under him, every muscle clenched as the orgasm hit her, tiny pulses clutching at his shaft as he rode it out with her. *Fuck!* It felt so damn good sliding in and out of her, and she wasn't coming down from this climax, she was spinning into another, screaming his name and wrapping her legs around his hips and dragging him down to settle into the heat of her embrace. *Jesus!* His blood flowed hot in his veins, expanded in his heart, roared in his ears, filled him with aching need.

Gabriel was losing control. His body was responding to her like the animal it truly was now, taking her hard and fast and deep, driving toward a climax that was relentless and primal. And she was only encouraging him, lost in a spiraling vortex of pleasure, her soft voice at his ear telling him how good it was, how she liked what he was doing to her, how much she wanted him.

Another stroke closer to heaven and every barrier between them collapsed. He no longer knew, or cared, where he ended and she began. In that instant her mind was open to his and without hesitation he flowed in; his mind was open to hers and he welcomed her in. A sweet cascading loop began between them, he feeling her pleasure in the hot, filling push of his shaft, she sharing the ecstasy he found in her slick, fiery core. He felt her surprise at the joining of their minds, her surrender to the indescribable sensation, her rush to climax. And, oh, God, he felt that climax, all of it, the piercing joy of the last seconds before it took her, the tidal wave of overwhelming release, the rolling clench of muscles that began in her spasming core and spread to every part of her body, the endless, mindless suspension of time while the orgasm claimed her.

Like an echo he felt the ripple of her pleasure through his own body, the squeeze of her sheath at his thrust, the grip of her hands at his back. In seconds the unbearable pressure that had been building at the base of his spine demanded its own release, and he exploded into her with a feral groan. He heard her answering moans of satisfaction as his hips bucked and his seed left him in hot, liquid jets. He pumped into her over and over, until he felt her come yet again, and still he didn't want to stop. It seemed like forever before his body finally shuddered to a halt, still semi-hard in the throbbing warmth of her flesh.

Gabriel lay inside her for an unknown time, feeling her hands moving slowly on his back, her breath at his ear. She was there in his mind as he shook with the aftermath of their lovemaking, unable to move, unwilling to leave her. Then, abruptly, he felt her withdraw. Her body tensed, and it was as if a cold wind had blown into the room. His brief, beautiful moment of peace dissipated as if it had been a dream, as if it had never been. His shields snapped back into place of their own accord, the long years of hard, disciplined training taking over. And his heart shrank in his chest.

Gabriel pulled back and rolled to his elbow. Lana sat up and drew her knees up around her chin. She was trembling, but there was fire in her green eyes.

"I gave you my body, Gabriel." She stared into his eyes. "I didn't give you anything else."

"Lana—"

"You said . . ." She stopped, fighting for control over the quaver in her voice. "You told me you thought it was wrong to enter someone's mind without their permission. Was that just a lie? Or don't the rules apply when you're already fucking somebody's brains out?"

He sat up, reached for her. "Lana, listen to me—"

"Don't!" She pulled back from him. "What exactly was your motivation, anyway? It wasn't enough for your ego that I was already screaming your name? You had to know from the inside what I was feeling?" She glared at him. "Just how much did you see while you were in there, Gabriel?"

A black pit formed in his chest and threatened to swallow his heart. Because, of course, he had seen it all—every fantasy she might have shared with him in the heated dark of an embrace, every secret he might have learned in the years of a trusting relationship, even the broken, hurtful memories she might never have revealed no matter how long she knew him or how deeply she loved him. He had seen her soul—and she had seen his, though she didn't realize it yet.

Gabriel saw her eyes widen with the truth. "You fucking bastard!" she sputtered, lunging for him.

Bitter regret rose up in him to meet her anger, and he grabbed her forearms before she could close her hands around his throat. "Goddamn it, Lana! I didn't force this! My shields dropped without my even being aware of it. Your mind was open. I couldn't resist slipping into it any more than I could resist climaxing."

"So now it's my fault?" Her hands balled into fists, and she fought against his grip. "Bastard! The last time I checked there was a difference between mutual consent and rape! Even if it is my mind we're talking about!"

"Lana, I lost control! I'm sorry. I swear, I didn't mean for this to happen."

"Get out." She shrugged out of his hands. Tears slid down her face.

"Lana, please." He was desperate, the hole in his chest expanding. "Believe me when I say this wasn't a casual thing. I would never have hurt you. I meant . . . I wanted so much more with you."

She looked at him, her eyes dark with his betrayal. "I wanted it, too, Gabriel. But for that I'd have to trust you. Get out."

There was nothing left for him to say—no heartfelt words of apology or regret, no artful explanations, no appeals to logic or promises for the future. She was done with him. He picked up his clothes and left her, the growing chasm in his chest having taken what was left of his heart.

CHAPTER THIRTEEN

Aboard the Bloodstalker, in Orbit, Earth, Sector Three

The human screamed and fell to his knees, blood spurting from his nose, from his ears. His eyes were wide and bulging with terror, streaming tears of blood, and still Kinnian would not let him go. There was nothing useful left in the man's mind, Trevyn knew. He saw what his brother saw—the skittish, meaningless images of a mind unhinged by unremitting pain and horror. Whatever knowledge this creature might once have possessed, whatever basic intelligence its brain might have drawn upon to process that knowledge, were gone forever.

When, at last, the man ceased breathing and collapsed to the deck, Kinnian cursed and kicked at the lifeless body. "Portol's balls but these humans are weak! They have no will at all! I slice through them like a knife through fresh *sofra* cheese. That's the third one in less time than it takes to cure a hard-on and still nothing!"

Trevyn snatched at one bit of information swimming in the flood of unrelated facts from the interrogation subjects taken from the house in Little Rock. "Perhaps we have the answer we need if only we frame the question a different way."

Kinnian turned to snarl in his direction. "What do you mean?"

"None of these men saw the boy leave the house. They can't tell us who has him now. But perhaps that's not important." Trevyn paced, thinking. "They all knew of another location, a facility significant to the organization that took the boy. The name of this facility was there in all of their minds."

Kinnian's brow lifted. "This 'Groom Lake'. Yes, it beats like a drum in their heads. You think the boy was taken there?"

Trevyn risked his own life with this theory, but he couldn't stand to watch another interrogation. "It seems likely. The house in Little Rock appeared to be nothing more than a stopover."

"I suppose it is possible. If so we would need only to find the facility and take the boy from there." Kinnian scratched at his beard. "You would have little problem locating it, I assume?"

"None whatsoever, my lord."

"Excellent! Then let us confirm this little theory." The captain of the *Bloodstalker* clapped his hands together, his eyes gleaming. "Guard! Bring in that last human!"

Trevyn schooled both his thoughts and his

expression to display enthusiasm for his own work. "With your permission, my lord, I'll begin the search to locate the facility."

His brother waved a dismissive hand, and Trevyn took his leave, grateful to be done with Kinnian and the smell of torture and death that surrounded him. He made his way down the corridor to the lift and up the three levels to his quarters without encountering any of the crew, for which he was also thankful. His muscles still quivered with the effort to control his loathing—for what he had seen, for what he had been a part of, for what he allowed to go on, day after day.

One day, Trevyn told himself. One day he would find a way to end it. And until then he would find a hundred small ways every day to mitigate what Kinnian did, to save those he could. His message had reached Gabriel; he had felt the barest whisper of his older brother's presence at the house in Little Rock. Yet he was certain Gabriel had not been the one to save the boy and his mother. The ones who had taken the humans had moved them long before any of them had gotten there. *Thank the gods*.

With a sigh, Trevyn sat down at his desk and opened his compscreen. In less than thirty seconds he found the general location of Groom Lake, Nevada. Within minutes he breached the security firewalls of the facilities in the isolated compound, including the organization, codenamed STEELWALL, currently in possession of the boy that was their target. He recorded all relevant schematics, satellite data and route maps.

He ordered the bridge to take detailed sensor readings of the location for further planning. Then he sent word to his captain that all was in readiness and informed the crew that he was off duty for the next shift.

Trevyn stripped off his uniform and boots and collapsed onto the bunk that filled one wall of his cabin. But sleep did not come. As he stared at the gray metal of the ship's bulkhead above him, he saw only the agonized faces of the men Kinnian had tortured that day. His mind flinched away from the thought of that expression on the sweet face of the woman they were hunting, of her screams echoing through the corridors of the ship as Kinnian found his uses for her.

Trevyn fell back on the Discipline of the Adepts, stilling his thudding heart, slowing his ragged breath as he fought to calm his mind. When his conscious thoughts were as smooth and placid as a mountain lake, he sank below the glassy surface and rode the currents of his mind's deeper patterns. He checked the traps and detours he had constructed to divert Kinnian's intrusions and reinforced them where necessary. Then, recognizing that his bloodthirsty sibling was still occupied with his human victim, Trevyn took a chance. He reached out across the tenuous link he maintained with Gabriel—

--and was swept up in a swirling storm of emotion: a physical desire so intense he was instantly hard and throbbing; a primal possessiveness that rose in a growl from his chest; a corresponding need to protect what was his, to enfold her in his arms and never let her go. He was swamped with sensation—warm, smooth skin, a scent like ginger cream, her taste on his tongue, her slick, hot hold on him, the sound of her voice in his ear, urging him on. Oh, gods, this was paradise! Gabriel was lost and Trevyn was lost along with him, wanting her, needing her, giving her everything he had to give just to hear her call his name as she fell apart in his arms.

She shattered, crying out as she arched beneath him, and Gabriel's shields collapsed. Their minds merged, while Trevyn watched in shock through the link he shared with Gabriel. It was all he could do to hold himself above the bond that was forming between the two of them. He struggled to maintain his own separate identity against the vortex of sexual intensity building between them. Lana—her name was Lana—was feeding off Gabriel's energy, even as he was feeding off of hers, coming again and again until Gabriel finally found his own release with a shout of joy.

When it was over Trevyn lay gasping, aching despite the ribbons of pearly seed glistening across the hard planes of his belly. And despite all his discipline, he could not keep himself from imagining that Lana might turn to him and part her sweet lips to accept his offering.

Hours later, making certain it was still safe, Trevyn tested his link with Gabriel again. He skirted Gabriel's volatile emotions with a delicate touch, avoiding the sexual pull between his brother and his lover. He hadn't meant to be part of what had happened between the two of them. It had been a riptide he'd found impossible to escape. He'd been carried along with it until he'd washed up on a lonely shore, battered and barely able to breathe. Once he recovered enough to return to this point of origin, he probed, fearful of what he might find.

And there they were—the first few adhesions of a permanent bond between Gabriel and Lana. They were as fragile as a morning's stillness, no more substantial than moonlight and shadow, but they had sprung into existence almost from the moment Gabriel had dropped his shields and let Lana in. Somehow Trevyn had sensed it, even then.

Gods help them all. Lana was an extraordinary woman, strong and brave and, by *T'mara*, so beautiful! She may even have had some latent psi talents of her own. But she was untrained, and because of the depth of emotion between them, she had opened a gap in Gabriel's defenses, a gap Kinnian would be certain to find and exploit.

Behind a wall of shielding, Trevyn dared to share his fears with Gabriel.

The answer came back, as hot as the blast of wind off a desert: *Stay away from her. I will protect what is mine.*

The bedside clock read 3:47 a.m., a time of night reserved for revelry, skullduggery, lovemaking or deep REM sleep. But Gabriel Cruz was involved in none of these. In the darkest hour of the night, he was involved in guilt, self-recrimination and an examination of the behavior that had cost him the affection and respect of Alana Matheson.

Every time he awakened with a jolt to remember why he was sleeping alone, his chest burned with remorse and his breath refused to fill his lungs. *Dios!* He'd been so thoughtless and stupid, and now he had no chance of ever explaining the things Lana would be picking out of her mind about him. He had exposed himself in the worst possible way—to an agent of the government, no less—and unless she dismissed him as insane, there was no way to cover it up again.

Of course, that was only part of the problem, the part he needed to explain to, say, Sam and Rayna, who as representatives of Rescue, could have him up on interference charges if they weren't also his friends. Like anyone working for that organization, Gabriel had a responsibility to keep the denizens of Earth ignorant of their place in the crowded little galaxy. They thought it was empty, except for themselves, and everyone else out there wanted them to continue to think so. One look at what she had learned from him and Lana would know better.

The bigger problem, by far, was that Gabriel *ached* with the thought of never being allowed to touch Lana again, of never having another chance to share her beautiful mind and sweetly responsive body. He had wanted her again as soon as he had left her, and it was a craving that was so much more than the need to bury himself in her over and over until he couldn't move. Being with her made him lose all control, not only over his body and his mind, but also over his emotions. That had never happened to him in all the years of his life.

He had always kept himself in reserve, his shields solidly in place, no matter what the provocation. He'd shared the beds of dozens of women, many of them human, many more of them not. He'd felt them give themselves to him in pleasure, in need, sometimes even in love; he'd heard them moan and scream as he took them over the edge. But nothing—*nothing*—compared to the feeling that had come over him when he heard Lana call his name in the throes of her passion. And nothing had ever felt like the conjoining of souls he'd experienced when they merged, body and mind. It was as if he'd been compelled by some primitive force he could not deny. To be with her. To be as one with her.

That same force compelled him to protect her as an animal would a mate. And as much as it angered him, Trevyn had been right to warn him. Kinnian would exploit his weakness. It was bad enough that he had brought Lana into any kind of proximity with his sibling. Only Kinnian's distracted rage at losing Asia and Jack had kept him from detecting Gabriel's presence at the safe house. But if by opening himself to her he had led Kinnian to Lana—Gabriel couldn't tolerate that thought. She would be a lamb to the slaughter, vulnerable, without any defense at all. That he would never allow. He scanned his mind's shields and made certain Lana's referents were well encircled. Kinnian might get through to him, but never to her.

Gabriel exhaled in frustration and punched at the pillow, determined to make the lumpy thing yield another hour or two of sleep. But it was not to be. An alert pinged on the comm unit beside the bed, demanding attention. He reached for it and spoke.

"Sam?"

"I'm sorry, *amigo*." His friend's voice rasped in his ear, the lateness of the hour affecting him as well. "I have something on that little task you assigned me."

Gabriel sat up and switched on the light. "Yes?" He padded over to the larger compscreen on the desk and powered up, knowing he'd need the maps and sensor data it contained.

"We have a black, 2008 GMC panel truck leaving the house a couple of hours before you got there. We're tracking it now. It was the only vehicle in or out that day. I'm sending the data to your personal comp."

"Good. Where is it now?"

"Stopped outside of Sallisaw, Oklahoma. They've been there for an hour, not sure why. Maybe just a break."

"Probably think they're home free by now. But where the hell are they headed?"

"They have to be taking Asia and Jack to some kind of research facility. We've been watching a number of places out west for years."

"You're guessing, Sam."

"No. We've ID'd a couple of the kidnappers. They're connected with a black ops group out of Groom Lake, Nevada. Seventy percent certainty that's their destination."

"You're monitoring that location?"

"Of course. Nothing yet. What about your girl? She and her crew been any help?"

He gritted his teeth. "Think that one's just about played out."

There was a pause on the end of the line. "Too bad. Seemed like a promising partnership."

Was that a hint of teasing in Sam's voice? If so, he was likely to be talking around a split lip next time Gabriel saw him.

"Seems like you need to mind your own fucking business, Murphy."

Sam laughed. "Whoa, there, *vaquero*! I'm not trying to get up in your business. But if you need a little advice in the relationship department—"

"I don't. What can you tell me about Kinnian? Any sign he's on to the truck?"

"No sign of a tail, sensor or otherwise." Sam was businesslike again. "The *Bloodstalker*'s in outlying orbit; we're busy playing hide and seek amongst the weather satellites."

Gabriel grunted. "I guess it keeps the shavetails

awake."

"Yeah, but we'll need an upgrade in the stealth shielding before too long. The Earthers will be on to us next time we try to do this."

As Earth's protectors, Rescue risked exposure with every operation. Gabriel found he needed the reminder. It was too easy to think of the planet's citizens as a collection of backward dolts. As this endless shipwreck of a day had proved, they were quite capable of outmaneuvering him without benefit of technology or enhanced psi talents.

He changed the subject. "Hey. How's Ethan holding up?"

"This is wearing on him, no lie. We haven't heard anything from the little guy since yesterday afternoon."

Gabriel's head snapped up. "Not since they left the safe house."

"No."

"Thanks, Sam. I'll talk to you soon."

He got up from the bed and crossed the room to the sink in three quick strides. He splashed water on his face, dismissed any thought of shaving and conceded precious seconds to brushing his teeth. Then he turned to the tasks of dressing and packing with focused haste. The vehicle carrying Asia and Jack hadn't speeded up between one part of his conversation with Sam and the next. Gabriel wasn't any further behind his quarry now than he'd been when Sam first called. But just knowing Ethan was no longer in touch with his son sent a spike of fear through him.

His mind offered him any number of reasons for the boy's silence—drugs , injury, death—but he shut down the useless cycle of speculation. He told himself he'd have time enough to figure out what had happened once he'd caught up to that truck. Right now, he had a more immediate problem.

He paused with his hand poised over the flat steel of the door to Lana's room. She'd told him to get out not less than four hours ago. It was still an unreasonable hour of the morning. He wouldn't blame her if she opened the door just to slap his face. If she opened it at all. He took a breath and knocked.

No answer.

He knocked louder.

A muffled "What the *fuck*?" from inside her room. Then, "'Get out' meant 'stay out', too, asshole."

Her voice sounded strained and hoarse, filtered by more than just the locked door and the blanket of night between them.

"Alana, open up. I have news about the case."

"I'm off the fucking case, Gabriel. Call the Bureau."

"Come on, Lana. This is important. Let me talk to you."

After a long, silent moment, he heard the bolt slide back, and the door swung open. Lana stood on the other side of the door in a tee-shirt and knit shorts, the bed where they'd made love still in rumpled disarray behind her. He couldn't help noticing the second of the two double beds was also unmade. She'd slept in that one, he deduced, the thought causing him pain.

His gaze moved to her face, and he tried to breathe. Slow. Deep. She'd been crying. She met his eyes with stubborn defiance, refusing his sympathy.

"What the hell is so important that you have to wake me up in the middle of the night?"

She'd stepped aside just enough for him to come in, so he did. He stood awkwardly in the middle of the room, trying to focus on what had brought him here.

"I got a call from Sam. I'd asked him to look at some satellite data to try and identify whether there'd been any traffic in and out of the safe house before we got there yesterday. He picked up just one vehicle—a black GMC truck. It left the house a few hours before we got there yesterday afternoon. He's tracked it to Oklahoma. They're still heading west, Lana."

She regarded him, hands on hips, eyelids dropped down over her sharp, green gaze. "You're sure about this?"

"One hundred percent. It was the only vehicle in or out yesterday."

"Of course, that's provided we're certain about the fact that Jack and Asia were there in the first place."

Gabriel swallowed. There was a way she could be as certain as he was about all of this. She had only to open herself to what she had seen in his mind and she would know what he knew. She had obviously refused to do that yet. She had closed it all off, built a wall around it. That wouldn't work for long, he knew.

"Lana, you know they were there," he said at last. "The van was in the garage."

She exhaled. "Okay. And this truck was the only thing in or out?"

"Since we got the tip on where they were located, yes."

Lana began to pace in the confined space between the bed and the dresser, her hands running through her blond curls. "Sam's tracking them by satellite?"

"Yes. He has them in Oklahoma right now."

She stopped to consider him. "Jesus, where the hell do you people get access to all this high- tech shit?"

Gabriel was silent. She had the answer to that question if she would just look for it.

She shook her head and resumed her pacing. "You know I'm PNG back at my office right now, right?"

"PNG?"

"*Persona non grata.* A.K.A. She Who Walks in Deep Shit. I got a special phone call from my boss after midnight last night informing me that I've been removed from this case forthwith. I've been assigned desk duty for the foreseeable future, pending reassignment—probably to the Bear's Breath, Alaska, sub-office."

Despite her prickly aspect, it was all Gabriel could do to resist reaching out to her. "I'm sorry, Lana."

"For what?" She glared at him. "I may blame you for a lot of shit, Cruz, but I only have myself to blame for getting thrown off this case."

"The safehouse . . ."

She blew out a breath, impatient with him. "They've been one step ahead of us the whole way, Gabriel. I've been over this and over it. We've beaten the percentages by a lot so far—thanks mostly to you."

He searched her face for any signs of sarcasm, but it was clear she meant what she said. Maybe it pained her to admit the man who'd hurt her personally had been useful to her professionally, but it struck him she'd spent a lot of years keeping her professional life separate from her personal life. He'd been relegated to "strictly business," which at least allowed him access. For some reason, this realization only intensified the urge to touch her, so much so that he took half a step in her direction.

She appeared not to notice—and she refused to meet his eyes. "Still, my boss doesn't see things quite the same way. All he sees is that this case is a gigantic fuckup. And I'm not sure he's going to want to hear anything new from me."

Gabriel shrugged. "Do you have a choice?"

At last she looked up at him. "No. I don't guess I do."

Trin, Center for Administrative Control, Consortium of Minertsa, Sector 10

The Ministerial Council was in an uproar.

The Oligarchy had called a rare face-to-face meeting of the nine Directors who managed the vast bureaucracy of the Consortium. Though no one could deny the circumstances were unusual, even dramatic, the Directors would have avoided any meeting if they could. Meetings in general meant inefficiency, lost profit and, most of all, the chance that something would be said that would affect one's status within the hierarchy. This situation in particular was fraught with danger for all involved.

And yet, Sennik looked forward to the meeting with calm. No—with relish. After all, his actions had precipitated the crisis that had brought them all together, though, of course, none of the others knew it. Now, if he simply sat back and let his fellow directors do what they each did best, his goals would be accomplished without further effort on his own part.

Silence reigned in the room as the Chief Oligarch rose to address his administration. *My friends. I bring you here today on a matter of grave importance to the Consortium, but also, as some of you may know, a matter of great personal sorrow to me. In the early segment of this solar cycle on Minertsa, at a time cloaked in darkness on the planet of Zalin where the tragic events took place, a number of brave Minertsans were brutally murdered, their human slaves were slaughtered like herdfish, and an entire manufacturing facility was laid waste. These horrific acts of savagery were the work of a small cadre of malfunctioning androids.*

Though most of the ministers in attendance had heard this much of the story, there was a gasp of horror from all of the throats in the room. The mere framing of the tale was enough to chill everyone with its implications. Sennik gasped along with everyone else and made an effort not to smirk.

Forty androids were awaiting shipment to their place of assignment, a mining colony in Sector 14, and according to reports, "went berserk," refusing to respond to commands, killing and destroying everything in their paths. The death toll at last count included 167 Minertsan workers, 544 human slaves and the founder and chief of research of Labor Futures, Limited, High Lord Vadis and his family. Lord Vadis was a close friend, and I shall miss him.

Sennik darkened his aura to the appropriate shade of purplish black in apparent sympathy and watched as his fellow directors around the table hastened to do the same. A few of them, he knew, would be slower than the others to adjust to the proper mood. They were already his allies in secret, though even they did not know to what extent he was responsible for the day's events: Rhondis, at Agriculture, who had scoffed early and often at the idea of replacing human slaves with androids; Tarrik, of the Ministry of Mines and Natural Resources, ever pressed for replacement labor in a dangerous occupation; Zipriss, Commanding General at the Ministry of Defense, an old warrior not yet ready for the new day. Until recently, the four of them had been under siege on the Council, often outvoted and outmaneuvered, characterized by their opponents as holdovers from an earlier era. That would soon change.

This is sad and disturbing news on many levels for the future of the Consortium. The Second Oligarch was as old as the swamps and showed it in her sagging skin and dull aura. But no one dared speak against her in Council. *The Zalin facility produced the majority of android workers in the Consortium and housed all of the research and development laboratories. Lord Vadis himself directed almost all of the research—he is irreplaceable. As for who will take over the assets of the company* . . . She shook her head. *That is a moot point. There are no salvageable assets beyond the credits in the company accounts, and any successor that might have taken Vadis's place is dead.*

Another, deeper exclamation went around the room. Here was one implication some people had not considered, though it had been Sennik's main goal.

Are you saying, Madam Oligarch, that we effectively have no android manufacturing capability in the Consortium as of today? This from the Director Prime of the Ministry of Health and Public Welfare, a female of little intelligence, in Sennik's opinion.

That is so. The Second Oligarch nodded. *If we wish to have an alternative to slave labor in the form of androids, we will have to purchase them from another source.*

That will not bode well for our balance of trade. The Director Prime of Commerce showed an aura that was gloomy and black.

Worse. General Zipriss wore an aura the threatening colors of a thunderhead. *We'd have to buy them from the* mrilling *humans on Terrene.*

Auras at once flashed bright green with fear,

underlit with the red of rage. Just as Sennik expected. Even the most liberal of his fellow directors could not accept such a thing. He let the pause lengthen as all considered this dark possibility.

Then he spoke. *My fellow directors, this is not the time to mire ourselves in the mud of negativity. The Consortium has sustained a severe blow today. Some of us have lost dear friends. We must take the time to mourn our losses, bind up our wounds and retrieve what we can from the wreckage. There will be time later to think of long-term strategies for meeting our labor needs. My ministry and I will be at your disposal when the time is right.*

There was silence while all present stared at him. Perhaps he'd overdone it? But, no, the Chief Oligarch was nodding, his black aura showing streaks of silver.

Spoken wisely, Director Prime. Let us take this solar cycle to seek comfort in the circle of family and friends. By the end of the cycle tomorrow we will have the complete report on what happened at Zalin. We can begin making plans to compensate for its loss at that time.

There were nods around the table and auras shining with the requisite respect and agreement as the directors rose to await the departure of the Chief Oligarch and his two ruling partners. Sennik darkened his own aura afterward as if in mourning or deep thought and avoided conversation with any of his fellows as he left the meeting room. It would have been just *too* difficult to hide his satisfaction throughout any extended interaction. And he could not afford to let his reaction be seen in a public place.

Perhaps he would ask his Director Second to join him at his home. Yes. Ilia had been a tasty morsel that day in his office. He could express his elation with her in a very satisfying way. He was barely able to control the flare of bright blue that shot through his aura at the thought of the evening ahead.

CHAPTER FOURTEEN

Outside Little Rock, Arkansas, Earth, Sector Three

Lana wanted to wait as late as she could before calling Frank Ballard. She was pressing her luck enough already without waking her boss at oh-dark-thirty. She packed up the car and went to the motel lobby for coffee, willing the minutes to pass until it was a decent hour of the morning to make the call.

Gabriel had been trailing her like a shadow. If it weren't for the case, when he'd knocked on her door in the middle of the night she might have opened up just to clock him one and slam it shut again. Every minute with him now was torture, remembering how he'd made her feel. Like no man had ever made her feel. Then remembering how it had all fallen apart— discovering him there *in her mind*, realizing he'd been there all along.

She exhaled a breath that came close to a growl, exasperated with him, exasperated with herself. She was just going to have to set this aside for now. She didn't have time to think it through. She didn't have time to feel the hurt or the anger. A woman and her child were depending on her to help them and, damn it, the actions of a slimeball, mindsucking, bastard, half-breed Thrane were *not* going to put her off her stride.

Lana stopped, her coffee cup halfway to her mouth. She stared at Gabriel, who was studying a roadmap, comparing it to satellite images on his computer. What the hell had she just called him? *Half-breed?* And what the hell was a *Thrane*?

With a sickening sense of inevitability—of doom, even—a new realization dawned in her mind. She set her coffee cup down with deliberate care and closed her eyes, fighting a wave of disorientation. He *wasn't just in* my *mind*, she thought. *I was in his, too.*

How that could be she didn't know. She had no psi talents. She didn't want any, either. And she most definitely did not want any part of rummaging around in Gabriel Cruz's mind.

Did he know about this? If not, she was not going to enlighten him. She could sense a huge pool of knowledge, of potential, of *connection*, waiting just below the surface of her conscious mind, waiting for her to tap in. Something told her it was all there for the taking—all the details of his life, all the contours of his psyche—just as hers were there in his mind. Why did that frighten her so much? She should be gloating, ready to use the dirty little secrets of his mind to bring him to his knees. For some reason, the idea didn't appeal at all.

Instead, in her imagination she built a thick, high fortress around that treasure trove, and around that a deep moat, and on the moat's banks an impenetrable thicket. She wanted nothing to do with what was behind those barriers, whether she discovered it by using her mind or just by asking Gabriel an innocent question. Gabriel was officially off limits. From now on, their relationship would be strictly professional, no matter how much that hurt.

"Aren't you going to eat?" Gabriel nodded in the direction of the breakfast buffet.

She scowled. "Not hungry. What time is it?"

"Just coming up on six."

"Guess I can't put it off any longer." She pulled out her cell and hit the speed dial for Ballard's home phone.

The old man skipped the growling and started right in on the barking. "Jesus Christ on a fucking crutch, Matheson, did I not make it clear to you just how much shit you're in? You have to piss me off some more by calling me before I've even had a cup of coffee? How about I assign you to scrubbing toilets next, would you get the message then?"

"No, sir, I'm quite clear on my current status. And if this was not vitally important, I would definitely not be disturbing you, sir."

"Vitally important, huh? What's the matter, got a cat up a tree in Iowa? Or maybe you need to blow up a ranch in Texas."

She dodged the acidic commentary on the other

end of the line and pressed on. "Sir, I have a lead on the possible whereabouts of our kidnapping victims. They were seen leaving the house before we got there yesterday—"

"Stop right there, Agent Matheson." There was no misunderstanding his tone. "Don't say another *fucking* word! Were you not ordered off this case last night?"

"Yes, sir. But—"

"What part of that is not clear? You are off the case. That means you don't turn up leads, you don't pass on leads and you most certainly do not follow up leads. It is no longer your case, do you understand?"

"Sir, can't you just pretend that I'm a citizen reporting a good lead? You wouldn't jeopardize the case just because I personally am"—she grit her teeth—"a screwup."

Ballard blew a huge sigh through the mouthpiece into her ear. "Okay, look. Normally, Lana, you are not a screwup. Normally, you are one of my best agents. How in hell you screwed the pooch out there in Little Rock I'll never know, but you did it royally, and as a result my ass is in a sling, too. But you can ease your little heart on one thing, girl. Your innocent kidnap vics? Turns out they're not so innocent. Mom has been ID'd as a person of interest by Homeland Security—they were the ones who sent a team to pick her up. Guess Junior just went along for the ride, and they'll send him home when they get around to it."

Lana's heart stilled in her chest. "What?" The single word was all she could manage.

Ballard chuckled. "Yeah. Nice of the assholes to let us know, right? I got a phone call just before I called you last night telling me to lay off, that this Asia Roberts was theirs. Guess I should have known when that former Green Beret turned up as one of the 'perps,' huh? Those guys don't always play nice when they make their pickups. I gave him hell about interagency cooperation and all that hoohah, like it's gonna do any good."

An oily black cloud threatened to steal her vision; a roar of sibilant static drowned out Ballard's chatty voice on the phone. Her thoughts raced off on a dozen tangents: the HomeSec story was obvious bullshit; none of her team's investigation had turned up any connections to international or domestic terrorism. The possibility of Asia's psi talent was a more plausible reason for a black ops section of government to want her. And now her own boss was ordering her to stand back and let them kidnap an innocent U.S. citizen and her child?

Finally the pure, white-hot flame of rage provided a point for her focus. And as she burned with it, a plan resolved itself in her mind.

She took it one step at a time. "But what about the van? And there were four men killed in that house—"

"Every one of them with drug records as long as your arm. HomeSec made the switch to a different vehicle, then left the van in the alley, figuring we'd track it eventually. They didn't count on drug dealers being stupid enough to pull it into the garage—or a rival gang hit on the house."

"Well, shit." She held back her disbelief and allowed only disgust to come through. "You're telling me I just threw my career in the crapper for nothing?"

Ballard grunted. "Just keep your head down. This'll all blow over eventually."

"Yeah. I guess all this is getting to me a little bit. I got a little banged up last night, and I'm feeling it today."

"Damn, girl! That wasn't in Trent's report!"

"Why doesn't that surprise me? I imagine you'll see a few things different in my report."

"Well, what happened? You okay?"

"Just a bad burn, some bumps and bruises. I was chasing down a perp and caught the tail end of the explosion."

Just as Lana had hoped, Ballard envisioned the worst. "Jesus Christ! Why didn't you check yourself into the hospital?"

"Well, the EMT wanted to take me in, but Trent needed to dress me down and I had to wrap up the scene and—"

Ballard interrupted with a long string of creative cursing. "You ain't got the sense God gave little green apples. You take some time off and heal up, you hear me? That's an order. I don't want to see you in this office for at least a week."

Lana poured on the charm, just to make sure. "Aw, c'mon, boss. What the hell am I gonna do at home for a week?"

"Who says you have to stay home? You're already in beautiful downtown Little Rock. Take a vacation, for all I care. Just don't come in to work. You almost got yourself blown up into tiny pieces for some HomeSec asshole. You deserve a little down time, courtesy of the United States government. Take it."

Gabriel was eyeing her with curiosity. Lana ignored him.

"You're the boss. What do you want me to do with the car?"

"Park it until you're ready to come home, then drive it back. I'll see you in a week or so." He didn't linger. The line went dead.

Gabriel lifted an eyebrow. "What is it?"

"Good news is I'm free to chase these bastards down." She swallowed the last of the coffee in her cup and got up from the table. "Bad news is, from now on I'm on my own."

She headed out the door, Gabriel on her heels. He caught her as she reached the car and opened the driver's side door.

"Where the hell do you think you're going?"

"That's my business." She slipped in behind the wheel. "Where can I drop you?"

Lana wasn't sure if she was prepared to leave him standing in the parking lot, but Gabriel apparently wasn't taking any chances. He threw his bag in the back of the car, slammed the door shut and jumped in the passenger seat before she could put the car in gear and take off.

A muscle ticked in his jaw. "You're not going anywhere without me."

"Watch me. I'll be damned before I sit in a car all the way to freakin' Oklahoma with the man who mindfucked me." The words shot out of her mouth, shocking them both. She sat shaking in the emotional backwash, anger and hurt close to carrying her beyond the limits of her control.

Fury sparked deep in Gabriel's black eyes. "What I did was a violation. I know that. But it wasn't deliberate."

"Just tell me. What the hell happened last night? How could you—" her voice caught; she stopped, started over—"how could you do what you did to me?"

Gabriel breathed out a curse in a language she didn't recognize and ran a hand through his hair in frustration. "Lana, you have to believe me. I could not control what happened last night. Keeping my shields up—maintaining my distance between myself and others—is a constant act of will. When we made love I couldn't think of anything but you. For the first time in my life, my shields dropped on their own, and before I knew it, we were . . . together." He looked as if he would touch her, but she bristled and he backed off again. "The last thing I wanted was to hurt you."

"Yeah. Well. Couldn't have proved it by me." The bright flare of anger subsided to a weary ache. Maybe he hadn't been able to control what had happened. That didn't excuse it. And the feelings she had for him? She'd just have to get over them. "We're done, Gabriel.

Understand? I'm finding the nearest rental car agency, and we're renting two vehicles. We're going our separate ways."

He shook his head. "We're not done. You need me."

"You arrogant son of a bitch!"

"Tell me about the phone call."

"Go to hell."

"You're off the case. That means you have no access to FBI resources."

She stared out the windshield. She had friends in the Bureau she could rely on, favors she could call in, but it wouldn't be easy. And she just had the one lead that Gabriel had given her. Who knew if Sam would continue to help her without his intercession?

"Lana. You need my resources. I need your expertise. Asia and Jack are still out there. Together we can find them and bring them home."

She turned to look at him and caught the glimmer of banked fire deep behind the cold surface of his dark eyes. This fight wasn't over, for either of them.

"Okay," she said. "For now."

The cell was dark, not merely the dark of night or of the unlit corridors of the training compound after hours, but the dark of deep places in the musty earth, the dark of shadows untouched by any source of light. He couldn't see the walls, though he knew they were exactly four steps in any direction from where he sat on the unyielding stone of the floor. He couldn't see his hand, shaking at the end of his thin, knobby arm. He might as well have been blind. If he were to spend more than a few weeks in the cell, he *would* be blind.

He shivered, naked, curled up upon himself in a useless effort to conserve his body heat. He'd been here before. He knew it would be a long time before they came for him. He had to survive until then. It was a test. It was always a test.

The first time he had made the mistake of trying to sleep. They had attacked through his dreams, and he had not been able to defend himself. The nightmares had bled over into his waking state as hallucinations he could not shake, terrors that would not release him. Rodyn had been forced to stop the exercise and bring him out of the cell. Then his teacher had beaten him for his stupidity. He hadn't fallen asleep again.

Now he waited, controlling his breathing as best he could. He monitored the levels of his emotions—the normal fears of the dark and isolation and cold that an eleven-year-old boy would feel. These he tamped down easily. They were his to control, after all. Not everything he would experience in this cell would be.

From one corner of the cell came a slither and

a sigh of sound, not very loud, just enough to make his head snap around. Then silence, as profound as the darkness. His heartbeat filled the space, pounding in his ears over the sawing of his breath as he strained to listen for more. *There!* A soft sibilance, closer now, and . . . and *thicker* somehow. It was a . . . a *snaky* sort of sound, he thought, and as soon as he identified it, his mind exploded with the image. There was not one serpent in the cell with him, but dozens, coiled and snarled upon each other all around him. The floor of the cell was alive with their writhing bodies. They had only to move a few inches and they would be on him! Some of them had to be venomous. They would bite him! He would die a horrible, choking, agonizing death!

He was standing in the center of the cell now, close to panic, certain he could feel the first of the reptiles on his feet. He wanted to scream, was certain he would scream at the first touch of scaly skin on his toes. Abruptly, in his mind the picture of the snakes at his feet was replaced with the stern face of his teacher, Rodyn's thin rattan cane raised to deliver a stinging blow. He almost flinched at the realistic image. He blinked. The snakes were gone.

Was Rodyn helping him? Or had his mind provided the image to banish the psi attack? He took a breath, fighting for control over the outward signs of his fear. Of course there were no snakes in the cell! That was ridicu—

He blinked again—and scrambled backward into the corner of the tiny room. A roar shattered the very air, cracking the stone beneath his feet and shaking a fall of dust from the ceiling. The creature trapped in the cell with him had sprung from a nightmare. Its hunched shoulders scraped the ceiling, its four legs were as big around as tree trunks and tipped in six-inch razor-sharp claws that clattered against the stone as it paced. Its jaws gaped wide with each thunderous roar to reveal row after row of yellow fangs, and its eyes glowed red as it studied him with intelligence.

He shook with terror, even though he knew in some part of his mind that the monster could not be real. The monster looked real. It sounded real. It even smelled real, its hot breath like the overflow of open sewers, but he knew, he *knew,* it could not be real. It took all the courage he had to close his eyes and summon the image of Rodyn and his cane again, but he managed it. He used the image to beat back the false reality of the monster sharing the cell with him, wielded it like a shield to clear a lucid space in his mind free of the interference of outside influence. Around that calm space he built a wall, tall and strong.

And when he opened his eyes again, the monster was gone.

There were other "visitors" that night, but he recognized them all for what they were. When the door to the cell swung open hours later, he was sitting quietly in the center of the floor, waiting.

Rodyn looked at him with something that might have been a smile. "You found nothing to disturb you during the night, boy?"

"No, Master." He rose to his feet.

His teacher's eyes narrowed, observing him in the flickering light of the lantern he'd brought. He handed him a robe.

"You're not cold?"

"No, Master." He slipped the robe over his head. "I built a fire."

In his mind, the merry flames still burned, illuminating the cozy room.

Lana jerked wide awake in the passenger seat of the rented SUV and sucked in a breath. Her heart was threatening to jump out of her chest, beating at about twice its normal rate while she struggled to reconcile the bright sunshine of the Oklahoma countryside outside the car window with the dark vision she'd just experienced.

Gabriel took his eyes off the road to glance at her in concern. "Are you okay?"

"Shit, no." She sat up and dragged both hands down her face. Then she turned to stare at Gabriel, unable to look away from those lines around his mouth that hinted at cruel determination until he smiled, at the shadows in his eyes that were the only sign of the pain he concealed so well, at the set of his shoulders, the strength of his hands. She saw everything about him differently now because she'd seen that little boy battling the monsters they'd sent to invade his mind. God knows she hadn't wanted to. *Damn him!*

"What is it?" She could tell by his voice that he knew. He was waiting for her to tell him.

"Who was Rodyn?"

His eyes flicked in her direction. "He was my teacher. I trained under him from the age of ten until I was 17."

"Trained. For your psi talents."

"Yes."

"You weren't just born with them?"

"I was born with potential, Lana. How that potential was exploited, for good or for evil, with control or without it, depended on my training."

She snorted. "We see how well that worked out."

His jaw tightened along with his hands on the steering wheel. "A loss of control on the order I experienced with you while I was in training would have marked me for immediate termination."

"Termination. You mean from training."

"I mean from life. The people who ordered my training in the first place distrust those with psi talents. For good reason. Without proper training and self-control, a person with a high level of psi talent is dangerous to those who have none. Even with the training and control the mandates require, some still choose to use their talents in all the wrong ways."

"Like the ones chasing Asia and Jack."

"Yes. Exactly like them."

Blood on the floor, spreading in a wine-red pool. The women screaming . . . Lana shook her head, trying to clear it of the shattering image.

"You have history with them," she whispered. "This is personal for you."

His expression revealed nothing.

A rush of untamed anger ran through her before she could catch it. Nothing seemed within her control any more, least of all her emotions.

"What is it about these men—Kinnian . . . and Trevyn, right? Why can't you just stop all the lies and tell me?"

"Yes, I have a history with them." His voice lacked any inflection that would have allowed her to interpret meaning from the words. "But it's also true that I took this case as a favor to Sam and Rayna. As for lying, it's going to be damn hard for me to do that from now on. Though I'm not sure you'll see that as a good thing."

Her temper flared, as hot as he was cool. She was furious, the rage she'd felt at his violation of her mind the night before compounded by the confusion she felt now as the bits and pieces of his life forced their way to the forefront of her awareness despite her best efforts to suppress them.

"Goddamn it, Gabriel! I didn't want any of this! You could have kept all of your secrets, but now I have all of this . . . this"—her hands waved in the vicinity of her head—"secret society, psychic cult *shit* in my brain, and I can't make any sense of it! I feel like I'm losing my mind!"

He started to reach out to her, but aborted the movement when he caught the warning in her expression. He let out a frustrated breath and returned his hand to the steering wheel.

"Alana, I know this isn't easy. Nothing I say will make it any easier for you. If I had wanted to keep any secrets from you, it would be impossible now. And, believe me, most things about my life would have been best kept to myself. I no longer have that choice, nor do you. I'm an intimate part of your mind now, just as you're a part of mine." He glanced her way, his expression grim. "You can't wall off that part of you, any more than you could block out your own memories or feelings. Even less, since your natural curiosity will want to explore what's there, and you have no remembered emotional trauma of your own to keep you from doing so."

She didn't need to have her own emotional trauma attached to those memories. She could feel enough of *his* to keep her from wanting to investigate what she'd acquired from him. Every glimpse of what his life had been only frightened her more. Every fragment of memory only served to increase her confusion about who, or *what*, Gabriel Cruz truly was.

Lana ran both hands through her hair with an exasperated sigh, releasing her unruly curls from any semblance of Bureau-mandated control. "That's just the thing, Gabriel," she said at last. "Maybe if I'd had some time to get to know you before this happened. You know, the usual way. I ask. You answer. I tell you a little story about how I got in trouble in fourth grade. You tell me how you like your steak. But this . . . I just don't know if I can handle this. It's too much."

He nodded, his eyes on the road. "I know."

All at once she felt as if her heart was breaking. A tear, sudden and inexplicable, rolled down her cheek. In the silence, her thoughts echoed.

My God, Gabriel, you were just a little boy. "Shit." She swiped at her face with shaking hands.

"Lana." He had a warm hand on her shoulder before she could stop him. Part of her ached to lean into that touch, but she hadn't listened to that part of herself in a long, long time.

She shrugged him off. "Leave me alone, Gabriel. Just . . . for God's sake." She turned toward the window and huddled in on the pain. "Leave me alone."

How could she cry for him? She had hidden it, was hiding it even now, but he'd seen.

God knew she had every right to cry for herself. For the senseless act of violence that took her mother—and the only family she'd ever known—when she was nine. For the horrors she'd endured in the succession of foster homes that followed. For the salvation of kindness she'd found in the last of them that had meant she would survive after all.

Anger and a kind of fierce protectiveness burned in Gabriel's chest for her. He had long ago acclimated himself to the emotional content of his memories. They no longer had the power to affect him. But he cursed himself for the moment of weakness that had brought Lana to this. How was it that a woman so strong she had overcome what he saw in her own mind could be so vulnerable she would weep for what she saw in his?

God help him, he didn't know what to do with the feelings she called up in him—the tenderness, the possessiveness, the ache of desire. He could feel the link between their minds seeking to reestablish itself, tendrils of pre-thought and connection reaching out from the deepest, least conscious part of his mind to hers. His autonomic nervous system slid into synch with hers, aligning their heartbeats, their breathing patterns, making allowances for their difference in size and genetic structure and still finding a compatible rhythm. Gabriel's heart sped up as he recognized what was happening.

He set it aside. What he thought he felt was impossible. It was just another of his body's reactions to being near her—like the erection he couldn't seem to lose.

He stole a glance at the remarkable woman who had shared his bed not 12 hours ago. He dared to reach for her soft curls; now that she was sleeping, she wouldn't reject his touch. She had forced herself to sleep, rather than give in to the emotions she felt. For him. In her heart she could not forgive his betrayal. She would never allow him close enough to hurt her again.

And though it broke him body and soul to admit it, Gabriel had to agree that was probably for the best.

CHAPTER FIFTEEN

Trin, Minertsa, Sector 10

The usual light lavender of Ardis's aura was shot through with magenta and deep red. Here in the hidden recesses of the Public Records Archive, Collections Building II, there were no other researchers at this time of the solar cycle to see the depths of her anger. There were no monitoring devices covering this angle of the room to record the breadth of her outrage. She could give free vent to her emotions for the time she was here, something she could not do even in her home, which she knew had been monitored for some time, probably since she'd started working with Sennik, certainly since she'd started having sex with him.

The sex, of course, was one reason for her anger. And her shame. Though she had planned for it, though she had encouraged it, though, indeed, everything depended on it, still she flushed bright orange when she thought of what she did with Sennik. Her body and mind responded to his manipulation as they were programmed by nature to do, and the pleasure was wild, indescribable, world-shattering. She left him every time shaking with the aftermath, barely able to function, aching for more.

Hating him with all of her being. Hating herself even more.

When this was all over, if, indeed, she lived to see it through, there would be a reckoning. Of this Ardis was certain. Her aura grew dark and glowering with that knowledge.

She returned her attention to the compscreen and the black of her aura was once again underlit with the dark red of her rage, pierced with occasional white-hot flashes of shock at Sennik's audacity. There on the screen was the data she had paid such a dear price to gain. She had bartered her self-respect in hopes of learning the access codes to Sennik's personal data files. In the previous solar cycle she had snagged the last of them from his mind. And in those data files she found the blueprint for destruction she knew the Director Prime had drawn with his own hand.

Fifty-six human adults. Twenty young ones. Specially trained and placed in positions of strategic importance throughout the Minertsan Consortium. A series of events, coordinated not through Sennik or anyone connected to him, but through an innocent-looking human boy, trained and encoded to function as a bioserver, relaying instructions on a precise timetable via telepathic connections. Assassinations, staged riots, sabotage of key facilities—apparently random acts of terrorism and murder. At the end of three solar cycles, the prominent voices in favor of opening the Consortium to outside influences would be silenced. Those who had dared to suggest an alternative to slave labor in the Consortium would be dead or blamed for the deaths of others, their businesses in ruin. The markets would be in chaos, reeling from the loss of crucial manufacturing and mining centers. Fear would rule the populace. The people would demand a change in leadership, a swing of the pendulum toward more control.

Sennik would be ready. And once he had restored control over the Consortium as Chief Oligarch, there would be no power in the galaxy that could stop him from taking whatever else he wanted.

What had happened on Zalin had been a test, Ardis realized. Sennik's happy mood afterward was ample proof of the success of that test. But he needed the boy for the rest of it. Until the boy was found, Ardis had time to do what could be done.

Still, that was so little! Exposing the plan was not enough. Ardis had no proof, beyond the files on the screen in front of her, files that could very easily have been fabricated. Sennik was a powerful being, with powerful allies. She was a minor administrator, and an investigation would reveal both her affair with Sennik and a very personal grudge against him.

Her only hope was with the humans, whose path had begun to merge with hers in the time of her mourning. Slindar had always said the humans pointed the way to the future. *My beloved Slindar.* Little had he known his own fate, and hers, would be so intimately intertwined with the humans'. . .

"I'm so sorry," the human had said, his facial expressions showing sadness, regret. She understood they had no auras to show such things. "There was so much fighting. We couldn't get through to the children. Slindar found a way through a back corridor and let us in, but he was killed before we could get out of there. We had to leave him behind."

"It is better that it happened that way." Her own aura was the dark purple of a fresh bruise. "He was seen as a hero for defending the facility."

The human—his name was Sam—nodded. "He was a hero, Ardis. Those children should grow up remembering his name."

"No." She shook her head. "I hope they forget everything about that place."

Slindar's death at Del Origa VII had propelled her on this journey. And now she would pass the torch to the humans traveling with her, to do what they could do to avert this looming disaster. A very few of the Minertsan targets were sympathizers. They could be warned to neutralize the human threats working for them. In some cases, the abolitionist organization Rescue might be able to extract the humans from their posts. But they were all racing against time. Kinnian and Trevyn Dar were hunters of a deadly and efficient reputation. They would have the boy soon. Once the child was in Sennik's hands, the Director Prime would waste no more time on preliminaries. He would set his plan in motion. And worlds would fall.

His mouth slanted hard across hers, his kiss hot and demanding. Beneath her his hips lifted in unyielding rhythm. His hands, tight on her waist, gripped her as if she would escape him. She moaned, caught between pleasure and pain.

"Ethan." She tried to slow him down, her breath coming in gasps.

"You can't leave me, Asia. I won't let you go."

The rough slide of his shaft in the slick heat of her core fed a flame that threatened to burn her to cinders. "I could never leave you. You mean everything to me. Jesus, Ethan." She burned, *God!* she burned, as he filled her and withdrew, over and over. He made her lose her mind, forgetting everything except the feel of him deep inside, pushing her closer and closer to the edge.

Without warning he rolled her onto her back and hovered over her, motionless. He hadn't left her; he was still inside her, hard, throbbing, but unmoving. She arched into him—close, so close.

"Ethan, please, God, don't stop."

"Tell me." His face was wet with tears, his eyes shadowed with torment. "Tell me, Asia. I have to know."

"I don't . . ." She breathed, barely able to think, "I don't know what you want. I don't know how to help you." He seemed so sad, so desperate, but they had been too long without each other, and this need would not be denied.

He groaned and surged forward, igniting the firestorm that had been smoldering in her body. She came with him, perception shattering as she clung to him, the memory of his tortured voice following her into consciousness: "Where are you, Asia? Tell me where you are!"

"Ethan!" She woke, gasping, shuddering with the shock of intense orgasm, alone in the dark and a heat so oppressive she could hardly move under the weight of it. She groaned and curled up on herself on the floor of the moving truck, the sense of loss immediate and piercing, squeezing her breath from her chest. She wrapped her arms around her waist, rocking with pain. She could still smell him, still taste him on her tongue, still feel the power of his climax, even as she felt his helpless need.

"Damn it, Ethan," she sobbed. "If I only knew . . ."

Asia rolled to her knees—and added dizzy nausea to the list of crazy, conflicting signals from her overwrought body. Stiff, aching muscles. Pounding head. A thirst so profound she felt it cell-deep. *Drugs*. She had been out for who knew how long—hours, at least. Maybe as much as a full day.

Jack! Embarrassment vied with concern as she glanced around the empty truck box for him. If he had seen . . . but, no, he was passed out in the opposite corner. A rueful smile tugged at her lips. Today would not have to be the day for that birds and bees talk.

Jack was sleeping heavily, his head cradled on one arm. She watched him, her heart aching. She would have spared him this if she could. Him and Ethan. If there had been a way to overcome Ethan's instincts to protect her, she would have climbed into the back of the van without a protest to save the two of them. But she had tried that once before. Ethan just wasn't capable of giving her up without a fight.

As before, there was water in the back of the truck with them. She tore open a bottle and upended it, draining it in seconds. Then she grabbed another bottle and crawled to where Jack lay huddled on a pile of blankets.

She lifted him into her lap. "Hey, buddy, time to wake up."

It took more than a minute of cajoling, jiggling and, finally, chafing at various pulse points to get him to come around. She blew out a breath in relief when at last his lids lifted a fraction and showed the blue of his eyes beneath.

"Thirsty," he mumbled.

"Got some water right here, baby."

"My head feels funny." His voice was stronger.

"I know, buddy. They gave us drugs to make us sleep. They wanted us to be quiet."

Jack sat up as if he'd been poked. "Where are we?"

"I don't know, Jack. I can't tell how long we've been driving."

He lurched to his feet and weaved to the front of the truck, pressing his ear against the panel that separated the cargo compartment from the front seat. He listened for a long moment, his face screwed into an expression of concentration. Then he looked at her with something close to panic.

"I can't hear anything!"

"What's wrong, honey?" She took his hand and made him sit down. "What's going on?"

"Mom, do you think we're in Arizona yet?"

She tried not to let her exasperation show. "I don't know, Jack. Maybe. Why?"

"Because that's where it's going to happen."

"Where *what's* going to happen?" Her voice took on an edge; she couldn't help it.

Jack just looked at her like she had no sense. "Something bad. Something really bad!"

As he spoke the truck swerved to the right, the tires below them rumbling over rough pavement. They were no longer on the interstate. Asia wondered just how long it had been since they'd left the highway. Jack's face had gone pale. For the first time since they'd been taken, he looked terrified.

She took his hands in hers. "Okay. We have to let your dad know where we are. Come on. You have a job to do."

He nodded, swallowed. His gaze darted to the front

of the truck and back.

"Jack!" She was stern with him, forcing him to look at her. "Settle down. Think. Do what you were taught to do." Beyond that she couldn't help him. She didn't know what it was he did, but apparently what she suggested was the right thing.

He calmed down. He closed his eyes.

Then the truck slid to a rough stop, and Jack looked up at her in horror. "It's too late."

Ethan dropped to his knees in the shower, felled by a bludgeoning avalanche of dread so dark and impenetrable he could barely lift his head. For long seconds there was nothing but overwhelming emotion—terror, raw and ungovernable; a panicky search for help.

They're coming! They're coming, and I don't know what to do!

Then silence, more frightening than the wail of a little boy's terror in his mind. Ethan began to tremble, every muscle locking up with shivery tremors, even though the water still pelted down as hot as he could take it from the showerhead.

Please, God, not after all of this, he prayed. *It can't be the end. Not now.*

An hour earlier he'd crashed on the couch in the den, the television tuned to something inane. The FBI agents had long since learned to leave him alone; he wasn't pleasant company, and who knew when he might turn out to be a viable suspect again. Sam and Rayna had given up on him, too, for the night. So he'd been alone when he'd dreamt of Asia and woke in the middle of an orgasm.

He'd wanted her so damn bad. The dream had felt so real. It had been as if he could still feel her wrapped around him. He'd had to jerk off again as soon as he got upstairs into the shower. And yet he'd been angry—so fucking angry with her, though God knew he couldn't blame her for any of this.

And now . . . *Jesus, Jack! What the hell is going on?*

Ethan pulled himself to his feet and slapped at the faucets to turn the shower off. He refused to believe there was nothing he could do to help his family. He dried off and got dressed, then picked up the fancy comm unit Sam had left behind for him to use.

Sam responded to his signal, but he didn't sound happy. "This better be important."

If it had been another time, he might have smiled. "I'm sorry if I interrupted something."

"Shit. Ethan. No, I'm sorry. I, uh, I didn't look at the readout. What's wrong?"

"I . . ." He stopped, started again. "I got a partial message from Jack. Then it cut off. They're in trouble, Sam. You're still tracking them, aren't you?"

There was just the slightest hesitation. "My crew would have told me if they'd lost track of them. Give me a second."

A soft murmur of voices—Ray's rising alto, Sam's

answering bass—confirmed he'd interrupted his friends' limited private time. Ethan waited, swallowing an ache that was equal parts regret and envy.

"I was calling up their current location on my compscreen," Sam explained when he came back. "Looks like something is happening. They're off the interstate. And they've stopped. Pulled up about fifteen minutes ago."

Ethan's heart dropped into his belly. "Where are they?"

"Middle of fucking nowhere in Arizona. No town, no stores, no houses, nothing."

"Breakdown?" *God, please tell me—*

"No way to tell."

"Jack was afraid, Sam. For the first time in this whole mess, he was terrified. And now I can't hear him."

"Okay, just calm down. It could have been anything. We already talked about the fact that they probably drugged him. He's likely disoriented. All this could be starting to get to him a little. That would only be natural."

"We need to find them, Sam." Ethan refused to be "handled." "Where is Gabriel?"

"They're catching up. We don't have a track on him and Lana so I'm not sure—maybe six hours behind?"

"Damn it, Sam! They might as well be on the far side of the moon!"

"No." Sam paused for effect. "I think I'd know."

"You can't send a team in from up there?"

"Ethan. Take a minute to think, man." Sam's voice was soothing, logical. "We're not positive this vehicle is carrying Asia and Jack; that part is just an educated guess. Even if we're right, we go blasting in with no plan and no cover and we'd do nothing but get them killed. If they're off-road now, they're probably going to ground again. That's a good thing. Trust Gabriel to do his job. Believe me, he's the best there is."

Ethan blew out a frustrated breath. "Okay. Just get in touch with Gabriel. Tell him to put on some speed."

"We'll do everything we can, my friend. Hey. You want to come up here and keep watch?"

"No. I don't know how far Jack can 'send.' I better stay close in case he tries to reach me."

There was another pause. Sam still didn't trust his communication with Jack. Ethan tried not to hold it against him.

"Okay," Sam said at last. "I'll let you know as soon as we learn anything."

South of the Navajo Nation Indian Reservation, Arizona, Earth, Sector Three

The doors in the back of the truck opened to reveal two men, their husky frames silhouetted by the deep orange, lavender and purple of the desert sunset behind them. One gestured to the other. "Get the brat."

Jack went rigid in her arms. Asia turned him toward her and wrapped arms and legs around him.

"Like fuck." She curled inward, giving the man as little to grasp as she could.

He wasted no time fighting her. He pistol-whipped her in the back of the head. Her arms would not obey her commands as her vision exploded in shards of bright white and neon color, then faded to black. She only blanked out for a second, but it was enough. She went limp, and the man pulled Jack, kicking and screaming, from her grasp.

"Fucking bitch." He kicked her in the ribs as he took Jack.

The boy was inarticulate with rage and fear, growling and spitting, writhing in the man's grip to no avail. Helpless and despairing, Asia watched them take him, seeing Jack as he'd been when she and Ethan had first fostered him—unable or unwilling to speak, so traumatized by what he'd been through that any frustration would send him into blind, feral rampages. All the progress he had made, all the love they had given him, and it was all going to be for nothing. They had stripped Jack to his essential terror in seconds, and it was going to end before she could do anything to help him.

She cursed and dragged herself to her knees, unable to make it to her feet. She crawled, fighting the nausea and the dizzy pain in the back of her head, ignoring the crushing disability in her side to get to him. Goddamn it, Jack was not going to die out there alone! He was going to know she was there for him. He was not an animal, a slave, a piece of garbage that the galaxy used and threw out. He was her son. And Ethan's. And they loved him.

She made it to the edge of the truck and looked out. They had dragged Jack to the lip of a draw. One of the men was pulling a gun out of his waistband. She rolled from the truck to the ground and started to stagger in their direction.

She shouted. "Jack!"

He looked up. Met her eyes.

Somebody grabbed her from behind. She struggled in an iron grip, fighting to get to Jack. "No! Get your fucking hands off me!"

The men with Jack looked around, dismissed her, went back to their business.

No!

The man with the gun raised his hand.

She felt . . . something . . . an electric charge . . . go through her, and the man behind her fell away. She turned her head to look. He wasn't there.

And when she turned back to look at Jack, the men around him just . . . vaporized.

Jack stood alone on the edge of the draw, his hands at his side, his face blank and pale. Asia stumbled to a stop, her heart thundering in her chest, unable to understand what she had just seen. She turned and looked back toward the truck. The vehicle sat unattended by the side of the road. There was no sign of anyone for miles except for Jack and herself.

She stared at the boy standing motionless not a dozen yards from her, his eyes on the ground. He had done this. *Oh, God*. Somehow Jack had done this and saved himself—and her. She took a shaky breath and ran to him. "Jack?" She knelt in front of him and reached out to put both hands on his shoulders. "Jack. Look at me."

After a long moment, he raised his eyes to hers. They were a dark, dark blue, so unlike his usual bright color that she pulled in a breath. And they were full of uncertainty. But Asia wouldn't let him think for a second that any of her reaction was due to a fear of him.

"I was so scared, Jack," she told him. "So afraid I'd never see you again. Whatever it was that you did to save yourself, honey, I want you to know that it was okay. I'm glad you did it. Because it means you're here now and we're both safe. You were very brave."

Jack just looked at her with those blue, blue eyes and a face so expressionless it could have been struck from the red rock of the desert that surrounded them. Even the brief doubt he had shown had faded into blankness. He had retreated again, to that place he'd found to hide when life was too painful to endure. It had taken all of Ethan's professional skill and the love of both of their hearts to bring him out of that cave the first time. Asia had no idea what it would take to coax him out again.

"Oh, baby, I'm so sorry." She pulled him into a hug, her tears rolling down her face to soak into his dark hair. After a minute she pulled back and brushed the tears from her cheeks. "Come on." She stood up and took his hand. "Let's get the hell out of here."

She was almost giddy as she trotted back to the truck and boosted Jack into the front seat. They were going to get out of this! This nightmare was almost over! She yanked open the driver's side door and scanned the interior. There was little of use—no cell phone, no map, no clue as to where they were. There was a GPS, though she wasn't sure they could use it without leading their kidnappers' colleagues to them.

She slid behind the wheel, turned the key in the ignition and . . . nothing. She pumped the gas and tried again. No crank. No catch. No click, even. The truck was as dead as its owners, probably for the same reasons. After all, Jack had been responsible for a breakdown before.

"I don't suppose you could fix this, Jack?" She gestured at the truck.

He shook his head.

"Are you sure? It's important."

The head shake was adamant this time. Then he looked out the window.

"Okay. Okay, Jack. I understand." But now they were stuck in the desert with night coming on and the likelihood of another car coming by on this pathetic excuse for a highway was—

"Oh, my God! I think those are headlights!"

She jumped out of the truck and stood in the road. These people were *not* going to drive by them. She waved both arms over her head, just in case they didn't get the message.

"Hey! We need help!"

A battered old pickup slowed its approach and swerved to the left side of the road. For a brief, breath-catching moment, Asia thought maybe they wouldn't stop, that the move to the left was just so they could get around her and go on. But she could hear a high, quavery voice issuing orders from inside the cab, a lower, younger one arguing back, and the truck slid to a dusty stop beside her.

She came up close to the open passenger-side window, where a wizened, bronze-skinned crone gave her a sunny grin. A young man of about twenty-five was scowling behind the wheel, sweat running from beneath a Stetson that looked like it had spent time under the tires of the pickup.

"Hi. Thanks for stopping."

"Trouble," the old woman said.

"Yeah, you can say that again." Asia nodded. "My son and I need a ride. Do you have a cell phone?"

The man shook his head. "Cells don't work out here. No towers. There's a phone at a store down the road. We can take you."

"Thanks. Really. Thanks so much." She ran back to the truck, gathered Jack in her arms and brought him around. The woman slid to the middle of the bench seat and made room for them. Asia climbed aboard and put Jack in her lap. Like most of the farm trucks she'd ridden in as a kid in Tennessee, the seat lacked a safety belt.

The young man put the truck in gear and rolled

back onto the road. Then he leaned forward to squint past the old woman at Asia. "You driving that truck by yourself?"

"Yeah, it's a rental." She lied as smoothly as she could. She saw no point in starting a long, unbelievable story about a kidnapping. "Got turned around at the last exit, started going the wrong way, I guess, then the thing just quit on me."

"Hunh." Then, "Timing chain, maybe." He didn't offer any support for his argument.

"Could be. It didn't overheat or anything."

The woman gestured at Jack. "Your son."

Asia smiled. "Yes. This is Jack. I'm Asia."

"Geneva Twohawks. That's my grandson, Hardhead."

"Keep it up, old woman, and I'll make you walk home." The man scowled. "Name's Will." He thought for a moment. "You come this far off I-40?"

"Yeah." Asia laughed. "Talk about lost, huh?" She had no clue how far off the interstate she was. "I just kept hoping I'd see a sign."

Will grunted. "Only sign you'd see out here would be fucking 'wrong way.'"

Geneva responded with a frown. "Huh. Comedian."

Having the windows open made for a noisy ride, so there wasn't much conversation once the truck got up to speed on the flat highway. Asia was grateful. Something about Geneva Twohawks's shrewd brown eyes made it hard to lie to her, and something about her grandson made it hard to tell him the truth. She was glad to be able to keep quiet.

A deep blue night sky sprinkled with stars had rolled out over the desert by the time they pulled off the highway into the pot-holed parking lot of a one-room store. Jack had fallen asleep in her lap and was a dead weight in her arms as she carried him inside. Asia was close to sleepwalking herself, fatigue and relief and a strange sense of disconnectedness combining to slow her movements and her thinking. Maybe it was the last of the drugs working their way through her system? She blinked like an owl in the yellow light of the store's interior and fought to sharpen her wits. She pushed forward to the counter. In a few seconds she would be on the phone with Ethan, and it would all be over.

Geneva and Will were already standing at the counter speaking with the tall, broad-shouldered man behind it, but he was shaking his head. He looked at her with sympathy.

"I'm sorry, ma'am." He had a voice as deep as the night outside. "Phone's been down since last night. Prairie dogs got in the connection box and chewed up the wires but good. I can't get a man out here to fix it 'til end of the week."

The man was still talking, but Asia was no longer listening. She had slumped to the floor in despair, Jack still draped over her shoulder as though dead.

CHAPTER SIXTEEN

Interstate 40, Somewhere near Gallup, New Mexico, Earth, Sector Three

She had wanted to cry like a helpless child.

Goddamn it, Lana thought, *I never even was a helpless child, and it was all I could do to keep from blubbering like one. What the hell is wrong with me?*

Her near-breakdown had occurred hours ago—though it seemed like days ago—in Oklahoma. They were a third of the way through New Mexico now, and her eyes felt like they were full of sand, her neck and shoulders were wrung tight as a dishrag, her hips and lower back were fused solid and her right foot was numb over the accelerator. She'd been driving for the last three hours; it was time for another change, thank God. But they were still hours behind Jack and Asia, who Sam said had stopped somewhere in the Arizona desert. She pressed the pedal a little closer to the metal.

God damn Gabriel Cruz anyway. Damn him for making her cry and double damn him for looking at her with that hunger in his eyes and triple damn him to hell for making her want him as much as he wanted her. She had never needed anyone—she still didn't, damn it!—so why did she ache to have his arms around her? It made no kind of sense.

Lana stole a glance at him. He was watching the dramatic desert scenery slide past the window, his tall frame wedged between the door and the dash, one forearm resting on a knee. At rest like this, his face looked as if he had never had reason to smile, as though he didn't know how. His was a face to break your heart.

Gabriel turned in her direction and lifted one eyebrow. "You okay? Need to change drivers?"

"I'll be okay for a while."

"We can stop and eat in Gallup if you want—change there."

"Sounds good."

There was a small silence.

Gabriel dropped a question into it. "What was your mom like, Lana?"

It was as if he had stuck a dentist's drill into her mouth and hit a rotten tooth. She shot him a look that should have fried him in his seat.

"Why the hell would you ask me that?"

He shrugged. "I thought maybe we could try to get to know each other the usual way. You know, like you said earlier. A little at a time."

"Kinda late for that, don't you think? You want to know about me all you have to do is rummage around in the pile of junk you stole from my mind."

"I could. But, as you found out, there's a lot in there that's not so easy to interpret."

She glared at him. "A woman lying in a pool of blood shouldn't be so hard to interpret."

"Context is everything," Gabriel answered softly.

"You want context?" She couldn't match his tone. Instead her words came hard and fast. "Okay, how's this for context? I'm nine years old. I get off the school bus. I'm thinking, I gotta show Mom the A I got on the spelling test today, and, oh, don't forget there's a Girl Scout meeting tomorrow. I go in the house, and there she is on the kitchen floor, her brains all over like a bunch of scrambled eggs and ketchup. I try to scream, but I can't breathe, my lungs just lock up. I can't move. I can't even close my eyes. I just keep seeing her there. When I finally figure out I have to do something, I go next door, and I try to tell the next door neighbor what's happened, and the bitch won't understand me. She thinks I've had a big attack of imagination or something. It takes her for-fucking-ever to *pay attention* and go back over there with me. Oh, then there's some screaming, boy, I'll tell you what!"

Lana finally wound down, the story having spilled out of her like poison. She took her eyes off the road to see Gabriel with his head back against the headrest, his eyes closed against the pain in her voice, in her heart. Of course, he knew. He was living it all with her now.

"Damn it, Gabriel, I had all this strapped down tight until you came along." Now the detritus of her life was loose and crashing around in her heart, causing new damage. It made her feel too weary even to weep.

He looked at her, more sympathy than she wanted in his dark eyes. "You could think of it as redistributing the load."

"No." The word had an edge. "This shit is mine. Don't you get it? I would never have shared it with you in the first place. You're a thief. Just because the stuff you stole is toxic doesn't make the theft any less wrong."

"I didn't mean to take it, Lana, and I can't give it back. Maybe you should think about letting some of it go."

Fresh anger, white hot and blistering, rose in her throat. "Let it go? What about your own puddle of blood, Cruz, you wanna let that one go? My mom was a suicide. Not so for that guy in your mom's foyer, huh? And I'm thinking you know who killed him."

She went still, her mouth gaping open in shock, as Gabriel watched her with eyes that had gone as black as death. Her mouth went dry. Her hands were shaking so much it was all she could do to keep the car on the road.

"Pull over."

"What?" Her head swung around to look at him, and her hand went to the spot under her left arm where her shoulder holster normally rested. "Why?"

He uncoiled from his recumbent position and was poised for action, every muscle tense. "Pull off the fucking road, Alana, before you wreck the damn car."

She did as he commanded, cursing herself for having left her weapons in her bag in the back seat. The man next to her now seemed very dangerous, the conversation they were about to have potentially explosive. Her sense of security had shattered. She wanted very much to have the comfort of that Glock close to hand before she next opened her mouth.

Lana stopped the car and turned to confront him. Gabriel was turned sideways, one arm braced on the seat back, the other on the dash, his face an angry storm cloud ready to break.

"What is it you think you know, Lana?"

Temper overran her fear. "What I *know* wouldn't fill a shot glass. What I'm guessing, though, is that you're *related* to those bastards who are chasing Jack and Asia—the ones who almost killed me. They're your *brothers,* right? And that body on the floor that I keep seeing? That was your father's work somehow. How'm I doing?"

She saw him take a deep breath and the anger in his face morphed into something close to pain. He ran a hand through his hair and looked out the windshield for a long moment before he faced her.

"Yes. Kinnian and Trevyn Dar are my half-brothers. They grew up with my father, Kylan. I lived with my mother. She owned a tavern in a port town. He was passing through." His voice took on a bitter edge. "The way she told the story it was a mutual attraction."

As he spoke she saw them—Kylan, tall and dark, teeth flashing white against a heavy beard; Kinnian, almost a clone of his father; Trevyn, clean-shaven and fair, sadness shadowing his deep-set eyes; and his mother, coffee-colored eyes like Gabriel's and a smile like an angel.

The faces were replaced by the scene she'd viewed

over and over. "The murder—what happened?"

Gabriel sighed. "My older sister's husband. A political assassination."

Her mind filled in the details. *Voran Ptorak had been a member of something called Rescue, with enemies too numerous to name. Gabriel's sister had been pregnant with his child. She delivered safely after the murder—a girl—but killed herself before the child's first birthday.*

"No one was ever prosecuted for the crime," Gabriel was saying, "but it was known to be Kylan's work."

Lana's heart thudded in her chest. "His work?"

"My father was a Hunter, a mercenary paid to track, kidnap, assassinate, sabotage and steal. My brothers carry on the family business."

"They use psi skills to do these things?" She asked the question though she knew the answer.

"Yes."

She looked at Gabriel for a long time, unable to speak. She hardly knew how to name the emotions that squeezed her heart until it threatened to explode in her chest. Anger, yes, and betrayal and a sadness so deep it seemed to have no bottom. Hurt and longing and need. Dismay and denial.

And yet, despite everything, a stubborn tattered scrap of belief—in him.

Still, she had to ask. "What about you, Gabriel?" She found his gaze and held it. "How is what you do any different from the family business?"

His face turned to stone. "Look inside, Alana. You know my heart if you would only look at it. I have no other answer to give you."

Asia opened her eyes and saw Geneva Twohawks's weathered face hanging over her. "Get up, Timewalker. We have no time to waste here."

"What?"

The old woman just grinned and told the others in the store, "She's waking up." She turned back to her. "Come on, Asia. Sit up, now, and have some water." She held out a bottle.

Asia took it and swallowed in grateful gulps. "Jack?"

"He's right here." Geneva pulled the boy into view. Jack stared at her, a slight frown his only indication of concern. God, he was so withdrawn.

"I have to get to a phone." She started to get up, but dizziness caught her halfway to her feet and drove her to her knees. She stayed there, reeling.

"Whoa, there, lady." The store owner hustled over to hover close enough to catch her if needed. "Take it easy. Just sit for a minute. You're probably a little low on water."

She settled back down onto the floor and put a hand to her head. She couldn't think.

"Look. My husband will be worried about me. I should have checked in by now. I need to get to a phone."

"Where is your husband anyway?" Will's voice was a suspicious drawl.

Geneva snapped something in a language Asia didn't understand.

"I'm just asking," he shot back. "Seems kinda strange she'd be out here all by herself."

Her heart began a slow thud in her chest. The lanky Indian was a threat somehow, though why she should feel that way, she didn't know.

"We're in the middle of a move from Nashville to L.A.," she lied. "He can't leave Nashville for another week."

The old woman gave her grandson another tongue-lashing.

"You're crazy." He gave Asia a last sideways glance and stomped off to another part of the store.

"Don't mind him." Geneva waved a hand in the young man's direction, dismissing him. "I know why you're here."

Asia's mouth fell open. "But, I—"

"Shh. You come home with me. You and the boy. You'll be safe there."

Asia shook her head and scrambled to her feet. "Thanks. We can find a motel."

"Will says he's going into Winslow tonight," the store owner said. "Guess you could go with him."

Asia nodded, hope rising.

"No!" Geneva gestured at the store owner. "Go on back to work, Joseph. I have to speak with Asia."

"Yes, ma'am." He was gone with a nod.

Asia squared her shoulders. "Miz Twohawks, thank you for all your help, but I need to ask your grandson to take me into Winslow with him."

The woman's eyes blazed. "You will not ask him. You will not go with him. He is a danger to you and your son."

"What? Your own grandson?"

"Will is my blood, but he has long since closed his ears to me. He listens to alcohol now, and drugs, to easy money and loose women. Can you tell me if someone speaking his language asked him about you, it wouldn't matter?" Geneva paused to let that message sink in. "He wouldn't take you somewhere safe. He would sell you to the highest bidder. Do you understand?"

"My God!" Asia felt the strength of her legs dissolve like so much sand washed away by strong rain. "How do you know?"

"It is my place to know." Geneva's smile was grim. "Come. You and the boy will stay with me. We can do what must be done to keep you safe."

Asia was shaking, her legs unwilling to carry her as she followed Geneva out the door. Will stood with the store owner, smoking and drinking a beer in the thin light spilling from the storefront.

His grandmother smacked him on the shoulder. "Hey, hardhead, we're going home."

"About time. You know I got to get to Winslow tonight." He looked at Asia. "I could take you into town, if you want. You could make that phone call."

Before she could answer, Geneva spoke. "It's late. She and the boy are exhausted. They don't need to be hanging around the bars with you. They're coming home with me. You call for her."

"Me? What's her old man gonna think, me calling?"

"He's gonna think you're a good man, making the call like that, that's what." Geneva looked up into her grandson's slack face. "He's gonna stop worrying so hard, maybe. And maybe you're gonna win some positive attention from the ancestors, for once."

Will scowled. "Shit."

Geneva turned to the store owner. "When Leonard Begay comes by tomorrow, tell him I need to see him and Martha."

"Yes, ma'am, Miz Twohawks, I'll do that. If I don't see them I'll let them know as soon as the phone gets fixed."

"You'll see them." She nodded and ushered her wards into the truck.

Asia looked back as they drove away from the lonely store, wondering if they had left the last of civilization behind them—or if it was just her mind she had left in the dust of the pickup.

Aboard the Bloodstalker, in Orbit, Earth, Sector Three

"You smell of sex, brother." Kinnian's lip curled in

a smile that was more derision than amusement. "Who was it—that stupid helmsman's apprentice you confined to quarters the day we hit orbit? Or the slut down in engineering you favor when you're trying to work out a thorny navigational problem?"

Trevyn sank into the chair on the other side of the desk from his captain and used all his skill to appear unaffected by Kinnian's perceptiveness. "There are advantages to keeping a woman confined to quarters." He let a smug smile slide across his face. "She was very grateful for the distraction." And, gods, he had needed her soft skin under his hands, her tight, hot core around his *draum*. He had needed her reality to ground him before his visions of another man's woman tore him apart.

"Ha! I'm certain she was! Maybe I need to pay her a visit myself, hmm?"

Trevyn's heart stuttered. "Give her some time, my lord." He tried to keep his tone light. "I left her with little energy for you."

Kinnian laughed again. "I don't doubt it, little brother! Maybe tomorrow!" His sibling heaved his body out of his chair and paced across his cabin to pour himself a draft of ale. He poured a second mug for Trevyn and passed it over. "I'm not in a giving mood, at any rate."

Trevyn drank, raising his eyebrows in question.

"When will our quarry arrive at Groom Lake?" Kinnian took up his stalking across the cabin again. "The wait is killing me."

"We have several more hours yet, perhaps as much as a full day dirtside. We can't know how fast the men are moving with the boy. Planetary technology is primitive; it requires frequent maintenance and refueling. Don't worry. They'll be there soon enough and everything is ready for them."

Kinnian stopped his pacing and glared at him. "What if you're wrong about this place?"

"I'm not wrong."

His brother bared his teeth. "And yet I sense your fear."

Trevyn shrugged. "What you sense is legitimate apprehension, my lord. The boy is powerful, and the men transporting him across many kilometers of uninhabited country have little idea of what he can do."

Kinnian cocked his head. "Are you saying you think the boy can engineer his own escape from them?"

"It's unlikely, but possible." He held up a hand to forestall his brother's impending fit of temper. "I'm monitoring communications in the organization that has him. If anything happens in transit, I'm sure I'll hear about it."

"By that time it will be too late!" The captain loomed over Trevyn's chair, an ion storm of fury. "We should have pursued the vehicle when we had a chance."

Trevyn thought it safer not to remind his brother that they'd had no information on the vehicle with which to follow it in the first place. "If the boy escapes his captors, his first instinct will be to contact the authorities and try to get home. We are monitoring *all* communications, my lord. We will be on him before those keeping him can clear their throats."

Kinnian froze, thinking it through. Then he relaxed and began to laugh. "Ah, Trevyn, you do have your uses. It is a wonder, though, that I haven't killed you before now, the way you make me sweat."

The younger man brought the mug of ale to his lips and drank it dry. "You should learn to trust me."

His captain's eyes narrowed. "Not bloody likely."

Trevyn grunted. *I didn't think so.*

In one swift movement, Kinnian stepped closer and grabbed him by the hair, forcing his head back to look up at him. "You are far too clever for your own good, brother. There is the stench of something other than sex about you lately. Betrayal, perhaps? Or perhaps simply ambition. Whatever it is, my gut tells me Gabriel's sudden reappearance in our lives has something to do with it. You always cried after our oldest sibling like a mewling babe."

Trevyn's eyes flashed—he could feel it, he couldn't help himself—but it was the only sign he gave of his reaction. He took his emotions, his knowledge and all his connections and buried them deep, as deep as any blue ocean, as unreachable as any dark recess in the planet spinning below them.

"Gabriel again," he said, as though he was merely annoyed. "What is it that disturbs you so much about our sibling?"

Kinnian held his gaze for one more second, then

threw him off. "Did you know Father had a plan to use our bastard brother to forge us into a weapon he could have wielded to take all of Thrane? You and I alone were too weak, not good enough. He had to have that son of a Terran whore to make it work. But Rodyn had turned Gabriel against us. The old slave hid the bastard. And Father spent our inheritance scouring the galaxy for Gabriel, trying to kill him, until the old *merox* died himself."

Kinnian took up his angry pacing again. "Our brother has grown stronger since the last time we fought him. I was certain I had a link to him, but I can't seem to open it. Every time I try, I'm diverted, or I'm entertained with drivel in a remote corner of his consciousness. He has set traps within traps to keep me from unlocking his secrets. It's frustrating."

No, it's heartening. Trevyn rejoiced in the depths of his soul. He only hoped Gabriel could maintain his defenses in the face of such an onslaught.

"Still, I've begun to sniff a weakness," the captain was saying. "The last time I made a run at him, there was something new, something"—he paused, almost tasting the air—"soft. I don't know what it is yet. But I will find it, Trevyn. As I am Kylan Dar's son, I will find it. And I will use it to rip Gabriel's mind into a thousand bloody pieces."

CHAPTER SEVENTEEN

The teacher turned to him, a glint in his gray eyes. "I say we owe the galaxy a civilized Thrane to make up for the butcher that is his father. What is your name, boy?"

"Gabriel Cruz, sir. And I am human, not Thrane."

Lana sat bolt upright in the unmoving vehicle, her eyes seeking light, her lungs gasping for breath in the airless void of night. The child that Gabriel had been had stood up for the part of him that was human, but Lana saw what the others that day had seen—part of him was not of this Earth. His father was Thrane, his brothers were Thrane, and his memories in her mind showed her everything that meant—the cruelty, the conquests, the centuries of war. The bloodlines, the psi talents, the laws that held them in check.

Then, more proof, if any had been necessary: the image she had first seen when she'd touched his scars, of the fight on the dark side of Azreeni VI. Just one of so many fights on so many exotic planets, the creature dying beneath him just one of so many other unimaginable, inhuman creatures he had seen in his lifetime. Image after image, place after place, memory after memory flooded her consciousness until she was shaking and weak. *Jesus Christ!* Was she crazy or was he? Aliens? Other planets?

And . . . holy mother of God, she had . . .

She clawed open the car door and stumbled out of the vehicle. It was all she could do to keep her feet—and the contents of her stomach—as she gulped in huge breaths of cold desert air. They were pulled just off a secondary road onto a flat stretch of hardpan, and she was alone. Stars wheeled overhead. God, it was quiet! Her heart was like thunder in her chest.

A flashlight winked a few paces away and began to bob in her direction. "Lana?"

Oh, Jesus! She wanted to run. She wanted to fight. She wanted to do anything but talk to Gabriel Cruz. Who wasn't human.

"Lana," he said, as he got within speaking range. "I found the vehicle."

"Don't come any closer." *Damn it, why didn't I go for my Glock?*

"What?" He kept walking. "What's wrong?"

She backed up until her butt hit the car's hood. "I mean it. Stay where you are. *Thrane.*"

He froze for an instant. Then he was on her, pinning both hands behind her as he loomed over her. Her training was useless against his size, his experience and the raging hurt she could see in his black eyes.

"Never call me that. Never!"

"Why not? It's what you are, isn't it? Something . . . alien. Just like the ones who are chasing Asia and Jack!"

His grip tightened on her wrists, and his hips slammed into her pelvis. His words came out in a feral growl.

"I'm nothing like them. I've fought all my life to be something more than a butcher or a coward, to escape my father's bloody legacy. And now when I look in your eyes I see it all staring back at me."

Lana's breath came in short, raspy gasps; her heart thrashed against her ribcage, unable to settle into a steady beat. He was too close, his lips inches from hers, his chest crushing hers, his hard length stabbing into her hip. Fear and anger warred with desire in her rebellious body. Her blood heated in her veins; molten fire pooled in her belly. She wanted to hate him; she wanted to fuck him. Christ almighty, she had no idea what the hell she wanted.

"Get the fuck away from me!" She pushed at him, if only to save the last shred of her self-respect. He didn't move. "Let me go!"

"I will never let you go, Alana." His breath was hot against her lips. "I can't let you go. We're connected, you and I, body and soul, joined in a way even I don't understand. And it's no more within my control than the rotation of this Earth."

His eyes held hers, and in that gaze was more heat, more longing, more certainty of loss, than Lana had ever seen. If she had doubted his humanity, he could have given her no more proof of it than that last, lingering look before he released her and turned away.

Shame—and desire—sent a hot wash of blood to her face, but pride refused to let her acknowledge it. She fought for control of her voice.

"Wait, Gabriel." She needed to understand all the ramifications. "What exactly does it mean for Asia and Jack that the . . . men . . . hunting them are Thrane?"

He turned back, cold rage icing his features. "It means we need to stop fighting like stupid children and find that woman and her child. Or my *alien* brother will turn her mind inside out, flay the flesh from her bones and take the boy beyond our help."

"The boy," she repeated in a whisper. Knowledge that had been Gabriel's forced its way to the forefront of her consciousness. "Jesus God!"

Gabriel drew a hand through his hair and blew out an exasperated breath. "*Dios*, woman, can we please just have this out now? Dig deep. Let yourself see what I know. And let's move on, for God's sake."

Searing anger swept through her. She pushed off the warm metal of the car to lunge at him. "Did it ever occur to you that what you 'know' might appear slightly *insane* to someone like me? Little gray aliens abducting humans for slave labor? Mindsucking warriors from another planet hunting an innocent human boy who just may have some kind of secret powers? No, wait—a whole galaxy full of other beings!"

She stood inches from him, staring up into the hard planes of his face. "Yes. I built walls high and wide around what you forced into my head, Gabriel Cruz. And no wonder."

He held her gaze a moment longer, his eyes as black and cold as the desert sky. "It will do you no good, Lana. The walls will crumble eventually. The truth is the truth, and it will come to you, sooner or later. Sooner would be better for Asia and Jack."

He turned and stalked into the darkness, his shoulders rigid. Lana watched him go, struggling to wrestle command of her body back from her emotions. When she could trust her legs to carry her, she went around the back of the vehicle to retrieve her shoulder holster. She pulled the pistol from her bag, checked the chamber and slammed home a magazine, then slid it into the holster under her arm. She wasn't going to be without it from now on. What she had with Cruz was no longer a partnership; it was a truce at best, and a tenuous one at that.

Sighing, she grabbed a flashlight from her bag and went to join him at the SUV parked at the end of a line of tracks leading into the desert. The headlights from their Jeep back at the road threw angled shadows against the sand, obscuring more than they illuminated.

She forced a businesslike tone into her voice. "What do you see?"

He shook his head, frowning. "Nothing. No bodies, no blood. They were here, I can sense them."

"Then what?" She filled in the shadows with her flashlight, seeing signs of a scuffle, foot traffic leading away toward a draw off in the near distance, then returning. More footprints led toward the road, but there was only the one set of vehicle tracks. "Could have been just a breakdown. Maybe they got a ride out on the road?"

"No. There's something else."

She looked at him, waiting.

"Power. Lots of it. The air is still charged with it, like the sky before a storm. Can you feel it?"

Lana stopped, opening herself to the night. *Yes.* A hum like walking beneath a high voltage tower.

"What the hell happened?"

But Gabriel wasn't listening. He had straightened, his attention on the road.

"We're out of time."

Headlights were approaching, too fast to make it back to their vehicle before the newcomers cut them off. "Shit." Lana scanned their surroundings. "Too late to make it to the draw. We'll have to make a stand here. Maybe they'll want to talk first."

Gabriel grunted, as if that was unlikely. She agreed with him. She pulled the Glock and stood with it out of sight behind the door of the abandoned vehicle while a big Cadillac SUV roared up and jerked to a stop in a cloud of dust.

Gabriel positioned himself between Lana and the men piling out of the Caddy, though he was armed only with his souped-up TASER. Lana counted four opposing them, all but one with automatic weapons. No insignia that she could see. She eased the safety off the gun and relaxed her forearm.

Lights flashed on, blinding her.

"Hands in the air!"

Holy Christ! That voice . . .

"What the hell . . . Lana?"

She started to move forward. *NO, Lana!* Gabriel's warning echoed in her head. *He's not what you think he is!*

She put aside her shock at sharing her consciousness with him. There was no time to argue, and at the moment the ability was damn useful.

Back off. I've got this.

"Jesus Christ! Mark!" She made it sound as if he'd just thrown her a life raft in a raging sea. At the same time she waved her empty left hand and used her right to stash the gun, barrel down, in the inside door handle of the truck. She came around the outside of the door, swinging it halfway shut, and raised both hands fast enough to satisfy the trigger-happy crew surrounding FBI agent Mark Jamisky. Again she scanned them for any sign that they were Bureau agents and found none.

Jamisky nodded to his men. "Relax, fellas, I know this girl." He glanced once at Gabriel before returning his attention to Lana. Two of the three with him shifted in Gabriel's direction.

Lana's throat went dry. "So Ballard took my lead seriously after all."

"Yeah." A crooked grin lifted Jamisky's mouth. His tell, as familiar to Lana as his voice in the dark had been. He was lying. "We've been a few hours behind these guys since Little Rock. But what are you doing here? You're supposed to be off the case."

Weapons had been lowered on the other side, but Mark was several steps closer, and her adrenaline was pumping like he was a stranger rather than her former lover. She lingered around the door to the truck and didn't dare look at Gabriel.

"I'm officially on vacation." She shrugged and gave him her most charming smile. "But you know me, baby. I couldn't let it go." She raised an arm and draped it on the frame of the truck door, letting her shirt fall open to reveal both the empty holster and her breasts beneath the thin tank top she wore. As she'd anticipated, the attention of all four agents centered on her chest, if only for a second.

Gabriel moved silently into a better position behind the gunmen. *Dangerous,* targita, *very dangerous.*

If I take him, do you have them? Because he's coming in, I can feel it.

Leave them to me. His confidence came through the link like a shot of adrenaline.

Mark stepped closer, his grin fixed, his gaze hungry. His big body loomed over her.

"No, sweetheart, you never did know when to let it go." His left arm snaked around her waist and hauled her in tight; his head dipped to take her mouth in a bruising kiss. She went limp in his arms, letting his tongue plunge inside her mouth. The action that had once been so familiar, even welcome, was such a violation now that Lana couldn't control a shudder. She covered it by clutching his shoulder in pretended passion with her left hand. Her right hand dropped inside the truck door to grasp the Glock.

He ground his hard-on against her and chuckled deep in his throat. "I really am going to miss this. You should have left it alone, baby." Lana felt his right arm begin to move.

But she was faster. She brought the gun around, stuck it in his ribs and squeezed off two shots before he could bring his own weapon from the back of his waistband. She stepped back and let him drop, the shocked expression on his face oddly pleasing to her.

Gunfire boomed through the roar her own shots had created in her ears, answered by the high-pitched sizzle of Gabriel's custom weapon. As she tore her gaze from Mark's fallen body, Gabriel was kicking over the third of the thugs who had been with Jamisky, making sure he was dead. She had been too focused on Mark to see what Gabriel had done, but the bodies were evidence enough. Numb and unable to move, she watched him check his handiwork with stark efficiency.

He leaned over Jamisky to take the gun from the dead man's hand. Then he looked back up at her. She was shaking, cold with shock, but he didn't approach her.

"Are you all right?"

She nodded, not yet willing to trust her voice.

"He was your partner."

"He was more than that once." She took a wobbly step.

Before she could fall Gabriel caught her and pulled her in. *Damn it*. She wanted to resist him, but she was freezing to death in the cold of the desert, shivering in the cold of her righteous anger. She needed his warmth.

His voice rumbled in his chest. "You had no choice."

"I know." She straightened and pushed away from Gabriel. "And I'll never forgive him for it."

Navajo Nation Indian Reservation, Arizona, Earth, Sector Three

Asia awoke alone, and for a long moment her mind would not supply a location for her body. She was no longer a captive, living at the mercy of killers in the back of a truck. She wasn't at home, either, with Ethan in the bed beside her. She sat up in a mild panic.

Jack?

A mid-morning sun lit the room despite the rough-woven curtains covering the one open window. She listened. From outside came the familiar, comforting sounds of rural life—chickens murmuring and protesting in the farmyard, a sheep bleating nearby, horses whinnying somewhere at a distance. Then she heard the old woman, talking in low tones as she went about her chores, asking a question now and again, though Asia didn't hear Jack answer.

At last things began to make sense. She'd slept late

in the tiny second bedroom of Geneva Twohawks's modest doublewide. Jack was already up and gone. Asia felt more than a little guilty for abusing the woman's hospitality. Geneva had been so generous to offer her home, her help, even—she had insisted—her clothes. Asia had spent the night in a faded green tee shirt advertising the 2005 Apache County Rodeo. At the end of the bed a pair of clean, elastic-waist dungarees was neatly laid out in place of her own filthy jeans. Both the tee shirt and the dungarees were at least three sizes too large. Asia shook her head and got up to get washed and dressed. Beggars could hardly be choosers, and she was lucky to be alive this morning. She was smiling as she went out to the porch to greet her rescuer.

The desert heat was already thick in the air outside. Asia had to shield her eyes against the sun to watch the old woman and her young charge cross the farmyard. It was obvious Geneva Twohawks had been forced to go about her usual business all morning with a small, curious, strangely silent shadow following a few steps behind.

"Morning," Asia said as they approached. "Sorry I was so late getting out of bed."

"You needed to rest." Geneva looked up at her and erupted into cackles. "Better not try to run, pants thief! Those pants will fall right off your skinny butt!"

Asia's mouth fell open in shock, and she stood for a moment frozen in embarrassment. She hadn't stolen anything! The pants had been at the end of her bed!

Then she caught the twinkle of sly amusement in Geneva's dark eyes. She'd had an elderly great aunt back in Tennessee who'd made her childhood miserable with the same continual teasing until she'd learned to respond in kind.

"What pants?" She tugged on the fabric at her thighs. "When I woke up this morning my jeans were gone, and all I found was this tent with legs."

"Ha!" Geneva laughed. The brown eyes sparkled. "Your clothes had so much dirt I used them to plant my garden."

Asia nodded. "Good idea. Much less work than washing them."

Still cackling, Geneva climbed the porch steps behind Jack, and the two came even with Asia. With solemn pride, Jack showed his mom the basket he was carrying. She captured her son and gave him a hug.

"Did you gather those eggs, buddy?" The boy nodded.

The old woman patted his shoulder in approval. "He's a good worker. Come. I'll cook breakfast."

Geneva pulled out a skillet and scrambled up the eggs with some onion and tomatillo from the garden. "You like frybread?"

"Anything is good." Asia wanted to be polite, but she had no idea what frybread was. "Thank you."

"Frybread is Dineh—Navajo—food," Geneva explained, apparently reading her expression. "I have coffee, too. And dry milk for the boy."

When it was ready they ate in silence, paying

serious attention to the food. Asia hadn't realized how hungry she was until she looked up from her empty plate.

The old woman smiled. "You both eat like hungry coyotes!"

Asia blushed. "This was very good. We're grateful for all your help."

"The Holy People sent you to me," Geneva explained. "I could not turn you away."

"Not everyone would have been so kind."

Geneva shook her head. "Not kindness. It's my duty to protect the people. The evil that stalks you threatens everyone."

Asia's heart began a slow thudding in her chest. Why would she think anything was stalking them? And "evil"? As bad as the Men in Black were, she would have a hard time calling them "evil." "Ruthless," "cold," "misguided," maybe. Even the psychiatrist who had kidnapped her on their behalf two years ago had had his own warped motivations. The Grays, now, maybe you could call *them* evil.

"Miz Twohawks, I'm not sure what you mean."

The old woman held up a hand. "I know you didn't have a breakdown on the road, Timewalker. You escaped the spider, but the snake lies in wait. The boy is trying to hide from this evil in the Spirit World, but it will find him even there. And though he is powerful, he doesn't know how to fight it. I can help you. That's why the Holy People sent you to me."

Asia looked up. "That's the second time you've

called me that—Timewalker."

"Is it not the truth?"

Geneva's bright, birdlike stare demanded an answer. Asia couldn't control the trembling that shook her thin, battered body. This Navajo woman she'd just met couldn't possibly know what had happened to her, an episode of loss so horrific it had changed her life forever.

When Asia remained silent, Geneva went on. "The hawks told me in a vision: Evil ones took you far from your home; made you their slave. You were rescued and brought back, but your time was not your own. You earned your name in battle, Timewalker. You are a warrior, almost as much as your son."

Tears slid down Asia's face.

Jack rose from his seat at the table and went to her. Without a word, he put his arms around her and buried his head in her shoulder. She wrapped him up, her cheek on the top of his head.

"It's okay, buddy," she told him. "I'm okay."

Geneva watched her, waiting, her gaze sympathetic, but stern. "You do not have much time. The boy is in danger."

"No." She straightened, struggling to regain control of her thoughts. "They don't really know about Jack. They just want me. I have help waiting for me at home. I just need to get there. My husband and I—and Jack— we have allies. They can help us. This is not your fight, though I thank you for being willing to make it yours."

Geneva's hand smacked the table in frustration.

"Foolish woman! The enemy you see is not the enemy who will defeat you! Those men in the truck? They are no threat to you. You saw what Jack did to them."

Asia stared at her in shock. "You know . . .?"

"It is no matter." Geneva dismissed it with a wave of her hand. "There are two others—brothers—who hunt you. They are not of this world. One is shadow, one is light, but is swallowed by the shadow. If they find you, here or in the Spirit World, they will kill you and use Jack to work a terrible wrong. Many people will die."

"*What?*" It was what she had feared since the moment she had sensed the power in Jack. That kind of power could be a means to an end, and in the wrong hands—"They want Jack?"

"They have been sent from far away to find him. They can hunt even in the Spirit World. And they will not stop until they capture their prey."

Asia licked at dry lips. Rescue had found Jack in a Minertsan processing center. Could the Grays want him back?

"How—no, don't tell me—another vision?"

"I have been the hawks' favorite since I was the boy's age. Without them I would not be a singer for the tribe. Few women are called, or allowed, even if they feel the calling. But the hawks were very insistent." Geneva smiled. "Eventually I even had to take their name before they would be satisfied."

Asia blew out a breath. "I suppose the hawks told you what to do about these two brothers?"

"Yes." Geneva got up to carry her dishes to the sink. She pointed out the window to a cloud of dust indicating the approach of a pickup on the road. "They said call a meeting of the elders and talk about it."

Gabriel was beginning to wonder how long he could survive living in close proximity to Alana Matheson. He had thought it would get easier over time, that his body would stop responding to the stimulus of her scent or her nearness. He had thought that he'd tire of sifting through the secrets of her life and her personality, that he'd eventually find no delight in the nuances of her intelligence or memory, that she'd begin to bore him.

But instead, every day, every moment with her heightened the tension, refined the torture until he was a vibrating string ready to snap off its posts at the slightest tweak. They did nothing but argue and snarl at each other. She hated him with a bitterness that was almost palpable. She tried his patience beyond all endurance. Still, he wanted her. He could think of little else. God, she was driving him crazy!

They had finished cleaning up the mess in the desert and rolled into Winslow long past midnight. Some kind of big event had filled most of the decent motel rooms in town. They'd finally agreed—after considerable argument—to share the last room available at an independent on the edge of town. The motel was clean, at least, and didn't appear to rent the rooms by the hour. The argument had bloomed again when they saw that there was a single, king-sized bed in the room, rather than the two doubles they had expected. The oversize shower made up for it, so they'd called a truce at last and collapsed onto the outer edges of the huge bed.

He'd awakened hard and hungry, shaking with the need to reach out and pull her into his arms. But she'd rolled away from him and out of bed without so much as a glance, padding off to the bathroom in the tee-shirt and soft little shorts she wore to bed, as if he was just another pillow on the mattress. He'd taken extra time in the shower later, but it hadn't helped. The edge he'd been riding for days was just as sharp as ever.

And then there was Kinnian. The assault of his brother's mind was like an ever-rising flood beating against the levees of his shields. A part of his consciousness was constantly devoted to patrolling his defenses, searching for and repairing the leaks that sprang up under the pressure of Kinnian's attack. If Gabriel had let himself think about it—and he didn't, not even for a second—he would have admitted to a healthy amount of . . . apprehension. Kinnian was strong and he was skilled—and he had the power of the Blood Legion behind him. It was only a matter of time before he found a way in. When that happened, Gabriel would need all his training and years of experience to defeat his sibling. If that was even still possible.

Gabriel stared at the map of Arizona spread out among the remains of breakfast on the table in front of him and considered that finding Asia and Jack might be the easier of the many problems facing him this morning.

"Why do you suppose we haven't heard from them?" Lana's hands were wrapped around a mug of coffee, her eyes on the desert outside the window. "It just doesn't make sense. This wasn't a transfer or a simple breakdown. We didn't see any other vehicle tracks out there. You say Kinnian doesn't have them. So where are they?"

"I would know if Kinnian had them." Even he seemed to need the reassurance of hearing it out loud, but he knew in his gut that Kinnian would lose no opportunity to gloat if he had the boy. "Everything points to an escape attempt. Jamisky clearly was not working for the FBI last night. He was working for whoever took Asia and Jack in the first place. Something went wrong. He was there to clean up their mess and find the woman, if he could."

Asia sighed and rubbed her eyes. A surge of protectiveness rose up to squeeze his heart as he watched her.

"Yeah, that was a pleasant surprise—Mark collecting two paychecks. But then he was ambitious, and he could be a devious sonofabitch, too. I'd always considered myself lucky to be on his good side. Guess my luck ran out, huh?"

"That's not how I see it. He's the one we buried in the desert."

The way her jaw clenched made him want the

D o n n a   S .   F r e l i c k

insensitive words back. He reached out and touched her arm.

"He gave you no choice, Lana. From the moment he saw us there, he meant to kill us both. That's the kind of organization we're dealing with."

She pulled her arm back. "I know."

"Okay, so they may have escaped, but they haven't checked in." Not even with Ethan. Gabriel had confirmed as much with a quick conversation with Sam earlier. He didn't want to consider why the boy had suddenly gone silent. His tone turned brisk. "They could be on foot, no access to a phone. They could still be in the hands of one or more of their captors, though it's hard to maintain control of that kind of situation. It's more probable they escaped and are in hiding with someone local, again, with no access to a phone."

"Jeez, what is this, one of your desert planets, spaceman? *Everybody* has access to a phone."

Gabriel was caught between amusement and irritation. "Obviously you don't know your own planet very well. Look at this map. Lots of empty space. That means no cell towers, no fiber optics, no cable. Just kilometers of wires. Phone service is not always reliable in areas like this."

"Like you're an expert."

He shrugged. "Empty space is empty space, no matter what part of the galaxy you're in." A slow smile touched his lips. "Technology does make a difference, though."

He could see her making the connections as she

stared at him. "It's Sam's ship. That's how you got all that great tracking data."

"Yes, but it won't do us a lot of good today. Too much area to cover, no known search parameters."

Lana gave herself a little shake. "Right. So we're left with a lot of plain, old-fashioned legwork, then, huh?"

"If by that you mean we have to use the vehicle to canvass these small towns and ask if anyone's seen our people, then, yes, that's what we're left with."

Lana sighed, gathering up the map. "Then I think we're in for a long day."

CHAPTER EIGHTEEN

Aboard the Bloodstalker, in Orbit, Earth, Sector Three

Commander Trevyn Dar prowled the bridge of the *Bloodstalker*, balanced in exquisite agony on the edge of a mortifying loss of control. His heart pounded, his blood raced, he *ached,* and no amount of shifting, pacing or distraction would ease him. It might cost him his life, but he was going to have to take the ship's pilot off this deck soon and fuck her until neither of them could walk.

The godsdamned woman could not learn to keep her thoughts to herself. She was thinking of all the things she would like to do to him—some of which she had already tried to considerable effect—and she was broadcasting her most intimate ideas to the entire bridge. The Thrane members of the crew were too horrified to be amused. They expected to die for the bad luck of having witnessed their commander's embarrassment. For his part, Trevyn just wanted her to stop thinking and start licking and nipping and squeezing and sucking. Gods, please, yes, *sucking*.

He didn't consider for more than a moment that it was Lana's face he saw in his fantasy, not the lieutenant's.

The communications officer interrupted his obsessive thinking. "Commander, flags have appeared on several of the comm links you are monitoring. Would you like to see them now or should I bundle them for you to view later?"

Trevyn could have read them via the wetware in his brain, but the interference from his helm officer made concentration difficult. He strode from the conn to his usual bridge station.

"Send them to my personal comm screen now, Vran."

He scanned the messages, communications traffic from within the organization STEELWALL. As he read he was forced to call upon every discipline he knew to maintain a neutral expression. The crew on the bridge would have expected him to scowl, or curse, at the news he'd received. But instead he felt like whooping in fierce joy, no matter that it was likely to cost him if not his life, then a good measure of his skin. Kinnian would certainly demand *something* in payment for his miscalculation.

The humans had lost their quarry. The boy and his mother had escaped into the desert. The team that had been with them had vanished; the team sent to retrieve them had not reported in. The boy was more powerful than the humans knew. In fact, none of their communications mentioned him at all. They were only interested in the woman and her "special knowledge."

Trevyn finally did release a curse at the humans' stupidity. The Minertsans had been using humanity as chattel for centuries and the best the human leaders could do was to brutalize or remain ignorant of the ones who could help them?

Still, this did not solve his immediate problem. The prey had slipped out of their grasp, and an easy catch at the confined facility of Groom Lake had now become a more time-consuming chase through the open territory of Arizona. Kinnian would be furious. And it was Trevyn's next job to tell him.

He straightened from his compscreen and turned to his communications officer. "Vran, take the conn. I will be in the Captain's cabin."

His beautiful but indiscreet helm officer met his eyes as he passed her station on his way out. What she saw there was enough to shut down the constant stream of her amorous thoughts. He noticed the pilot returned her full attention to her instruments as quickly as possible. Even she could read what was in his mind and wanted no part of it.

He made his way to the captain's cabin, knocked twice on the metal hatch and entered when he heard the bellow from inside. He took up a position in front of the desk and waited for Kinnian to turn from the compscreen to speak.

Kinnian gave him no chance. The captain spun with a snarl and laid a backhand across his face.

"*Pultafa!*" he cursed. "*Shalssiti pultafa!*"

Trevyn's head snapped back as Kinnian's fist connected with his cheek. His teeth rattled, and he tasted blood. And yet, stupidly, he stood his ground, his legs unable or unwilling to move. His brother struck him twice more in the face, knuckles smashing into his nose and mouth until the blood spurted over his chest. He staggered back, but he did not fall.

"You limp-dicked, bastard cast-off of a human whore!" Kinnian grasped him by the shoulders and kneed him hard enough to drive his balls up into his abdomen. Trevyn sank to his knees, fighting for breath, the contents of his stomach rising in his throat. Kinnian began to swear again and at the end of the string of curses, he aimed a kick at Trevyn's exposed ribs. Agony exploded in Trevyn's side as the ribs caved inward. On his hands and knees, Trevyn called on a lifetime of training to get him through the pain, to give him the strength to survive until he could pull in one more sustaining breath.

At last he looked up at his sibling. "If you had wanted me on your knees before you, my lord, you need only have asked."

Kinnian's fist slammed into the back of his head. "I told you. I warned you that this would happen. But no, you had a plan. And now the quarry is on the run again. What is the plan now, you worthless *fmat*?" The captain of the *Bloodstalker* loomed over him. "Tell me before I strip the flesh from your bones and bleed you to death."

"I know where they escaped." His split lip made

forming each syllable a struggle. "A STEELWALL team should be arriving there soon to start its own search. It should give you some pleasure to question them. Meanwhile, the boy cannot hide for long. He will be trying to get home. I will find him."

Kinnian regarded him. "Very well. We'll go now and see what we will see. Organize a landing party."

"Yes, my lord." His pride demanded he stand upright. He used the last of his courage to push himself to his feet.

"It is well that you remain useful, Commander." Kinnian lifted his lip in a sneer. "You have no idea how close you came to death today."

Trevyn spit blood from his mouth and tried to pull in a breath around his wounded ribs. His brother was wrong. Only he knew just how close he lived to that black pit and how little it would take to step over the edge.

"I serve at your will, my lord." He bowed and took leave of his murderous sibling.

Navajo Nation Indian Reservation, Arizona, Earth, Sector Three

Visitors had been arriving at Geneva Twohawks's place all morning in their dusty pickups and ten-year-old Jeeps. The old woman had sent out the call, and the elders of her community had answered, leaving their homes and their personal obligations to do what was needed for the benefit of their people. They'd gathered under an open-sided shelter in the shade of a twisted piñon pine behind Geneva's trailer. Some of the women had brought food to be shared, and a tall, steel enamel coffeepot was kept boiling on a small fire to keep everyone supplied with coffee. People stood in quiet groups and talked or sat on rough wooden benches and mismatched folding chairs, throwing an occasional glance in the direction of the outsider who was the cause of all the fuss.

Asia had nodded in polite response to the greetings each person extended as he or she arrived. She'd smiled at the shopkeeper from the night before, who had offered her a cheery wave as he joined the throng. Beneath her smile she was anything but comfortable. Just how many people was Geneva going to bring into this? How much was she going to tell them? And what the hell was the point of all this anyway?

Jack was frozen in place beside her, his face blank and unresponsive. He had gone to the Spirit World again, Geneva said, "hiding from us." She didn't seem concerned, and the elders simply nodded when they saw him. But Asia was worried. If the brothers that Geneva spoke of could find him there, he wasn't safe. And God knew she couldn't help him if they attacked him in a dimension she didn't even understand.

By some unspoken agreement it was finally determined everyone was in place. An ancient, nut-brown man, his silver hair hanging in a long braid, made as if to stand. The two younger men on either side of him each took an elbow to help him, and the gathering came to attention.

Geneva, sitting at Asia's side, explained: "Jeremiah Nakai is the eldest *hata'lii* of the tribe. He's gonna ask the *Yei*—the Holy Ones—and the ancestors for a blessing so we don't screw up today."

Asia thought that was probably a good idea, no matter what else happened.

The old man's thin, high crooning was more song than speech, full of entreaty and well-worn ritual. Asia looked down as Nakai prayed and saw Jack watching him, transfixed and fully present.

Nakai tottered to his place and sat down again. Geneva Twohawks stood.

"Elders. Thank you for coming here today. What I have to tell you is very important to all the people, though some of you will doubt me. All of you know that the hawks speak to me. They have chosen me as their voice, and I have always tried to speak as they have told it to me."

Asia scanned those assembled. There were nods of assent from many in Geneva's audience, but one man watched her with open hostility. He sat on the edge of his seat, as if he couldn't wait to speak.

"For a while the hawks have been speaking to me about these two outsiders." She inclined her head in Asia's direction. "The woman they named Timewalker, because she was stolen from this world by evil beings, forced to walk in a different place and time before returning to find her home and her family were lost.

The boy they call the Striking Stone, because others would use him to start a fire to end the world. He has the power to walk both in this world and in the Spirit World, and he can use this power to see and to speak over great distances. But he is just a boy, and there are evil ones hunting him who threaten us all. I am asking that we use our knowledge of the Spirit World to protect him in the battle to come."

Geneva turned to Asia with a small smile. "I'm going to repeat some of that in our own language." She shrugged. "Some of the older people prefer to speak it. So the discussion will probably be in Dineh also."

Asia smiled back. "I understand."

She glanced at the man she had seen watching Geneva with such animosity. He stared back at her, his eyes black and cold. He looked away, toward the speaker, but it was clear he was only biding his time. New voices droned on in the language of the Navajo, each of the elders taking a turn responding to the problem that had been presented to them. Asia settled back against the warped metal of the chair in which she sat and closed her eyes, hoping that it didn't seem impolite. Jack slipped to the floor beside her and began to amuse himself with a pencil and paper that Geneva had given him earlier.

Asia was impressed that no one so far had batted an eye at the whole time-walking/Spirit World-battling/evil hunters-baiting aspect of the strangers among them. An equal number of WASPs from her home town would not have taken this so well. And yet the issues were profound for this little community. They were at risk even now, just by giving strangers shelter from their kidnappers, who were no doubt scouring the desert for them. Geneva was proposing they stand up and fight the "evil ones," with what weapons Asia didn't know, and with what consequences *no one* could possibly know. It made no sense.

Asia opened her eyes and sat up, waiting for a plump woman in a pale blue polyester pantsuit to finish her speech. She couldn't allow these people to put themselves at risk, no matter what Geneva said; she had to put a stop to it. When the woman sat down to nods all around, Asia started to stand up. Geneva clamped a hand on her thigh and shook her head. By the time she'd recovered, she saw the man she'd been watching was on his feet.

"Elders. Please forgive me for speaking in the language of the outsiders, but I want to be sure this one understands what I say." The man's baleful gaze was aimed straight at Asia and Jack. "I came here today even though I had sick animals on my ranch and fences to mend. I came because the people said a matter of great urgency would be discussed. And yet I see we are here because two outsiders are in trouble. They have brought trouble to us. We talk of evil openly when we have been taught that to speak of evil brings evil among us."

A whisper went through the assembly, of agreement, or of fear, Asia couldn't tell.

"If evil follows these two it must be because they did something to attract it." The man's logic was relentless. "That is what the old ones tell us. If we keep them here, the evil will come to us. They are outsiders, not Dineh. We have no obligation to protect them. Let them go to their own people for protection. Our ceremonies are not for outsiders."

The man took his seat again and the murmurs grew louder, more insistent. Asia could see plenty of nods in the crowd.

Before anyone else could stand and defend her, Asia was on her feet. She refused to look at Geneva, who she was certain was ready to toss lightning in her direction.

"Elders. I thank all of you for coming today, and I especially thank Geneva Twohawks for her efforts on my behalf and my son's." She had paid careful attention to how things were phrased, and she followed suit. "All that she has said about me is true. I believe what she says about my son. But some of what this man says is true, too. The people who are searching for us are dangerous. Just the fact that my son and I are here puts all of you at risk. I believe there must be other ways to defeat the ones that hunt us without putting you all in danger. Just help us return to my husband. He and our friends can protect us. Please. This is not your fight. I beg you, don't put yourselves in the line of fire."

There was silence as all in the gathering studied her face for signs of *what? Intention? Sincerity? Insanity?* Asia waited, unsure whether she'd committed an unforgiveable breach of etiquette or deeply offended Geneva, whose face was as unreadable as Jack's. Only the man who had opposed her presence seemed satisfied. He sat with a smug little smile on his face, waiting like all the others.

A man nearly as tall as the shelter's low ceiling, with shoulders as wide as a wrestler's, stood to face Asia. He was a younger man, his hair black and glossy, his features as sharp as the intelligence in his eyes.

"My name is Leonard Begay." His deep voice was a match to his size. "I'm the County Sheriff as well as a singer for my tribe. I think I know about being in the line of fire. Sometimes, if you don't stand up and defend yourself when you have the chance, you find yourself dragged out of your own house in the middle of the night and shot in cold blood. You may be outsiders, but the ones who hunt your boy want him for a purpose that affects all of us. My dreams tell me we will all be drawn into this battle, whether we wish it or not."

He paused and looked around at the others. "Everyone here can feel the boy's power. If he is taken by the evil ones, when we fight this battle we will lose. Better to fight now, with the boy on our side."

There were many nods and murmurs of agreement around the room. Asia felt the sting of tears in her eyes and dropped her head. Jack got up from the floor and took her hand, pulling her back to her seat.

She looked up at Begay. "Thank you."

The sheriff nodded and sat down.

Next to her, Geneva Twohawks smiled. "You see how it must be. The Holy Ones sent you here for a reason."

The tenor of the discussion changed now as the voices grew more animated. The man who had objected continued to argue, but he seemed to have few supporters. Jack still clung to Asia's hand, and after a moment her head snapped up, eyes wide. She looked from one speaker to another in shock, her ears confirming what her mind could not conceive. The elders were speaking the language of the Navajo, but she understood every word. Geneva was grinning at her as if she held a secret.

Asia looked down at Jack, who looked back at her with a slight smile on his face. "Are you doing this?"

He lifted one shoulder.

She let go of his hand—and the words swirling around her lost their meaning. She grabbed his hand again—and comprehension flowed back into the conversation. Her mouth was suddenly dry, her muscles trembling. But she held on for dear life. Because the elders were discussing what would have to be done to defeat the brothers that hunted her son.

"Why not just perform the Night Dance?" suggested a younger member of the group. "That should bring the boy back from the Spirit World and anchor him here. Then the evil ones can only fight him in this world and the sheriff can protect him."

"No!" Geneva's voice sliced through the murmur of reaction. "The boy draws his strength from the Spirit

World. Cut him off from it and he cannot defend himself at all. Asia, tell them what these creatures are capable of. Do you think Leonard Begay can protect your son from the ones that stole you from your home the first time?"

Her heart shrinking in fear, Asia shook her head. "They can move across time and space. They have weapons and tracking abilities that go far beyond our science. Believe me, I know this from personal experience. We wouldn't have a chance of protecting ourselves here without the help of my friends. They have similar weapons. But who would be the stronger? I can't answer that question."

"Through the Enemy Way, we might be able to draw out the evil spirits and destroy them." Leonard Begay's dark eyes met hers, seeking to reassure her. "It's one of our most powerful ceremonies."

There was a lot of agreement with this viewpoint, many speaking in support of the idea. Several people even went so far as to begin to make plans for the ceremony, suggesting roles for those in the room, assigning tasks and so on.

All talk ceased when Jeremiah Nakai raised a hand. "Leonard has made a good suggestion." The old man's thin voice carried clearly despite the waver of age. "But I am thinking about this in another way. We use the Enemy Way to help those who may be carrying the weight of evil spirits in this world. We send those spirits back where they belong so the people can live their lives free of that burden here in this world.

"This is a different problem. This boy is under attack by evil ones who can move in both worlds. We cannot destroy them in this world. We must destroy them in the Spirit World. The boy is not only the target. He is also the weapon. How can we help him fight his battle in the Spirit World? There is only one way to do that. We must go there with him."

The silence of a cathedral fell under the corrugated metal of the shelter, broken by the occasional bleat of the sheep in a nearby pen. Asia felt Jack's hand fall from hers as he reached for the drawing he'd been working on throughout the morning. He brought it up and placed it in her lap. She glanced down and was astounded. He'd never shown a talent for art before, but the details of this drawing were far beyond the normal abilities of a six-year-old. Horror walked the page—a creature that looked like a cross between a bear and a dinosaur, with four tree-like legs, massive jaws filled with rows of jagged fangs and long, ripping claws at the ends of its forelegs.

She heard Geneva gasp and turned to see her staring, her eyes wide. "What's wrong?"

A word Asia did not understand slipped from Geneva's lips. Then the old woman grabbed the paper, crumpled it and threw it in the fire outside the shelter. Jack watched her do it without emotion.

"What?" Asia demanded.

"Demon." Geneva's hands were shaking. "Some call it the Beast of the Four Winds, but most will not name it at all for fear of waking it from its slumber. And if the evil ones can call this one to the fight, then we battle to save both this world and the next."

"Portal's Balls, but this planet is a godsforsaken heap of burned out cinders!" Kinnian swiped at the river of sweat rolling down his face. "I see nothing but star-blasted dirt in all directions! Why are we here?"

Trevyn weathered the storm of bad temper from his captain and pointed toward the horizon shimmering in the heat. "A team of men from STEELWALL is investigating the site of the boy's disappearance just over that rise. If we approach on foot through this draw we can take them with minimal casualties." He made a point of meeting his brother's gaze. "You did want to question a few of the men, did you not, my lord?"

Kinnian spat into the red dust. "Let's get it over with, then. D'Lac!" When the lieutenant of the guard snapped to attention he gestured up the draw in the direction Trevyn had indicated. "The enemy is just over that rise. We want them alive."

"My lord!" D'Lac saluted and led his men ahead through the shallow cleft in the desert left by the occasional flash flood. Trevyn, Kinnian and the captain's personal guard followed close behind.

They moved through the unforgiving landscape, the heat a weight pressing down on them from above and rising to meet them from below. His body armor, light though it was, chafed against Trevyn's bruises and the cracks in his ribs. His head was spinning, and his knees buckled with each step. But it wasn't the heat or his injuries that threatened to send him to the sand. And it wasn't the thought of what Kinnian would do to the men of STEELWALL once he found them. Trevyn had read about the organization and what it did; its agents probably deserved whatever Kinnian had planned for them.

No. What had his heart flailing and his blood surging in alarm had little to do with what was going to happen and everything to do with what had already happened in this crucible of sun and sand. The place still sang with power and vibrated with the electromagnetic signatures of those who had used it. He could still taste each and every one of them on the air, unique and separate—the boy, immensely powerful, but untrained and unfocused; his mother, fiercely protective, with powers of her own; Gabriel, stronger every day as his bond grew with Lana; and Lana, so innocent, so much at risk.

Trevyn felt his heart drop into a deep, black chasm in the center of his chest. Kinnian would sense the same things he sensed; know the same things he knew. It was only a matter of time before he found his way to Lana and destroyed her.

Up ahead the first of D'Lac's men topped the lip of the draw, and the laser rifles began to fire. A few of the STEELWALL men screamed as the volley hit them; most dropped as they stood, stunned into unconsciousness. It was over in seconds, with no casualties among the troops from the *Bloodstalker*. A simple operation, one they had accomplished countless times on dozens of planets. Trevyn pressed his lips together and suppressed a sigh.

He gestured at D'Lac, indicating the men sprawled closest to him. "Rouse these two."

Kinnian strolled over to begin his inquisition once the men had regained consciousness. "Good afternoon, gentlemen." He grinned. "Lovely day."

The men were professionals. They said nothing.

"I don't suppose either of you would care to tell me what you've been able to find out here in the desert today?" He looked from one to the other. "Save us some time?"

"Sure," said one. "I'll tell you. A whole shitload of nothing. If that's what you're looking for, then I guess you've found it."

The other one crooked a smile at that, but otherwise kept quiet.

Kinnian looked around. "It does seem a little desolate at that. Not much to look at. It would seem we're all wasting our time out here. So I have only one other question for you. Which one of all of these men would be your, um, leader? Your captain, lieutenant, chief—I assume you know what I'm after?"

"Well, shit, man, I think you went and shot him." The talkative man's companion smirked. "Bad luck."

Kinnian offered them a wide grin. "Oh, yes, I quite agree. That is bad luck. I'll just have to begin with you, then."

He placed his hand to the man's temple, and the man began to scream.

Sometime later Trevyn was standing at the edge of the draw. From behind, it must have appeared that he was overseeing the disposal of the bodies, but in truth his eyes were unfocused. He was deep inside himself, shielded from all others, particularly from the one who clapped him on the shoulder in unbridled glee.

"A most productive afternoon after all, my brother," Kinnian crowed. "We are close. I can almost smell our quarry, can't you?"

"You learned something from the men?"

Kinnian snorted. "Hardly. They were useless. And now that the organization has lost a third team? They should change their name from STEELWALL to SHITHOLE!"

"What, then?"

"Please, Trevyn, you can't tell me you don't feel it." His sibling studied him. "Have I rattled your brains so thoroughly you sense nothing?"

"I sense the boy's phenomenal power. He killed the first team, didn't he?"

"Of course, he did, you idiot, but that's not what I mean. Our dear brother has been here. Oh, yes. Yes, he has. His track is like the whip of lightning across the sky—it makes the hairs stand up on the back of my neck. And he's not alone, Trevyn." Kinnian turned to him and grinned, the black ash of death in his eyes. "He has a woman with him, a human so close to being his bondmate the air is full of the scent of sex. How delicious is that? I can't wait to meet her."

Trevyn returned his intense, inquisitional stare with a dull reflection of boredom. Behind that bland shield he fought to control his every physical and neurological reaction—heartbeat, respiration, pupil size, cranial pulse, electroencephalographic markers. He could not let Kinnian see what he knew. If he had any chance of helping Lana now he had to keep his sibling out of his head.

At last Kinnian's lips curled upwards, and he turned away. "Send a team into the nearest town. Gabriel and the girl must be holed up there somewhere. Go with them—I don't want anything overlooked. I'm going back to the ship." His grin widened. "I'm going to conduct a little search of my own."

CHAPTER NINETEEN

Lana had gone through the motions of her job all morning, flashing the credentials, saying the words, maintaining her expression and her body language in the open, non-threatening, professional manner she'd been trained to use when encountering the public. But it was no use. She was a walking train wreck, her mind in turmoil, her emotions simmering just under the placid surface of her outward calm. Her skin felt too tight for her face, her chest too tight for her hammering heart and laboring lungs.

She had killed a man last night. She had killed Mark Jamisky, an FBI agent, her former lover, last night. The man sitting next to her in the car had killed three other men and together they had buried them all in the desert and rolled their vehicle off the edge of a craggy ravine to destroy the evidence. She was in this thing so deep she would never work her way out of it, and she was beginning to wonder where it was going to end. Nowhere good, was the only possible answer.

Gabriel pulled the car into the pitted parking lot in

front of a sun-bleached roadside store and turned to look at her. "You okay?"

"Sure. Just peachy." Lana didn't want to talk to him about how she felt. She didn't want to talk to him about anything. She unlatched the seat belt and stood up out of the car into the Arizona heat.

The store was marginally cooler than the desert air, thanks to the wheezing A/C unit in a hole in the wall over the register. The teen-aged girl sitting under the unit looked like she appreciated the difference, though, and would be ready to fight for her cool spot.

Lana approached the counter. "Afternoon."

"Hi." The girl's face showed that she recognized them for the aliens they were. Well, Lana thought, at least she was half right.

Lana showed her credentials and watched the girl's eyes grow round with surprise. "I'm Special Agent Alana Matheson with the FBI. I wonder if I could ask you a few questions?"

The girl swallowed. "Sure. I guess."

"We're looking for some folks, a young woman and her six-year-old son. We think they might have been in an accident or had a breakdown somewhere out here maybe yesterday afternoon or evening." She pulled out the picture of Asia and Jack she'd been showing around all morning. "Any chance you've seen them?"

To give the girl credit, she looked at the picture. A lot of people didn't bother.

"No. But I wasn't working last night. I went home at lunchtime and my dad took over."

Gabriel had been prowling the aisles, stopping and listening as if to far-off thunder. He lifted his head to catch Lana's eye and gestured for her. She excused herself and went to join him back by the drink cooler.

"They've been here." He pitched his voice for her ears only. "Yesterday evening at the latest. They were alone, though. No sign of the kidnappers."

"That doesn't make sense, Gabriel. If they'd escaped, why didn't they call? This place must have a phone, access to the police?"

He lifted his shoulders. "All I can tell you is what I feel. They were here."

"Shit." She ran a hand over her tamed curls. "Okay."

She plastered a smile back on her face and went back to the girl. "You say your dad was here last night? Where is he now?"

"Um, he's at a big elders' meeting, I think, way out on the res. He won't be back home until late, Mom said."

"Is there any way we can reach him out there? It's important."

"Well, no, I don't think so. There's no cell service out there and Miz Twohawks doesn't have a phone."

"You do have a phone here, though, right?"

"Sure, yeah. I mean, usually. It hasn't been working for the last few days. The guy's supposed to come and fix it today or tomorrow."

Lana and Gabriel exchanged a look. Gabriel got to the question first.

"Can you tell us how to get to Mrs. Twohawks's place?"

The girl looked broadsided by the question. "Uh. Yeah. I guess. Well, you are FBI and everything, right?"

"You want to see the creds again?" Lana lifted an eyebrow in inquiry.

"No, that's okay." The girl set her shoulders as if she'd made up her mind. "The old lady lives a ways from here, I don't know, maybe an hour? I can show you on the map. I've been there a few times with my Mom and Dad."

Gabriel unfolded the map and laid it out on the counter, and the girl showed them. They committed the route to memory, stocked up on water and snacks and left her to her TV and A/C.

As Lana slid behind the wheel, Gabriel ducked his head into the car. "I just remembered something. I'll be right back."

She watched him go back into the store, the muscles moving like water under his tee-shirt and jeans. Sudden desire speared through her chest, taking her breath in a gasp. Her mind was filled with the memory of his mouth on hers, hot and demanding, his skin under her hands, his voice deep and warm in her ear. He had filled her, stretched her, stroking deep and slow until she begged him, *begged* him. Oh, God, she wanted that again. More than her stupid pride. More than her life.

What in the living hell is wrong with me? She shook her head, rubbing her hands down her face. She had never felt this way about a man before. She had to get away from him before she did something insane.

Gabriel came back out of the store and folded himself into the passenger seat. He glanced at Lana with a frown.

"You okay?"

"Why wouldn't I be?" The repeated question was getting on her nerves. "What was it you forgot?"

He twisted the top off a bottle of water and guzzled half of it down. She watched his throat move as he swallowed and felt her own mouth go dry. *Damn it to hell!*

"We couldn't risk anyone else learning where Asia and Jack are." He shrugged. "Now the girl just won't quite be able to put together the details the way she did for us. No harm done."

"Son of a bitch!" Anger rose up into her throat and choked her. "You went into that girl's mind—just fucking blew right in and took what you wanted! Just like you did with me."

She would have said more. She wanted to say more. But he turned with surprising quickness and grabbed her arm.

"No! No, Lana. This was deliberate. It was business. I skimmed the surface of her mind and erased a few minor details that are of no consequence to that girl. What happened between us was different."

She shook him off. "You told me it went against your personal code to enter a person's mind without permission, then you jumped in mine with both feet.

How can I trust anything you say?"

"You tell me." His eyes blazed with dark fire. "Open your mind, Lana. Open your heart. You have to know what happened between us affected me as much as it affected you. A lifetime of training broke down that night—you saw what I endured to build those shields and they were gone in seconds. *Think*. What kind of emotion must exist between us to do that?"

He cursed in frustration and scrambled out of the car, slamming the door behind him. Lana followed him as he paced across the sun-washed lot, gravel crunching under their boots.

"What the hell, Gabriel! You're just going to throw that at me and walk away?"

He turned on her. "What's the use? You won't listen. You won't see. Just like so many other things in your life you refuse to look at. You hide them in a dark corner of your mind, thinking you've dealt with them. But let me warn you. My brother is a master at finding those things and turning them into monsters."

She came to a halt and stared at him. "What the hell does your brother have to do with this? And what things? What are you talking about?"

Gabriel paced in the ragged shade of a few stunted pines, caught between anger and some emotion she could not identify. "I hurt you. It was the last thing I wanted to do, and I'm sorry. But I didn't extract your deepest secrets to cause you pain. I didn't magnify your fears until they destroyed you. I didn't make you relive your mother's death until you lost your mind. *I am not my brother.*"

He was shaking now, and Lana finally understood. He was not only furious at her, he was afraid for her.

"You think Kinnian is after *me*?"

"I think if Kinnian ever found you, you would learn what mind rape truly is."

She met Gabriel's gaze for a long moment. A depth of knowledge pooled like a black, limitless sea just below her conscious mind. Dangerous things swam below the surface.

"You're nothing like your brother." She started to turn away. "And you don't have to worry. I got over my mother's death a long time ago."

He grabbed her hand. "You need to look deeper, Lana." The way he was looking at her made the bottom drop out of her stomach. "If we hope to defeat Kinnian, you can't hide from what you know."

She pulled out of his grip. "And what is it you think I know?"

"There's a connection. I know you feel it. All those moves you made as a child, from city to city, from state to state. What was your mother running from all those years, Lana?"

She wanted to scream in frustration. "Why would it matter what the hell she was running from? She was a diagnosed paranoid schizophrenic who ended up killing herself. End of story."

"And what if the story was more complicated? Did you know that your mother was the patient of a doctor in Nashville named Claussen? Eighteen months ago this Claussen was . . . prosecuted . . . for selling the records of his patients to a black ops agency of the government. Asia Roberts was one of his patients."

"Asia Roberts . . ." *Oh, hell no.* "Are you suggesting my *mother* might have had some kind of psi talent? And someone was trying to kidnap her?"

"You're an investigator. What does the evidence suggest to you?"

She stared at Gabriel, unable to process what he was telling her. She could only tremble in shock. All those years of running, her mother wild-eyed with fear at every knock at the door. Never allowing Lana a friend; never allowing herself a moment. Until time had finally run out. Lana had always believed what everyone had told her, what it had *looked* like, for chrissake. Her mother was *crazy*. But what if she'd just been trying to stay alive? What if, like Asia Roberts with Jack, she'd been trying to keep her little girl out of the hands of a deadly enemy?

She didn't want to speak, but the words wouldn't be stopped. "You're saying this case is related somehow to my mother's death over twenty years ago."

"I think the same organization that kidnapped Asia and Jack was after your mother, yes."

And the suicide . . . NO. She refused to think about that. The whole idea was too much.

She blew out a breath. "See, that's the problem, Gabriel. You put all this fantastic theory together from looking in my head. And you should never have been there in the first place."

Gabriel stared at her for half a second. Then he exploded.

"Christ, yes! I admit it! I've already apologized for what I've done. But what I saw in your mind is a part of me now. I put that together with what Ethan knew, and I did some digging. That's my *job*, Lana."

"No, Gabriel, your job is to help me find Asia and Jack. I'm not part of your investigation." She turned and strode back across the bleached gravel toward the Jeep. She'd had enough of Gabriel Cruz and his high-minded bullying.

She heard his boots on the gravel behind her seconds before he spun her around to face him. "If I 'investigated' you it was only to learn how to protect you. We're running out of time, Lana." He stopped, took a breath. "The closer we get to Asia and Jack, the closer Kinnian gets to us. I feel him even now."

Lana looked up into Gabriel's face. New lines had appeared around his dark eyes.

"Okay." *What was it he'd said about fighting like children?* "Okay, I get it. Maybe I could let some things go. And maybe from now on we could set all this personal bullshit aside and just focus on the job."

She could see Gabriel struggle with himself. Clearly her solution wasn't quite what he had in mind, but he set his lips in a thin line and nodded.

They made their way to the vehicle, and Lana slipped in behind the wheel. She pulled out of the parking lot, put the A/C on blast, and headed into the sun.

A few miles down the valley highway, Gabriel looked up from his map and pointed. "Take this next right."

"What? It's not even paved."

"That's what the girl said. The map has it going almost to the old lady's door."

Lana cursed under her breath but took the turn, grateful she hadn't let the rental car agent back in Little Rock talk her out of a four-wheel-drive. The road began to climb right away, lifting above the desert floor with its patches of broom grass and occasional cactus into hillsides dotted with piñon pine and juniper. The lowering sun gave it all the surreal golden glow of a John Houston Technicolor. Too bad the plot of this movie was something more out of Sam Peckinpah, Lana thought. Or maybe Quentin Tarantino.

Lana shut down her fevered thinking and focused on the here and now. The questions Gabriel had raised—about her lost childhood, her mother's sanity—had no answers. She should know, she'd been asking them long enough. She just followed the twisting gravel and red dust of the road and let it take her higher, over the broad breast of the mountain.

A much-abused Ford F-150 passed her as she came down off the crest of the ridge, crowding her to the outer edge of the narrow road. But once she got past the highest point the road widened for a bit, the result of recent maintenance, perhaps. The trees were a little thicker on this side of the mountain, too, and came closer to the road. It seemed cooler for a while, or were those clouds gathering for an afternoon thunderstorm?

The road was winding down the mountain into another little valley, dry, but protected on all sides by low mountains. Lana could see a number of homesteads below, ranches with livestock and barns, with houses or trailers and here and there a traditional Navajo *hogan*. She had read somewhere that people still used them for ceremonies, though she didn't think anyone still lived in them. Still, who knew? She'd run into some cabins back in the hills of Tennessee that were so primitive they might have been unchanged from Davy Crockett's time.

The road was growing rockier, the trees had thinned out and thunder was rolling over the shoulder of the mountain now. She exhaled. Maybe she should have let the big man drive. She glanced over at him, thinking Gabriel had gone awfully quiet. He was staring sightless at the road ahead of them.

"Gabriel? You okay?"

His only answer was a low murmur of words she did not recognize and the same uncanny stare.

"Hey! You're starting to worry me here, spaceman. What's going on?"

His words emerged as a kind of chant, repeated over and over. What the hell was he doing? Then he fell as silent as death, his eyes closed, and he went boneless and limp in the seat.

"Holy shit! Gabriel?"

She didn't dare take her hands from the steering wheel; she couldn't risk looking away from the road for more than a few seconds at a time. The road had become a one-car track snaking its way around the mountain in a tight series of hairpin curves. Steep and unrelenting, the curves worked their way down, with only the battered, rusting guardrail between life and disaster. There was no place to pull over, no way to stop.

Lana heard Gabriel moan and glanced at him in alarm. His hands were fists, his body one taut mass of muscle. His eyelids were fluttering as if he were dreaming. Was he having another attack like that day at the rest stop? With a searing, white-hot slash of pain she saw what he had seen that day, she felt what he had felt—the ripping invasion, the unbearable agony. And for one perilous second her body was no longer her own. Her hands went numb and unfeeling on the steering wheel. Her eyes went blind except for a vision of that face, the face of an enemy so implacable, so fearsome, fighting him seemed impossible.

She heard a sound—the crunch and pop of gravel underneath the car—and with a start of horror her eyes flew open. *Jesus Christ Almighty!* The front right tire was at the edge of the precipice. There was no guardrail at this spot, nothing to keep the Jeep from going over, and down that side was nothing but a thousand feet of brush-covered mountain slope. In a panic she swung the wheel to the left. The Jeep slewed sideways, all four wheels spinning and skittering in the gravel. She fought with it, ended up back on the right shoulder again, and slid into another tight curve. She tried the brakes—the tires spun for a few desperate seconds before they caught and began to slow her down. Then, *thank God,* the road eased out of the last of the hairpin curves and hit a short straightaway.

They were still high above the valley floor, and beside her Gabriel was pale and unresponsive. She was shaking so badly she could hardly trust herself to take the vehicle off the road and park it, much less guide it through another series of those damn death curves. With a grateful exhale she spotted a wide semi-circle of red dirt at the start of the next bend. She slowed with exquisite care and pulled into the rough sanctuary. Trembling, she shut off the engine and turned to deal with Gabriel.

She touched his shoulder. He was rigid and unyielding, his muscles clenched tight, a fine sheen of sweat over his skin. His belly and chest rose and fell with rapid breaths, as if he was running a marathon, and his face wore an expression of predatory concentration. She almost withdrew her hand, afraid to disturb that magnificent focus. But she felt compelled to warn him. Because somehow she knew that just as this dreaming hunter was stalking his prey, something else was stalking him.

He arched in the seat, his back bowing and twisting, the tendons in his neck pulling as tight as bowstrings. A sound emerged from him, more animal than human, a growl, a howl of frustration. And he collapsed into huge, wracking tremors, a seizure that threatened to break his bones and tear him apart.

"Jesus, Gabriel!" Lana scrambled from her seat and straddled him, grasping his flailing arms to keep him from crashing through the car window. She hit the lever to lower the seat to give them room, even as his spasms threatened to throw her sideways into the gearshift. Then, just as suddenly as it had begun, the seizure stopped. Panting, she looked down at his face.

He wasn't breathing.

"Oh, God, Gabriel. Don't you do that. Shit! No! Don't you do it!"

She hitched herself higher onto his hips and centered herself over his chest. She put her palms over his heart and leaned in, feeling the whole car shake with the force of her compressions. She counted out loud, to keep from thinking of anything else.

"One, two, three, four, five, come, on, you, bas, tard, don't, do, this, to, me, eleven, twelve, thirteen, fourteen, fifteen." She gave him a breath. Then she felt for his pulse. There it was—weak and thready, but there.

She sat back on his hips, staring at his chest as it lifted—once, twice.

His body dissolved from beneath her, replaced by cold, gritty stone. Vertigo spun through her head as the Jeep disappeared from around her and left her alone on her hands and knees in a dark so complete her vision starved for light. She would have screamed, but she could find no breath to bring to it. Instead she could only cower, there in the dark and the cold, struggling to understand what had happened.

"Gabriel!" She wanted to shout, but it came out a whisper, and the silence threw the name back in her face. Somehow he'd brought her here, or she had followed him, and whatever danger he was in was hers now, too. That thought provided an anchor for her untethered mind, and gradually her frantic heartbeat began to steady, her breath began to slow. She raised her head, and at last she could see the outlines of walls, a tunnel carved out of living rock, its sides narrow and jagged.

She stood, her legs shaking, and listened. There was a constant, bone-deep booming of surf against stone beneath her feet. A sharp sizzle-and-crash every few minutes that seemed to fill the whole cavern. *And there!* the distant clash of metal, and the mutter of male voices. She stretched out a hand and began to move toward the sound.

A pale, diffuse light opened up in front of her, as if she simply willed her path to be lit, and the darkness fell in step behind her. Though the passage twisted and turned like the gut of a snake, she had no trouble following the sound of the battle raging ahead. The metal rang louder than a blacksmith's forge, and beneath the clanging Gabriel grunted and cursed. She ran, reaching automatically for a gun that was no longer there. S*hit!* What were the rules in this place? She could have light, but no weapons?

Lana turned a corner, and where the tunnel widened, two men armed with heavy swords faced each other across the rocky cavern floor. Gabriel looked like she had never seen him—taller, more muscular, his face and body like that of an ancient gladiator, rather than the more modern man she'd known. He was wounded, bleeding from his thigh and sword arm, bearing what looked like burns on his chest and back. His opponent wore the face she had seen in her visions, and now that she saw him, she knew. Kinnian was evil, as evil as any murderer or rapist or kidnapper she had ever encountered on the job.

And he was winning this fight.

The Thrane leapt onto a rock to take the height advantage from Gabriel and grinned. "You surprise me, brother. I had no idea that slave who taught you gave you the secret of reanimation. I could have sworn you were dead—how did you break that chokehold?"

He gripped his sword with two hands and sliced down toward Gabriel's neck. Gabriel sidestepped and parried with his own, smaller curved broadsword, then changed directions and swung at Kinnian's feet. The Thrane was forced to jump at Gabriel and just missed impaling himself on the long dirk Gabriel carried in his left hand. He deflected it in time and swung again at Gabriel's head, only to find the blow blocked again. The two men backed off.

"You have little idea of what I can do, Kinnian." Lightning struck at the Thrane's feet, forcing him backwards. Gabriel pressed his advantage, attacking in a flurry of blows with the lighter sword. Kinnian was hard put to deflect them. But he was bigger, stronger. When he recovered his composure he came back, and every blow with his heavier sword beat Gabriel further down. Once or twice Gabriel got in under Kinnian's guard for a quick swipe with the dirk, drawing blood and bringing a sharp hiss of pain from his opponent. But Lana could see he was tiring, his sword arm quivering with fatigue. He couldn't last much longer.

Kinnian could see it, too. His grin was savage as he raised his sword over his shoulder and came in for the kill. Lana couldn't help it, a gasp escaped her, echoing off the fractured cave walls. For a single instant, the Thrane's black, hate-filled eyes were turned in her direction. Lightning flashed—had Gabriel merely raised his hand?—and Kinnian flew backward into the wall.

Growling, his face a mask of rage, Kinnian threw out an arm. A bolt of white-hot energy disintegrated the cavern wall, and reality rearranged itself.

Lana found herself exposed and vulnerable on a windswept crag overhanging a roiling black ocean. Kinnian and Gabriel were gone. She fought to look around, but rain slashed into her face, stealing her sight. Day or night? It was impossible to tell. A storm was piled high and thick against the broken bluff where she maintained a slim hold, and clouds shut out the light. A long fall below, waves boomed and crashed against a solid wall of rock. There was no beach on which to land a boat, only an outlying comb of rock erupting from the ocean bed a short distance from the cliff that frayed the incoming waves into leaping flumes.

Shivering, she moved her feet on the slippery rock, step by careful step, lowering herself over the splintered surface until she could squeeze between the overhanging cliff and an abrupt outcropping of rock. She heard voices. She lay on her belly to look.

Through a gaping crevice in the rock below her face she could see Gabriel had only just survived the explosion that had brought them to this new battleground. He was battered, bleeding.

And though Gabriel held the higher ground, Kinnian laughed. "Shall I just cut your legs out from under you, half-breed? I don't really feel like chasing you to gut you."

He took a swipe at Gabriel's knee, Gabriel stretched to deflect it and Kinnian grabbed the back of his neck to pull him off the rock. Gabriel missed a fall to the ocean below by inches, but lost his sword, sacrificing the weapon to clutch the cliff face and save his life.

Above them, Lana watched in horror as Gabriel struggled to pull a knee up and lift his body over the rim of rock, only to have Kinnian roll him over and straddle his chest. The Thrane pinned Gabriel's arms under his knees and put the edge of his sword to Gabriel's throat. She watched a thin line of red blood well up under the blade and her heartbeat machine-gunned in her chest; she couldn't breathe. *Christ!*—that bloodsucker was going to kill Gabriel and here she sat doing nothing!

She could hear him. How could she hear him? The wind was roaring, the waves destroying themselves against the uncaring rock. But she heard every word.

"Oh, yes. I'm going to kill you, brother. But first I want to know all about her. Her name. Her face. How she smells, how she tastes. How she feels all snug and tight and hot around your dick. Because before you die you're going to see me *ruin* your little human in every way possible. First she's going to beg me to fuck her. Then she's going to beg me to kill her. And believe me, my brother. I'm going to do what she begs me to do."

Gabriel struggled, his hips bucking, his chest twisting, but it did no good. The sword didn't move. Lightning flashed all around them, but it was as if some invisible force deflected the current. Lana could see there was another battle going on, a war of wills, a murderous, underhanded street fight between sharp-edged minds. She didn't know whether Gabriel was strong enough to win that battle. She only knew she had to help him.

Her hand closed on a fist-sized piece of black rock, its edges so rough they tore at her skin. She got to her knees, then to her feet, and raised her head over the outcropping. It would be a tough shot, the angle not straight down, but coming back in toward the cliff face. She lay out almost upside down over the wet, canted slab, her legs dangling behind her just enough to balance the weight in front, her head swimming as gravity tugged at her inner ear. She slipped—and caught herself by the skin of her forearms spread over the rock in front of her. The weight of the back half of her body was losing ground to the front half, and the tops of her thighs were scraping the edge of the slab as she slid further out.

Adrenaline flooded her system, her blood roared in her ears, her heart thudded under her ribs. Her right hand shook and dripped blood as it clutched the missile. She rose up on her left, aimed and caught Gabriel's horrified expression, gazing up at her as she let fly with the rock.

"You fucking sonofabitch!"

The rock bashed Kinnian in the back of the head. He flinched, a split-second's movement, and Gabriel freed his dirk to stick it in the bastard's neck. Blood sprayed. The big body rolled over and down, falling toward the madly-leaping ocean.

She grinned, wanting to shout in triumph, but the simple act of drawing breath was enough to tip the balance toward disaster. She slithered down the face of the rock, thighs and forearms scraping without hope for purchase on the wet, smooth surface. Too late she found the breath to scream and fell, hurtling toward the black maw of the ocean, blind and flailing with terror. Lightning flashed and she was swallowed up . . .

. . . but not by the unforgiving waves. Time and space, instead, had turned inside out.

"I've got you, Lana." A voice murmured in her ear. "Just breathe, *querida*, it's okay. I've got you."

Strong arms were wrapped around her, holding her close to a hammering heart. She could just move her lips to whisper his name.

"Gabriel."

"Yeah, it's me, baby."

She sat up, rocking back on his hips to look around in wonder. The storm-swept sky, the slick, jagged rock, the thunderous, reaching waves—all gone. And in their place, only the frantic beating of her heart and the solid strength of his chest under her hands.

"Sweet Jesus." She struggled for breath. "It felt so real."

He met her eyes, but could not hold her gaze. Fear and blazing emotion were quickly hidden behind his dark lashes.

"Your mind is more powerful than you know; even more powerful than I suspected."

Her hands gripped his shirt. "I was falling . . ."

"If I hadn't brought us out of it, the shock would have killed you."

She began to shake, unable to control the tremors. Her body had reacted as if the situation had been real, pumping her full of adrenaline. Now she suffered as the chemical leached from her cells, leaving her empty and cold.

Gabriel pulled her back down again and held her tight, one hand tunneling roughly in her hair. "Whatever possessed you to come after me, Lana? What the hell were you thinking?"

She raised her head. "I wasn't thinking. It just happened. You stopped breathing. I did CPR to get you started again. Then all at once I was *there*."

He touched her face, his jaw clenched. "I've done this to you."

She shook her head, confused by his reaction. "But

this is good, right? Kinnian is gone."

"No. We won this battle. But he escaped the way we did. He'll be back."

Ice crept along her spine at the thought of meeting Kinnian again, but she refused to back down. "Maybe we were meant to fight him together, Gabriel."

Anger sparked in the black depths of his eyes. "I'll never let him near you."

She saw the possessiveness in him and desire leapt up to meet it with a suddenness that took her breath. Her focus narrowed to his scent, the rise and fall of his chest, the heat of his skin under her hands. A fever rose in her blood that threatened to overwhelm all rational thought. She was drawn to this man like no other, by a force she could no longer resist. She burned too much to deny it now.

Gabriel reached up to take her mouth, and the hot, velvet slide of his kiss set her blood on fire. Her breasts ached for his touch, the nipples tightening to stiff points beneath her thin shirt. Her core exploded with need as his hands kneaded her buttocks and pressed her into the hot ridge of his growing erection.

His hands slipped under her shirt, found the catch of her bra. In seconds the shirt was over her head and his mouth was at her naked breast. His tongue circled her nipple. Drew it into the warm, wet cavern of his mouth. Suckled. Nipped. She felt every tug and pull as a pulse of liquid heat between her legs.

He lifted his gaze to hers. "I won't wait any longer for you, *querida*." He moved beneath her. "Tell me you want this."

Her belly clenched as she ground against him, aching for him. "Yes. God, yes."

Outside the storm had broken over them, thunder drumming over the mountain, rain coming down in sheets. The windows of the car had fogged, enclosing them in a private world of passion. Lana moved off of Gabriel's chest long enough to strip out of the rest of her clothes, then she straddled him again. Her breasts brushed his chest as she paused, heart bursting, pulse pounding in sweet anticipation.

Gabriel's expression was dark with hunger, bright with a kind of wild, predatory desire. Lana could see he was maintaining control by the sheerest margin, his chest heaving as he dragged in breath, sweat pouring off his skin. Knowing that he was so close to some kind of madness nearly sent her over the edge. *She* did that to him. That untamed need she read in his eyes, in his body, was for *her*. And something primal in her threw off all its chains and roared in response.

His hand moved to her belly . . . lower, to the center of her desire. His thumb circled the tender nub, making her gasp. She didn't need his petting. She was ready for him, had been ready for him for days. She wanted him inside *now*. He centered himself at her entrance and arched upward to join them and *oh, God!*

His arms encircled her hips, holding her in place for his thrusts, and *Jesus!* it was just the *right* place; he was sliding in deep and finding her with every stroke. His mouth wandered over her neck, his teeth scraping and biting at the tendons, his tongue soothing the tiny hurts, and every sharp delight ended in a flood of molten fire between her thighs. She moaned his name, feeling the spiral of her climax begin to spin higher . . . and higher . . . out of her control toward a place where ecstasy overcame fear, where passion overturned reason.

She screamed as the orgasm tore into her with the force of a hurricane, pleasure wracking her from the inside out. She sobbed his name as wave after wave rolled through her core and her sheath clutched at his thick shaft. She heard him curse, the sound a breathless groan. His pounding strokes became brutal, relentless. Her fingers bit into his shoulders, and she held on as his body went taut and he found his release at last.

She rode it out with him, the pleasure so intense she could only give in to it and pray she survived. It was a force of nature she could not control. And in the end it left her devastated. Ripped apart. Wide open and vulnerable.

She collapsed against Gabriel's chest, tears running down her face, unable to keep herself from crying. She couldn't have told anyone why she was crying except to say that the experience of sex with Gabriel had affected her nearly as much as her fall from the cliff.

But Gabriel didn't ask why. He just wrapped his arms around her and murmured softly to her—words she didn't recognize or understand, sometimes in Spanish, sometimes in languages no one on this Earth had ever heard. All she knew was that the things he said and the way he held her made her feel safe like no man had ever done before. Gabriel Cruz made her feel loved. And that just made her want to cry a flood.

CHAPTER TWENTY

Trin, Minertsa, Sector 10

Ardis sat in her usual seat in the great hall and let the sights and sounds of the Venue flow around her. The Venue itself was unchanged, its graceful architecture as appealing to the senses as ever. But the atmosphere in the hall—the *emotional* tenor of the place—had undergone a profound change from a typical night ten solar cycles ago. From any night before Zalin.

Before the incident on a minor planet of the Consortium, it was possible to think of an empire built on something other than slavery. Factories might be run by robots, farms tilled by androids, transportation and mining and shipping and sanitation scutwork performed by ranks of mindless drones. It was not such a stretch of the imagination to think that civilization might proceed without the need for the enslavement of lesser species.

But that was before Zalin, before "reliable" machines had run amok, murdering and destroying everything in their paths. What happened at Zalin had been pure, uncontrolled slaughter—and who knew when or where it might happen again. The factory owner and his poor family had paid the price of his experimentation. With human slaves you could rely on time-tested mind-control techniques. They had been proven over centuries of use. Tradition had its benefits.

Zalin had destroyed not only the manufacturing base for an android workforce but the *idea* of an android workforce. Ardis had only to look around the Venue to see the results. Humans no longer sat among the Minertsans and representatives of a half-dozen other races in the galleries of the Venue. The Venue, like the streets of the capital city, like every other gathering place in every other city on every other planet in the Consortium, had become a hostile, dangerous place for humans.

No matter what their "legal" status, humans were no longer free in the Minertsan Consortium. They were slaves, whether anyone currently owned them or not. It was already common practice to take them into custody on the slimmest of pretenses. Curfews and segregation laws set them apart. Ardis knew that it was only a matter of time before the sweeps began, arresting and deporting whoever was left to the labor camps or the mining planets. It was all part of Sennik's plan.

The only question was how long Sennik would wait before he implemented it. The hunt for the one who was the key to his plan had dragged on too long. He was growing impatient; Ardis could sense it in him.

And public reaction to events on Zalin had been so gratifying, he'd said.

She shuddered despite the swampy warmth of the Venue's sensory backdrop. The setting of the piece was to be a primordial salt ooze before the rise of the Consortium. Her aura flared with just the briefest hint of deep purple and black before she could call it back. In the days when they were just beginning their lives together, these pieces, with their clever heroes and their clear depictions of good and evil, had been her young husband's favorites. He had been an idealist, her Slindar. In the end he became the hero of his own story, though few knew it.

The house lights went down. The music went up. The spectral vibrations began. Ardis waited, and within seconds a human male slipped into the seat beside her.

She turned to him, but before she could speak, hands like steel claws gripped her arms, lights blinded her and she was pulled from her seat. The man next to her was snatched up, too, but with brutal efficiency. The Thranes in the uniform of Consortium Military Security snarled and beat him, even though he offered little resistance. Those that surrounded her merely maintained an unbreakable hold on her elbows as they escorted her out of the great hall.

Ardis couldn't help herself. Her aura flashed the greens and yellows of her fear as they led her out, the the pale orange of her embarrassment as all turned to look at her. She was terrified, but that she dared not show. It was reasonable that she would be confused.

But her true emotion—her horror at the thought that they had been discovered—could not be betrayed. She fought for control, knowing her reaction would mean life or death, not only for herself, but for dozens of others.

Soon enough they reached the outer atrium of the Venue, and as the doors sighed shut behind her, Ardis's courage drained from her like the tide from the shore. For waiting in the lobby was the Director Prime of Consortium Military Security herself. The First General's aura was the bright gold of satisfaction.

Ardis did what she could to show the proper respect with her aura and her body language.

The First General nodded to her. Then she turned to the Thranes holding her. *Idiots! Release her!* Her colors warmed. *I apologize for their . . . ardor . . . Director Second Ardis. They were instructed to ensure your safety during our operation.*

Ardis threw a tight net of control over her burgeoning emotions. She allowed her aura to drift back toward its neutral lavender, though she left it streaked with the colors of fear, curiosity, and a more than healthy respect for the First General. *Of course, Director Prime. I admit I was rather . . . taken aback. May I ask what operation I was unwittingly a part of?*

The woman who had practically built the security ministry from the mud up showed an aura full of sunny indulgence. Ardis had heard she had a sense of humor.

Our intelligence has led us to believe human operatives have been meeting here at the Venue for some time to exchange information and so on. We have been following this man for several solar cycles. We believe he made contact with someone here tonight to receive sensitive information from inside the government.

No! Ardis made certain her aura reflected her shock. *Were you also able to catch his contact?*

The First General's aura darkened with smug certainty. *That information will be forthcoming. Never fear.*

Ardis inclined her head and deepened her aura with the magenta of respect. She studied the crumpled figure of the human awaiting the final attention of the Thranes. He lifted his head a fraction to glance at her. She met his eyes for a tiny slice of time and looked away. No one noticed. But Ardis knew. They would learn nothing from this man. He would be dead before they returned to the CMS headquarters less than a kilometer from the Venue. He had been trained to break open a blister inserted in his skin and release a deadly poison in the event he was taken. From the look he had given her, he had already done his duty.

Her life—and the conspiracy—were safe.

Navajo Nation Indian Reservation, Arizona, Earth, Sector Three

Dancers followed the drums in a circle of dusty ground a short walk from Geneva Twohawks's compound. The drumming and dancing had been going on for hours. The fire burned high as the singers shuffled and stamped in the proscribed movements, calling on the *Yei* and the ancestors, asking their help in the coming battle. Asia had long since stopped asking anyone to explain the songs or the movements of the dances. As Geneva had put it, they were covering all the bases, using all the most powerful songs from the deepest ceremonies to ensure they had the Old Ones' attention.

Off to the side, two rounded huts, the traditional *hogans* of the Navajo people, had been prepared as sweat lodges for the purification ceremonies set to begin at dawn. Geneva had told Asia that even she and Jack would be expected to participate. Asia couldn't help a shiver of apprehension as she considered what was to come. Here, under a sky full of familiar stars, among people who only wanted to help her, she felt lost, alone. The power all around her, even the power inside her, was so alien, so far beyond human. Even Jack, so small and warm in her arms, could not give her the comfort she craved.

She needed Ethan.

Asia let her mind go. She let her being dissolve in the rhythm of the drums and the rise and fall of the voices of the singing. She closed her eyes and sank into herself. She reached out. And like a miracle, she found him.

Jesus! Asia? My God. The wave of emotion that came through the link from him was like opening a door onto the desert heat—love and longing and relief and lingering fear, a fear that had ground him down, hour after hour, until he was close to madness. The question flitted through his mind: how had she reached him after all this time? But just as quickly, it was dismissed. It wasn't important.

Where are you? Tell me you're okay. Tell me Jack's okay.

Yes, I'm okay, baby, really. And so is Jack. We're fine. She tried to project calm and a sense of well being, but guilt and the dark knowledge of what they faced welled up inside her and threatened to break through. *We're safe. We escaped the kidnappers, and we found help. We just . . . we can't get to a phone. We're in the middle of the desert.*

She sensed his confusion, his desperation. *Where? Tell me where. We'll come and get you. Gabriel and Lana are not far. They're looking for you.*

Asia felt her way through the link. Lana was the FBI agent on the case. But Gabriel . . . Gabriel was something more. Hope flared in her chest. *Sam and Rayna brought this Gabriel in? Why didn't you tell me?*

Ethan's mind projected the sardonic uptick of his mouth so well she could almost see it. *As I recall our only conversation so far was in the middle of an orgasm. Not that I'm complaining. Just leaves little time for details.*

Details like how we're accomplishing this, you mean? In truth, she didn't know. Maybe her contact with Jack, maybe just the sound of the drums, the smell of the wood smoke riding the desert night. *If you were here with me it wouldn't seem so strange. The Navajo people I'm with seem to be operating on a different plane.*

Navajos? Are you on a reservation? Tell me where you are, Asia. Gabriel can be there within hours. God, I can't wait to have you back.

She wanted to tell him. Her heart ached and her body shook with the desire to tell him and end this. To go home, to be with him. To feel him holding her, kissing her, loving her. But she knew she couldn't have any of those things. Not yet. Here, with Geneva and her people, she had worked out a strategy. They had weapons they could use against an enemy they understood. Ethan loved her, he loved Jack, but he was only flesh and bone. He had no weapons to fight the battle they were facing.

The man Sam and Rayna had brought in, however . . . *This man Gabriel—does he know what hunts us? Can he fight them?*

Confusion. Killing rage. Dread so dark it matched her own. She monitored the emotions sweeping through Ethan's mind as he tried to make sense of her question and knew right away she had made a terrible mistake.

You're trying to hide something, Asia, I can feel it. What's going on that I don't know about?

He didn't know about the brothers. Damn it to hell! She fought to order her thoughts, to keep the truth from him.

Ethan, Jack's become so powerful, so withdrawn. They were going to kill him and he . . . She gave up trying to explain verbally and sent an image of what had happened in the desert and the emotions she had experienced at the time—her fear, her relief, her compassion for her son.

She sensed Ethan's shock at what he'd seen. *Jesus. It must have been terrible for him. He's withdrawn again, hasn't he?*

--*Geneva Twohawks, the Navajo elder we're staying with, says he's hiding in the Spirit World. He's like he was when he first came to us.*

--*You have to come home, Asia. I can help Jack here.*

She took a breath, readying herself for the battle to come. *I can't. Not yet. And you can't help Jack this time. The people I'm with know better what we're facing. They know how to fight it.*

She was tired now, and her head ached like a bitch, but Ethan wouldn't let her go. *You and Jack need to be home where the people who love you can take care of you. Damn it, Asia! What is it you think you're fighting?* Waves of agonized longing came at her through the link. *What aren't you telling me?*

She hadn't wanted to hurt him, but her control over her thoughts was not complete. Now it seemed no matter what she did, Ethan would suffer.

--*Who are they, Asia?* Immovable demand joined the hurt in Ethan's presence in her mind. *You're not hiding from the Men in Black anymore. What are you running from?*

She exhaled. *Two brothers. Aliens. They want Jack. The Navajo elders have told me they'll use him to start some sort of galactic apocalypse.* She rubbed at her throbbing temples. *I know how crazy it sounds.*

She could read Ethan's weary acceptance in his thoughts. *Two years ago, yes, I would have signed the committal papers without a second thought. Now nothing surprises me. But if these brothers are aliens, then Sam and Ray would have the technology to defeat them. Gabriel is in place to help you. Let him bring you home where we can protect you. If we have to we'll go up to the ship. We'll relocate. Whatever it takes.*

Frustration made her want to jump to her feet and pace, when she could only sit on the hard ground with her eyes closed and act as if she was in peaceful meditation. *That's just the problem. This fight won't happen with guns or lasers or even ships in space. In ways I can't even begin to grasp, it's going to take place in a world we can only reach with our minds. The Navajos understand this. If I stay here, we have a chance of defeating the brothers on their own terms— in the Spirit World, with Jack's power. If I leave, we have no defense.*

Ethan had reached his limit. *Asia, none of this makes sense. Just come home to me.*

She let him feel her sadness, her guilt—and her determination. *I can't come home until this is over. I can't risk your life, too. It will all be over in a couple of days. We'll be home then.*

--Asia! Don't do this alone. You have to let me help you. Please.

--Not this time, baby. I love you.

And as she closed him off from her mind she felt his emotions wash over her—anguished, desperate love, stark fear, and, staining everything like blood, the dark pain of betrayal.

Gabriel Cruz owed few people in the galaxy. Many people owed him—their lives, their freedom, their place in the way of things. Until today, only one or two—Sam Murphy for certain, his teacher had he lived—could have laid a claim on him. Now this woman—a tiny thing, really, though her heart was as big as the sun that warmed her planet—had yoked him with a debt he could never repay. She had saved his life. Not once, but twice in one day. She had drawn the everlasting wrath of an unstoppable, sadistic enemy to save him. And how had he repaid her?

By taking her, hard, without preamble—and by the side of the road, for chrissake. What a perfect romantic he was! The one saving grace was that he had managed not to violate her mind again, though only by the fiercest application of will. And that couldn't last long.

Because the worst was yet to come.

Gabriel recognized the signs. He wouldn't be able to

hold it back long. The *T'haridon Set*, the Forging Fire. He'd put the process in motion with his loss of control the first time. Their proximity, her innate talent, her shocking ability not only to appear at the scene of his battle with Kinnian but *to affect its outcome*, and finally this last foolish surrender to his desire for her had carried the process through its inevitable stages. And now the two of them would see its undeniable conclusion. The bond had already formed between them. It could not be consummated in fire as it had been for generations of his father's people. So it would be broken in agony. To save her life if he could.

His body, still inside hers, was already hard again. He'd never gone slack, and wouldn't until he'd seen the mating time through. His feverish mind wanted to replay the scenes of their lovemaking, wanted to show him her glowing skin, the soft, firm globes of her breasts under his palms, the indescribable joy in her face as she came for him. He gritted his teeth and thought instead of the disciplinary cell at the Academy on Thrane—its cold, dank walls, its earthen floor, the smell of . . .

"Gabriel, you're cold, baby." She rubbed at the skin of his arms. "You've got goosebumps all of a sudden." She sat up, and he slipped out of her, now only semi-hard. "Come on. We should get back on the road."

He gathered her into his arms again, if just for a moment, and brushed a lingering tear from her cheek. "Are you all right?"

She smiled at him, a shy little smile that lit up her

green eyes. "More than all right." Her eyes dropped to his throat and widened in horror. "Jesus Christ, Gabriel!"

His brows came together in confusion for a second. But as her eyes and hands scanned his body in rising concern, he realized what was happening.

"What the hell?" She ran her fingers over an angry red streak slashing across his ribs. "Tell me this isn't from your fight with Kinnian!"

"Do you want me to lie?"

She looked at him. "How?"

He shrugged. "A doctor would define it as psychosomatic injury."

"Like hell! Those are *real* bruises on your throat where he choked you! Fresh scars on your ribs and your thigh where I saw him cut you with the sword! They look like they hurt like a sonofabitch!"

His mouth quirked upward. "They do."

Her eyes glittered with feral light. "I saw Kinnian hit the water. Will his injuries be real?"

"His training would have spared him the worst of it, but yes. He's likely in a regen tank right now."

"Good." Her voice was a growl.

"*Targa.*" Heat flared in his chest that had nothing to do with his desire for the little wildcat. "Did I mention they never leave a rival alive? It is always a fight to the death for them."

She grunted as she scrambled into the driver's seat and wriggled into her clothes. "Makes perfect sense." She glanced at the clock on the dash then craned her neck to check the scudding clouds outside the windshield. "Damn it. By the time we get to Mrs. Twohawks's it'll be way past dark. We're likely to get ourselves shot." She sounded exhausted.

The trip to the old woman's was out of the question now. He couldn't be around others for at least 24 hours, possibly longer. It was too far to go back to Winslow; he'd be deep in the fever long before they got there, and the vehicle was too confined a space.

But there was an alternative. "Change in plan."

She looked up from tying her boot, one eyebrow lifted.

"We've had enough excitement for one afternoon. How about we call it a day?" He stretched carefully. "We could stay over somewhere, go on to the old lady's tomorrow."

"Aren't you forgetting something? Asia and Jack are out there with nothing but an old woman and her shotgun to keep them out of a shitstorm."

"Asia and Jack are safe with Geneva Twohawks. I can feel it. No one knows they're there. Kinnian tried, but he couldn't get into my mind to access what I know, and he'll be forced to rest now and regain his strength for a few hours. We should do the same." The last sentence was a lie. Gabriel wouldn't be resting, and neither would she, if he knew anything about Lana Matheson. He would have to fight her off to do what was necessary to save her.

She studied him. He let her see a little of what he was beginning to feel—the fever rising, the minute tremors in his arms and legs.

"Maybe you're right." She was fighting her own fatigue, he could see it. Her face had gone pale and tiny furrows had appeared between her eyes. "But we're in the middle of nowhere. Where the hell do we hole up?"

He pointed at a sign by the side of the road, swinging in the wind from the storm.

She squinted to read it. "'Last Ranch B&B, ten miles ahead.' Cute. Bet they have ruffles on the curtains, too." She nodded once. "Okay, it's a plan. At least I don't have to drive back over that freaking mountain in this rain."

"No. I've had enough." He opened his door and ran around to the driver's side. "I'll take it the rest of the way."

"My hero." She sighed and slipped into the open seat.

He adjusted the seat and the mirrors and pulled back out onto the road, grateful that she had agreed to go along. The rest of the evening would not be so simple.

Though there were no other guests at the bed and breakfast, Gabriel asked for accommodation in the "Creekside Cabin." The heat in Lana's gaze as he registered them brought the blood in his veins to a slow boil, but he chose the isolated little cottage for reasons very different from those she assumed. Any screams tonight would be his and not those of ecstasy.

He played his role to the hilt for the benefit of the inn's owners. He made sure they knew he and Lana needed privacy, asking to have some sandwiches sent out to the cabin rather than having dinner in the main house. The innkeepers were happy to oblige. It wasn't long before he and Lana were settled behind the locked door of their cabin for the night, supplied with anything a young couple might need for a romantic evening.

Gabriel had used every last scrap of his strength accomplishing it. Now he stood trembling with chills under the steamy spray of the shower, his hands splayed over the tiles to support himself. A few minutes ago he'd been burning with fever; now he couldn't seem to get warm enough. Waves of weakness washed through his body. He couldn't trust his legs to hold him, his hands to grip the slightest weight.

Only his cock was strong, full of life and blood, heavy and hard and aching. His whole body pulsed with his need; his mind buzzed and shrieked with it. From the few shreds of reason left to him he knew he was fighting an instinctual drive, the inborn compulsion to complete the mating bond. To join with Lana, body and soul, mind and spirit. To forge a union between them that only death could break.

But she was human, damn it, not Thrane. She shouldn't have to be bound by his alien biology, forced into a commitment she couldn't possibly comprehend. And there was Kinnian. The moment the bond was complete, she would be fully revealed to him. It would be like throwing a kitten into a cage with a tiger.

He shivered, though the water was like a fall of hot needles on his sensitive skin. If he denied himself long enough, if he controlled his body and his mind through the time of *T'haridon Set*, if he just endured, he might break the bond that had already formed between them. It was said to be possible, even for full-blooded Thranes. He was only half-Thrane. She was fully human. He had to make it work.

Gabriel took a deep breath, exhaled in a long, shaky sigh. He reached out and turned off the water. His skin rose in goosebumps. He grabbed a towel and dried off. Took another and wrapped it around his hips, poorly concealing his erection, huge and rigid despite his perception of cold.

Lana was busy laying the food out on a low table in front of the cabin's glowing fireplace. She was turned away from him as he entered the room, her blond curls spilling down her back, her curves wrapped to entice in the thick robe provided by the inn.

"Hey," she said, without looking around at him. "You know, I was starving earlier, and this stuff looks great, but I seem to have lost my appetite."

The thought of food made him ill. He only wanted to devour her. His hands clenched at his sides.

She straightened and turned to look at him. "Oh, my God, Gabriel." She took a step toward him.

He held up a hand. "Don't." The sound was less than human.

"What is it?" She stood poised on the balls of her

feet, as if she was going to have to fight, as if she was going to have to run. "Are you sick? Did Kinnian do something to you?"

He shook his head. He couldn't find his tongue. His thoughts were scattered. The words he needed to explain himself just would not come. He stood, shaking, unable to keep himself from wanting her *so much* it stripped him of all resolve.

But then she moved, taking another step in his direction, and he had to do what he'd vowed he would do. "Lana, no. If you touch me, I swear, it will kill me. Be still and let me get through this."

Her eyes roved over his naked body, and Gabriel would have sworn his skin burned as if she touched him. He saw her take note of his tremors and his pale skin, of the massive erection tenting the thin towel around his hips. He could see her confusion in the deepening lines between her brows.

"Tell me what's going on, Gabriel."

"I'm sorry, *querida*." His throat tried to close up on the words. "I'm afraid this night is not going to be what you expected. I'm not going to be very good company. In fact, you're probably going to have to tie me to the bed for the night and stay as far away from me as you can. Seeing you here like this . . . I don't . . . I'm not sure I can do what's necessary otherwise."

She smiled, just the tiniest crook of her lips. "Hey, *Cubano*, I'm not averse to a little bondage between friends. Could be kinda exciting." Her voice was low and soothing, running like cool water over his flayed and bleeding nerves. "But you have to tell me first what's got you so freaked. I know it can't be that gorgeous hard-on you're carrying, because we both know what to do with that."

His cock jerked at her attention, at the idea that they would do anything about it. He hissed and took a step back toward the bed. He knew she was trying to tease him, to distract him. She couldn't know it was pure torture. His skin was on fire, the towel like sandpaper where it touched him.

"Lana, stop." He was desperate to halt her slow advance. "You have to let me explain." His hands went to his head, ran through his hair until he nearly pulled it from his scalp. He wanted to scream; he held onto his control by a thread.

"This . . ."—he gestured at his body—"this is a kind of . . . fever common to my father's people. It's called the *T'haridon Set*."

"The Forging Fire." At once her eyes registered perfect understanding.

His mouth opened, but he could not speak. Of course she would know. The knowledge was there in her mind—from his.

"You need to consummate the bond between us." She took a step closer.

He scrambled backward. "No! That can't happen!"

Her jaw set. "If the bond isn't completed, you could die."

"If we complete the bond, Kinnian will find you," he shot back. "You'll be defenseless against him. He'll rip you apart, Lana. I can't stand the thought of that—of my selfishness being responsible for what he'd do to you."

Comprehension dawned in a bloom of anger over her face. "So, what's your plan, Gabriel? You fight the Fire until the bond is broken—or until your body gives out, whichever comes first?"

"It's the only way."

"And if you die tonight? How do I fight him then?" Anguish showed through the flare of temper.

"I won't die." He shook even as he said it, chills and his need for her wracking his body.

"You can't be sure of that. You can't be sure I won't die with you."

He stared at her, his heart racing, his mind spinning. "You're human. Nothing should happen to you."

"We're connected. You said so yourself." Her eyes sparked with green flame. "Already I'm starting to feel what you feel—the fever, the shakes, that . . . that *hunger* for you. How can I tie you to that bed and watch you go through this bone-crushing pain alone? While all the time I'm aching just as much, burning for you just as much? How am I supposed to keep myself away from you?"

Holy Christ, he could see it now. The flush of fever in her cheeks. The tiniest of tremors in her hands. It was starting with her, as it had with him.

But she didn't understand. "This isn't about scratching an itch, Lana! The bonding is forever. For the rest of our lives. There's no divorce, no second-guessing, no waking up in the morning wondering what the hell you've done. We hardly know each other."

She shook her head. "We know everything about each other, Gabriel. Every secret, every hidden desire, every fear, every memory. Whether we want to or not. You've already taken care of that."

"Shit!" Shaking so much he thought his bones would break, he turned away from her. "I never meant to bring us to this point. You are the one person I would have protected from this. You hated me once. It would be better if you kept on hating me."

"Yes, I hated you. But I loved you even more. I just never realized it until I saw Kinnian poised to take your life today." He felt her at his back, her touch cool and soothing on his tormented skin. "This is what I need. All my life I've been alone. I never knew how alone I was until you . . . broke me open . . . so you could get inside. I couldn't understand it, and it made me mad as hell—how it could feel so right having you there, like you were meant to be part of me. How you could see all the shit in my life and still want me."

He heard the rustle of cloth as her robe fell to the floor, felt the tug of her hands on the towel around his waist. She turned him to face her, her naked body so close to his that his arching shaft pressed hard against the skin of her belly.

Her hands lifted to frame his face. "Gabriel. I need you inside me—in my body, in my mind, in my heart. I don't ever want to be without you again."

His resistance crumbled into the flames. He tried to make one last plea for sanity, though his blood burned and his lungs gasped for air.

"Kinnian . . ."

"Separately we're no match for Kinnian." She slipped her arms around his neck to press close. His body shook with the urge to take her. "Together, who knows what we can do."

"My fierce, beautiful *targa*." He opened himself to her, found her mind without shields, and was swept up in a rising flood of emotion—*enfolding love, unshakable faith, blazing courage, piercing, shattering need*. This was the woman he knew at a depth no one else could know; the woman whose soul was in his keeping forever; the woman he now realized he loved as he had never loved another being in his life; his bondmate—forever.

Gabriel let her feel everything he was feeling, surrendered all of himself to her, as she had done for him. He felt the Fire rising in his body and in hers, demanding completion. His hands, greedy for the feel of her, slid over her hips to cup her bottom. He lifted her, spread her thighs to encircle his hips, and held her poised over his blunt, seeking crown. He covered her mouth with his, slipped his tongue inside to plunder the warm cavern of her sweet taste, craving it as much as he ached to feel the heat of her body around him. And when he couldn't wait any longer, he centered himself at her entrance and lowered her down over his shaft.

She was hot and wet for him, her folds slick and pulsing with her need, and she gripped him as he filled her. They groaned together, joined body, mind and soul, every movement, every pleasure multiplied as he felt himself in her and she felt herself engulf him. The fire built quickly, so quickly he had no time to dampen the flames. Her core was already contracting in orgasm as he lifted her and lowered her again onto his swelling shaft. Just as she gasped his name, he let go and exploded deep inside her, his release staggering him, almost bringing him to his knees.

It was only the beginning. He knew it, and he could read the comprehension in Lana's mind as well. She wasn't afraid, though their mutual need threatened to sweep her away on a riptide of passion so overwhelming she would never be the same.

He carried her to the bed, and she moaned as he laid her beneath him. "Don't leave me, Gabriel." She wrapped her legs around his hips and arched into him, forcing him deeper inside her.

"Never," he swore, stiffening again in the tight grasp of her core. He withdrew, then he pushed inside again, loving the feel of her welcoming warmth, loving the way she shuddered and cried out as he stroked her.

God, he filled her with heat and need and sweet longing until she thought she'd never get enough. She could feel his love for her in the touch of his hands at her breasts, in the brush of his lips at her throat, in the hot slide of his hard length into her slick softness. It was there in his mind as he brought her closer and closer to the brink; there as he held himself back from his own edge.

Then the orgasm detonated deep inside and rolled through her, taking her breath, taking her body, taking her conscious mind. Indescribable pleasure pulsed in waves from her frantic core outward through her chest and hips and along her spine. And she couldn't stop. The waves went on and on, each one more intense than the next, as Gabriel rode them with her.

Lana screamed his name and clutched at his shoulders, writhing and bucking as her orgasm took her. He was in her mind with her, feeling what she felt, and his shaft jerked and wept inside her in response. There was no need to hold back, he knew he would recover in minutes, but he hated to leave her mid-stride. He wanted to take her as far as she could go, to leave her spent and sated before he found his release. But *Jesus!* her core was so hot and wet with her juices and every clench of her inner muscles tightened his balls and made him throb with need.

This had to end, but she wanted it to go on forever. She was sobbing now, mindless with pleasure, Gabriel's name on her lips as he slid endlessly in and out of her. She looked up at him, saw the strain in the muscles of his chest and arms, the sweat glistening over his skin. She opened again to his mind and knew she needed to feel him shatter the way she had.

And the second she thought it, he let go, driving forward in one last desperate thrust, roaring with release as his come pumped deep inside her. He pulled back and pushed inside once more, gasping as his seed spilled again and again, hearing her moan in sweet response.

His body, his heart, were aflame with unendurable passion. Every barrier of his mind was being burned to slag in a furnace of union, a crucible of joining. Everything was hers now, every detail of his life, every nuance of his soul, given into her care. And in her acceptance, in her sweet, brave, open affirmation of him, he found peace.

The blood on his hands, the blood on the floor . . .

The blood on the floor, the sorrow, the fear, the endless running . . .

. . . all swept away in cleansing, purifying fire.

His, she was his. Everything she had, everything she was. Nothing held back. Forever. God, I love you, Gabriel.

I love you, *mi amor*. Forever.

CHAPTER TWENTY-ONE

Winslow, Arizona, Earth, Sector Three

Trevyn sat in the dark chill of the dirtside bar and stared with hooded eyes at the loose-hipped girl on the catwalk. He was hard, aching with need, but not from the stripper's pathetic efforts. And not from deprivation, either. He was fresh from the arms of a willing partner, picked up in a place not far from here. He had left her close to comatose with pleasure, thinking he'd finally sated the hunger that drove him.

He'd been wrong. And now he feared he knew why.

Somewhere nearby Gabriel and Lana were burning in the Forging Fire. They were locked in the hours-long sexual marathon of the *T'haridon Set* that would join them body, mind and soul until the end of their days. Trevyn had been caught up in the flux at the beginning of their attachment. Until the bonding was complete and their emotional parameters were reset, he would be a part of their upheaval. It was taking every bit of his control not to be drawn into what was happening between them. His mind was responding to that control. His body was . . . not.

Events had about them a sense of the inevitable now, of *trohar*, what the humans called fate. He sat in this bar, watching what he did not want to see, because that which he had warned against had happened. It was almost as if the bond had taken on a life of its own, helping Gabriel defeat Kinnian in their first round, so that the bond could be completed. Now the bond would be fully in place for the final round—so that Gabriel and Lana could defeat Kinnian? Were the gods so interested in the outcome of this contest?

Clearly Kinnian *had* been defeated in his first encounter with Gabriel. He'd even admitted to the real reason for it, cursing "that human bitch" as he lay up to his neck in fluids in the regeneration tank. Kinnian had sought out Gabriel across their link, launching an attack he was sure would catch their brother by surprise. But Kinnian had been the one surprised—by Lana's presence, by her ability to influence the mindfield, and he suffered for it now. Trevyn allowed himself a smile. He'd been tempted to put Kinnian out of his misery permanently, but though his brother was injured, he was still no fool. The captain of the *Bloodstalker* had surrounded himself with his most loyal lieutenants on constant watch for just the kind of thing Trevyn was contemplating.

The defeat only bought them time. A planetary day, perhaps. As soon as the bond was complete, as soon as Kinnian recovered, the hunt would be on again. Trevyn doubted Gabriel's ability to protect Lana's mind from Kinnian. There would be a weakness in his protections, and Kinnian would find it. That, too, was inevitable. Surely Gabriel must know it.

At any rate, Lana and Gabriel were not in this town. Trevyn had found their hotel room, still reserved under a false name, their DNA and EM markers still detectable. But they were not there; their vehicle, their weapons, their communications devices were gone. His men were watching the place, in case they returned. Trevyn suspected they had been out in search of the boy when the *T'haridon Set* had imposed its own imperatives.

So here he sat, a prisoner of their desires as much as they themselves were at this hour. He lifted the glass of amber liquid to his lips and propelled it down his throat with a quick toss of his head. It stung like a swarm of angry *zarunds* on its way to his unquiet stomach.

"Hey, Zack, set the man up again." The young man who owned the voice did not presume to sit. He kept his distance, lounging against the bar an arm's length from Trevyn. "And a Bud for me."

"You payin', Rez, or you tryin' to stiff this poor sucker?" The bartender was glaring at the newcomer with open hostility and made no move to get him a drink.

"What did you call me?"

"You heard." The bartender turned his gaze on Trevyn. "You know this guy?"

"He don't know me, but he wants to talk to me." The newcomer bared his white teeth in what passed for a grin. "Word is you been looking for something. Think I can help you find it."

Trevyn lifted his chin to dismiss the bartender. Shaking his head, the man behind the bar set a shot of whiskey and a bottle of beer in front of them and left.

Another complication, Trevyn thought. He let his unhappiness show and turned to the man beside him.

"What is it you think I'm looking for?"

"Name's Will Bates." The man held out a thin brown hand. Trevyn ignored it until he withdrew it. "I got friends around town say you been checking out the hotels, looking for somebody."

"And what business would that be of yours?"

"This ain't such a big town, mister, uh . . .?" Bates raised an eyebrow.

"Call me sir."

"How about I just call you asshole and this conversation is done, huh?"

Trevyn reached underneath the bar for the front of the man's shirt and jerked down hard. Bates' face made brutal contact with the bar rail, splitting his lip. Trevyn put an arm around his shoulders to hold him in place and spoke into his ear.

"You approached *me*, Mr. Bates. I insist upon a certain level of respect. If you have something to say, don't waste any more of my time. Get it out. Quickly."

Trevyn scanned the room and found it almost deserted this early in the afternoon. The bartender, unconcerned, continued to wash glasses at the other end of the bar. Bates had no friends in sight to back him up. Trevyn released his hold enough for the man to talk.

"Okay." Bates looked up, wiping at his bloody mouth with a shaking hand. "I just thought if you were looking for a couple of Anglos—a woman and a little boy—I might know where to find them, that's all. She said she had a husband. I thought you might be him. Thought there might be a reward or something."

The images Trevyn had leached from Bates in an unfiltered stream had showed nothing of the kind. They had revealed unbridled greed, unthinking selfishness. This man didn't care why Trevyn was looking for the two innocents he had come across on the road by accident. He didn't care what might happen to them after he'd "delivered" them. In fact, he'd been warned they should remain hidden by an older woman seeking to protect them. Bates wanted the payoff, to hell with the consequences for anyone else. But give him credit for one thing—he had what Trevyn was looking for.

Trevyn backed off. By some unlikely law of physics, the shot of whiskey had been spared in his interrogation of Bates and sat waiting for him on the bar. He drank it down. Gods, he hated himself for what he had to do next.

He laid a hand on the young man's arm. "Tell me where."

South of the Navajo Nation Indian Reservation, Arizona, Earth, Sector Three
Gabriel wanted her again.

His body, relentless in its demands, had long since pushed hers past simple exhaustion into a trance-like semi-consciousness. She responded, sometimes with fire, sometimes with languor. Sometimes she even turned to him and urged him to begin again, spurred by a need as great as his own. But she was only human, and what should be pleasure was now approaching punishment.

Lana stirred in his arms, aware of him. He cursed himself for waking her. She made a little purring sound and moved to turn and face him, but he held her tighter.

"Shh. Try to sleep."

"Sleep is not on your mind. Or mine. I want you."

"It's too soon, *querida.*" He said the words, but his body betrayed him. His hard length pulsed between them. He longed to bury himself deep inside her, to feel her slick and hot around him. He wanted to move with her until she screamed her satisfaction in his mind, until his own ran down her thighs.

Lana moaned and rotated in his embrace. "You can't think like that and expect me to ignore it, *Cubano.*" She pushed him onto his back and straddled him. She was smiling, but he saw the evidence of the *T'haridon Set* on her body—the marks of his possession on her perfect skin, the beginnings of bruises where he had held her, fierce in his need, and she had pushed back, even wilder in hers. And through their link he could feel the raw soreness underlying the ache where her sex met his. She had no skills to hide the secrets of her mind from him. She was as throbbingly close to climax as he was, but to welcome him inside as she wanted to do would cause her pain.

Gabriel sat up and gathered her to him as he swung both legs over the side of the bed. Lana yelped and wrapped her legs around his hips as he carried her to the bathroom.

"What the hell? Gabriel!"

He squatted by the oversized Jacuzzi tub and turned on the water. He continued to hold her in his lap as the tub filled, refusing to let her go, though she watched him in bemused silence.

After a moment he met her steady, green gaze. "I will never hurt you, Alana. Not even when you think it's all right."

He kissed her, a soft, tender slide of the lips at first, then a deeper, sweeping exploration of her sweet mouth as she urged him on with little hums of pleasure. At last he stepped into the steaming tub with her, settling them both into the soothing water. Then he let the water fill until they were both chest-deep in heaven. Gabriel hadn't realized how great a toll the night had taken on him until his muscles began to unwind in the blessed heat.

"Now, my sweet bondmate, I am going to teach you one of the great pleasures of sharing a bond as we do." He stroked her arm as he said it, delighting in the way her nipples peaked to attention with even so innocent a touch. "For us, sexual pleasure doesn't have to require pain, or effort, or even touch. We can share pleasure as fantasy in the bond, in our minds. Here, or even if we were separated by endless kilometers."

Lana turned to look up at him, her eyes sparkling. "Fantasy? Are you bored with me already?"

"Never, *querida*. It's a matter of simple practicality. I won't hurt you, but the *T'haridon Set* hasn't yet run its course. For either of us."

She sighed. "You have a point. I ache all over. And I still want you."

"So. Show me a fantasy. Let's play together."

Laughter shook her. "Oh, my God. And I was worried about my childhood secrets."

He smiled behind her head, where she couldn't see him. "Would it be easier if I chose one for you? How about the two cowboys? That seems to be your favorite."

"Jesus, Gabriel! No! Well, not for the first time, anyway." Her whole body was flushing red, but she was intrigued. Her thoughts ricocheted for a moment, then coalesced and focused.

Ah! Yes. Your office! He slipped into his role at once: *a dangerous man with criminal ties and something you need. A forbidden liaison, a semi-public place, coming together in a blaze of uncontrollable lust...*

. . . Lana opened her eyes. She still lay in the heated water of the bath, Gabriel's arms wrapped around her, the steam rising to fill the room. Yet her pulse pounded, her core, drenched with the proof of her arousal, throbbed with the last throes of her orgasm. Gabriel's warm hand still cupped her mound, but she didn't think he'd physically stimulated her to climax. As he'd promised, the fantasy had been sufficient.

"My God." She could barely find enough energy to speak.

He kissed her just below her ear. "Oh, yes. A very, *very* nice choice, *mi amor*. You are extraordinarily talented both in this world and in the mindfield. So talented, in fact, I think we may have burned through the Forging Fire at last. How do you feel now?"

"Warm. Satisfied." She sighed. "Like I could curl up next to you and sleep for a week."

A murmur of agreement rumbled through his chest. "But I think we'll have to settle for a couple of hours and make up the difference with food. I feel like I could eat an entire *psoros*."

She thought for a moment and captured the image of a shaggy, four-legged ruminant running a grassy plain, then a carcass being roasted over an open fire. She could even taste the smoky, heavy flavor of the meat. Her stomach growled.

"I think I agree. Sleep first or eat first?"

"Better sleep first. We can't afford to be out long. Our hunger will wake us."

She was nearly asleep already in the warm comfort of his arms and the hot water. "We should get in the bed."

"Mmm. In a moment."

--*So how does this thing work, Gabriel?* Her heart sped up as she opened herself to the presence she felt in her mind. It had seemed so effortless in the heat of passion; now she was suddenly shy. *Will you always be . . . here like this?*

His warmth filled her, reassured her. *Your thoughts are your own, Lana;* y*ou'll learn to communicate what you want, to keep what you want to yourself. You know I won't violate your privacy. The link is strongest at the level of emotion. Can you feel it?*

The connection between them was like a live wire, humming with vital energy. Love flooded her heart.

--*I feel it*, k'taam. K'taam. *That's the proper word, isn't it?*

Gabriel smiled. *Yes. The word "beloved" is often used between bondmates. It must have been on my mind.*

He sat up and turned her to face him. "There's something else in your heart, *k'taama*. Let me answer that question so there can be no mistake. We may have no paperwork to show we are married, but we are joined forever. No matter where we are, we will always be aware of each other. You belong to me and I to you in a way no human marriage vows could ever enforce. And I'm sorry you had no choice in this."

Lana lifted a hand to stroke his cheek. "If I had been given all the time in the world to think about it, I would have made the same choice. We belong together. And I thank God for the bond that will keep us together, no matter what. Something tells me we're going to need it."

Trin, Center for Adminstrative Control, Minertsa, Sector 10

Sennik sat at the center of an aura the color of his planet's primeval mud and struggled to keep the blood red of murder from leaking out and revealing his innermost thoughts. This meeting was not going well.

--I tell you we are losing momentum, and with it the strategic advantage we held just ten solar cycles ago. General Zipriss of the Ministry of Defense showed an aura black with rage and shot through with heavy, bilious greens. He felt he was being betrayed. *We must move to secure what gains we have made.*

--If we move too fast, we risk exposure before we are ready. Sennik injected calming lavender into his aura. *The plan is on schedule, never fear.*

--The plan! That's all we ever hear from you, Sennik. And yet, we are never privy to any details. Director Prime Larrik of the Ministry of Mines and Natural Resources had long been an ally, but he was no fool. And his neutral aura of silver-gray was unreadable. *Were you aware that Vadis had set up a partnership in secret with a group of investors outside his immediate family? The factory on Paridius is almost ready to begin production.*

Auras around the table went dark with shock and

consternation. Even Sennik was unable to control his reaction.

Agriculture's Rhondis was bright red with anger. *Those* mrill-*fucked abolitionists are behind this, as sure as I am born of mud. They are everywhere!*

--Do we know who is behind the investment, Larrik? Sennik would cut their throats personally.

Larrik lifted a hand in indifference. *It may be as Rhondis says. But there are also many of our own fine citizens who wish to see a change in the way of things and believe there may be profit in it as well.*

The General's aura went as dark as a thundercloud. *Would that include you, Larrik?*

The Director Prime of Mines allowed the slightest tinge of red to darken his silver aura. *The labor requirements of my department are the most demanding of any in the government, General. They cannot be met by any means other than forced human labor, no matter what my personal wishes or beliefs may be. The Minertsan Consortium cannot survive without slavery.*

--Indeed. And isn't that why we are all here? The deep, royal blue of loyalty and patriotism bled into Sennik's aura. *I can assure you all that the plan we have agreed upon is proceeding on schedule. We have planted the seeds of discontent. Soon we will reap the benefits of chaos. Continue your work as you have always done. Prepare for the future. The new cycle will turn upon our vision of a new Empire.*

When the others had filed from his office, he

wasted no time taking the necessary steps to ensure his promises had something of substance behind them. *Ardis. Connect me with Mezin Xe on Savagne. His private code.*

His aide was as efficient as ever, but Sennik resented the time spent waiting for the connection to be made. He resented having to take this action at all, for it meant that his elegant plot was in need of reinforcement and repair. His Thranes had failed him, still mucking about on Earth somewhere in search of the boy that was the key to his plan. He could not afford to wait while they scoured the cursed planet for the child. Zipriss was right. They were in danger of losing momentum. Sennik had to use his backup plan.

--Director Prime, Board Chairman Xe is in the comm window for you now, sir.

Sennik looked up and activated the window in his field of vision to display the elongated head and neck, the green skin and vertical irises of the Savagnoir, director of one of the galaxy's wealthiest commercial conglomerates. The exploitation of raw resources on primitive planets, the manufacture of weapons and entertainment technology, cutting edge research into genetic manipulation and chemical transmutation, even the simple transportation of goods throughout the galaxy—*everything* was XEX's business. And if it was not, and it was profitable, then XEX's chairman very quickly made it his business.

A slurry of sibilance was translated in Sennik's mind. *I've been expecting your call.*

--Chairman Xe. It seems I will have need of the backup unit to the one that was destroyed on Del Origa.

--I anticipated that. Work began on a second transmitter as soon as the first one was destroyed.

Sennik felt a small thrill of hope. *Your reputation for efficiency is well deserved.*

--Perhaps. But there has been an unforeseen obstacle to progress. It has entailed some delay.

--What sort of obstacle and how long a delay? The Director Prime did not bother to couch his inquiry in polite terms. He was under too much pressure of his own.

--Both of a minor nature, I assure you.

Damn these other-worlders! No auras to read, no inferences to be drawn through the layers of translation. Sennik could tell nothing from the words he heard in his mind.

--What has happened, Chairman Xe? I must insist that you be specific.

The Savagnoir dipped his head twice, the equivalent of a shrug. *The human engineer that built the unit is no longer in my . . . employ. His expertise has been difficult to replace.*

--But surely not impossible?

--Not impossible, no. But it will take time to complete your transmitter to its original specifications.

Sennik seethed, his aura the color of untracked space. *How long?*

A long hiss sounded through the audio pickup as thin membranes slid down to cover Xe's yellow eyes. *A better question might be how much, my friend.*

--You would hold me hostage to your profit now?

--Think of your own gain, Director Prime. My commission is but a small part of what you stand to take in this. I believe the humans have a saying: Time is money.

Red, vivid as a wound, shot through the black of his aura. *I need this unit now, Xe.*

--I can have it to you by the end of this lunar cycle if the price is right.

Fucking pirate! *Name it and I will send you the credits by transfer.*

Xe's hiss of satisfaction needed no translation.

Ardis backed out of the translation program as efficiently as she had tapped in. No trace of her intrusion remained behind; neither Sennik nor Xe would ever know she'd been listening. And when the Director Prime swept past her on his way out of the building, her aura shone a bland lavender and violet, tinged with the bright blue of sexual interest she was required to show him now at all times.

She was pleased to note Sennik's own aura was tinged a sickly yellow, despite his best efforts to maintain his neutral silver-gray. He was disturbed by his meeting and his conversation with Xe. Still, the

Director Prime would have what he wanted in less than three solar cycles, though the negotiation made it clear he'd paid more than he'd planned.

She'd read the specs. The sophisticated communications networking device would take over the functions the boy, ID 425907, had been programmed to serve, coordinating signals to the human slaves Sennik had in place throughout the galaxy. Using the device risked exposure, where the boy would have been untraceable. But having the transmitter gave Sennik one advantage—it would allow him to begin his campaign of destabilization without further delay.

She had to do something. It was no longer possible for anyone else to save the situation. There was no time to develop an elaborate plan or hope for intervention. Only Ardis was close enough to Sennik to stop him. She knew what Slindar would have done.

Xe had mentioned a human engineer—the one who had developed the transmitter. Recently such a man had famously escaped XEX control on Savagne. It was said the same shadowy organization that sent humans to meet her in the dark at the Lorenda Venue had engineered his escape. If that was true, then she had a way to contact him. And if she could only have enough time, she might have a way to sabotage the transmitter and put a stop to Sennik's plan.

CHAPTER TWENTY-TWO

Navajo Nation Indian Reservation, Arizona, Earth, Sector Three

Asia had entered the sweat lodge with a breaking heart. Oh, she had covered the hurt with anger, but Geneva and the other elders had seen through it and treated her with firm, but tender, care. Jack could not be with her, they'd explained with infinite patience. He would be with the men in the other *hogan*. She would spend the day undergoing purification in the women's lodge. It did no good to protest that he was only a boy, years from puberty and a man's obligations. Despite his youth, Jack was at the center of all their preparation.

At least Jack had seemed to understand. He hadn't been afraid to leave her. She had hid her tears from him, but now she struggled to hold them back in the dark and heat of the sweat lodge. Packed shoulder to shoulder, hip to hip, with Geneva and the other women of the tribe, dressed only in a towel, Asia felt isolated, alone, as she had for days. This was not her world; this was not a world she understood. But Geneva Twohawks had said what they did here would save her son, so she would do what had to be done.

At the center of the *hogan*, heat emanated from the pit of red-hot rock, forcing the sweat from Asia's pores, searing the air that she breathed, prickling her scalp and stinging her eyes. She let the heat wash over her and through her, let it infuse the singing and the drumming until they became one thing and pushed out the thought that threatened to strip her of all her courage. Thought was her enemy. She had no use for it if it couldn't help her defend her son. As words drained from her mind and left her empty of thought, sweat drained from her body and left her empty of poison. Agitation drained from her heart and left her empty of fear. Toward the end, even her soul seemed to drain away, until her awareness drifted and was caught in the web of another place and time.

Outside the lake house the rain swept through the trees, whipped by a wind that held the cold promise of winter. But a brave fire was crackling in the huge hearth, and Ethan's arms were warm around her, his voice soft and reassuring in her ear.

"They can't have been human to hurt you like they did." His hand stroked her hair. "My Asia, my sweet, beautiful Asia."

A night, almost two years ago, a memory she had sworn no one would ever take from her mind. She had known by that time that the alien Grays had taken her, but the larger picture had yet to be revealed. She had been battered and confused, on the run and recovering from a loss that had taken her to the crumbling edge of a pit of self-destruction. Ethan had been there to pull her back and to hold her in the firelight as afternoon turned to darkest night, whispering her name.

She sat up. "Ethan?"

He smiled. "I'm right here."

"But you're not real." She looked around. Every detail was the same, more vivid than any dream. The soft glow of firelight on the pine paneling. The smell of wood smoke. The moan of the wind outside. "None of this is real."

"It's as real as you need it to be." He touched her cheek, demanding her attention. "And so am I."

Guilt and sorrow coiled around her heart. The last thing she'd wanted was to hurt him. "Ethan, I'm so sorry. You know I have—"

He raised a finger to her lips, silencing her. "We don't have much time. I don't want to argue."

She stared into his eyes, eyes the color of deep Northern oceans, and suddenly knew why she was here. Not to explain herself or justify her actions or convince Ethan to let her go, but to say the things she might not have a chance to say to him ever again.

She took his hands in hers. "You brought me

back from a very dark place, Ethan Roberts. And every day you give me new reasons to be grateful for that. I love you. Never forget that."

Ethan's gaze returned her love in equal measure. But his grin was playful.

"Hold that thought."

Awareness returned to Asia with the sudden snap of a breaking dream. She opened her eyes to find the inside of the *hogan* unchanged, except, perhaps for the heavier scent of sweat and sage, of piñon pine and red rock. Many of the women sat with eyes closed, swaying or nodding in rhythm with the drums and their own pulses, some walking in the Spirit World, as she had been.

Geneva Twohawks, however, sat watching her. "You have seen something?"

She hardly knew where to begin.

At that moment, a young woman came to the doorway of the lodge and worked her way around to where they sat facing the stone fire pit. "Elder Twohawks. There are some people here to see you. One man says he is the Timewalker's husband. Sheriff Begay is with them."

Her heart expanded to break through her ribcage. "Ethan!" What Ethan had said in her vision made perfect sense now. She moved to get to her feet, but Geneva held her in place with an iron grip on her forearm.

"Wait. We cannot be sure it is him. The evil ones—"

"It's him! That's what he was trying to tell me in the vision."

"Then you cannot see him until you have washed." Geneva nodded at the girl, dismissing her. The girl went with a short bow.

"What? I haven't seen him in days! I'm sure he won't mind that I haven't had a shower!" Asia made as if to stand again and again was pulled down. The old lady was stronger than she looked.

"The sweat lodge is for purifying the body. Removing poison—fear, heartache, weakness." Geneva's stare probed deep. "Would you pass all that on to him now? Already he will have to carry his own poison with him into battle—there will be no time for him to go into the sweat lodge before we go to war. It would have been better if he had not come here, but since he is here you must go to him clean. It is the best you can do for him."

Asia didn't want to wait another second to see Ethan, but the old woman was adamant. The two of them rose and left the lodge, emerging into the heat of the late afternoon, a heat that felt almost cool on her skin after the sauna of the *hogan*. Geneva led her around the back of the lodge to a screened-off area equipped with buckets of water and basins, soap and towels for washing. The cool water felt like heaven on her overheated skin, but she hurried through her bath, spurred by the sound of Ethan's voice, arguing with several of the men in the outer compound.

God, she had to see him; she had to feel his arms

around her. She wanted him so badly she was shaking and breathless, barely able to manage the heavy basins of water. But at last she had washed the heavy sweat from her body and shampooed the shine back into her hair. She dressed in the clean jeans and tee-shirt someone had laid out for her and ran for the center of the compound.

Jack was already there, his small, pale arms slung around Ethan's neck as Ethan knelt to enfold him. The man she loved stood with their son still wrapped around him and held out an arm to include her. She ran to him, buried her face in his chest, put her arms around him and Jack and tried hard not to fall apart. She breathed, and every breath carried his scent deep into her being. So familiar. So real and present, where for so long he'd been nothing but a distant dream.

She looked up at last to see his face. "I can't believe you're really here."

His eyes, dark with concern, met hers. "They wouldn't let me see you. Are you okay?"

She started to explain about the ritual, or to make some joke about the bath, but the words wouldn't come. Tears slid down her cheeks as she nodded.

He pulled her back into his chest and held her, his voice a gentle murmur in her ear.

Geneva Twohawks approached them, wearing a grin that seemed unsuited to her usually solemn face. "Come. She and the boy need food and drink. We can talk as we eat."

They began to move toward a big open-sided tent at

a distance from the compound, where tables and chairs had been set up and food was laid out for the many people attending the ceremonies. Asia turned her head to see Rayna and Sam trailing along with them and stopped long enough to receive hugs from both of them.

Rayna squeezed her hard. "How many times are we going to have to save your ass, girl?"

"How did you find us?"

"We heard from Gabriel a couple of hours ago. He should be here soon."

Asia couldn't fault her friends for coming. God, she needed Ethan so much. But she feared for him, too. She couldn't protect him here.

"I told Ethan to stay away until this was over."

Ray shook her head. "You ought to know by now you couldn't keep him away. He wouldn't hear it from us either. Nothing would do but we all come out here in the freaking desert to bring you home."

Asia sighed, close to tears again. "Damn it."

They entered the tent and found seats at one of the long tables with Geneva, Leonard Begay and several of the other elders. They were brought plates of food and plastic cups of water. Asia found she was both famished and parched after her time in the sweat lodge. She did the food justice despite her emotions, washing it down with cup after cup of water.

Ethan sat between her and Jack, his thigh tight against hers under the table, as if he had to be in constant contact with her. His warmth, his nearness, resonated in her body in tiny tremors. She wanted all of these people to disappear so she could be alone with him. Selfishly, she didn't even want Jack to come between them. She just wanted Ethan. She wanted all of this to be over so she could feel him holding her, so she could feel him moving inside her, so they could sleep at night safe in their own home once again.

One glance at her and Ethan must have known it. "Asia, let me take you away from here." His hand touched her hair. "You're tired, you need to rest. If you don't think it's safe at home, we'll stay on the ship with Ray and Sam."

She wanted to, God knew she did. But she shook her head.

"I can't."

His lips compressed, though he said nothing. Asia didn't want to fight with him. Not now. Not here, in front of all these people. Her heart shrank in her chest, shriveling in despair. How to make him understand?

"Ethan, this place, these people—this is our only chance against what hunts Jack."

"How can you be so sure?" He glanced around, then spoke so only she could hear him. "These people aren't fighters, Asia. I don't see any weapons, any places to hide. Why are you here?"

"Something bigger than we are brought me here because this is where Jack needs to be. Yet despite everything, we may still fail." Anger rose to meet his stubborn resistance. "That's why I asked you to stay away. If you came hoping to change my mind, there's still time for you to leave."

His whole body went taut. "I came because I couldn't stand to wait at home while you were in a fight for your life two thousand miles away. I came because I'm your husband and Jack's father, and I'm supposed to protect you. I came because that's what a man does. Can you understand that?"

His voice had not risen above a low rasp, but the way his gaze had locked onto hers, the way the two of them were entwined in an intensity of emotion, could not be missed, even in the noise and conversation of the tent. Faces turned in their direction, then looked away. Conversation dropped as people held their breath.

Asia ignored them all, held by the hurt—and the love—in Ethan's eyes. "Yeah, baby. I can understand that." She reached out to touch his cheek. "And I'm sorry we have to stay, but I'm so, so glad to have you with me."

The late afternoon sun hung low in the western sky, spreading deep yellow light like melting butter across the valley floor. The heat rode the light in waves that washed across her skin and dropped deep into her lungs with the air. Lana squinted behind her sunglasses, unsure whether it was the light or the heat that pinholed her vision.

"That must be Miz Twohawks's ranch up ahead."

She pointed off to the left. "There's nothing else for miles."

Behind the wheel, Gabriel lifted an eyebrow. "Looks like half the county is here." He slowed and turned off onto the dirt drive that led up to the property.

Trucks, Jeeps, horse trailers and old dented cars of all descriptions lined the road and sat parked in the desert leading up to Geneva Twohawks's home. A number of permanent outbuildings huddled behind the house—sheds, a barn—as well as several pens for livestock. There were also two of the rounded huts used for traditional ceremonies by the Navajo people. Fires built outside the *hogans* indicated they'd been used recently.

Gabriel parked the car and looked at Lana, waiting.

She nodded at an open tent outside the compound's perimeter. "Everybody's out back."

They left the car and made their way toward the tent. Lana ignored the impulse to keep her right hand near her shoulder holster and let it drop to her side. She could sense Gabriel's state of mind as if it were her own. He felt no threat here among these people, though he knew they were all in danger. She found herself relaxing under his influence.

Several people noted them as they passed and nodded, but no one stopped them. Lana tilted her head.

"Would you think I was crazy if I said it was as if they were expecting us?"

"No. They're preparing for something."

"And we're part of it."

"Yes."

Their link told her he was disturbed by the idea. "That's what Sam meant when he said Asia was convinced she was safer here, that these people had some idea how to fight Kinnian."

Gabriel met her eyes, and suddenly she understood. These people were allies. Her bondmate hesitated only because he feared he couldn't protect them, because his sense of responsibility now included them.

Lana sent a wave of warmth along their bond. *Together we are stronger*, k'taam. *All of us.*

They entered the tent, and all conversation stopped. Every face turned to stare at them, not in hostility, not even in curiosity, but in expectation. Sam and Rayna jumped up from the table nearest them and came to greet Gabriel with smiles and hugs, while everyone else at that table stood waiting.

Gabriel wasted no time in explaining the change in Lana's status. He tucked her under his arm.

"Sam, Ray. You've met Alana before. She and I are bonded now."

Sam's jaw dropped. Ray elbowed him before she smiled and stepped forward for a hug.

"Something told me you two would hit it off. Or kill each other. Congratulations."

Lana laughed and hugged the tiny woman back, registering the strength of her grasp with some surprise. Rayna had scarcely moved when Sam rushed in and scooped Lana up into a bear hug, a huge grin on his face.

"God knows he needed this! Nice job, Lana!"

Lana felt a strange hollow twinge in the vicinity of her heart and turned to see Gabriel watching her, pride and love warming his dark eyes to the color of sweet chocolate. He allowed her a small, private smile and a wave of intimate feeling through their bond before he turned to face Ethan and the woman and small boy that had been the focus of their desperate search.

Gabriel nodded to Ethan, his face solemn. Ethan, caught in the same mood, returned his nod, but did not speak. The tracker turned to the slender woman beside Ethan and again inclined his head.

"Ma'am. Believe me when I say that Agent Matheson and I did all we could to find you and bring you to safety. It seems that circumstances have brought us all to this place and time. Perhaps that is for the best. I pledge my life to your son's protection in what is to come. And to yours." He shifted his gaze to Ethan. "If you will allow it."

Ethan held out a hand to him and when Gabriel took it, he offered a brief smile. "In these past couple of weeks, my family has valued your help, and Lana's, more than you know, Gabriel. We need you more than ever now. Thank you."

Asia smiled and reached up to hug him, then turned to hug Lana, too. "Thank you, both. You have no idea how much it helped to know you were looking for us."

Lana looked down into the biggest pair of blue eyes she'd ever seen—and met more wisdom than she could ever have guessed. "You must be Jack."

"The Holy Ones said you'd be coming." He stared up at Gabriel. "With him."

Gabriel got down on one knee to speak with the boy. "And what did they say about me?"

Jack grinned. "They said you can kick butt!"

"Jack Roberts!" Asia looked appalled. "You haven't said a word in days and that's what you choose to say first?"

Gabriel only laughed, but Lana felt she had to answer the boy. "I can tell you from direct experience that the Holy Ones are correct."

"The Holy Ones have much to say about these two." Geneva Twohawks had risen from the table to join them. "Much that everyone should hear."

Asia drew her closer. "This is the woman who has been sheltering us, Geneva Twohawks. Her people have devised a strategy."

Gabriel nodded. "We'd like to hear it."

Geneva held up a hand. "Elders, hear this. People, listen to what the hawks have told me. The help we have been waiting for has come. These two stand now as one, bringing the strength of heart's fire. But we face a battle to the death. And if heart or mind fail and even love cannot hold, the Nameless One will be loosed upon the waking world with none to stop him. Then even the Old Ones will not be able to help us."

CHAPTER TWENTY-THREE

Trin, Minertsa, Sector 10

Ardis slipped through the doors of the Public Records Archive a mere segment of a solar cycle before closing time. *Mrillingas* take it! She had little time to finish what she'd come to do, but there was no help for it now. Sennik had kept her in the office long past closing time working out the final details of his plan— the plan she sought to divert.

At this time of night, there were few researchers in Collections Building II and none in the area of the archives she chose. She found the most isolated desk in the loneliest corner of the room, one she knew was out of sight of the monitoring equipment. Then she initiated interaction with the compscreen and proceeded to nullify the system's security protocols.

Somewhere in the vast web of communications linking Minertsa with the galaxy beyond was an elusive, nearly invisible thread tied to an organization so secretive even Ardis did not know its name. Her goal tonight was to gain access to that thread and make direct contact. Her usual contacts with the group, so long maintained only by meetings at the Lavenda Venue, had been cut off since the night of her partner's arrest. But an emergency contact had given her what she needed. And tonight, she hoped to speak by internodal link to the human who could tell her what to do.

There! All barriers were down. Ardis entered the correct codes and sent the initializing message. Her aura flared with the intense aquamarine of her excitement.

Madam. Excuse the interruption, but we will be closing the Archives in half a segment.

Though Ardis rushed to dampen her aura back to lavender, she failed to bleach all of the tell-tale color from her emissions. She turned to acknowledge the staff member, but did not dare respond.

The male was young, a guard in uniform. *Are you all right, madam? You seem unwell.*

--Oh, yes. Forgive my excitement. It seems I may have found the information I have been seeking for some time. Archival research can be so tedious, you know.

Now the young male's own aura was tinged with the light blue of amusement. *I quite understand, madam. I will complete my own degree program in the next quadracycle. I am pleased for you.*

Ardis inclined her head. *Thank you. Perhaps you wouldn't mind if I just finished up here quickly?*

He caught the hint and bowed out. *Not at all. I'll*

try to give you a few extra hundredths.

Her pulse pounding, Ardis went back to the compscreen and found an answer to her opening greeting. *Miracle!* The humans had found the man she sought.

--I am Martin Blake. How can I help you?

Ardis stared at the compscreen. Such a simple question. Such a complicated answer.

--My superior has recently commissioned a second prototype of a device you once designed to his specifications on behalf of your former employer. It was a type of EM transmitter keyed to human brainwave patterns. The first example was destroyed during the attack on Minertsan facilities at Del Origa VII. Are you familiar with the device to which I refer?

--Yes. Are you certain the second device can be delivered?

--It has been guaranteed by your former employer. A great deal of credit depends on it.

--Then it will be delivered. Xe never misses a chance for profit. When?

--Two solar cycles now.

--There's no time to stop the shipment.

--That is why I contacted you. You must tell me how to sabotage the machine from here.

--Impossible. If your boss is who I think he is, he won't let anyone near that thing. He has a lot invested in this. A whole team of Rescue commandos couldn't get to it.

--He will be expecting a whole team of commandos, Martin Blake. He will not be expecting me. However, I acknowledge that it would be easier to disable the machine from a distance, as I would not have a legitimate excuse to be in the vicinity. Would that be possible?

There was a pause in the telemetry as Blake considered the request. Then a single line appeared on the screen.

--How good are you with reflexive, multipartite synthesizing program coding?

Ardis's aura began to glow a fierce gold.

Navajo Nation Indian Reservation, Arizona, Earth, Sector Three

Trevyn watched the desert sky grow dark over the cluster of shacks that sheltered his brother's prey. Red and orange and deep purple threw the ragged edges of the rooflines in sharp relief against the horizon, while behind him squad after squad of men dematerialized from the ship and reformed in ranks in the draw. When the light was gone they would attack.

"Where is that piece of shit you found in town?" Kinnian's black eyes glittered in the dying light. "He should be here to join the fun."

"I took the information I needed from him, then I killed him." It was a lie. Trevyn had left Will Bates drugged and handcuffed to a bed in a motel room in Winslow. If he himself lived out this night he would release Bates in the morning.

Kinnian grunted with satisfaction. "Good. A traitor should always be the first to die. Though I must say you surprise me, brother." His gaze slid sideways at his sibling. Trevyn felt the pressure of Kinnian's probing at his shields.

He held fast. "I'm tired of this chase. Time for it to be over."

"Well said." Kinnian's smile spread like 'bot oil over his face. "Grab the boy. Kill the others and be done with it."

Trevyn gripped his emotions tight. There was more. He waited for it.

"Ah, but Gabriel and his new bride—did I tell you I discovered her name, Trevyn? Yes. Alana."

Kinnian watched him like a spider. Trevyn refused to move a muscle of his face. He did not blink or swallow. He did not frown or smile or twitch. He merely breathed. In. Out. As if the information was of no interest to him at all. As if he could not care less that it meant that the killer beside him was one step closer to finding the woman who had a hold on his heart, as well as Gabriel's.

"Alana, Alana, Alana. Tonight I will torture your Gabriel until I am as hard as a bulkhead. Then I will make him watch as I take your mind so you beg me to fuck you over and over again. We'll do it every night, my darling, until I grow tired of you, then I'll send the both of you to the mine pits of lzpatra. That will be fun, don't you think, Trevyn? Want in on the action?"

Trevyn, so sick with nausea he tasted the bile in his mouth, lifted an indifferent shoulder. "Perhaps. I haven't seen her yet."

Kinnian howled with laughter. "Ever discriminating, eh, brother?" He slapped him on the back. "You haven't seen her yet!" He leaned closer, hatred sparking from his eyes. "I tell you I don't care if she's ugly as a *nuntoc*. I will ruin her, body and mind. Just to see Gabriel's face."

And yet, with no training at all, this woman had bested him in her first experience of the mindfield. Of course, that was part of the reason for Kinnian's fury.

"Are you certain you're feeling completely recovered, my lord? Perhaps I should go in with the troops first to secure the ranch."

"No!" Kinnian whirled on him. "Gabriel and his bitch are *mine!* You can see to the boy." He turned to yell at the company commander. "We go in as soon as it is dark."

Trevyn's hand fell to his dirk, sheathed on the left side of his belt. The moves played deep in his mind, behind the barriers that protected his innermost thoughts. Two steps, now three, to bring himself even with Kinnian. A closing of the fingers to grip the weapon, the fall of his arm to bring it to his right side. In the clinch, left arm around his throat, stab to the right kidney to shock, then a killing slice across the throat. He could hold his mind quiet long enough.

And the consequences? To hell with them. He was second in command. If he took the boy and got their payoff, the crew would follow him.

He took a step. Two.

Then across the desert sand, drums began to sound. Kinnian spun to stare at him.

"What the fucking hell is that?"

On the edge of the compound, where the dust of the corrals and the driveways became the scrub of the desert, the drum circle had been established, with a leaping bonfire at its center. All of the Navajos except the very oldest had joined the circle of dancers turning in patterns at the limit of the fire's light, their voices rising and falling in the ancient call to the Holy Ones for help.

Gabriel stood several paces outside the circle and watched the darkness in the desert beyond the firelight. Lana slid an arm around his waist and waited with him.

He nodded at the last of the purple light fading in the western sky. "We don't have much time."

Sam, back on board the *Shadowhawk*, monitored a force of 60 massed in a shallow draw about a kilometer southeast of where they stood. Kinnian would wait until dark to attack with conventional forces, believing they were defenseless. Gabriel's strategy was to strike first—in the mindfield.

"The plan is a good one." Lana squeezed his side.

"The Navajos know this land—the canyons and the hills are as familiar to their minds as their faces in the mirror."

Gabriel shook his head. "These elders may have traveled in the Spirit World, but they've never had to fight in it. And Ethan and Asia—"

"Will be with us. And with Jack, who has more power than any of us."

"He's untrained."

"You'll help him."

He turned to look at the woman who was bonded to him now for as long as he lived—took in her golden, curly hair, contained in a knot at the top of her head; her green eyes reflecting the flame of her courage; the easy strength in her body; the warmth that lived in her heart and soul. If he could keep her from this fight, safe in some protected hideaway, he would do it. Yet there was no one he'd rather have fighting at his side. Smiling, she sent a wave of liquid heat along their bond. She knew his heart—and felt the same way.

He glanced back out into the desert, unable to shake the bitter awareness of another presence.

Lana followed his gaze and shivered. "He's here. I can feel him."

"We'll be done with him tonight." Gabriel turned to pull her into his arms and kissed her, gently at first, then with a longing and a need that threatened to crush him before he got it under control.

He broke off and met her eyes. *I love you,* k'taama. *Stay close to me tonight.*

And I love you, k'taam. *As close as your heart.*

He clasped her hand and turned back to the spot near the drummers where Geneva Twohawks, Ethan, Asia, Jack and several others waited. They sat, and Gabriel cleared his mind.

Surrounded by the drums and the smoke, the singing took him.

CHAPTER TWENTY-FOUR

In the mindfield, no physical coordinates

Bright sun overturned the darkness. Choking heat replaced the cool desert night air. Canyon walls rose on three sides around him, forming a box of jagged stone with a narrow strip of cloudless blue sky at the top, a floor of gritty sand at the bottom and a narrow slit at one end to allow entrance or exit. Shadows slanted across the canyon walls, hiding his people in the ledges and rock falls well above the canyon floor. Below them was the killing field they'd prepared in their minds for Kinnian and his troops.

Gabriel faced the tiny knot of people who would fight beside him. "We'll only have one chance, a few seconds at most. His crew is connected to Kinnian, just as we are all connected. They will follow when I spring the trap. Do what you can before Kinnian gets everyone out of here."

Ethan and Lana held automatic weapons. Asia carried a small, but serviceable Glock. Jack was hidden in a tiny niche in the rock, safely out of the path of flying bullets or the laser weapons favored by Kinnian's crew. Gabriel had explained to the boy that once the trap was sprung his job was to hold an image in his mind of this place filled with Kinnian and his men, reinforcing the "reality" of the setting and keeping Kinnian there long enough for them to do him real damage.

"This is probably the only time you'll get to use that." He nodded at Lana's gun. "Close in and mind-to-mind, they're too hard to control. We tend to favor bladed weapons or pure energy blasts."

Lana tilted her head. "That's what I saw you using against Kinnian before—the lightning?"

He nodded.

"Too bad there's no time for a little training session."

He smiled and stood up to wave across the narrow canyon to Leonard Begay. "Ready?"

Leonard waved back. "All set."

The others set their sights on the swath of sand below, and Gabriel reached deep in his mind to connect with the power he needed. Like a fire in his soul, he felt Lana. He felt Ethan and Jack and the others like a wall at his back. He heard, far away and deep in his blood, the drums beating and the Dineh elders singing, feeding him strength. He took a breath and plunged, seeking the thread that would link him to Kinnian. He cut through the barriers that protected them all, seized the link and pulled.

In the bottom of the canyon, Kinnian appeared out of nowhere, surrounded by sixty of his men. A shout rose all around him, drowning out Gabriel's own order.

"Now!"

Fire and rock and bullets rained down on the men in the canyon, killing a third of them where they stood. The rest scattered and shielded, acting on instinct, seeking cover from an attack that had taken them from the draw where they had been gathering for their own assault to this unknown place. The most experienced and skilled among them returned fire, scoring and blistering the canyon walls with lasers or blasting at the rock with bursts of blue-white energy thrown from their hands.

Only Kinnian stood his ground, looking up at Gabriel with a hatred so black it darkened the sky. He raised a hand and lightning shattered the canyon wall just above them.

Gabriel dove for the person next to him—it was Ethan, his weapon trained on the last man standing below—and threw him to the ground as the cliff above them cracked and lost cohesion.

The landslide he expected arrived as a soft fall of dust on their backs. He raised his head to see Lana grinning at him. She shrugged.

Gabriel turned to check on his people. Asia was gathering Jack into her arms from his hiding place, and though everyone was now covered with a fine layer of red dust, all seemed unhurt.

He turned back to Lana, and in an instant, the sun was taken from the sky, dropping them into pitch darkness. The heat was taken from the air, wrapping them in a fetid, damp cold.

Disoriented, he could only think to freeze and bark an order to do the same. "Don't move!"

No one spoke, but he could sense them all still with him.

Lana touched his hand. *It's the cave where Kinnian fought you before, isn't it?*

--Yes. He owns this island on Thrane. "We have to go back to Navajo land. There's a switchback trail leading up a mesa called Laughing Mother. Do you all see it?"

"No." Ethan's voice came out of the dark. "Wait. Grab my hand, Jack. Okay, I've got it. All these damn trails look the same to me."

Gabriel focused on what he knew of the trail from old man Nakai's mind and took them there, even as the black cave they were in began to echo with the sound of heavy boots and the shouts of Kinnian's men. In a heartbeat, Gabriel and the others found themselves on a broad, flat overlook off the main trail up the mesa, the sleeping desert spread out below them in the silver light of a full moon.

Ethan stood with his arms around his tiny family. "What the hell just happened?"

"Kinnian tried to take back the home field advantage."

"And we're supposed to go on all night like that? What if he beams us into the middle of an interstate next time?"

Gabriel grunted. "Not his style, fortunately."

"Ethan has a point, babe. This isn't very productive." Lana nodded at the boy. "Can't we use Jack to block him?"

Gabriel shook his head. "It's too dangerous. We risk Kinnian getting a separate hold on him." *And, damn it, I can't feel Trevyn at all. Where the hell is he?*

Lana said nothing, thought nothing, but her heart shared his unquiet. Deep down, he could tell she felt a haunting sadness at the thought of Trevyn that even she did not understand. Gabriel studied her face for a moment, then put it aside.

"There is something we might try, though." Gabriel paced, his thoughts reaching back to his training, then running ahead to their problem. "With Jack's raw power, I might be able to deflect Kinnian's next attempt to move us and land us all somewhere else."

Lana was there ahead of him. "We need a defensible site."

"No. We need a battleground."

Lana met his eyes and, after a second's thought, nodded. Ethan and Asia watched him, waiting.

He explained. "If we try another ambush, Kinnian will just escape to another venue and try to draw us there." He glanced at Ethan. "As you say, it could go on all night with no resolution. Or he could catch us in a trap from which we could find no way out. Our goal should be to make him fight—engage him with blades, make him think he has a chance of winning."

Asia shook her head. "With blades? Are you crazy? He would have every chance of winning!"

Gabriel's lips twisted in a wry smile. "Thanks for that vote of confidence."

"I have to agree, Gabriel." Ethan looked unconvinced. "This isn't a meeting of the Society for Creative Anachronism. What the hell do we know about fighting with swords?"

"You won't have to know a lot. I'm going to give you each a weapon to work with and imprint the basics in your minds. Jack's job will be to disarm your opponents from his hiding place. Lana's mind already has my sword skills. Her body just doesn't have the experience of mine as yet—the muscle memory, you might say. If we can isolate Kinnian and bring him to our chosen battleground with a minimum number of his men, we can do this."

Ethan frowned at him. "And if we can't?"

"Then I'll take us out and bring us back here. Keep that option in the back of your minds in case something happens to me."

He saw Ethan and Asia exchange a look—a glance, nothing more—but it pulled at him in a way he would never have believed possible before his bonding with Lana. Those two, their son, everything they had, depended on him. What if he wasn't strong enough?

Two are stronger than one, k'taam.

He smiled at her, his *k'taama,* then he set to work, materializing two heavy wooden staffs and two of the curved Pharisian broadsword/dirk pairs he favored for battle. Lana took up her sword and knife with a grin, while Gabriel did what he could to make Ethan and Asia proficient with the staff in a few short minutes.

He held off Kinnian's repeated attempts to find them through the link they shared, but his little team didn't have long. As he watched Lana execute a perfect swirling cut-and-thrust combination he felt a strong tug on the link, warning him that his brother had broken through at last. He gathered his troops.

"It's time! Jack, grab my hand!" The boy touched him just as Kinnian yanked them toward a place of his own dark choosing. Gabriel drew on Jack's power, felt it like a cauldron bubbling deep inside him, and visualized a sun-dappled grove of aspen and piñon pine at the base of the mesa.

The grove materialized around him, his people in place between the clear, shallow stream that defined its northern edge and the sheer sun-lit rock wall that was the mesa on the south. An instant later Kinnian and five of his men appeared at the western end of the grove, braced for battle. Gabriel stepped out from behind a jumble of red rock and lifted his sword over his right shoulder in readiness.

Kinnian grinned, a flash of white in the center of his black beard. "Ah. The smell of freshly-bonded female. Nothing like it in the galaxy." One hand slipped obscenely to his crotch. "I can't wait to have some."

Before Gabriel could stop her Alana had stretched out a hand from her hiding place in the trees to his right. "I'll give you some, you asshole." Lightning bloomed at Kinnian's feet.

The man sidestepped with a laugh, but Gabriel gave him no more time to trade quips. He closed the distance between them and swept his sword at Kinnian's neck in a bright blur of motion. The blow met a block raised just in time.

Kinnian's blade slid inside the strike and sliced across the body armor protecting Gabriel's ribs. Gabriel twisted to catch and deflect the deadly edge before it carved any deeper. With a grunt Kinnian broke off and swung his heavy blade back around toward Gabriel's head. *Shit!* Gabriel's block came up too slow and his arm crumpled under the weight of Kinnian's superior strength. The two blades pushed closer and closer to his neck—then he dipped his shoulder and struck quick as an adder with the dirk in his left hand. *Ah, a hit!* Kinnian's blood erupted over his fist.

Kinnian cursed and sprang away from him, giving Gabriel time to glance around the grove and check the progress of the fight in other quarters. Lana was very near him, holding her own against two swordsmen whose swords kept disappearing at critical moments. Both were wounded, one was not going to last much longer, and Lana seemed unharmed. Deeper into the grove, Ethan and Asia were back-to-back and fighting off two others who couldn't seem to keep a sword in their hands. A third man lay unconscious or dead at their feet. Jack was nowhere to be seen, but his effect was certainly being felt.

A flash of light and heat, a concussion of sound and power, took Gabriel off his feet and threw him through the air. The hard ground caught him an unknown distance later. He rolled and came up spitting blood. His hands were empty, his head was spinning. Kinnian was almost on top of him. He struggled to clear his head, to find his feet.

Then he heard her voice in his mind . . . *NO!* . . . and saw the blue-white glare as Lana ducked under the swing of her opponent's sword and hit Kinnian with a pure blast of power. His sibling flipped backwards and landed face down in the litter of leaves on the floor of the grove a few meters away, his grip loose on the hilt of his sword.

Gabriel manifested his own weapons and staggered to his feet just as Kinnian began to stir. Lana was dispatching her last opponent; she didn't need his help. Ethan and Asia were equally secure. His battle was with Kinnian, as it had been from the beginning.

He ran at Kinnian, sword raised, saw his brother stand and turn with murder in his eyes, his own blade at the ready. Then he saw an awful, pitiless grin spread across his brother's face. The ground began to shake as if the mountain behind them had left its foundation and begun to wander the desert.

The boy hidden in the grove behind him began to shriek. And Gabriel didn't need to turn to see what had begun to rip and tear at the trees, what had begun to roar with a soul-shattering noise.

VRadkrystion. World Eater. The Nameless One.

Alana met his eyes. So brave. *We'll find a way. Stay close to me*, k'taama.

As close as your heart, k'taam.

The Thrane laughed. "Very touching. Don't die too quickly, brother. I have plans for you and your lovely bondmate."

And then, without another word, Kinnian disappeared with the woman Gabriel had pledged his life to protect.

Trin, Minertsa, Sector 10

Sennik could not contain his excitement. His aura flamed with the bright aquamarine, the brilliant gold, even the deeply sexual blue of his emotions as he completed the routine tasks of his last segments as a lowly government minister. When Minertsa had completed its rotation this cycle and he greeted the star of his birth once more, Ren Sennik would be ruler of the Consortium Entire. His aura flared white-hot in triumph.

The Savagnoir had not let him down. Several million credits had changed hands and Xe had delivered the device on time as promised. Sennik had not even bothered to have it brought down to the planet surface. He'd merely had it transferred to another ship's hold in stationary orbit around Minertsa. He would activate the device from his own computer—through an impossibly complex tangle of intermediaries, of course—and sit back and watch the results. If anyone got close to discovering the source of the EM pulses that were causing the chaos throughout the Consortium, the drone ship would be ordered to leave the system and self-destruct.

Sennik had to admit this backup plan was almost better than his original scheme, despite the expense. Of course, there was no telling what the boy would have been capable of over the long term. But, then, the child was human and inherently unreliable.

The segments seemed to crawl by. How had he survived so long in this sulfurous mud flat of an existence? His new life awaited him—the recognition and power he deserved, the order and respect Minertsa deserved. Of course, he would not be leaving everything behind. A man of his stature required a consort of beauty and intelligence. Someone discreet. Someone to enhance his prestige, to demonstrate his status. He had decided Ardis would make a suitable companion, at least temporarily. The bright blue in his aura deepened into an unmistakable azure.

Unable to contain himself any longer, Sennik left his work and strode out of the office. The object of his thoughts was bent over her own computer screen at her desk outside his door.

Ardis, my love. I am much too harsh a taskmaster

to keep you so hard at work at this late segment.

The female looked up at him with a start. Her aura flashed a quick yellow/green before returning to her usual calm lavender. Then she blushed with a very attractive midnight blue. He was surprised to find his own color grew more intense in response. What an extraordinary female!

It is still early, Director Prime. I have those reports to complete for the Ministerial meeting in the morning. You wish me to be thorough.

Yes. Thorough is what he wished her to be in her attention to his sex, which even now was swelling and leaving its sheath. He slipped into her mind, flowing past her barriers as easily as water over a streambed, and stroked with teasing pressure at her pleasure center.

She hissed, back arching, as her aura bled midnight blue and deepest purple. *Ren!*

My love? He stroked again, ruthless, unrelenting. He took her hand and wrapped it around his sex, forcing her to his will.

We cannot do this here! Her breath heaved in her chest.

She was coming, he saw it in her mind. The white-gold of triumph flashed through his aura. He thrust himself into her sweet mouth and pushed further into her mind until he felt her shatter around him. Only then did he let go, the force of his release shaking him, shaking her. Ah, yes. This was good, so good! To have her like this, so completely at his feet.

Like the world. Like the many worlds of the Consortium. Soon now.

In the mindfield, no physical coordinates

Something was wrong.

Lana knew it as soon as her foot hit the first rotting step up to the back porch. Her legs grew heavy and didn't want to carry her the rest of the way up to where the battered aluminum storm door sagged in its loose hinges, failing to keep the cold out of the kitchen. She'd been so happy on the bus. She held the spelling test in her hand. An A. It had been a good day, for once.

It wasn't going to stay that way.

"Mom?" Silence answered. She stood on the porch, shaking, wanting to run. The inner door was open, gaping like a slack jaw. In the kitchen a glass had shattered. Shards sprayed across the linoleum of the kitchen floor, met and mixed with the blood. Jesus, so much blood. A sea of it under her mother's lifeless body. Red rivers of it running down the uneven floor to the grimy baseboards.

She tried to scream. Nothing would find its way from her constricted lungs but a breathy, keening moan. She tried to look away. Nothing could keep her from staring at the horror that would haunt her for the rest of her life. She tried to move. She trembled and shook, but she could not take a step away from her mother's murdered body.

Murdered? *She gasped, staggered.* Murdered! *She took a step into the kitchen, no longer seeing with the eyes of a terrified nine-year-old. And what she saw was a revelation.*

The blood. There was too much of it. *It couldn't all be her mother's. She'd fought before they'd shot her in the head. She'd wounded, perhaps killed, one of her attackers. Maybe the black ops team had killed her in self-defense; maybe she'd simply refused to be taken alive. Lana could see it now, but the evidence would have been easy to miss in the days before DNA testing. The Nashville cops had no reason to think murder when suicide was the logical call. She didn't blame them.*

But Gabriel had been right.

"Thinking of Gabriel so soon, my sweet Alana?" The growl was close to her ear, borne on a yeasty exhalation of warm air. "I'd hoped to have more fun here at the scene of this whore's suicide."

She dropped a fist back and down, aiming for Kinnian's groin. He was standing so close behind her she couldn't have missed, but his mind was quicker and in a heartbeat the scene changed. Her fist flailed at the empty air, her momentum causing her to stumble, and when she looked up again, Kinnian was straddling a woman, one hand wrenching her head back by the hair to expose her throat to his dagger.

Before she could help herself, Lana screamed and lunged forward.

"Careful!" Kinnian laughed and flourished the knife. Blood welled on the skin under the blade. "You have so much to say to your mother, don't you, my love? So much to tell her, now that you have the chance?" He jerked at her hair, and the woman—her mother, she saw that now—whimpered.

Another step. "You bastard!"

The knife sliced deep, and her mother screamed. "You are slow to learn, woman! Very slow to learn. And your mother will pay the price. I will make her suffer in ways you cannot yet imagine. Until you lose that arrogant pose."

Lana breathed deep and thought of her mother, lying in a pool of blood and shattered glass on a floor in a house in Nashville, Tennessee on a winter afternoon long ago. That was the reality she knew, the reality she had *lived* for more than twenty years. She felt it. She believed it. And in an instant, she made it happen.

"My mother is dead, you bastard. You can't touch her anymore." She reached out her hand and blasted the man standing before her. He flew backwards . . .

. . . but Lana landed with a jolt on her back,

her hands and feet strapped to a table in a hall of stone—dark, dank, lit with candles and torches and warmed only by the cheerless fire in a hearth at one end of the cavernous room.

Kinnian loomed over her and smiled. "Nicely played. But as you see . . ."

Lana surveyed the room and made a point to laugh, though her temples throbbed with the effort. "You've got to be kidding. What is this, *Dungeons and Dragons*? Or is this your throne room, your freaking majesty? Have you thought of moving out of the twelfth century? You know, central heat is nice."

"I prefer this sort of . . . arena . . . for some activities. The stone absorbs both blood and screams quite well."

"Yeah, well. Absorb this, asshole." Lana imagined herself on her feet with a sword in her hands and found herself facing him. The look of surprise on the Thrane's face was worth everything she owned.

She pressed her advantage with a swipe at his neck, but he manifested his own sword with blinding speed and blocked hard enough to bring her teeth together with a snap. Before she could strike again, he'd knocked the sword out of her hands. He backed her against the table and pushed his own blade against her throat to hold her in place.

He grinned at her, a horrible parody of Gabriel's smile on his lips. "By the gods, you are full of Marala's own fire! No wonder Gabriel burns for you. And I'm going to experience all of that time of Forging Fire between you, my little dragon's cunt. Every secret shared, every shattering orgasm. I'm going to dig deep and take it all. Why not just give in and enjoy our time together, eh? Gabriel will never have to know how you begged for me, how you came for me."

She struggled, even though the blade ate at her skin. "I'll never give in. You'll have to kill me."

"Oh, I won't have to kill you, but you will give in. I'm so much stronger than you are, Alana. My body, my mind, trained and honed for battle, just like your lover's. I'll be inside you in every way possible, and you can't stop me."

Though the effort sent sharp spikes of pain through her skull, she manifested a gun in her hand. Pointed it at his gut. Pulled the trigger.

He laughed and backhanded her across the room. Her vision blanked, the ceiling spun over her head and the taste of metal was thick in her mouth. She tried, and failed, to get to her feet before he found her again.

"You see now what I mean about the stone and the blood?" He stood just far enough from her that she couldn't take him down with her legs. "You should know your mind is far too weak to attack me with a handgun, even at close range. If we had more time, I'd explain why, since my brother was too busy fucking you to properly train you. But then, I'd rather fuck you than train you, myself!"

"Yeah, since I'd just use that training to kill you, you bastard."

With a swiftness that gave her no warning, Kinnian stepped in and delivered a vicious kick to her midsection. Ribs gave under the assault, leaving her curled in on herself in crushing agony.

"You have quite a mouth on you, I'll admit. I intend to put it to better uses."

Lana closed her eyes on Kinnian's gloating face. Closed her mind to the pain that slashed through her body. Focused all her thought and energy on the grove of aspen and pine where she'd last seen Gabriel, on every detail of color and light and smell and sound. For a split-second she was there—*my God, what was that roaring?*— then her head shattered into jagged fragments of unbearable pain, and she was back in Kinnian's hall.

The Thrane had her pinned to the stone floor. The unyielding ridge of his erection ground into her hips. "Oh, yes, my darling Alana. I will break you into tiny pieces. And Gabriel will find nothing left to save."

CHAPTER TWENTY-FIVE

Lana was gone and Gabriel's only thought was to follow her. If it was into Death he would follow her without a breath of hesitation. She was his bondmate, his heart, his life, and there was no other choice for him. He stilled, tracing the thread of their connection in his soul, readying himself for the projection that would take him to her. For an agonizing time he could feel her terror and her rage, then, all at once, he could feel nothing but his own despair. Their link had been blocked. All he knew was that Lana was still alive. Her death would have stopped his own heartbeat.

--Gabriel! Help me! I can't get to my Mom and Dad! He's almost here!

The cry dragged him back into his body and his own danger. Gabriel scanned the grove, but couldn't see the boy. *Stay down! I'll find you!*

As big as a freighter, the monster towered above the quaking aspens and bellowed in fury. Its massive head swung from side to side, searching for prey, jaws opened wide to reveal rows of dagger-like teeth. With each step the

VRadkrystion took, the ground thundered and shook, trees and brush splintering to dust beneath the beast's feet.

For one more precious second Gabriel could not move, could not think, could not act to save himself or the humans whose lives depended on him. He was paralyzed, twisted with fear for Lana. Kinnian had her, and it was too late—too late, God *damn* it!—to follow them. Hell was on top of him, and he had to protect the boy, though it ate like acid at his soul to think of Lana . . . no, he couldn't. He wouldn't.

"Here! Jack! Ethan!" He ran toward where he'd last seen them in the grove, though none of them were anywhere visible now. "Asia! Where are you?"

The beast roared and turned toward him at the first sound. He almost didn't hear Jack's thin shout from the rocks to his left. He scrambled up to the boy just as the World Eater screamed and crashed through the stand of trees in front of them, whirling in place to destroy with its tail what was left of the grove and any cover they might have taken in it. Fractured pine and splintered aspen rained over their shoulders as the creature rampaged through the trees, seeking the source of their scent.

"Where are your parents, Jack?"

The boy, pale and trembling, pointed. Barely

concealed behind a fall of rock twenty meters away lay two bodies, dead or unconscious, Gabriel could not tell. "Ah, Jesus." He glanced up at the ravening monster. There was no hope of getting to them unseen.

"Okay. Step one. Defense." Gabriel envisioned a heavy palisade of thick oak logs surrounding the rock outcropping where the couple lay, with a bristly outer fortification of sharpened thick metal stakes erupting in all directions. As it sprang into being, the beast whirled and surged in that direction with the speed of a starfighter.

"Christ, no, not yet!" Gabriel threw out a hand and hit the beast in the flank with a blast of energy. The thing slowed, turned . . .

"Run!" He grabbed Jack and pelted for the defenses, pulling the boy into his arms to carry him when he wasn't fast enough. But the VRadkrystion was faster, thundering up behind them like an avalanche. Gabriel cast a high wall in the beast's path. The creature roared and crashed through it, leaving the wall in shattered fragments.

Gabriel fell to his knees, releasing Jack. "Run, boy! Get behind those walls!" Jack hesitated, so Gabriel pushed him, propelling him in the direction of his parents. It wasn't far—only a few meters now—maybe he could hold off the beast that long.

The thing bellowed and reared over him—so close he could see the coarse fur rippling over the muscles of its massive chest, so close he could see the dirt under each of its sword-length claws. He dropped and rolled to the right. A tree-sized forelimb swept by him, the claws inches from his face. He reached up and scorched the thing's belly with a stream of fire from his fingertips, releasing a stench of burning fur. The beast screamed and curled in on itself, clawing at its wound in pain.

Gabriel ran.

The breastworks that protected his people loomed high before him, looking secure enough to stop an army. Legs pumping, lungs burning, he scrambled up the steep face, not daring to look back.

Above him through a gap in the palisade, he caught a glimpse of Jack's horrified face. "Hurry, Gabriel! He's right behind you!"

His fingers and toes scrabbled for purchase while the ground shook beneath him. He tried imagining himself behind the palisade walls, but the beast bore down on him with more than the terror of size and gnashing teeth. All of Kinnian's evil, all of the power of the Blood Legion filled the VRadkrystion, damping Gabriel's life force, slowing him down. He climbed, but the top of the earthworks got no closer. He fled, but the beast kept getting nearer. He was losing this fight.

A heartbeat later, a fistful of hot blades raked through his back as the beast's claws caught him. Blood gushed, soaking his thighs. A scream erupted from his throat; he lost his grip on the loose, scattering rock of the slope, and slid downward.

Then the landscape exploded with blue-white light. The VRadkrystiron howled in outraged anguish and fell back. And when Gabriel opened his eyes, he was behind the barrier.

Jack stared down at him. "Your back is bleeding."

Gabriel groaned and rolled to his knees. He tried to focus, but his thoughts refused to align. Pain and despair were overwhelming him. He stared up through a bleary fog at the boy.

"We need help. Where are your parents?"

Jack turned his head. Asia had an arm around Ethan's shoulders, helping him sit up. Both of them looked as if they had been drugged. Gabriel crawled the few feet it took to get to them.

"What happened?"

Asia glanced up at him. "I was back in the mines of Gallodon IV, but it wasn't a place I wanted to visit a second time. I followed Jack's . . . pathway back here."

Gabriel nodded. "You have a strong connection. And he's powerful for one so young."

Ethan was shaking, his reactions just short of clinical shock. "My leg—it was as if the accident was happening all over again. It was like a nightmare, and I couldn't . . . I couldn't wake up."

Sharing Ethan's mind told Gabriel just how badly that accident four years earlier had traumatized him—how it had scarred him body and soul until Asia's love had healed him.

"Kinnian has access to our deepest fears through the power of the VRadkrystrion. You have no shields to fight him."

The beast roared and ripped at the fortifications, sending earth and metal flying. His quarry hunkered down as best they could and endured a pummeling hail of debris.

Asia gasped as she raised her head. "My God, Gabriel! Your back!"

The agony ran too deep for control, and he had no energy to spare for healing. He shook his head.

"No time to worry about that now. We have to send out a call to the others. It will take all of us to fight this thing."

He clasped hands with Jack and the others and focused one part of his mind on a call to the Dineh for help. His link with Lana was still blocked, but he went deeper into his mind, behind the most secret protections he possessed.

Trevyn, if you still live, please help me. Find

Lana. For God's sake, help her before it's too late.

Trevyn went still, the desperation of his sibling's call pouring into him like ice water through a hole in his skull. The force of it shook him, wrenching his attention from the other battles he'd been directing, unseen and only subtly felt. He'd whipped in and out of dozens of fights, distracting, disabling, altering the field of battle to change the outcome to favor the inexperienced Navajos. His own men were dying because of him, but he couldn't bring himself to care.

He had left it to Gabriel to protect Lana, but no one could hold out against Kinnian for long. He'd known it had to come to this. Trevyn wasted no time in conversation with Gabriel. He reached out across the link to Kinnian's mind . . .

. . . his cock ached to fuck her. Her legs were spread beneath him, she was ready, ready! He could feel her hot and wet at his tip, and he pushed. She gritted her teeth and twisted away, denying him entrance. He could force himself inside, but that wasn't the plan. Oh, no! Her mind would yield first. He picked his way through her outer defenses, tossing away the fractured pieces of her shielding as if they were eggshells. She screamed, resisting him.

He saw that there were more guarded areas of

her mind, secrets protected, elements of her personality jealously hoarded. He would have those, too, soon. For now, he only wanted the open treasure house of her pleasure. He thrust at the primitive parts of her brain that governed her sexual response. She gasped, and her body arched upward, nearly taking him in. He laughed. I told you, my little dragon's cunt. *He stroked at the sensitive synapses again. She came, convulsing under him with unbearable need. Now beg me . . .*

"Kinnian!"

Trevyn ran across the echoing chamber to grasp his brother by the shoulder and turn him into his punch. Kinnian rolled off Lana's shuddering body and came up growling. Trevyn gave him no time to recover, manifesting a six-foot ironwood staff bound with metal at both ends and using it to break Kinnian's right elbow before he could bring up a sword to attack.

Howling, Kinnian counterattacked. White-hot energy shot from his left hand, his right hanging useless at his side. Trevyn threw up a quick shield, then hit his sibling with a blast of his own. Kinnian rolled out of the way, but Trevyn followed and struck him in the ribs and the knee with the staff.

"You traitorous pig! Killing you won't be enough!" He threw three more blasts in Trevyn's direction, staggering him. "If you were brave enough to fight with a sword, you'd be dead already." He manifested a sword in his left hand and charged.

Trevyn sidestepped and clipped him in the back of the head, splitting open his skull. Kinnian dropped like a butchered *psoros*.

The third son of Kylan of Thrane stood and watched the life's blood drain out of his brother into the stone of an unfeeling planet. Then he bent to the unconscious body of the woman he loved, a woman who was bonded to his oldest brother. Her bondmate might not survive this day to do what was necessary now. It fell to him to enter Lana's mind one more time, to undertake yet another violation to preserve her sanity. With a touch as light as a nightbird's wing, he spread healing balm over the raw wounds Kinnian had left behind. Lana would remember—to attempt to erase the memories would only cause violent whiplash later—but from an emotional distance that would make it easier to bear. It would be as if she'd already had years to heal.

When it was done, Trevyn picked her up and left that place of horror, praying her bondmate was still alive to appreciate what he'd done.

Trin, Minertsa, Sector 10

It was time. Ardis watched her compscreen as Sennik called up his program and initiated the proper sequences. The display showed the minister's actions, shadowed by the codes she and the human scientist Blake had injected to bend the program to their bidding. She didn't bother to shield or alter her shining aura. Sennik was in his office, deep in his task. He wouldn't know or care how she felt. Until it was too late.

The commands scrolled down, one by one. The stealth codes followed in their wake. The computers aboard the ship circling high above her planet acknowledged receipt. The countdown began. Ardis waited, her breath shallow and fast.

A few segments later the data began flooding in. Accounts were being depleted. Secure files were being opened and shared. Secrets were being revealed. Startled inquiries were already flowing between government offices. The Consortium was being shaken to its foundations. But not as Sennik had planned. No. Not at all according to Sennik's plan.

Ardis felt the scream deep in her mind. Serene, she rose and went into the office of the Director Prime.

He was manipulating data on several computer screens, all to no avail, his aura a horrid dark yellow-green. *It's some sort of* mrill-*fucked comp attack! My personal accounts, my files, everything! I've been posted to public nets; smeared all over every active government screen!*

--Chaos serves your purposes, does it not, sir?

Sennik stopped his frantic motion and stared at her. *What do you mean?*

--Did you not plan to coordinate similar attacks on others with the device you purchased from Xe? She waved an elegant hand at his master screen. *The targets have been changed. And I regret the sabotage orders have been deleted from your program.*

His aura exploded with bright red rage. *You!* He leapt up and started in her direction, then stopped, frozen, unable to move a single muscle not connected to his autonomic nervous system. Lime-colored terror swirled through the crimson of his anger. *What are you doing to me?*

--I am controlling you, as you so often controlled me.

She could sense the rise in his pulse, his blood pressure, his respiration—all signs of his struggle to gain release from her will. She had hidden her skills so well, for so long, even she hadn't been certain her mind was truly stronger. Now she felt her confidence swell.

--You can't. Let me go!

--They will be coming for you soon, Ren. They'll want an explanation for all of this—the plan, the chaos, the deaths and destruction on Zalin. They'll say they want the details, but they already have all that. Everything is in your open files. What they really want is justice. But that I will have already taken for myself. And for Slindar.

His aura flared. *I am a hero because of what*

happened on Zalin. Zalin was proof that this Consortium needs what only I know how to provide.

--*You are a fool!* Her aura burned hot with the silver and gold of her impending triumph. *You provide misery and slow decline. Your time is coming to an end. I only wish Slindar had been here to see it.*

--*Slindar! And who is he?*

Her chin lifted. *He was my mate. The only man I ever loved. And it's for his sake that you will do this last thing—his and the many humans you've killed.*

Ardis stepped to the antique glass case and chose a serpentine jade kris, a blade more than two thousand circuits old. She turned and pressed it into Sennik's limp hand, ordering him to hold it.

He stared at it in horror. Then he watched it, eyes widening, as it rose and moved closer to his throat. *Ilia, no! You can't mean to do this! Please . . .*

Whatever else he might have said was lost as the blade slipped into the sphenis artery at the side of the throat. The blade, still sharp after so many circuits, severed the artery with one stroke, cutting off blood to the brain. Sennik fell, the blade still in his hand, his dark green blood spurting in powerful gouts over the floor. He was dead long before the blood stopped flowing.

When Ardis was certain of that fact, she turned and left the building, well ahead of the government officials and military police she knew to be on their way. By an indirect and complicated route she arrived at Slip 298B of the commercial section of Minertsa's secondary spacedock within approximately one segment. There was a pad beside the hatch closing off the floating catwalk to the ship. She keyed in the code she'd been given.

The face that appeared on the screen in response was a surprise. "Ardis? You made it!"

Her aura glowed with aquamarine, with gold. "Blake. It is you." She heard a strange quaver in her voice.

The human—her friend—smiled. "Wow, things are really popping, thanks to you! Hang on. I'll be down to get you."

She had been sad and frightened to leave her home, though the humans had said they'd find a place for her. Now, she realized, her feelings had changed.

Her aura flushed bright with joyous pink, shot through with a hint of deep, midnight blue.

In the mindfield, no physical coordinates

The beast was enraged, insane with pain and frustration. Gabriel watched as it whirled in a storm of dust and thunder, snapping its jaws at the bolts of sizzling light splashing against its flanks. The VRadkrystion was surrounded, crowded by tall, pointed fortifications and beset by attacks from all sides, and yet the thing would not give up. The beast threw itself against the breastworks time and again, injuring the humans behind them, but doing little to damage itself. It may have been confused, but it was far from dead.

Ethan shouted at him over the din. "This isn't working."

The beast rushed the fortifications at the far side of their circle. Gabriel heard the screams of more of their people. People would be killed soon, if they hadn't been already.

"I have to get closer. It's the only way."

Geneva Twohawks stared up at him. "We were not able to heal you properly. You are slow. The World Eater is fast. Not a good plan."

Gabriel barked out a laugh. "True. Do you have a better one?"

Her eyes slid to the boy who was throwing energy bursts through a hole in the defenses with Leonard Begay.

Ethan took a step forward, his jaw clenched.

The old woman shook her head.

Gabriel wished it were otherwise, but he couldn't seem to find a way to tap the boy's power. He'd had no training—and Gabriel had had no time to teach him. Jack could throw energy with the best of them, but the VRadkrystion ignored his hits like all the others.

Long ago, his teacher had told him the little he knew about the VRadkrystion: First, never fight it. Second, if you must fight it, try not to die.

Third, the beast has only one true vulnerable area, on the inside of the back thighs—good luck reaching it.

He sent out the order to all the others to keep the beast's attention to the far side of the circle. The blasts intensified, infuriating the monster, leading it to charge against the barricades within a small arc furthest from Gabriel's position.

Gabriel slipped out from behind the defenses he'd struggled so hard to reach and slid down the slope of the embankment. He circled behind the beast, skimming the shadows at the foot of the palisade where he had a chance of cover in case the monster turned.

The others knew his intentions. When they saw he was ready to make his move they redoubled their efforts to distract the beast with a barrage of energy bolts and a hail of conjured rock and fire. The thing responded with a sky-splitting roar and hurled itself at the wall in front of it.

Gabriel tore across the open circle toward the maddened beast, his focus on the massive tree-trunk-sized hind legs. The monster was standing, pushing at the palisade. The people behind the wall were screaming, some of them trapped beneath the splintering logs. Gabriel was closer . . . closer . . . *there!* He came around the side of the beast and reached out, hitting the thing square between the legs with a crackling bolt of actinic light from his fingertips.

The VRadkrystion bellowed and keened—then pivoted to come down on all four legs in the midst of the destruction it had caused. It screamed and stomped, turning to find its tormentor—and Gabriel could not move fast enough. He backed up, fell, clambered over the debris just ahead of the beast's marauding feet. He rolled and cursed himself—*Get up, you bastard, get up! GET UP AND RUN!*

But the monster had seen him now, and its hunting cry went up. It turned toward him, and the sound of its jaws snapping was the sound of death. Gabriel thought of Lana as he stared up at dripping fangs. *I'm sorry,* k'taama.

Then there was a sound like the high-pitched whine of a hundred engine thrusters, and a flash of blue-white light so bright Gabriel's vision blanked. Heat seared his skin, followed by a bone-deep concussion and a blast of wind-driven sand.

Gagging on a renewed stench of burning flesh and fur, Gabriel rolled to his hands and knees. He blinked hard to try and clear his vision, because it seemed there was no shadow of a beast hovering over him. That's when he heard it:

Laughter. Cheering. A six-year-old's excited voice rising above the crowd.

He staggered to his feet and saw people emerging from behind crumbling barricades, embracing each other, dancing with joy. Some of them were headed in his direction, for which he was grateful; he could use the help. Finally, at the top of the tallest palisade, he saw Jack Roberts, slayer of monsters, arms raised in triumph. For the first time since he'd met the boy, maybe for the first time ever, Jack was smiling.

Of the VRadkrystion, he could see nothing left at all.

Moonlight pooled in liquid silver at the base of the bluff and spread like the widening ripples from a dropped stone until it hit her legs. Lana sat with her back against a crumbling wall and stared, trying hard to make sense of the objects bathed in the pale light. Adobe walls, missing their doors and windows. Fallen rocks. Her bare feet, her naked legs.

There were few sounds to go with the sights. Only her breathing. *And his.*

She scrambled to a crouch, her heart pounding, seeing him at last. "Who are you?"

He stood and backed away from her, his hands held away from his body. "I won't hurt you, Alana."

She stood, ready to run. Then she looked down, horrified. Her body was as naked as her legs. She shut her eyes and manifested a tee-shirt and jeans. A pair of shoes.

"Sonofabitch!"

"I'm sorry! I just had time to move you here. I didn't think about the clothing."

She advanced on him. He stood his ground. In the moonlight she couldn't see much of him, only that he was tall and well built, with a strong, clean-shaven jaw. He wore a uniform like that asshole Kinnian's, though, and that was reason enough to want to kill him. She manifested a sword and swung for his head. He brought up a metal-braced staff to block it.

"Stop! I'm here to help you!"

"Like I believe that." She thrust the sword at his gut. He sidestepped and rapped her wrist. She dropped the sword with a curse and fell to her knees.

He held the staff in a loose grip, watching her. "Before you attack again, take a moment to search your memories. My name is Trevyn. I am your bondmate's younger sibling—and ally. I found you with Kinnian. I killed him. Do you remember now?"

Flashes of memory showed her scenes of horror. Kinnian looming over her, poised to destroy her, ripping away at her mind. The way she had responded to him . . . bile rose into her throat.

"No, Lana." There was sympathy in Trevyn's quiet voice. Understanding. "You had no more control over your reaction than you had over your heartbeat or the blink of your eyes. You denied him access to your deepest self—that is what is truly important."

She looked up at him and even in the moonlight she could see Gabriel in him. She struggled to speak, in the end finding only two words in the tangle of her conflicting emotions.

"Thank you."

He said nothing in response, and for a long, silent moment he simply watched her, his gaze hungry and desolate. It was as if he conducted some debate deep inside himself as he stood over her.

Lana recognized the danger she was in and gathered her feet under her. "Why did you bring me here, Trevyn?"

Trevyn shook his head. "I brought you here to keep you safe. Come. Gabriel must need our help by now." He held out a hand.

She reached out to take his hand, but before she could stand, a shadow bloomed behind him, and a bright gleam of metal pierced the center of his chest. His breath left him—a sigh of shock and despair—and he slumped to his side.

Lana grasped at Trevyn's falling staff as she rolled to her feet. A voice and a form came at her out of the moonlight.

"You humans have a saying: 'quid pro quo.' Though I believe in this case I have done my brother one better."

Lana didn't wait for Kinnian to make his move. She struck at him with the heavy staff, aiming for the hand that held the sword, for his elbows, his knees. He was slower than he had been, the effect of the blow to his head that was still not fully healed; still he parried every blow and watched for the opportunity to disarm her. She was sweating with fear and effort, while he easily countered her, move after move. Frustrated, she gathered her energy and cast it at him in a blue-white arc. He cursed and fell back, almost dropping the sword. She followed up with a flurry of blows that got inside his parries, banging at his elbows and ribs.

"Enough!" He exploded with a concussion that flattened her against the side of a ruined pueblo. He started forward, his grin white against his face in the night. "Now you're mine."

Just as quickly there was movement and someone blocking his path. "No. She's not."

Gabriel!

His arm swung, metal flashed and there was a sound like an ax biting through soft pine.

Kinnian's head left his shoulders and flew several meters into a pile of rubble, leaving his body to drop like an empty bag.

Gabriel turned and fell to his knees in front of her. He threw away the sword so he could catch her as she launched herself into his arms. She spent a long, blissful moment feeling his arms around her, his heartbeat under her ear, his reality. She was aware of him in her mind, gently probing. She resisted showing him the worst of it.

He hurt you. Anger and guilt burned in his mind.

It was a fight, like yours with the VRadkrystion. You were wounded, too. We'll both recover.

I should have been there. Let me help you.

No. Later. Just hold me now. Just let me know it's over.

I'm so sorry, k'taama.

I'm not. She saw his memory of the victory over the World Eater. *We did what we set out to do. We won.*

She felt him exhale, the tension draining from the muscles in his back . . .

Navajo Nation Indian Reservation, Arizona, Earth, Sector Three

. . . and then they were sitting before the fire in the dance circle outside Geneva Twohawks's compound.

Several of the youngest dancers still shuffled around the well-tended flames. The drummers and singers kept up with the steady rhythm and the rise and fall of the chant. Here and there around the circle people were standing and beginning to move off in search of food and drink. Some didn't move at all and were being tended to by caregivers.

Gabriel stood and stretched, his body stiff with long hours of sitting, his muscles taxed with the knowledge of injury and overuse.

Lana groaned as she worked the kinks out of her back. "God, how long have we been sitting there?"

Gabriel smiled and lifted a hand at the sky behind her. Dawn streaked the eastern horizon with pink and lavender.

"Christ." She ran a hand through her unruly curls. "I feel like I could eat one of those—what are they called? Zorros? And sleep for an entire week. Where's everyone else?"

"Safe, for the most part. They're already in the food tent."

She started in that direction, but Gabriel held her back. "I have one more job to do."

He felt the warmth of her understanding. "Trevyn! Where is he?"

He pointed in the direction of the draw where their enemies had hidden. "I want to go look."

"I'll go with you."

"No. It'll be dangerous. I'm not sure how many will have found their way back from the mindfield. They may be injured, confused, certainly without leadership."

"All the more reason for you to have backup."

"She's right, *amigo*. You're not going in there alone."

They turned to see the big starship captain saunter up, followed by most of the encampment.

Gabriel frowned at him. "Sam? Aren't you supposed to be monitoring things from your bridge?"

"Ethan gave me a shout when the party was over. Figured you might need a little help with the mopping up."

"I'd hoped to recover Trevyn's body, maybe see to the ship."

"Sure, man. I've brought a team. Let's go."

Gabriel turned to make another attempt to tell Lana to stay behind, but he could see it would be useless. She was already checking and reholstering her Glock, putting on her game face in preparation for another fight, this one in the "real" world. As they fell in behind Sam and the platoon of armored troops from the *Shadowhawk,* Ethan, Asia, Jack and the Navajo people who had fought with them through the long night watched them go. Gabriel could feel their energy—their love—surrounding him like a shield.

They moved out into the flat desert scrub, heading for a dark line in the gray light that marked the open end of the draw where the *Bloodstalker's* men were holed up. They hit the broad ditch and dropped over the lip in pairs and threes. Then they started down into the gulch, weapons at the ready, eyes straining in the purple shadows.

Gabriel moved to the front of the line, exchanging a silent message with Sam. The captain maneuvered to keep step with him, protecting Lana from any fire from the front.

Cute. Think I haven't managed a firefight before?

Indulge me, querida. *Just this once. My nerves are shot.*

You know what? Mine, too. I'll give you this one.

Darker shadows flitted in the murk up ahead and murmurs came back to them. The Thranes were moving their dead and injured.

Gabriel called a halt. Sam sent troops crawling up and around the flanks as far as they could go without being seen. When he'd given them enough time to get into position, the *Shadowhawk* platoon hit the enemy with a blinding array of phos-lights and shouts of "Freeze! Drop your weapons!" in Thrane and Galactic Standard.

There was an answering shout of "*Marazt!*"— "Peace!"—and the Thranes began dropping their weapons and stepping back.

Lana put a hand on his arm. "Gabriel!"

He'd heard it, too. Though the voice was weak, the command it gave was not. "Trevyn?"

A man stepped from between several others, bloodied and leaning on a head-high staff. Several officers stood to either side of him, as if ready to catch him, but he shrugged them off. They scowled and exchanged worried looks.

Trevyn hobbled a few more steps and held out a hand to his brother. "Gabriel. I am glad you survived."

Gabriel ignored his hand and embraced him. As soon as his arms went around him, Trevyn trembled and collapsed. Gabriel eased him to the ground, Lana rushing to hold him from the other side.

"We'd thought you dead, my brother."

"It seems we Dars are not so easy to kill."

Gabriel grinned. "My old teacher always said cut twice, measure once—for the coffin, that was."

"Wise advice. And I think I will improve my skills with the sword after all."

"It does have advantages over the staff."

"Hey, I wouldn't knock the staff." Lana smiled at Trevyn, squeezing his hand. "That thing saved my life twice last night, thanks to you."

The Thrane looked up at her, then quickly looked away. "I was honored to be of service to my brother's bondmate."

One of the officers hovering at Trevyn's side could wait no longer. "My lord, we must return to the ship. You need medical attention."

"The others?" Gabriel heard steel in Trevyn's voice and felt pride for his sibling.

"All have been seen to, my lord."

"Very well. Give me a moment." Trevyn smiled at Gabriel and Lana and leaned on them as he struggled to his feet. Though he made an effort to shield it, Gabriel felt his pain through their contact. "I am captain of the *Bloodstalker* now and heir to our father's title. I find I have little enthusiasm for the family business, however." He glanced at Sam, supervising the last of the transport of Thranes to their ship. "I may have to look for a new line of work."

Gabriel raised an eyebrow. "Retirement is not common on Thrane."

Trevyn grunted. "Retirement is unknown on Thrane. And I will have rivals even on my own ship." He clapped a hand on Gabriel's shoulder. "Be well, my brother." Then he took Lana's hand and brought it to his lips. "My sister. May your bonding be a long and happy one."

As the swirl of the dematerialization beam took him, Gabriel saw him glance at Lana one last time with heartbreak in his eyes. He thought to search his link with Trevyn for the answer to that expression, but he let his brother keep his secrets of the heart. Gabriel had no doubt Lana was his alone.

They made their way back to the compound, weariness beginning to weigh them down. In the tent, the victorious fighters were wolfing down eggs and steak and frybread, sharing their stories of how they had each engaged the enemy. Gabriel and Lana helped themselves to heaping plates of food and cups of coffee and found the Roberts family and the Dineh elders at one table near the front of the tent.

Jack was already asleep with his head on his arms on the table. Lana sat down next to him and reached out to touch his dark hair.

"Tough work blowing monsters up, huh?"

Asia's arm slipped around his small shoulders. "Pretty amazing."

"For us—and for him." Ethan caught Gabriel's gaze. "He's still so young and we have no experience with this. How are we supposed to help him through it?"

"He needs training. I can help you find a teacher. Other than that, your love is all he needs."

Asia looked up, her smile showing her relief. "Thank you—both of you. You never gave up on us. We'll never forget it."

Geneva Twohawks placed a hand on his shoulder. "Neither will my people. We will sing many songs about the bravery of the man who led us to this victory." She lifted her voice and turned to face the tent full of her battle-weary friends and neighbors. "Hear me, elders. Listen, all my brothers and sisters in arms. Tonight we have shown ourselves worthy in the eyes of the Old Ones. We have defeated a great enemy and protected our people. We have destroyed an evil that has preyed upon not only our world but many others. We must never forget their names—Spirit Hunter and his mate, Fire Heart; Timewalker and her husband, Still Water; and most of all young Striking Stone, killer of the Nameless One. These people were once outsiders. Now they are all Dineh, great heroes of our people. Let us sing of them, and this night, forever."

EPILOGUE

Nashville, Tennessee, Earth, Sector Three

A few days later they left the bungalow in Nashville with its little family safe again inside. On the sidewalk in front of the house, the summer sun spilled yellow light across the lawn, warming their shoulders.

Gabriel lifted his face to the cloudless sky and sighed. "I have one thing I'd like to do before we leave."

Lana tilted her head at him. "I thought Sam was waiting for us. I'm all packed."

"Are you in such a hurry to leave your home?" Gabriel smiled at her, hiding his worry. She had given up everything for him with so little objection.

"Well, I . . ." She glanced at the houses up and down the street. Then her eyes found his. "My home is with you now, Gabriel. Wherever that is."

"Still, there is one place on this planet I'd like to see again before we leave. Sam will wait."

There was a taxi driver at the curb with his engine running. Lana raised an eyebrow when she saw him.

"Is that for us?"

"You no longer own a car, remember? And this is a

one-way trip. We'll have the ship pick us up from there. I believe you call it 'beaming aboard,' though exactly why is lost to me."

He had given the driver their destination ahead of time, so he had the pleasure of laughing at Lana's frustration when they pulled away from the curb with no clue as to where they were going. He distracted her with kisses and conversation and took the precaution, too, of shielding the place in his mind. His *k'taama* had become quite adept at slipping in and out of his thoughts, at sharing his emotions. She was comforting and stimulating at the same time. He hardly knew how he'd lived without her.

The taxi reached an intersection and followed the turning to the left to head out of town. Lana looked up at him with a bright, knowing grin.

"We're going to the Narrows."

He lifted his shoulders. "Maybe I only want to take a ride in the country."

"Fine." She settled back against the seat. "But I want to stop at the Narrows and look at the river."

"Your wish is my command, *mi amor*." Anticipation tightened his chest.

He picked up Alana's soft hand and held it resting on his thigh as he watched the countryside slip past the window. The fields, full and lush with growth; the trees, green and bending in the mid-day breeze; the road, curving ahead into the summer's heat. This place, Lana's home and Ethan's family's, so very different from the desert where Geneva Twohawks's people lived. He catalogued every detail.

Soon enough, they turned down a smaller side road, and finally left the road altogether for the dirt track that led to the river. The driver rolled to a stop in the gravel turnout below the bridge where Gabriel had talked with Lana their first day together.

He turned from the front seat and frowned at Gabriel. "You sure this is the place, man?"

"Yes, this is it." Gabriel and Lana got out of their seats and went around to the back of the vehicle. "You can just drop us here."

The driver popped the trunk and came around to gawk at them while they removed their few small bags from the back. "You just want me to leave you out here in the boondocks? How you gonna get back?"

Gabriel held out a wad of cash. "Don't worry. We have some friends meeting us here."

The driver looked them up and down. "You don't look like you're going fishing to me."

Lana laughed out loud. Gabriel just smiled.

"We're not." He gave the bills in his hand a tiny wave.

The driver gave it up and shook his head. He took the bills, his eyes widening.

"Thank *you*, sir. Y'all have a nice day." He slammed the trunk shut, got back behind the wheel and left them alone.

The bend in the river was just as it had been the first time he'd seen it, with the sun throwing diamonds off the rippling water and a fan of sandy pebbles at the river's edge. Insects hummed in the afternoon heat, and from the reeds nearby he could hear a bird—Lana's memories told him it was a redwing blackbird—repeating its call. Beneath it all was the burble of the water over the stones—soothing, sensual, unchanging.

Lana slipped her arm around his waist. "This is what you wanted to see one last time?"

He turned to her. "No." He pulled the clasp from her hair and let the golden strands fall around her shoulders. "You, standing in the light of your sun, in this place that has meaning for you. That's what I came to see."

Her lips curved upwards as she stepped back from him. Piece by piece, she began to remove her clothing, her eyes never leaving his. His pulse quickened, his blood heated as little by little her body was revealed there in the sun. First her shoulders, the creamy skin sprinkled with tiny freckles. Then her breasts, full and round, the tips tight with arousal in the stimulus of the open air. The smooth plane of her belly, the tantalizing curve of her hip. The taut length of her leg. And finally, her thighs, opening to the nest of curls that hid what he longed to explore.

When the last stitch had been shed, she laughed and ran for the water. He stripped and followed her in, and they tangled together in the stream, smooth, warm skin contrasting with the cool, flowing water. Her mind welcomed him as quickly as her body, letting him feel the liquid heat of her need for him deep in her core as her legs folded around his waist and pulled him closer.

Molten fire spread from his chest to his groin and made him shake. He was poised at her entrance, unable to hold back. *Querida.*

Yes, now, baby. Don't make me wait.

She moved, he thrust and he was in heaven. Deep, deeper. Again and again. So hot and slick and clutching him as if she would never let go. Her heart beating with his. Her soul linked forever to his. Nothing in the universe but the two of them. Feeling her spiraling out of control, the way her body in the beauty of orgasm made him want to give her more and more until he shattered under the wonderful pressure of it.

Lana floated in the water, her legs still wrapped around Gabriel's warm body, his arms still holding her close. Under her lips, the pulse at the side of his neck was returning to its normal, steady rhythm. And around them, now that she had stopped moaning, the insects thrummed, the blackbird sang, the river gurgled as they always did, undisturbed.

She swallowed a small lump in her throat.

She was ready to go, she really was. She had lost faith in the agency she'd given years of her life to, and it was only a matter of time before her actions in the Arizona desert caught up to her. She'd handed in her resignation with little regret. Nothing held her here now. Her life was with Gabriel. There would be other beautiful places in the universe. But to think that this might be the last time she would see *this* place. The last time she would hear a blackbird sing—

--K'taama. *We can come back anytime in our minds. It's the reason I came here today. To make certain I remembered every detail. For me, as much as for you.*

She let go of the tears she'd been holding back, grateful that she wouldn't have to put into words the emotions that gripped her.

He held her for a long time, then lifted wet fingers to wash the tears from her face. "Come. You're shivering. And Sam won't hold the ship forever."

Lana pulled away from him and used the river to clean up as best she could. "God, I must look like crap!"

Gabriel was already onshore and stepping into his jeans. "You look beautiful, as always." He tossed her a towel as she waded out of the water.

"You lie, but at least you came prepared."

He watched her as she finished dressing. "Ready?"

She took a last look around, then nodded. Her mouth went dry.

He reached for his comm unit. "Cruz to *Shadowhawk*. Do you read?"

"This is *Shadowhawk*. Go ahead, Mr. Cruz."

"Tell Captain Murphy that we're ready for pickup at these coordinates."

"Aye, sir. We are standing by D-Mat on your mark."

"Understood." Gabriel positioned her close to him. "On my mark in three . . . two . . . one . . . mark!"

Lana felt a strange tingling, like her entire body had

suffered a sudden return of circulation after the blood had been cut off. Then the scene in front of her went black, to be replaced with a new one: the interior of a smallish room that appeared to be lined with milky blue glass. There was a door and next to that a window looking into the room, the control room for this "transporter." She expected to see Mr. Scott appear any time now.

Instead, the door opened to admit Sam and Rayna. Lana drew in a breath as she caught her first sight of the big man in his role as captain of the *Shadowhawk*. He wasn't wearing a uniform, exactly, since, Gabriel had explained, his ship was his own, not a military vessel. But the black pants and padded overshirt he wore had a paramilitary feel to them and only accentuated his wrestler's physique. Rayna was wearing something similar in a softer, reddish color. She looked lovely—and deadly.

Their smiles, though, lightened the effect. Sam stepped forward with a grin and took her hand. "Welcome aboard." He nodded at his friend. "*Amigo.* Just about left you behind."

Lana saw Gabriel shrug as she and Rayna exchanged hugs. "Some last minute things to attend to."

Sam looked from Gabriel to Alana, then glanced down at his wife. "Gotcha. Well, no more putting it off—we're about to leave orbit. Want a last look at the old rock, Lana?"

Something squeezed her heart, but she managed to

find her voice. "Yeah, actually, I would."

They moved through the busy ship's corridors to what looked like a set of elevator doors. The "lift" took them up three levels to the bridge. She stepped off the lift, and there she stopped, captured by the image on the huge forward viewscreen.

Her mouth fell open, her breath hitched, and every preconceived notion of what it meant to be human fell away into space. Because there, hanging in the blackness of the void, lit by the rays of a congenial, yellow sun, was a beautiful, blue-green orb. Earth, home to billions of beings, including, until this moment, one Alana Matheson-Cruz. Tears stung her eyes.

Captain Murphy had settled into the center seat at the horseshoe-shaped equipment console that dominated the bridge. He busied himself with checking data on the computer screen at his station.

A woman at his left looked up from her readouts. "Ready to leave orbit when you are, Captain."

"Very well, helm. Set course for Jump Node Alpha Ten and take us out at three-quarters ion drive."

"Aye, sir. Setting course. Accelerating to three-quarters ID."

Lana looked back at Gabriel. "Ion drive?"

"We use it within solar systems, for small runs. Longer distances need pulse drive and the use of the jump nodes . . . uh, something like wormholes."

Rayna led the way to some empty seats above and well away from the main bridge stations. "Observation stations," she explained. Lana found the tiny woman was mostly observing her. "You okay?"

Lana watched as the planet of her birth slipped away behind them. Then she looked up at Gabriel, his eyes full of love and sympathy. She nodded.

"I will be."

Earth grew smaller and smaller as they cruised through the solar system, until it was just another dot in the black of space and the sun was just a bright, cold light on the far side of the system.

"Approaching Jump Node Alpha Ten in jump minus three minutes, Captain."

"Thank you, helm. Prepare to engage pulse in J minus one point five."

"Aye, sir. Pulse at J minus one point five."

"Switch viewscreen."

"Switching screen."

Ahead, the screen showed a luminescent swirl of dust and gas spiraling toward a spot in space.

"Is that it? The jump node?"

Gabriel nodded. "It will take us 1.7 light-years to the crossroads in Alpha Darion, where we will transfer for the trip to Terrene."

"But it's so close to Earth! Why haven't we seen it?"

"The screen is deceptive. The node is small—not much bigger than this ship. And the electromagnetic pulses it emits are of a type your scientists are still learning to interpret. There's an echo effect that makes them seem like they come from much farther away. Of course, we contribute to that effect."

"'We'?"

"Too complicated to explain. Trust me, it's for your own good."

"J minus one point five. Engaging pulse drive."

Deep within the ship, a bone-shaking hum began. Lana's heart pounded, in fear or in exhilaration, she wasn't sure.

"Buckle up, *querida*."

She reached for the straps that came down over both shoulders and across her thighs and secured the clasps with shaking hands. Then she reached for Gabriel.

"Pulse drive fully operational. All systems go for jump in thirty seconds and counting."

"Acknowledged, helm. You are good to go for jump when ready."

"Aye, sir. Jump in ten, nine, eight . . ."

Stay close to me, k'taama.

As close as your heart, k'taam.

". . . six . . . five . . ."

Good. Because this is where the adventure really begins.

". . . two . . . one . . . jump!"

THE END

ACKNOWLEDGEMENTS

This book would not have been possible without the expert background advice provided by former FBI Special Agent Robert Holman. Mr. Holman's patient explanation of the FBI's protocol in investigating kidnapping cases, drawn from his own personal experience in the field, gave Lana Matheson and her colleagues a grounding in real life. Any misinterpretations of FBI procedure are my own.

As always, thanks to my critique partner, Linda Thomas, for keeping me on the straight and narrow. Gabriel would not be the man he is without her!

A special shout out to my beta readers: Laurie A. Green, Petra Blazer, Jessie Wenger and Graeme Frelick.

Thank you to the amazing Deborah Kreiser for performing her editing magic.

And, finally, a heaping helping of gratitude to my agent Michelle Johnson, champion and cheerleader.

www.ingramcontent.com/pod-product-compliance
Lightning Source LLC
Chambersburg PA
CBHW051531250626
47157CB00001B/7